FELONY IN FULLERTON

A Ruby Ray Mystery

Debra L. Brunner

Debra L. Brunner

Cover design and art by Debra L. Brunner

Illustrations by Debra L. Brunner

Published by **Coral Cloche Press**
Orange County, CA

Paperback edition ISBN: 9798218220112

Printed in the United States of America

FOR LANCE

iii

The dapper doctor who captured my heart decades ago
and continues to keep it safe and sound. I cherish you.

Ruby's Fullerton

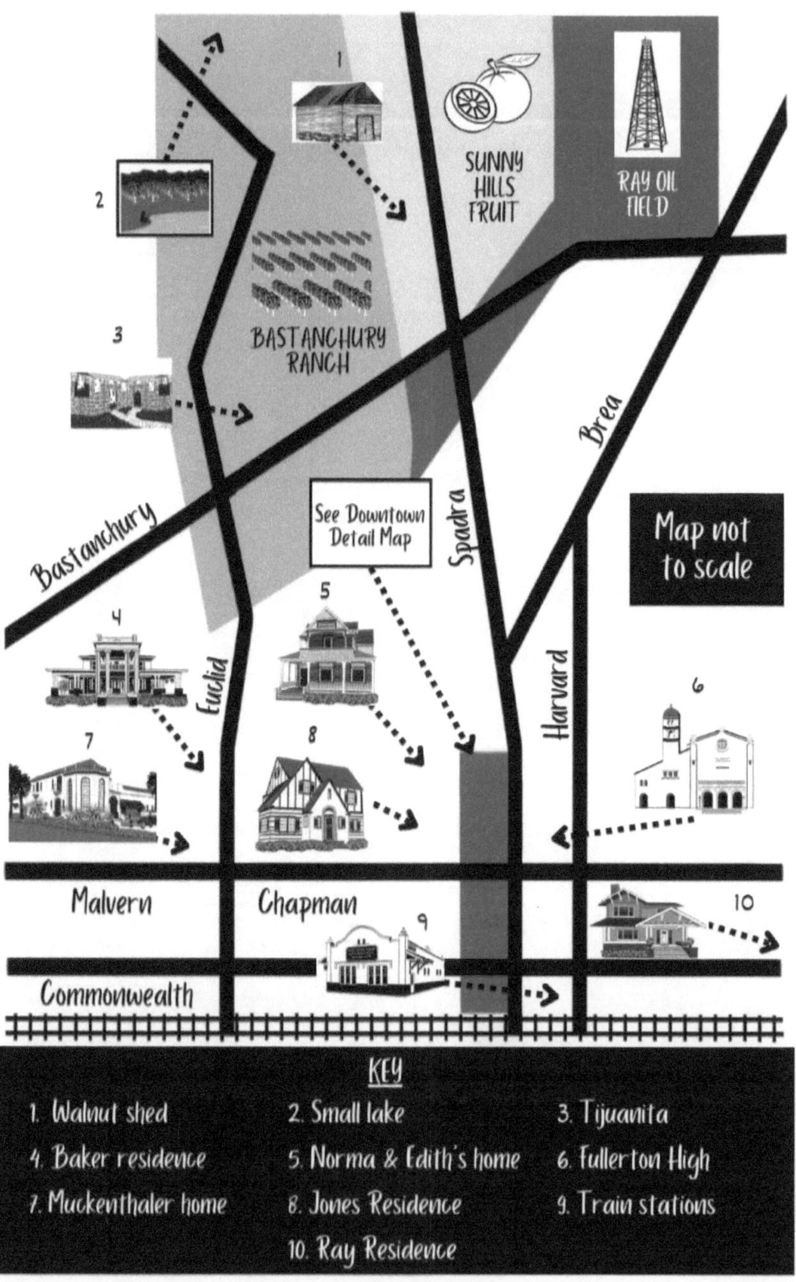

Downtown Detail

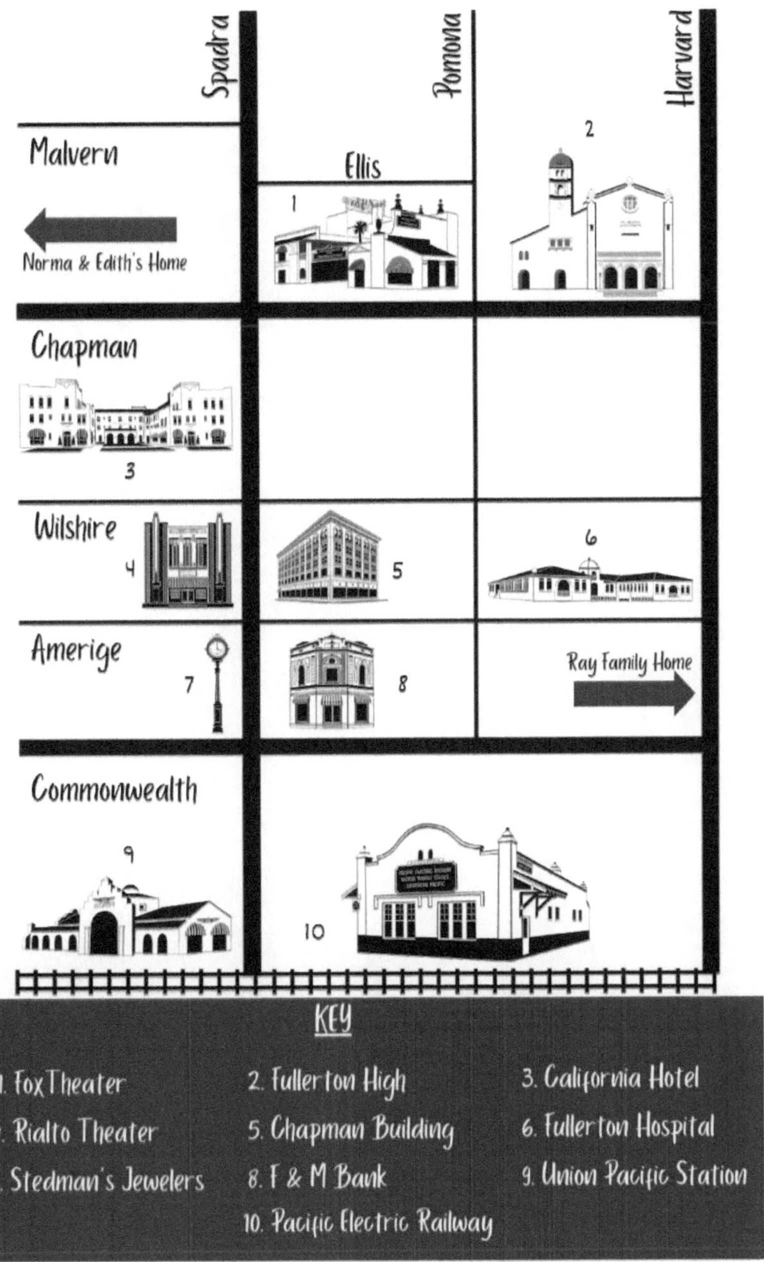

Debra L. Brunner

PROLOGUE

FRIDAY, MAY 9, 1930, SHORTLY BEFORE MIDNIGHT

Four pairs of feet click and clomp along the concrete path, their slow, monotonous rhythm reminding Dottie of the drumbeat played in movies as a prisoner walks to his execution. She shivers. After a while, the pavement ends, and the staccato beats dull to steady muffled thumps on the soft earth.

"This dirt will ruin my shoes!" Polly grumbles.

The others ignore her, having grown weary of her complaints. Weightier issues occupy their minds. So, they channel their mounting tension into a forward march through the darkness. Minutes pass as cool white cones from their flashlights sweep back and forth across the flat landscape. Suddenly, a shuffle disrupts the steady thud of their steps.

"Ouch! Why did you stop?" Dottie's chocolate bob swings forward while she bends to massage the top of her foot through the soft leather of her shoe. "Your heel dug into my toes!"

"It's freezing in here!" Blonde curls encircle Polly's piqued countenance as she rubs her bare arms.

"I told you to bring a warm coat," replies a strapping, chestnut-haired young man.

She sniffs through her raised, perky nose. "For Pete's sake, Earl, it's May! I thought you were joking."

Dottie comments irritably, "It hailed today." Her flashlight swings wildly about as she adjusts a fur garment around her trim form.

"You can wear mine, Polly." A slim youth slides his arms out of a slightly frayed wool cardigan and drapes it around her shoulders.

Polly softens, "Thanks, Leo. You're a peach."

Dottie turns toward Earl. "Are you sure no one will catch us here?"

"Nah," Earl waves his flashlight dismissively. "But let's go just a little further to be sure."

"This place gives me the heebie-jeebies." Polly shivers and slips a delicate arm through Leo's, as he directs the beacon of his dented flashlight toward the path ahead.

Earl's six-foot-one form brushes past to lead the foursome, his guitar case swinging casually in his right hand. But, in the darkness, the other three students fail to notice the nervous glance he throws over his shoulder.

After several minutes, Earl stops. "Alright kids, you can lighten your loads."

Dottie's gamine figure turns in a full circle taking in their surroundings under the bright beam of her flashlight. She carefully lights a kerosene lantern and places it at her feet, the warm light further illuminating the clear space. She remarks cautiously, "I think this will work."

"Of course it'll work!" Earl declares testily and reaches up to remove his leather gym bag from his broad shoulder.

Leo drops a hefty canvas duffel, which sloshes as it hits the ground. Polly sets down a Louis Vuitton case with care and looks up critically. "I dunno. There should be stars."

"Stars are always there, whether we see them or not," Leo comments with a friendly smile.

"I know that!" Polly barks.

Leo flinches as if slapped.

"Gees, Polly! Get a grip! Leo's the only one who's not completely fed up with you," Earl snaps.

Dottie turns toward the others. "We really shouldn't be at odds."

Earl blows out his breath. "You're right," he concedes, and reaches for his guitar. "Why don't I play the song I've been working on, settle our nerves." He opens the battered case to carefully remove a mahogany Gibson. After a few adjustments with the tuning keys, he begins to play. The others arrange a blanket on the dusty ground and listen. The tune begins with a peaceful, soothing melody, but as his strumming slows further, the notes become bittersweet. When the song ends, they sit in silence for a few moments, each preoccupied with their own private doubts.

Leo quietly comments, "I'm not so sure we should do this."

"Too late to back out now," Earl claps him on the shoulder with forced bravado.

Polly sighs dramatically, "My father's going to kill me."

"Maybe Polly and I should bow out. You and Dottie can do what you want," Leo suggests warily.

"Look, we're all having second thoughts. We'd be foolish if we weren't," Dottie remarks. "But it's all or none."

Earl insists "We're doing this."

"Easy for you to say," Leo mumbles under his breath.

"What's that supposed to mean?" Earl scowls.

Dottie attempts to smooth the tension. "This could affect Leo and me more than you and Polly. That's all."

This only riles Earl further. "Cuz I'm just a piano tuner?"

"That's not what—"

Without warning, a sharp boom explodes nearby.

Polly shoots a frightened glance over her shoulder and cries out, "What was that?!"

CHAPTER 1

THURSDAY, MAY 8, 1930

Another glorious day graces Fullerton, California with a cloudless sky and a cool breeze carrying the unmistakable fragrance of the last remaining orange blossoms. As I cycle down the lane toward our home, my thoughts return to the unseasonably emerald hills that accompanied me earlier on my ride. By May, the verdancy has typically faded from the surrounding foothills, as have the cheerful swaying heads of orange poppies.

Lost in reflection, I misjudge the distance of a tree root breaking through the asphalt that, when connecting with my front tire, sends me hurtling into a nearby hedge. I no sooner land on my hands and knees when I hear a squealing, "Oh my deeeear, Ruby! Are you alright?" Mrs. Lagersmock, a bell-shaped matron tightly gripping the leash of her faded fawn pug, Biscuit, hurries across the street and launches into a soliloquy about her shock over witnessing such a terrifying collision. She assures me that I must have broken something and refuses to acknowledge my repeated statements to the contrary.

I quickly examine my bicycle. Finding no damage, I note with appreciation the latched lid of the wooden basket secured to my handlebar. Thankful that my groceries haven't been scattered across the pavement, I hop back on and give a quick wave while rolling away. In truth, I'm so shaken by this woman's well-intentioned panic that I don't realize I've sustained an impressive abrasion below my right knee until I walk my bicycle up the path to my home.

Placing my hand on the whitewashed gate, I carefully avoid the exposed splinters, remnants of the most recent Santa Ana winds that were also atypical for this time of year. Once I maneuver the bicycle through the gate toward my office, a periwinkle single story cottage, I notice that, yet again, the hydrangea buds are pink instead of the blue that were originally planted. A horticulturist once explained to me that the pH of the soil determines the flowers' color and that our loam must be quite alkaline. For three years I've diligently raked my used coffee grounds around the roots to increase acidity, but thus far my efforts have failed. I must revisit this issue with my green-thumbed friend the next time I see him.

After arriving at my doorstep, I lean through the upper half of a Dutch door, having left it open earlier to air out my cottage, and set my handbag and gloves on a nearby table. I head to the "kitchen" with my string bag of groceries. Honestly, I should call it a "kitchenette," for the space is no more than a corner of the single larger room. A narrow two-legged sink stands under a bright window alongside a white cabinet. I place a box of crackers in a lower bin and a tin of coffee on the work surface next to the single burner stove. I usually serve crackers and cheese to the women who attend my reading parlor twice a week, something I began years ago to provide tutoring for women who never learned to read. The snacks at these meetings, however, have become something of a baking competition between the ladies who attend, so I really needn't bother with anything beyond coffee and a cold beverage.

Once my kitchenette is in order, I wheel my bicycle to the sleeping porch of Uncle Charles' two-story Craftsman house. I've had the bike for more than a decade and try to avoid sun exposure that would damage its paint and leather seat. I enjoy riding and would like to keep the bicycle a while longer. After returning to the cottage, I locate a small first aid kit in the medicine cabinet of the washroom and attend to my knee, all the while chastising myself over my inattention while riding. Properly salved and bandaged, I begin to remove my cloche hat when I hear a jingle from the bell next to the gate. Looking out the window I recognize Miss Graham and Miss Holmes, local teachers who have worked with my cousin Dottie over the years. I promptly approach the door and hold it open with a smile of welcome.

"Good afternoon, ladies. Please come in and have a seat." I look past them at the empty street. "It looks as though you walked here from town."

"Thank you, Miss Ray," the younger and fairer of the two replies as she sits and removes well-worn cotton gloves. "We came directly after school."

"Oh, Miss Graham, you must call me Ruby. How can I help you?"

"Well then you must call me Norma," she smiles up at me.

"And please call me Edith," her tall slim companion offers a hand to shake before sinking into a nearby chair. "We heard about your services and thought that perhaps you could help us with a…" she pauses to send a nervous glance in Norma's direction, "a delicate matter that has created quite a lot of turmoil for us both."

Delicate matters seem to have become my specialty as my career has evolved over the years. It began with assisting battered and mistreated women that I encountered through my tutoring sessions, women who needed to disappear into a safer situation someplace else. But in recent years, my work has included sleuthing and covert observation, such as uncovering evidence that the person pawning the silver was not the accused housekeeper but was, in fact, the homeowner who had developed quite the gambling problem. I suppose some would call me a "private investigator," but I prefer the term "inquiry agent," as it best describes the less formal operations I conduct on behalf of my clients, well outside the domain of police involvement. I suspect from Edith's tone that they too would like to avoid getting law enforcement involved.

To make these ladies more comfortable, I suggest, "Before discussing your concerns, can I offer you some refreshment? I made some lavender lemonade earlier this afternoon."

"That sounds lovely," replies Edith. "I'm quite parched after that walk."

I return moments later with a serving tray. "I apologize for the store-bought cookies," I nod toward a stack of Mallomars.

"No bother, Ruby." Norma smiles reassuringly. "I haven't had a Mallomar since Edith and I were students more than 15 years ago, but I remember being quite fond of them at the time."

Edith examines the dark chocolate mound on the plate that I hand her. "As I recall, they were brand new during our last year at Smith College, but you could only get them September through March."

I chuckle and admit, "Yes and that's still the case. They only ship them during the cool months, so I hoarded a stash a couple of months ago. Somehow though, when I was growing up in Manhattan, we could get them year-round."

"What brought you to California, Ruby?" Edith queries while resting the plate on her lap.

"Unfortunately, I lost both of my parents in a car crash when I was sixteen." I sip my lemonade before continuing. This is never an easy tale to share, nevertheless I continue in hopes that these women will feel more comfortable with opening up to me about their "delicate matter." "As an only child and no grandparents to take in, my father's younger brother, Charles, graciously welcomed me into his home."

"Oh, I'm so sorry to hear that," Norma replies. "That was kind of him and his wife. They would have had small children at the time."

"Actually, my Aunt Beatrice died of the Spanish flu earlier that same year." I reflect on how devastating 1918 was for so many people nationwide. "I think Uncle Charles and the children needed me as much as I needed them."

"Oh, how tragic. I am so sorry," Norma declares empathetically.

I notice Edith's curious gaze at a seascape hanging above the divan. "My aunt Beatrice painted that," I tell her.

Edith quickly turns toward me, her hazel eyes bright with interest. "Your aunt was an artist?"

"Yes, in fact this cottage was built as her studio. She finished that painting in 1915." I point to a colorful oil painting on the wall behind the divan.

Edith stands to get a closer look. "It's a masterful work of impressionism. Where did she paint this?"

"Well, my aunt was quite fond of the shore, Laguna Beach in particular. If you look closely, you can see the tidepools in the background." I join Edith at the painting.

"What a coincidence! Edith and I are planning to move to Laguna," Norma, now standing beside Edith, declares.

"That is a coincidence," I agree.

"It's true," Edith remarks. "It's been my lifelong dream to make a living as an artist. But instead, I chose education as a more practical occupation. I actually started college a bit later than my peers. Unlike Norma, I was not quite clever enough to earn a scholarship." Edith turns from the painting and smiles warmly at her friend. "So, for years I worked as a shop girl to save money. Once at Smith, when not taking education courses, I enjoyed every art class I could get, whether studio or history."

"She's modest. Not only is she brilliant, Edith is also a gifted artist," Norma praises.

"I'm not surprised," I comment and smile at Edith. She clearly has a good eye and exudes intelligence. I do understand her choice in career, however. Occupational options are limited for unmarried women with a college education. "So, what brought you both to California?"

Norma answers, "My father was killed in a construction accident while working on the Amerige Block in 1920. Do you know the area I'm talking about? Those brick and glazed tile buildings over on Commonwealth?"

"I do remember that, now that you mention it. I was a senior at Fullerton High at the time. It was very early in the construction of the buildings, if I'm not mistaken." Searching my memory for more details, I continue, "Your brother Frank didn't have any classes with me since he was a year younger, but we all felt terrible for him."

Gazing down at her clasped hands Norma goes on. "After my father's death, I was the only family he had. We lost my mother when Frank was a toddler, and our other brother, James, died in battle during the war. So you see, there was no question about my returning to Fullerton."

"And Edith came with you?" I shift my gaze from Norma to Edith, my eyebrows raised in question.

"Yes, well…," Norma blushes.

"Where she goes, I go," Edith proclaims with a look of devotion in her warm eyes as she squeezes Norma's hand reassuringly.

Meeting her gaze, I nod with comprehension, "I understand. It can't be easy in a town like this."

"Quite." Edith replies softly.

"I'm glad you know you can trust me with your secret, particularly in these suspicious times," I reassure them earnestly.

Norma audibly exhales and chuckles, "You see Edith, that wasn't so bad."

"I told you." Edith laughs then tells me, "We've heard that you're very kind."

"Thank you, Edith." As we return to our seats, I suggest, "Why don't you tell me what brings you here today."

Norma turns toward Edith, who nods encouragingly. "The long and the short of it is that all the money we've scrimped and saved has been stolen."

"Stolen?" I blink and lean forward, nearly toppling the cookie plate I have just rested upon my knee. "My goodness! Please tell me what happened."

"When Norma and I relocated here," Edith explains, "Frank was about to be evicted from the house he'd shared with his father. The man's accident was due to his intoxication, so no compensation was offered."

"Oh dear." That explains a great deal.

"Indeed." Edith gives me a knowing look. "We secured lodging at a boarding house about a mile from the high school. Norma and Frank have the upper floor suite with two bedrooms, while my ground floor room mirrors that of another teacher."

"For ten years we have saved every penny by, quite literally, stashing our savings under our mattresses." Norma explains.

"I'd say that was a wise choice in hindsight," The stock market crash last fall decimated the savings of so many, including close friends.

"Precisely. But a few petty thefts in our neighborhood a couple of months ago led us to rethink our fiscal management, so to speak." Norma's body stiffens. "We decided that we would open an account for our savings at Farmers and Merchants Bank, but we were quite rudely informed that as single women we could only do so if a male relative co-signed."

"We've had the vote for a decade yet are still dependent on men for our financial decisions," Edith interjects with frustration.

"Outrageous but true." I consider my own situation. It's my understanding that, at the very least, women need the permission of their husbands or male relatives (if unmarried) to open a savings account. But the bank manager at F&M erroneously believes that women are a financial risk and insists on male co-ownership for all accounts. "What did you decide?"

"The logical choice was for me to open the account with Frank as co-owner. We have no other male family in the area," Norma replies.

"And he was only too eager to assist," Edith rejoins, shaking her salt-and-pepper head.

Norma tuts, "You know he only wanted to help."

"Does Frank know of your relationship?" I query hesitantly.

Norma shakes her head, eyes wide. "I hope not. We've been so vigilant." She pauses. "Up until telling you, that is."

"Of course. You'd lose your livelihood and residence at the very least."

Norma nods sadly. "That being said, it's been our dream to buy a home together, just the two of us, and we finally had the financial resources to do so. Given the difficulty we had at the bank, however, we couldn't imagine that two women could own their own property."

Edith's open palm motions toward Aunt Beatrice's painting. "But last weekend we visited the art colony in Laguna Beach and, during the course of conversation, discovered that other unmarried women have bought homes there. Laguna is a haven for free thinkers. We should have realized this sooner. One artist in particular told us that she would help us make the connections we need to purchase a small cottage, as well as find teaching positions nearby." Edith turns toward me with a smile. "And I could start painting again."

Norma nervously smoothes her sandy colored hair. "Two days ago we thought we were alone in the parlor when Frank overheard a conversation we were having about this. He became quite irrational and accused me of abandoning him when he was down and out."

Edith comments, "Frank has had difficulty keeping jobs for several years."

"From what I recollect, he was a well-liked boy who stayed out of trouble." I think back to our high school days.

Norma agrees. "When he was younger, just after Father died, he was eager to prove his manhood and took any job he could get while finishing school."

"Then what happened?"

"Well, when the California Hotel opened in 1923, he was hired as a bellhop but quickly fell in with the wrong sort, if you know what I mean. After multiple warnings he was fired for drinking on the job and was quite lucky they didn't report him to the police." Norma's shoulders slump.

"You mentioned that he was angry about your plans, but you're both adults. Did he think you would live together indefinitely?" I question.

"I'm not sure what he's thinking these days. Until recently, Frank and I were quite close. From the moment I returned to California, he was so loving and respectful. Lately, however, he's become quite erratic and impulsive." Norma sighs as Edith reaches over to pat her hand. "But I never thought he'd steal from us."

"How did you discover that Frank stole your money?"

Edith leans forward to explain. "We went to the bank yesterday to make a deposit and were told that he had closed the account that morning. When pressed, the bank manager reminded Norma quite firmly that Frank's name was on the account, and that, as a male, he was considered the primary shareholder." She rolls her eyes. "Then the manager glared at me suspiciously and asked about my interest in the situation. Not caring for the direction of his line of inquiry, we left immediately."

"Did you ask Frank about this?"

"Yes, he admitted to taking the money but when asked about his intentions, he vaguely said that he has plans for us but then refused to discuss it further. He later left the house, and we haven't seen him since." Norma raises her open palms and shrugs her shoulders.

"Do you think he has spent the money?"

Edith bristles. "After he left last night, we searched his room but were unable to find any trace of the funds. We have no way of knowing what he's done with it."

"How much money are we talking about?"

"$2,073.28," they reply in unison. "Enough to buy a small home," Edith adds.

I release a long whistle. "That's a lot of pennies."

"Tutoring after school and on weekends has supplemented our income from the school. Of course, male teachers earn much more than we do." Norma exhales with irritation.

"Any idea where he may have gone?" I query.

"I doubt that he's left the area, but he drove away in our car. I figured he needed to cool-off, but he still hasn't returned." Norma answers.

"What type of car is it?"

"It's a tar black 1919 Ford Touring with an electric start. Norma's father pulled out all the stops, even though he couldn't afford it," Edith remarks.

Norma reaches for her pocketbook then passes me a folded sheet of paper. "I've made a list of people who might know where Frank is or what he has done with the money. I've also given you the name and address of Stan Jones, who's the foreman for the company that's building the new auditorium at the high school. He hired Frank a few months ago to do odd jobs."

I peruse the list, noting the impeccable penmanship characteristic of educators. Then, recognizing a familiar name, I question, "Elizabeth Martin?"

"She's the one who referred us to you." Norma explains. "I called her after Frank left the house yesterday, so she knows about the missing money. She can give you additional information about Frank. Maybe tell you something we forgot to ask."

I raise my eyebrows in question, which encourages Norma to continue. "Elizabeth was Frank's high school sweetheart until his troubles began. But they stayed good friends after they broke up. She didn't know where he was when I spoke with her last night, but knowing him as well as she does, she may be helpful to you."

"I'm sure you are correct." I forgot that Elizabeth, a dear friend since our days in the Girl's League at the high school, dated Frank all those years ago. "What is Frank's relationship with each of the others?"

Norma points a neatly trimmed fingertip to a name on the list. "Frank met Floyd Phillips at the hotel. He goes by 'Fipps.' They both started working there around the same time, but Fipps kept his job and worked his way up to security. He comes around the house from time to time to visit Frank."

"And Wallace Mains?" I ask.

Edith replies, "Wallace moved into the room across from mine just prior to the beginning of the school year. He also teaches at the high school."

"I'm not sure if he knows anything, but he and Frank have become quite friendly with one another," Norma explains. "Incidentally, I'm sure that he overheard the disagreement yesterday afternoon."

"Thank you for the information, ladies. This is an excellent start, and I will visit these folks tomorrow if he hasn't returned by then."

Edith then glances at me and quickly averts her gaze. "What about remuneration?"

I gently explain, 'Basically, when I've done all that I can with your request, you can decide what my efforts are worth."

"How unusual." Norma leans back, her eyes wide with surprise.

"This work is more of a mission than a vocation for me as far as I am concerned. I am willing to charge a fixed rate for my more affluent clients, but I would like to be able to help anyone who needs me."

"Thank you," both women reply in unison.

"If there's nothing else at the moment, can I offer you a ride home?"

After gathering their belongings, Norma and Edith follow me to the long driveway running between the house and cottage. There parked under a covered port is a highly polished black behemoth resembling a man's flat cap.

"What is THAT?" Norma asks incredulously.

I proudly proclaim, "This is a 1925 Balboa, the only car ever produced in Fullerton."

"Oh, I remember those. Didn't I read that, following the Orange County Auto Show, no Balboas were actually sold?" Edith questions, clearly an automotive buff herself.

"The truth is that a few prototypes were built and possibly sold. My uncle invested heavily in Balboa Motor Corporation after seeing a model of this touring car at an exhibit in the courtyard of the California Hotel. Before the BMC went belly up, he persuaded their executive board to release one of the prototypes." We each open a solid heavy door and slide onto a leather seat. "It doesn't reach 25 miles per gallon, as promised, nor is the engine 'supercharged,' but it gets the job done."

As we back out of the driveway, I turn to Norma, who is seated next to me in the passenger seat. "Can I ask you a question pertaining to your work?"

"Absolutely. What do you want to know?" Norma cranks down the window allowing a breeze to enter the stuffy cabin.

Pressing the clutch with my left foot, I shift into first gear. "It's about Dottie. I know that you've taught her over the past few years, and correct me if I'm wrong, she's currently in your senior English composition class."

"That's correct. Is something the matter?" Norma asks with concern.

I quickly glance at Norma then back to the road ahead. "Well, you see that's just what I'm trying to determine. She seems more secretive than usual, and my Uncle is quite worried. How is she getting on in class?"

"As always she's an exemplary student, very involved in discussions and not at all reluctant to share her writings with the class." Norma turns her body sideways toward me. "That being said, I have noticed that outside of class she is usually in the company of Earl Adams. He's quite a bit older than the other seniors."

I make a right onto the main boulevard. "Well that would explain her reluctance to accept her college admission for next year. She's been talking about Berkeley since she was eight. Yet when she received her acceptance letter to their chemistry program, she appeared more circumspect than enthusiastic." I sigh heavily. "I'd hate to see her sacrifice her dream, all because of a boy."

Norma pats my shoulder. "I'll keep an eye and ear out for you on campus."

"Thank you, Norma. I would appreciate that." I smile. "And please give me a call if Frank returns."

"Of course," she replies. "We will call immediately."

After a few more turns, I pull in front of their boarding house, a shingled Queen Anne with a wide porch and elaborate gingerbread trim. After exiting the car, they both turn and thank me for my assistance. I assure them that I will give their situation my complete attention and will be in touch soon. While pulling away, I glance out of my rearview mirror and watch as they lean into each other, shoulder to shoulder, and slowly trudge up the path toward their home.

CHAPTER 2

Salmon and magenta clouds drift sedately across the western sky as I stroll away from the carport. I stop to pick a few dark green avocados from low hanging branches, then head for a weathered wooden bench near a jacaranda tree. I notice that a few lavender-blue blossoms have begun to appear. Chuckling, I recall the tale Uncle Charles once shared with me.

When first purchased, the bench was placed underneath the tree, but my aunt soon noticed a sticky residue accumulating on the oak seat. Glancing up, she observed a fine mist falling from the canopy of violet petals, so she held up her palms to capture the mildly perfumed dew in her hands. Moments later, her bliss was interrupted by the gardener, who had entered the yard.

"Ma'am, that there honeydew ain't nectar. It's aphid droppings."

Horrified, my aunt tearfully raced into the house and would not be persuaded to leave the bath for hours. Of course, years later she was the first to recount her mishap with laughter when friends or family visited their home.

Setting my handbag and avocados on the bench, I remove my right glove and grasp a shiny Lincoln wheat penny from my coin purse. A few steps down the cobblestone path lead me to a diminutive wishing well built of stone that was quarried during the construction of drilling rigs at one of my Uncle's nearby oil fields. Closing my eyes I wish for the health, safety, and happiness of my loved ones and then, reaching under the scalloped shingles of its pitched roof, release the penny into the shallow depths of the jolly well. I'm certain that Jack and Dottie swipe the pennies from time to time, but over the years this simple daily ritual has staunched some of my anxiety on their behalf, for I am more sister to Dottie and mother to Jack than cousin to either of them.

Returning to the bench, I peel away my other glove and settle against the seatback. Looking down at my hands, knuckles furrowed on digits slightly too short for the width of my palms, I feel as though

I am seeing my mother's hands. When did that happen? Without warning, I am caught in a wave of anguish so visceral that tears immediately distort my vision. While over the years these moments of heartache have become less frequent, I feel them just as deeply every time. I give in to the emotion, finding comfort in the now familiar grief. After a while, arms wrapped across my chest, I give my shoulders a quick squeeze then dry my eyes with a handkerchief, careful to avoid the delicately crocheted trim. All this talk today about death has gotten to me. With shoulders squared, I stand, gather my belongings, and stride toward the house.

Once upstairs, I step into the bathroom to splash cool water on my face. I gaze into the mirror above the pedestal sink to inspect my eyes for redness and find only the reflection of jade green irises. Primping my strawberry blonde bob, loosely curled away from my heart-shaped face, I am reminded of comments others have made noting my similarity to the actress Marion Davies. Dottie's convinced that the face on the poster for the upcoming movie *Florodora Girl* could be me. But I sigh as my attention wanders to the bump resting on the bridge of my nose, for I'm certain that Dottie is only being nice.

As I turn from the sink to grab a hand towel, I spy something quite unexpected in the bathtub. A hand-sized pinecone with broad greenish-brown scales is resting under two feet of water. Puzzled, I reach in and begin to seize the prickly mass when a sharp downturned beak protrudes near my pinkie. Shrinking back, I bellow, "Ja-ack!"

Rapid footsteps approach from the hall and a lanky 13-year-old in wide-legged trousers and a brightly colored argyle vest enters and leans casually against the door frame with affected coolness. "I see you've met Bob."

"Bob?" I sputter incredulously.

"Why sure! Bob the alligator snapper. Those jaws'll bob a finger or toe if you're not too careful."

"You could have warned me when I walked past your room. I almost lost a well-regarded digit." I wiggle the fingers on my right hand.

Jack's short golden-brown curls bounce as he shakes his head. "Aww heck, Ruby. Where's the fun in that?"

"Sooo, how did you happen to acquire this, um, snapper?" I query, still uncertain of its genus.

"Traded my rosey boa for him. This new kid says they're in all the ponds and lakes in Tennessee. I think Bob may be the first alligator snapping turtle in California," Jack proclaims proudly.

Waving a hand in the direction of the tub I insist, "Well he can't stay in there."

"Righty-o! I have a bucket in my room." He carefully lifts the hissing terrapin from the water. "I kinda figured he wanted to swim around here for a while, but he just sits there like a dumb rock."

"Be sure to wash up before coming down for dinner. Who knows what sort of germs you could catch from that thing."

With a lopsided grin, Jack leaves a trail of water droplets on the waxed hardwood floor as he returns to his room. I roll my eyes while turning back toward the sink in disgust and scrub my hands with a bar of soap. Feeling more hygienic but no less unsettled, I head downstairs to check on dinner.

As I near the kitchen, I am mollified by the savory aroma of roasted chicken and the raspy yet calming voice of Louis Armstrong singing "When You're Smiling." Nan, our housekeeper and surrogate grandmother, adores her small radio and hums along while stirring a bubbling saucepan. At once she notices my presence. "Sounds like ya met Bob."

"Whatever are we going to do with that boy?" I inquire with mock seriousness. In truth I adore Jack's passion for all creatures, regardless of their size or germ count.

"I reckon he'll be a biologist or a zookeeper." Nan predicts as her wrinkled fingers brush loose gray strands away from her flushed face. "Either way he'll be happy as a clam."

I remove an apron from a hook behind the door and slip it over my head. "What can I do to help?"

Nan points a wooden spoon toward the colander in the sink. "Those taters need mashin'."

After tipping the steaming spuds into an enamel mixing bowl, I fetch the zig zag masher from a deep drawer in the cabinet. "Why isn't Dottie helping?"

With a nod toward a closed door, Nan explains, "She's in there studyin' with Polly Baker. B'sides, I could do this in my sleep." She may be nearing seventy, but she's no less spry and not the least bit frail.

After finishing the potatoes, I slide open the pocket door and call into a dining room that is brightly lit by an Art Nouveau chandelier. "Dottie, we'll be ready for dinner soon. Clear away those books, please, and set the table."

"Sorry Ruby. We lost track of the time. Can Polly stay for dinner?" Dottie snaps shut a composition book while Polly stacks several dense tomes on the sideboard.

"Absolutely. Polly, you know you are always welcome here."

She smiles sweetly while helping Dottie cover the mahogany table with an ivory tablecloth.

Uncle Charles saunters in from the adjoining parlor, tall and fit as a man much younger than his mid-forties. Tapping the top of my head with a rolled *Santa Ana Daily Register* he exclaims, "Well young lady, it's been a very good day on the market."

"Let me guess, Standard Oil, U.S. Steel, and General Electric are all up." I feign an indifferent tone, but in truth I am genuinely interested. My parents left me quite comfortable financially, having both received substantial inheritances from their own parents. So over the years, I've invested in quite a number of stocks.

"You forgot Coca-Cola." Uncle Charles tugs at his earlobe as he playfully teases. "To this day I cannot believe that I allowed a 16-year-old to invest such a handsome sum in bubbles and syrup."

"It was one of the only company names I'd ever heard of at the time," I laugh.

"Well, those stocks certainly served you well last fall." Charles reflects.

"Not panicking served us all well." I thoughtfully praise. "You—"

Jack bounds into the room. "Bob's finally eating! That raw chicken did the trick. Wanna see?"

With a wink and a smirk in my direction, Uncle Charles turns and follows Jack.

A short while later, a sharp *brrring* interrupts the clanking of cutlery and murmur of polite conversation during dinner. "I'll get it!" Jack leaps from his chair and bolts toward the living room.

"Walk please. There's no fire." Uncle Charles chastens.

"Ray residence. Jack Ray speaking." After a pause we hear, "Sure I'll get her." Then he hollers, "Dottie, phone's for you."

Uncle Charles reaches inside his gray plaid coat and pulls out his pocket watch. "Who on Earth would be calling during dinner time? Make it quick, Dottie."

"Yes, Dad. I apologize." Dottie bows her head as she hurries from the room.

Jack leans across Dottie's now vacant chair and, with a blush, asks Polly what she thinks of the new radio program *Believe It or Not.* "That Ripley guy has some creepy junk." He then nervously averts his eyes from Polly's disinterested gaze.

"It appears that his interests have broadened," I note under my breath to Uncle Charles while nodding to Jack. My uncle grins while buttering a biscuit.

Minutes later Dottie returns. "That was Nick."

"Nick Nixon? Gloomy Gus? I don't know why you bother with that guy," Polly pouts while cutting a glazed carrot.

"That's not nice, Polly," Dottie admonishes.

"Well, he's so dull."

Uncle Charles looks up from his plate, his mouth set in a frown beneath a dark brown pencil mustache. He does not tolerate unkindness.

"I'll admit, he seems like a curmudgeon, but that's because he's terribly shy and very serious about school." Dottie defends her former classmate and Latin tutor, Richard, who prefers to be called "Nick" by his peers. "He was considerate and patient with me sophomore year before transferring."

Polly shrugs her shoulders, "To each his own."

I lean across the table toward Dottie, "My heart aches for that poor boy. First Richard's family lost their lemon ranch, then his little brother died. I ran into his aunt Carrie the other day at Alpha Beta, and she told me that he's having to give up his lifelong dream of attending an East Coast university."

Dottie quickly raises her hand to her mouth, "That's terrible! Nick recently wrote to me about winning the Harvard Club of California Award. I assumed he'd be going."

"Apparently Harold's consumption has relapsed, so he's reentered the sanatorium. Even with the scholarship, Richard's family just can't afford to send him to Harvard."

"I suppose with his brother away, he's needed more than ever at the market." Dottie unconsciously pushes vegetables around her plate.

"Didn't he mention any of this during your conversation?" I inquire.

"He wouldn't. He's very private, especially about his family." Dottie turns toward Polly, who is enthralled with the conversation, "Please don't say anything to anyone about this."

Polly sighs with disappointment, but she crosses her heart. "What did he want anyway? I didn't know that he calls you."

"That was a first. There wasn't time for him to send me a letter, so his dad let him use the market phone." Dottie reaches for the pitcher to refill her glass with lemonade. "He's taking his girlfriend to the Fox Theater tomorrow. She's a student at our school. Anyway, he wanted to know if we could meet up after that."

"Well, I'll be!" Polly declares while tilting her pretty head. "Saaay, let's go see the movie too. I hear it's good. It has something to do with a gal having second thoughts about getting married."

"Which movie is it?" I question. "That describes both *One Romantic Night* and *A Notorious Affair*."

"The one with Lillian Gish," Polly replies.

"*One Romantic Night*," Dottie and I, both quite fond of films, declare simultaneously.

"Well, it's a plan then." Polly dusts off her hands. "I'll tell Leo tomorrow at school"

Uncle Charles regards Dottie. "That's a shame about Nick and Harvard. He's a bright young man." Then, following a loaded pause, he asks, "Speaking of college, have you made a decision about Berkeley?"

Put on the spot, Dottie blinks sharply. "Um…well Dad, I'm still not sure."

I interject, "Dottie, you've yearned for this opportunity for so long!"

Uncle Charles nods in agreement. "The deadline for accepting the offer is May 15th. This is your choice Dottie, but what's the alternative? You didn't apply to any other universities."

Dottie hesitates, casting a sidelong glance at Polly, then mutters, "Can we talk about this later?"

Noting her discomfort, Uncle Charles surrenders. "Alright for now, but we will discuss it this weekend."

"I for one would have loved a stint at Berkeley," I sigh. Studying English and logic at the junior college on the high school campus wasn't at all the same as going away to a university. But while I feel some regret, I harbor no resentment. The children were young, and I was needed at home. Out of curiosity I ask Polly, "How about you? What are your plans after graduation?"

About to take a bite, Polly replaces her fork on her plate. "My father decided that I'll work in his office until I marry someday. Business is booming, and he needs some help with the accounting." Somewhat defensively she adds, "I'm not half bad at math."

"Neither are you, Polka Dot," Dottie's father winks at her. Uncle Charles began calling Dottie "Polka Dot" when, at age four, she became fascinated with accordion music at a local Oktoberfest celebration in nearby Anaheim. Her parents bought her a miniature squeezebox for Christmas which she played nonstop for two weeks. While her interest waned over time, the nickname stuck.

"Da-ad!" Dottie complains with embarrassment then shoots a pointed glance in Polly's direction.

Uncle Charles dramatically clutches his heart and elbows Jack who's chuckling next to him.

"It's okay, Dottie. I think it's sweet," Polly says wistfully. From what I know of Fred Baker, her father is a cold, commanding man not prone to nicknames or endearments.

"Say Polly," Jack shyly cuts in, "I saw your dad's interview in the *Times*. He—"

Interrupting Jack, Dottie turns to her father and sweetly asks, "Can we be excused? We have to study."

Uncle Charles waves a dismissive hand and reminds Dottie, "It's a school night. No guests after eight."

As both girls gather their dishes and scurry into the kitchen, I notice Jack staring forlornly at his napkin. "So, Jack, what's this about Mr. Baker in the *New York Times*."

Jack's face visibly brightens as he retrieves the paper, already turned to the correct page, and passes it to me across the table. "Remember the cult thing under Mr. Baker's orange trees last month?"

"How can I forget? It was all anyone could talk about for two weeks."

At the time, the *Fullerton Daily News Tribune* reported that one of Baker's employees, Bert Lemming, encountered a group of trespassers in the grove while making his nightly rounds. He claimed that they were "Satan worshippers," and fearing that his own life might be sacrificed as part of their dark ritual, he fired two blanks into the air and successfully drove them away. Mr. Lemming returned to the site later that evening with Mr. Baker and the police, where they found ceremonial objects and candles.

I glance at the headline in the *Times*, "Cults In Southern California: A Disturbing New Trend," and recall why earlier I had not chosen to read any further. The article opens with the investigation of the Blackburn Cult last year which unearthed the bodies of a teenage girl and her dogs from beneath the flooring of a house in Venice, CA.

"Yikes!" I recoil and turn to Jack, whose expression is one of morbid fascination.

Loathe to expose myself to additional gore, I skip several paragraphs until spotting Mr. Baker's name and read aloud, "'We've been patrolling the area for months since bootleggers began cutting though on their nightly runs. But this is the first time we've seen anything like it,' states Mr. Frederick Baker, owner of Sunny Hills Fruit Company. Police Chief Wendell Houston concurs, 'There was no evidence of cult activity in Fullerton prior to this incident. Ours is a quiet, wholesome town.'" The rest of the article covers the arrest of a self-proclaimed "prophet" in Seal Beach, a neo-spiritualist commune in San Diego, and additional cult activity in Los Angeles. The author closes with a cautionary statement to "those susceptible to exploitation, including widows, young idealists, and the nouveau riche."

"Well, I don't suppose there are many of the latter left these days," Charles observes while rising from the table.

"True." I slowly begin to stack plates and bowls for clearing. "But it does make me wonder why now? Why here?"

"War, plague, financial crisis, unemployment...it's no surprise that some turn away from conventional purveyors of meaning." Charles gently pats my back. "Enough serious talk this evening. Why don't I start up the radio while you finish with the dishes."

Yawning as I head up the stairs a few hours later, I notice a light shining under Dottie's closed bedroom door. Without waiting for a reply to my knock, I push open the door and discover Dottie asleep at her desk, head resting on crossed arms. A small desk lamp with a pagoda shade provides the sole source of illumination in an otherwise darkened room. One book from a stack of weighty volumes is open beside her.

I turn down robin's egg blue bed covers, and Dottie awakens, stretches her arms, and rolls her shoulders. "I wasn't planning on falling asleep so soon."

"It's 10:00 on a Thursday night. Just how late were you planning to stay up?"

"Lots to get through this evening," Dottie yawns.

"Are you studying chemistry?" I inquire, curious about the overlarge books. Dottie is gifted in mathematics and science, but she finds chemistry to be particularly interesting and plans to study "the building blocks of everything" (as she puts it) in college.

"Not tonight," she replies briefly and stacks the books on the floor next to her desk.

I hand Dottie a pair of pajamas from a drawer in her armoire. She loosens and pulls off the tie of her school uniform, which are mandatory for girls (but not boys) at Fullerton High. While not yet successful in persuading the school's administration to abolish this mandate, thanks to the FHS Girls Uniform Dress Coalition (an offshoot of the Girl's League), female students now have a voice in the design of their uniform, something I would have greatly appreciated years ago. After Dottie has draped her skirt and blouse over a gesso screen angled in a corner of her room, she unselfconsciously slips a pale pink chemise over her head and tosses it into the laundry hamper. She pulls on the turquoise blue pajamas and plops on her bed, then removes a silver-backed Edwardian hairbrush from her nightstand. The smooth gleam of the brush and matching hand mirror indicate that they have been recently polished.

"Your mother would be pleased with your care of her vanity set." I accept the proffered hairbrush and park myself behind Dottie on her bed. With a start, I realize that several years have passed since we last engaged in this nightly ritual of smoothing her silky locks.

Dottie sighs, "I miss her. I remember how it felt to sit on her lap and how her laugh always sounded like a bell to me. But the only image

I have for her is that picture." She points toward her nightstand at an engagement photo of her parents.

"You look very much like her, especially now as a young lady. Jack, on the other hand, inherited her playfulness. But you both possess her charm in your own unique ways," I reflect.

Dottie abruptly turns to face me. "It's so strange. Even though mama's been gone for so long, I feel closer to her than Polly does to her own mother who's living."

I place two fingers under her chin and gaze directly into her eyes. "Your mama's still here. Don't you feel her all around us? A love like that doesn't vanish."

Wiping away a single tear, Dottie answers, "I do. And I know how lucky I am to have Dad, and you as well."

I resume brushing Dottie's hair as she faces forward. "Is Polly having trouble at home?"

Dottie nods vigorously. "Yes! It's a nightmare. Her father is furious that she's dating Leo Taliaferro. He says that Leo's mom doesn't belong here and that his dad is a papist wop, whatever that means. And Polly's mother supports her father without question."

Tensing with fury, my words explode before I can consider their impact. "That man is a hateful bigot hiding behind his wealth and position in town."

Wide-eyed, Dottie pivots to face me. "Mr. Baker is a bigot?"

I recall an incident I witnessed in town where Mr. Baker harangued a busboy for accidentally knocking over a glass of water on the table. A few drops landed on a stack of papers Mr. Baker was discussing with another businessman. Mr. Baker called the young man every derogatory term I've ever heard, as well as some that were new to me. When the busboy fled, Mr. Baker barked a laugh and said, "What can you expect from these immigrants?"

Uncle Charles has witnessed numerous similar instances. However, in the interest of Dottie's friendship with Polly since childhood, Uncle Charles and I have been careful to avoid voicing our concerns about

Mr. Baker in Dottie's presence. Nonetheless, we have monitored their relationship with vigilance.

I nod. "Very much so."

"You know, Ruby, Mr. Baker is always kind to me when I'm at their house, but I have heard him yell at Mrs. Baker and people who work at their house. He seems sweet to Polly, but she says that when no one outside the family is there, he sometimes becomes enraged."

"Is she afraid of him?" I probe.

"She hasn't said so, but I think she is right now," Dottie declares with concern. "She asked me to stay over tomorrow night because he won't yell about Leo if I'm there. I would have stayed there tonight, but it's a school night."

"Oh Dottie, after what you just told me, I don't want you over there at all. Perhaps Polly can stay here instead." I suggest with uneasiness.

"I'll ask her tomorrow, but if her dad says, 'No,' can I stay over?" Dottie pleads.

"Let's talk to your father about this in the morning. In the meantime, shall I tuck you into bed, like the old days?" I attempt to lighten the mood.

Dottie leans in for a warm hug and slips under her covers, which I then push snugly around her. I inhale the sweet honey fragrance of her hair as I kiss her forehead. "Good night. Sleep tight."

"Don't let the bed bugs bite," Dottie rejoins with a grin then closes her eyes.

CHAPTER 3

FRIDAY, MAY 9, 1930

Uncle Charles modernized our kitchen several years ago, starting with the addition of a sunny breakfast nook which was all the rage in new homes at the time. This morning the lemon alcove is brightly lit by a bay window projecting onto a back garden that is currently awash with cheery azaleas and irises. The built-in benches and table extend further than most bungalow nooks, which allows me to spread multiple newspapers alongside my coffee, a pot of Cordelia Knott's boysenberry jam, and a plate of fried eggs with toast.

"Listen to this." I raise the *Santa Ana Daily Register* for Nan to see the headline. "President Hoover is considering a Californian as his next nominee to the Supreme Court."

"Well, I'll be! That Parker fella didn't sit right with me," Nan sniffs.

For the first time in 36 years, the Senate has rejected a President's nominee. The tally two days ago was close, with Judge John J. Parker losing by only 1 vote.

I nod. "From what I've read he's not too keen about labor groups, and the NAACP opposes him over an inflammatory comment he made about 'negroes' participating in politics some years back."

"Who's the California judge? Have ya heard of him?" Nan wipes her freckled forehead with the back of her hand and returns to kneading bread on a large wooden board.

"What's this about a California judge?" Uncle Charles strolls in and plucks a fleshy strawberry from a bowl Nan has set aside for shortcake after dinner.

"Federal Judge Curtis Wilbur is being considered for the Supreme Court vacancy," I answer. "According to this, when Wilbur was on the LA County Superior Court he did a great deal for juvenile welfare. He even wrote a children's book."

"Hoover won't nominate Wilbur." Uncle Charles pops the entire berry into his mouth then attempts to reach for another but is swiftly thwarted by a swat on the hand from Nan. Truthfully, they've adored one another since she joined the household twenty years ago. "He'll choose Owen Roberts instead."

"But of course! He'll be a shoo-in." Owen Roberts has been at the forefront of the Teapot Dome scandal as special Government counsel. Since 1923, the public has been shocked by the level of government corruption revealed during the series of hearings, including illegally obtained oil leases on government land and conspiracy to defraud the US government.

"This unsavory business gives honest oilmen like you a bad name." Having lost my appetite, I push away the remaining egg and toast.

"The rotten apple spoils his companion," Uncle Charles quotes Benjamin Franklin.

"I wonder when we'll have a female Supreme Court Justice," I muse. Since the last decade a handful of women have been appointed to judicial posts.

"Stuff and nonsense! What next? A female Senator…or President?" Suffrage was difficult enough for Nan. At the time she despaired, "How do I know how to vote?" But I've noticed on every Election Day since, Nan heads to our polling place wearing a determined look and her best frock.

"Yes, eventually. I'm not talking about sending a man to the moon. After all, women have been appointed to state supreme courts already." I notice the color rising on Nan's face and don't wish to upset her further. Changing the topic, "Where are you off to this morning Uncle Charles?"

"Would you believe I'm meeting with Fred Baker at my office?" He replies with one eyebrow raised.

"Whatever for? I've heard his name entirely too much lately," I moan. "Dottie brought him up last night."

"Baker didn't say, but I suspect it has something to do with that Muckenthaler lease." A few weeks ago, my uncle's oil company leased

150 acres of land in northeast Fullerton to a good friend of his, Walter Muckenthaler, whose wife's family is also in the oil business. "Walter plans to grow walnuts."

"That must have riled Mr. Baker. Doesn't he also grow walnuts?" I inquire.

"He did. But he lost the walnut business due to blight a few years ago. I think the bigger issue is that the property butts up against one of his orange groves."

"Well, good luck with that conversation."

"Thanks," Uncle Charles laughs while shaking his head. "Back to what you said about your conversation with Dottie. You know I've never felt comfortable with that friendship, but Polly is generally a sweet girl and means a great deal to Dottie."

"What, specifically, concerns you right now?"

He rubs his chin and takes a deep breath. "Well, he has a reputation for being hot-headed, and I happen to know that he's amassed quite a gun collection over the years."

"Whatever for? It's not like there's much hunting here in Southern California?"

"As I understand it, he wants to make sure he can protect his loved ones." Charles shakes his head. "Personally, I'd be more afraid of having all those weapons under my roof."

"Hear! Hear!" I concur. "Let's hope that Dottie spends as little time as possible over at the Baker residence."

He nods in agreement. "So, what are your plans today?"

Since I didn't receive a call this morning from Norma or Edith about Frank's return, I must assume he's still missing. "I'll be in town later this morning. I have a few interviews for a new case. Do you want to meet for lunch at McFarland's?" I propose.

Uncle Charles bends to collect a lightweight hat from atop his dark leather briefcase. Adeptly tossing the fedora upon his head, he accepts my invitation then strides across the black and white checkerboard floor toward the back door. Tipping his hat and swinging his briefcase he bids us adieu. "Ladies, have a wonderful day."

I rise to fold and stack the papers then carry my dishes to a deep cast iron sink. After placing a rubber stopper in the drain, I turn both handles of the swing spout faucet and scatter a palmful of soap flakes into the rapidly filling basin. As per our morning routine, Jack, Dottie, and Uncle Charles have placed their plates and cups on the counter, which I transfer to the soapy water. Gripping a waffled cotton washcloth, I immerse both hands and feel the tightness in my neck and shoulders begin to soften. Since girlhood, I have found the warmth and rhythm of washing dishes to be soothing.

While walking past me to retrieve a loaf pan from the cupboard, Nan gently pats my back. "If ya don't mind, I'd like to take them there newspapers to my nephew's house later. He wants to paint the baby's room."

"Thank you for asking, Nan, but you're always welcome to them. That baby will be here before they know it." Her great nephew and his lovely wife are over the moon about the upcoming arrival of their first child. "Speaking of your family, will Addie and May be coming today?"

"Yeah, thanks for letting 'em change their schedule." Nan's great nieces give our house a thorough cleaning every Monday. This week, however, the twins were visiting their parents in San Diego for their 20th birthday.

"Of course, Nan. Not a problem." I assure her. "Would you like me to pick up anything at Alpha Beta while I'm downtown today?" Nan refuses to shop there because of their system of organizing the groceries alphabetically, which she finds confusing. "Can ya believe they had my denture adhesive right there next to diaper powder?" she once complained.

"Not today, Ruby, but thanks." She stacks the newspaper near the back door.

"Alright, well let me know if you change your mind. I'm heading up for a bath and won't be leaving for another hour or so."

"Figured you'd want a bath this morning, so I scrubbed the tub before leaving last night. It was filthy from that abominable creature." Nan shudders.

I reach into the refrigerator and retrieve a small bowl I prepared this morning of avocado mashed with honey and cream. "Oh, Nan you truly are the best! A good soak sounds perfect."

While drawing a bath, I uncork an amber glass bottle of bath salts which I sprinkle generously into the swirling water. That accomplished, I scoop three fingers into the avocado mixture and begin to apply the concoction to my face. I discovered the softening and toning benefits of "alligator pear" masks when attempting to reduce skin breakouts in my late teens. Since then, every spring and summer I treat myself to this little luxury.

Slipping into the warm cocoon, I rest my neck against a rolled hand towel and close my eyes. After several deep breaths, I notice my stream of thoughts begin to slow and feel a tingling lightness radiate from my throat and heart to my head and limbs. I lose track of time and only begin to surface from this peacefulness when my body reacts to the chill of the water. Once dry and wrapped in my silk kimono, a birthday gift from Dottie and Jack three years ago, I walk next door to my bedroom. Peeking out the window I notice dark clouds and decide against riding my bike into town today. Thus, free to wear a dress, I first step into a recently purchased foundation garment tailored to accentuate a higher waistline and the natural contours of the bust. As a shapely woman, the silhouette of the new decade is much more suited to my curves than the boyish straightness of the Twenties. I unsuccessfully search the bottom of my cherry armoire for my white center buckle heels and deduce that Dottie has borrowed them again without asking. With a sigh of resolve, I grab leather oxfords and slip them over my stockinged feet. I collect a shallow-crowned hat with a tipped brim, a pair of gloves, and a serviceable yet stylish handbag. I'm now ready to embrace a day of interviews, starting with my pal Elizabeth.

Driving west down Commonwealth Avenue, I'm forced to stop for several minutes by a convoy of cement mixers and dump trailers slowly making their way toward the construction site of the new Santa Fe Depot. From what I've heard, the rail station's Spanish architecture will include arches and a mission-tiled roof, as well as a much-needed covered platform. Exceedingly larger than the current station (built in the last century), the new depot should accommodate Fullerton's rapidly growing populace. Just this morning I read that Fullerton may be the second largest city in Orange County, narrowly beating Anaheim by three citizens.

The downtown area is busy this morning, so available parking is limited. I squeeze my car between a Packard sedan and a Chrysler Plymouth, the latter rather new from its appearance, when a flyer promoting a Mother's Day sale at Stedman's Jewelers blows directly onto my windshield. I realize at once that I have forgotten to order a corsage for Nan and resolve to remedy that oversight this very morning. With my handbag dangling from the crook of my elbow, I exit the automobile and pluck the itinerant paper from the window.

After a few steps up Spadra Road, I open my purse to retrieve a silver Elgin pocket watch that had belonged to my mother. Delicate clematis vines encircle the monogram "C," for Clara, but the engraving has faded slightly over the years. Upon the loss of my baby brother in 1905, my father purchased this half dollar-sized timepiece and asked the jeweler to modify the case so that a photograph of Stephen could be placed inside. When I inherited the lovely watch, I overlaid the picture with a photo of my parents so that my family is always with me. I click open the pocket watch and look up. About fourteen feet above me on a cast iron pedestal looms the broad face of Stedman's clock. After a minor adjustment (my timepiece tends to run 2 minutes fast), I snap the watch closed and head into the jewelry store.

"Why good morning, Miss Ray. We haven't seen you in a while. Please don't tell me the emerald has fallen off your pendant again. I was quite certain the prong setting would hold better than the bezel." Billy Stedman, always a delight to chat with, smiles up at me from his work bench with an array of silver loupes projecting from his spectacles.

"Oh no, Mr. Stedman, the pendant is fine. I just wanted to return this to you." I hand him the traveling flyer. "The breeze was tossing it about on the street."

Removing his glasses, he tightens his lips and shakes his head. "I see. Well, I certainly hope the young man I hired to post them on streetlamps didn't just dump them around the corner like the last kid."

"This is the only one I spotted so hopefully not." A certain policeman in our town is notorious for issuing citations for littering, intentional or not.

"Are you in a hurry or would you like to join me for a cup of coffee?" Mr. Stedman pinches the bridge of his nose between closed eyes. "I could use a break at the moment."

"Oh, that would be lovely, but I have a lengthy list of stops this morning." I reply regretfully. "Another time?"

"Of course," his face relaxes. "Have a good day."

"You as well." The bell above the door gives a merry jingle as I exit.

At the next intersection, I turn left and head west on Amerige Avenue. I notice the sky is darkening, and the breeze has stiffened into a steady wind. "Oh dear," I mutter to myself for I neglected to bring an umbrella this morning.

I stop before a red brick commercial building and peer into a shop window on which *Remember Your Mother* has been scribed in white shoe polish. I sigh audibly. Mother's Day is a difficult occasion each year for so many. Those who have lost mothers. Those who have lost children. Those who never had a mother. Those with motherhood in their hearts who never had children. For the Ray household, Mother's Day usually entails a trip to the beach or the local mountains. Over the years we've found nature to be an excellent balm for our spirits as we mourn the women we dearly miss on this trying holiday.

Opening the double doors, I enter Foster's Ladies Apparel and immediately find myself assailed by an eager young sales lady. "Welcome, how can I be of assistance? If you'd like, I can show you our new line of berets, the latest—" Miss Thorpe, as her name badge indicates, is interrupted by another feminine voice, one that I know quite well.

"Bessie, would you mind folding the silk scarves that just arrived?"

Miss Thorpe nods, but I notice a decline in her perk as she meanders to the back of the store.

Elizabeth Martin's delightful grin reaches her uniquely golden eyes as she bounds forward to embrace me. "Ruby! It's been too long," she exclaims while tightening her arms about me.

After sharing a warm hug, I hold her at arm's length to take in the perfectly coiffed titian bob and chic elegance of her ensemble. "My dear, you are as stunning as ever. I am flummoxed that Hollywood has not yet launched you into stardom."

Elizabeth chuckles, "Well it's definitely not for lack of trying." For years this enchanting and talented actress has taken the Red Car from our Pacific Electric Railway station to Los Angeles for interviews. She secured a few bit parts as an extra on minor films but has not yet landed any speaking roles. When not working at Foster's, Elizabeth performs in local theater productions, always as the female lead. Her most recent performance in a musical at a venue in nearby Brea was lauded by the local papers, with particular accolades mentioned for her singing.

"If Ada can make it, you certainly will." Ada Williams, Fullerton's Miss Valencia of 1928, was quickly snapped up by Fox Film Corporation following the beauty competition. In lieu of completing high school, she appeared in her first film and married the son of a motion picture producer the very next year. Mrs. Ince, as she is now known, is regularly mentioned in the local newspapers and is supposedly filming a movie with Constance Bennett.

"In case you haven't noticed, I'm not a blonde like Ada, but we'll see." Hollywood is currently partial to platinum locks, Carole Lombard being a perfect example.

"How is your family?" I query. Elizabeth lives with her parents and younger brother in a small house on Truslow Avenue. I recall a conversation with Elizabeth early on in our friendship. "Papa shortened our surname from Martinez to Martin when he and mama moved here from Arizona." As a young man with light hair and fair skin, he realized that no one suspected his Mexican heritage. John Martin was able to get a good job whereas Juan Martinez could not. Landlords for homes outside of the Truslow area, however, took one look at the tawny complexion and lustrous black hair of his wife and refused to rent them housing. Like her father, Elizabeth has been able to "pass" and bring home decent wages to help support her family. However, she loathes the charade, and her heart aches for her mother, brother, and neighbors who face prejudice and suspicion daily in our community.

"Jim was accepted to study medicine at the College of Osteopathic Physicians and Surgeons in Los Angeles. Honestly Ruby, he's a genius," Elizabeth beams.

"You and your parents must be so proud." I recall the bright young man who graduated as the first Mexican American valedictorian at Fullerton High School in 1926. Since that time, he has won numerous collegiate academic awards while studying biology and chemistry.

"Just yesterday he was informed that he's graduating summa cum laude from Whittier College." Dottie claps her hands in admiration.

"That's so wonderful. I am truly thrilled for you all." At that moment, a trio of women, what my uncle would call the "bridge set," saunter through the door and begin griping about the rising waistlines of the latest fashions. "At least the hemlines have come back down," one dowager remarks.

Noticing Elizabeth's nervous glance toward the bunch, I suggest, "Perhaps we can sit for a nice long chinwag during dinner. What time are you off this evening?"

With a look of appreciation she glances at her wristwatch. "I lock up at 6:00. Shall we meet at Mah Jong Cafe?" She then locks eyes across the store with Bessie and crooks a finger.

"Excellent! I haven't had chop suey in ages." I walk toward the door and turn to wave, but the posse has already surrounded Elizabeth with complaints.

CHAPTER 4

Back out on the avenue, my gloved hand flies to my crown as a strong gust threatens to snatch my hat. I blink away a few drops of precipitation while looking heavenward at charcoal clouds. One block ahead I make a right on Spadra Road and duck under the yellow and white awning of a stationary store next to the florist shop. Purple lilacs and a rainbow of freesias adorn the window display along with a pasteboard sign reading, "A Mother's Love." Again, my heart sinks. Looking past the arrangement, I spy Hazel wrapping a satin ribbon around a tall vase of magenta orchids. Sensing my presence, she raises her head, smiles broadly, and extends a friendly wave. I enter the shop.

"Ruby! How lovely to see you!" She abandons her work and embraces me, as I tighten my arms around her. Like the rest of my family, I don't shy away from hugs.

"Hello Hazel. How are you and your darling children?" At last count, Hazel and her husband had produced six offspring under the age of eight.

"Oh, they're swell. Jane's in third grade, and the baby just started to walk." Hazel's widowed sister moved in with them a few years back and cares for the children so that Hazel can work. Her husband, unemployed since last summer, has never been one to pitch in with his children. "Women's work," he objects. If only he knew how involved Uncle Charles has been since Dottie and Jack were tiny.

"Read any good books lately?" Hazel was one of the first women I tutored in reading back when she was a newlywed. Since then, she has become quite the bibliophile, preferring Agatha Christie's Hercule Poirot above all else.

"No time at the moment." Hazel replies with regret. "Perhaps when little Tommy is older. He's such a handful when I'm home." If I remember correctly, Tommy is the toe-headed tyke prone to accidents, largely due to his fearlessness.

She walks back to the worktable and resumes twisting the ribbon into a loopy bow. "Say, is your reading parlor still open? I have a friend who's interested."

"Yes indeed. Every Monday and Wednesday evening in the cottage, just like always." Over the years I have maintained a steady flow of one to two clients each night, all of them women who, for one reason or another, left school illiterate. I don't charge for my services. After all, I never trained to be a teacher, but I find great satisfaction helping others, like Hazel, discover a passion for reading.

"I think of you often. I've used your sound play with the older kids, and now Jane is using it with my four-year-old." Hazel reports with pride.

Years ago, when Dottie and I were teaching Jack to read, Nan would stroll into the living room where our books and wooden letter blocks were scattered on the floor and just watch. One day she sighed, "I sure wish I learned to read. Teacher told me I was too lazy." Her soft blue eyes conveyed the lasting damage of this remark. Appalled that an educator would say such a thing to a child who struggles to learn, I offered to help her, even though I was just a college student at the time with no training in education. It immediately became apparent that, when attempting to sound out words in *McGuffey's First Reader*, Nan could not hear the sounds themselves. I don't mean that she was deaf or hard of hearing, but when I asked her questions like, "What sound does 'dog' start with?" she had no idea. I also discovered that she couldn't rhyme words to save her life. So that's where we started, with the assistance of a college friend who was studying teaching. Over the years this developed into something I like to call "sound play" where we break words into sounds, change words by substituting or omitting sounds, and blend sounds together into words, all without using letters themselves. Once the sounds are mastered, clients seem to catch on to *McGuffey's* phonics more easily.

"That's wonderful to hear. It's hard to believe your children are becoming so grown up." I point toward a deep bucket of white and pink carnations. "I hope it's not too late to order a corsage for Mother's Day."

"Of course not." Hazel pulls a canary order slip and fountain pen from the top drawer of the work counter. "Most folks will wait till tomorrow. How many and what colors?"

"Just one please. White." I'm not quite sure when or how the tradition began, but women wear corsages to honor their mothers, pink for those still living and white for those who are deceased. I always buy one for Nan, as she enjoys wearing the ruffled bloom on her best Sunday dress each Mother's Day while attending her Baptist church. "I'll pay now since I'll probably send Jack over to pick it up tomorrow afternoon."

Hazel's hand shoots out, preventing me from opening my handbag. "For you Ruby Ray, it's on the house."

"Will Mr. Blumenthal mind?" The florist, not known for having a generous spirit, is in fact quite fond of Hazel.

"What he doesn't know won't hurt him." Hazel winks at me.

Appreciating a roof over my head for the time being, I stay awhile and watch in amazement as Hazel expertly clips, twists, and secures a variety of blossoms to create impressive arrangements. Eventually, the drizzle appears to let up, which I take as my cue to exit. "Don't be a stranger," Hazel calls after me as I leave.

I inhale deeply as the rain has left a trace of petrichor in the air. I wish someone could bottle this fragrance. Its clean, slightly metallic freshness is one of my favorite scents. I look up to watch swiftly moving slate gray clouds which contrast with a brilliant cerulean sky. Not wishing to get caught in the rain a second time, I make a beeline across the congested street toward my car. Thankfully, Fullerton drivers are polite and will slow for pedestrians. Approaching the row of angled automobiles parked along the curb, I notice with dismay that my driver's door has been pinned in place by a Rickenbacker Boattail Coupe. "How rude!" I exclaim and open the passenger door to slide across the leather seat.

Although I expect to wait for the slow-moving traffic to pass, I am pleasantly surprised that a driver has stopped to let me back out of the parking space. As soon as I shift into first gear and begin to roll down Commonwealth, the motorist maneuvers his car between the Rickenbacker and Ford. I bite my lip with concern that parking will also be scarce near McFarland's. Once on Spadra, I notice a commotion ahead at Wilshire Avenue. After several minutes, I make my way past overturned crates of oranges that have toppled from the back of a pickup in front of the imposing five-story Chapman Building, once the tallest in the county. My tires bump over rolling citrus while downshifting to slow. Chuckling to myself, I imagine the view from the arched windows of the top floor overlooking a mishmash of pulp and juice shrouding the busy street below.

Finally reaching Chapman Avenue, I realize with disappointment that street parking is unavailable. I decide to take my chances with the small lot behind the Fox Theater and am rewarded with an empty space. Glancing in my rear-view mirror, I reapply carmine lipstick and give my curls a bounce with my fingers. I reach into the glove box and retrieve a small black leather notebook which I promptly tuck into my handbag. After lunch with Uncle Charles, I plan to visit Mr. Phillips at the California Hotel which isn't too far from the cafe.

I round the corner and pass the Firestone service station whose neat row of metered pumps reminds me to refill my car before heading home later. On a whim, I enter the Italian courtyard of the grand Fox movie house and examine the posters for upcoming films. At once, I spy the bright yellow advertisement for *Florodora Girl*. I suppose the image of Marion Davies does resemble me, especially her wide, round eyes. Also on display is a poster for Howard Hughes' new extravaganza *Hell's Angels*, which promises thrilling dogfights filmed in the air along with technicolor footage.

Adjacent to the theater, McFarland's Cafe is a popular lunch spot for citizens, businessmen, and local elected officials alike. Upon entering the bustling diner, I examine the tables and booths for Uncle Charles. "I must be early," I mutter to myself and rifle through my purse for my pocket watch. Preoccupied with this task, I startle as a broad hand roughly caresses my right shoulder. The contents of my bag scatter across the linoleum floor. Bending down to retrieve a twirling tube of mascara, I look up into the pleased mug of my accoster.

"Hello there, Ruby. Let me help you with that." Randall Leech's self-satisfied smile displays darkly stained misaligned teeth.

Feeling my gorge rise, I swallow with disdain and scoop up the remaining objects. "No need Mr. Leech." I stand and place my fist on my hip, lifting my chin and eyebrows to ward against any further unwelcome advances.

Nonplussed by my confidence, Randall's face reddens as he looks away then stares down at the floor. "I can see that." He recovers his bravado after a moment and, with a smarmy tone, observes, "It looks like you're here alone. Would you like some company?" He doesn't give up easily.

"How is your wife, Mr. Leech? I haven't seen her for some time."

In truth, I know precisely where his wife has escaped to, having assisted her with securing a new job and residence in Pasadena. After years of blackened eyes, purple wrists, and untold internal injuries, Ida Mae Leech decided that if she didn't leave, she would surely kill Randall in his sleep. She had tried to report him to the police, but she was told that they "don't interfere with family matters." After that, a friend of hers in my reading group sent her my way. Given Randall's nearly constant surveillance of Ida Mae, she was forced to sit upon our escape plan for weeks, until one day he awoke with a horribly abscessed tooth. As soon as he left for the dentist, she seized a suitcase she had hidden in their hen house and headed for the train depot. The ticket agent, a former classmate of mine, allowed her to place a call to me on the station telephone, so I had an opportunity to see her off.

Now visibly uncomfortable, Randall mumbles, "Oh, well, uh...about that. She's visiting her sister." He scratches his greasy scalp and releases sizable flakes of dander.

He has no idea where she is.

Spotting Uncle Charles with not one but two umbrellas in hand, I sigh with relief and turn to direct a prim smile of affected politeness toward the louse. "Have a good afternoon, Mr. Leech."

"What was that all about?" Uncle Charles inquires while the hostess grabs a pair of menus and leads us to our table.

"Frankly that man should be driven out of town on a rail," I declare contemptuously. I brush at my shoulder wishing to disinfect myself with a hot bath.

"Did he harm you?" A look of alarm flashes across his face, and he whips his head toward the door to see Randall exiting the premises.

"He was fresh, but that's neither here nor there. I'm referring to his treatment of his wife." Aside from myself and the ticket agent, Uncle Charles was the only other person involved with Ida Mae's relocation, having helped with the funds for her to start a new life.

His panic fading, Uncle Charles opens the menu and remarks, "Unfortunately men like him are all too common. They view their wives and children as property."

Out of the blue, a crack of thunder rumbles the cafe while the lights simultaneously flicker. "Please tell me God has cast judgment on that wretch," I comment sardonically. But I can see Randall through the picture window scurrying across the street to escape the sudden deluge.

Thelma, our usual waitress, arrives and says drolly, "Well that was unexpected." She removes a pencil from behind her ear. "What'll you have for drinks?"

"Coca-Cola for me."

Uncle Charles shakes his head and chuckles, "I'll have coffee, please. Black."

Once our drinks arrive and our food has been ordered, I question Uncle Charles. "So, what did Mr. Baker want today?"

"Just as I suspected. He complained about Walter then informed me that he'd like to lease a section of my oil field. You know, the southern area where the wells have gone dry?" Uncle Charles blows across the surface of his coffee, steam rising with each breath.

"Are you seriously considering this?" I sip through a straight paper straw wishing, yet again, that someone would invent a bendable straw that doesn't restrict the flow.

"Not in the least. Fred Baker is the last person with whom I'd do business," he answers in a lowered voice, not wishing to be overheard. "His request, however, has got me thinking about cultivating that land for agriculture. Maybe a dozen acres for grapefruit or tangerines to start."

I nearly choke. "You? A farmer?"

Uncle Charles holds up his palms toward me. "Now hear me out. That land is just sitting there unused. I could hire someone, perhaps a farmer who's lost his land. Lord knows there are plenty of folks without work at the moment."

I tip my head in agreement.

Adroitly balancing a large tray laden with plates and bowls in one hand and a collapsible chrome stand in the other, Thelma interjects, "Hope you're hungry." After settling her load on the stand, she places a grilled ham and Swiss sandwich and bowl of corn soup in front of Uncle Charles. With silver tongs she transfers a dill pickle spear from a serving dish onto his plate.

"Club sandwich with a half an avocado on the side." She sets down my lunch then asks, "Pickle?"

Shaking my head, "No thank you. But I will take mustard."

Thelma deposits a jar of French's on the table before me, followed by a cup of vegetable bouillon. "Anything else?"

"That's all for now, Thelma. Thank you." Uncle Charles replies, and we dig into our lunch with relish.

Midway through our sandwiches, Uncle Charles pulls a newspaper toward him that a prior guest has left on the table. After glancing at a headline, he passes the paper to me. "It would appear that the Eighteenth Amendment may be a sticking point in this fall's elections."

"Are you surprised?" I peruse the article and read that a republican gubernatorial candidate in New Jersey is considering a "wet" campaign. "Well look at that. You're not the only republican opposed to prohibition."

"Of course not. The law just opened the doors for hoodlums and speakeasies to make a killing. The Bureau's done a terrible job with enforcement, and crime rates have continued to skyrocket, especially in big cities. This 'noble experiment,' as Hoover called it, has gone on long enough."

"Was Fullerton wet or dry before prohibition?" I am fairly certain I know the answer, but as a high school student at the time, I didn't give the issue much thought.

"Most definitely dry." Uncle Charles confirms my suspicion. "Anaheim, on the other hand, was wet. After all, their founding fathers were Germans."

"So, do you oppose prohibition entirely or just federal enforcement." We've never discussed this before.

"That's an excellent question. Personally, I think the amendment should be reversed. I highly doubt that those congressmen who voted for its ratification realized that even beer and wine would be banned." Uncle Charles stirs his soup and leans forward to swallow a spoonful.

"Would you support legislation that legalizes all alcohol with the exception of hard liquor?" While I've long known of my uncle's progressive leanings, this conversation is broadening my perspective of him.

"Absolutely not. What would be the point? States should control and enforce liquor laws, including their sale and consumption." Uncle Charles raises a hand at Thelma as she passes by and requests a menu. He then turns back toward me. "Still hungry? We can't solve the country's problems on an empty stomach." An entreating smile plays on his lips.

"Hardly empty. You're worse than Dottie and Jack when it comes to dessert." I begin to laugh but am startled by a thunderous concussion that reverberates through the diner, and the overhead lights switch off. Typically ignored as background noise, the electric hum of kitchen appliances ends abruptly, as do conversations at each table and booth.

Howling winds shriek as an agitated young man throws open the front door and bellows, "Lightning bolt hit the big theater sign," referring to the colossal three-sided neon and ironwork structure that straddles the roof of the Fox Theater.

"Earl Adams, you get in here right this minute. Do you wanna catch your death?" Thelma barks and rushes toward him with a dish towel.

The dashing youth tries to avoid her ministrations, but Thelma is drying his face and hair before he has a chance to raise his hands in protest. "Aww, cut it out, Auntie."

"Why aren't you at school?" She pauses to give him a stern look. "Let me guess. You were tuning a piano."

"I was heading back to school when the lightning struck. And yes, I was in fact tuning a piano." Earl stiffens his spine and attempts to reclaim his dignity. "I am nineteen after all. I can do what I like."

So, this is the young man who has captured Dottie's affection. I can't say that I blame her. He's a young doppelgänger for Gary Cooper in *The Virginian*, six feet at the very least with romantic liquid blue eyes.

"Yes, well, all I can say is—" but Thelma's choice words are cut off by a clamorous pounding. Folks leap from their chairs and run toward the windows to view hailstones, some as large as marbles.

CHAPTER 5

An ankle-deep river rushes down Spadra Road cleansing and carrying away the remaining detritus from the earlier citrus incident. Not wishing to saturate my oxfords by walking across the newly formed waterway, I head for my car behind the theater. The downpour and hailstorm let up just as we finished our slices of peach pie, so Uncle Charles' spare umbrella manages the current drizzle quite nicely. Once settled behind the steering wheel, I activate the vacuum powered windscreen wipers to clear melting pellets of ice. Thankfully Balboa Motor Corporation opted for this novel feature. Manual wipers are tricky to operate, especially while driving.

The three-story California Hotel sits a couple of blocks south of the Fox Theater on the opposite side of a waterlogged street. My tires send up a spray as I ease into a spot against the curb before the first of two square turrets. "Well, it's no use," I mumble while examining the flood beneath my open car door. I quickly splash through the pool and jump onto the sidewalk.

Once standing in the topiary lined courtyard of this Spanish Colonial gem, I notice uniformly darkened windows along the u-shaped building suggesting a power outage at the hotel as well. This may not be the best time to visit Mr. Phillips, but I am determined to give it a try. After all, as a shareholder of the Fullerton Community Hotel Company, am I not entitled to an extra measure of courtesy by the staff? I may have been raised to eschew preferential treatment, but I am not opposed to capitalizing on my good fortune in the interest of my clients.

A flustered elderly gentleman at the concierge desk replaces the receiver of an ebony candlestick telephone and hurriedly scribbles a note. Motioning to a bellhop, he instructs, "Please take this message to Mrs. Plunkett in apartment 17. The weather has detained the train so her husband will not be joining her for dinner." In addition to guest lodging, the California Hotel offers roughly two dozen rooms for long-term residents, as well as space for small shops.

The cherry cheeked bellboy tips his brimless cap with an eagerness to please and races toward a carpeted staircase. "I wish I had his energy," the concierge sighs exhaustedly then focuses heavily-lidded eyes on me over half-moon spectacles. "Good afternoon miss. How may I be of assistance?"

"Good afternoon to you sir. I am Ruby Ray. I know you are quite busy at the moment, but I hope to speak with Mr. Floyd Phillips." I flash my sweetest smile and lower my head with deference.

His eyes widen with recognition upon hearing my name. "Why of course, Miss Ray. Please feel free to wait in the lobby while I send a boy to locate him." He extends an arm toward an elegant assemblage of plush velvet chairs and settees.

Lowering myself onto a purple and gold tufted armchair, I examine the opulence of my surroundings, the physical actualization of Mr. Chapman's vision. This "Father of the Citrus Industry," as he has been dubbed, was the first mayor of Fullerton and, rumor has it, a descendant of Johnny Appleseed as well. I will never forget the palpable sense of anticipation we experienced while the town's populace gathered for the hotel's groundbreaking ceremony eight years ago. Jack and Dottie took turns astride Uncle Charles' shoulders to view the spectacle, which Jack later referred to as "an awful hullabaloo over a patch of dirt." Thankfully there was a great deal more to look at when hundreds of people gathered from all over Southern California for its grand opening a year later.

When the bellboy returns, I overhear the concierge order, "Please locate Fipps and tell him he has a visitor," after which the solicitous ladd sprints toward a door marked "Employees Only." The senior shakes his head and resumes plodding through his busywork, while mumbling, "Probably on a smoking break."

Moments later, a gangly fellow in his late-twenties steps through the aforementioned door, notices my attention upon him, and straightens his stooped shoulders. "You asked fer me?" He then proceeds to scan my body starting with my ankles until his gaze settles upon my chest.

I extend a hand and attempt to redirect his gape, "Why yes, Mr. Phillips. My name is Ruby Ray."

"Fipps." He accepts the handshake, grasping my hand slightly too long before releasing. Next, he removes a pork pie hat, runs bony fingers through a dark red mop of curly hair, then replaces the cap. A partially smoked cigarette sits behind his ear. Apparently, a tidy appearance is not a job requirement for plainclothes security at this hotel.

"I hope this isn't a bad time, Mr….uh…Fipps. If I could just have a few minutes."

He ogles my form again. "Take all the time you need."

What is it today with predatory men? "I'd like to ask you a few questions about a friend of yours…Frank Graham?"

Fipps' eyes instantly narrow as his spindly shoulders begin to swivel away from me. "I dunno nuttin' bout him."

Placing a hand on the sleeve of his shoddy suit, I dissuade him from walking away. "That's not what his sister, Miss Graham, told me."

Straightening so that his lean frame towers over me, all trace of the casual cad is gone. "What she hafta say?" I now understand why hotel management chose him for protective services. He has the intimidation routine down pat.

Refusing to be cowed I suggest, "Let's sit down to discuss this. I'm sure you could use a breather after such a busy afternoon."

Taken aback by my unexpected response, Fipps slowly slumps onto a loveseat as I return to the armchair. Now we are on the same level. "My friend Norma asked me to speak with you since you're such a good chum of Frank."

"I dunno bout that." He gives me a sidelong glance. "I sometimes stop by. That's bout it."

"Yes, that's precisely what Miss Graham said," I affirm. Fipps appears to relax somewhat.

"Apparently Frank left home the other day and hasn't returned. You can imagine Norma's worry." I lean forward and lower my voice conspiratorially, "Between you and me, I think he needed a break from her."

He smirks, "Yeah could be."

"Norma says you know where he is," I remark with a casual tone implying doubt.

"Baloney." Fipps rolls his eyes and dramatically waves a hand at the suggestion.

"That's what I thought." Recognizing his lie, I pause for a moment then switch tactics. "Well, I'm sorry to have bothered you." I begin to rise.

"That's it?' He blinks sharply.

"Well...yes. Thank you for your time." I reach out for a second handshake as Fipps stares at me in bewilderment. After walking away three paces, I turn with a raised index finger, "It just occurred to me. Frank used to work here if I'm not mistaken."

Taking the bait, "Yeah. Bellhop."

"That's how you met?" I walk back and perch on the arm of the loveseat he still occupies, turning his weakness for feminine attention upon him.

"Sure. We got hired together." He stretches an arm in my direction along the back of the loveseat.

"But then you worked your way up. Security...very impressive." I nod with feigned admiration.

He puffs up with pride. "Yep."

"But Frank couldn't hack it." A comment not a question.

"I dunno. He's a good guy. Just can't catch a break." Fipps removes his hat and sets it on his knee. Now I have him.

"You know what, Fipps?" I brush an imaginary speck of lint off of the arm of the seat. "I think you're a swell friend to Frank."

He beams, "Well, sure. He's a pal."

"I just wish…" I whisper coyly.

"What?" He leans toward me and stares openly at my lips. "Whaddya wish?"

Here goes nothing. "I wish I could tell Norma that Frank is alright," I release a slow breathy exhalation, cringing internally the whole time.

Fipps instantly puts up his guard and stands as he recognizes my attempt to wrangle him. Clearly, I've underestimated this guy. "You tell her he's right as rain, but I ain't sayin' where he is cuz I dunno."

Rising alongside him I give it one last try. "Thank you for your help. If you see Frank—"

Fipps cuts me off. "We're done, doll." He shoves his hat over his unruly mane and stomps away with clenched fists.

I shiver and mutter under my breath, "He really isn't one to mess with."

The storm has passed, filling the air with an earthy freshness that, while not quite petrichor, uplifts the spirits nonetheless. One block south of the hotel, I am able to traverse the broad boulevard with minimal impact to my leather uppers since the waters have greatly receded. Farmers and Merchants Bank is housed in a Beaux Arts masterpiece with decorative pilasters and terra cotta molding. Early dignitaries and ranch owners in our community, such as the previously mentioned Mr. Chapman, founded F&M as the first bank in Fullerton and continue to lead as officers on its board of directors. That being said, it is Mr. Clifford Snodgrass, bank manager, who rules the roost. And so, for that reason, I seek out Howard instead when I stroll through the unique diagonal entrance carved into the corner of the building.

Howard Pinney (emphasis on the "nay") has been middle-aged since high school. By fifteen his hairline had already retreated to the top of his crown. Consequently, his glabrous scalp, coupled with an unfortunate beak, have long given him the appearance of a turkey vulture. During the years we attended high school and junior college together, I never once heard Howard utter a sound, his severe bashfulness preventing him from speaking to girls. However, his academic standing and meticulous attention to detail qualified him for a clerk position at the bank. Thankfully, over the years his confidence as a speaker has improved, and he's able to talk with men and women alike.

Noticing me at once through the iron grill of the teller cage, Howard nods with a shy smile and returns to his current transaction, while two other customers wait patiently along a velvet rope suspended between two brass stanchions. I join the queue and bide my time as the next account holder approaches the marble counter and is greeted by Howard, "Good afternoon, Mr. Ondaro. How can I help you today?"

After handing Howard a withdrawal slip, the burly young Basque launches into an animated monologue about the unexpected weather. "What a day, Mr. Pinney! Whacky, I tell ya! After lunch we're playing pelota, like always on Friday, when BOOM!" Howard's head snaps up with a start as the chap slaps a palm on the counter. "Lightning smacks the fencing on toppa the court."

"How alarming," Howard responds with polite interest. He then looks over the written order and points with a gold fountain pen to a blank box. "Please sign here, Mr. Ondaro."

The ranch worker inattentively inks his name then continues gesticulating, his expansive shoulders threatening the seams of his coat. "Well, Marko blows his wig and makes tracks for the farmhouse when a hailstone conks him on the noggin. As big as a fist, I tell ya!"

The elegant woman ahead of me peers over half-rim glasses and, with a pinched expression, raises her eyebrows at Mr. Ondaro's hyperbole.

Howard dubiously examines his customer. "Is your coworker alright?"

"Well, a course he is. We iced his noodle with the same stone what hit him," the fellow guffaws. "Now he's copacetic."

Suppressing a smirk, Howard quickly counts out thirteen dollars and fifty cents and passes it between the bars. "Is that all Mr. Ondaro?"

The lad slides the cash into a pocket of his trousers then shoots Howard a grin. "I can tell a kiss off when I hear one. Abyssinia next week!"

Howard chuckles good-naturedly. It appears that Mr. Ondaro is fully aware of the teller's fondness for absurd slang.

Finally, next-in-line, I believe that I will actually avoid Mr. Snodgrass, whose paternalistic despotism I find tiring. For years, my futile efforts to gain independence over my accounts have consistently been met with derision. Mr. Snodgrass firmly believes that women are incapable of managing their money and would squander the entirety of their funds on frivolity if given the chance. I know for a fact that I will glean no information from him about Norma and Edna's missing funds and would prefer that he is nowhere around when I quiz Howard.

However, fortune is not smiling upon me, for behind my shoulder a hypernasal voice utters with practiced insincerity, "My dear Ruby. How may we be of service, young lady?"

I breathe deeply and try not to roll my eyes as I turn around to meet his sour expression. "Why hello, Clifford. I didn't see you there." His puce face darkens at the informality of my greeting, so I continue with mock innocence, "Are we not on a first name basis?"

Mr. Snodgrass clears his throat with force and ignores my question. "To what do I owe the pleasure of your visit today?" His beady eyes, centered above protuberant pouches, bore into me with antipathy.

"I could say that I would like my uncle's name removed from my accounts, but we both know how that would go," I reply casually while removing a glove one finger at a time.

Outraged, he sharply wags his index finger. "I've told you time and again, as a single young woman you cannot—"

"Yes, I've heard it all before," I wave a hand. "Perhaps you can unlock the vault so I can access 'my' safety deposit box. I believe I am permitted to examine its contents without adult male supervision. Am I correct?"

He nods begrudgingly, "Mmm, yes." After a pause he grumbles, "You have your key?"

"Believe it or not, Mr. Snodgrass, I do indeed."

Once ensconced in the secure vault, I slowly mill through my belongings. My plan is to linger here alone until Howard is free. A glance through the barred window of the thick door reveals that the queue for the teller window has lengthened, and Mr. Snodgrass is assisting customers in his office as well. I open and close a number of velvet boxes containing shimmering jewelry that belonged to my mother and grandmothers. With the exception of formal dances in high school and college, I have had no occasion to wear these radiant heirlooms.

My hand brushes past a large yellowing envelope then returns to flip open its flap. I withdraw a heavy cardstock document and run my hand across its surface, lingering over my name neatly typed in purple ink. Upon my parents' deaths, this deed transferred an 1896 row house in the Upper West Side of Manhattan to me, a minor who would come into full possession of the property when reaching the age of majority on my 21st birthday. Not wishing to sell my childhood home, Uncle Charles decided to hire a property manager to lease the house until I was old enough to decide for myself, and for years the house has generated a monthly income for me.

After my 21st birthday, during a transition between tenants, I visited the only home I'd ever known until age sixteen. The purpose of my visit was both sentimental and practical. I would decide whether to sell or continue leasing. As the taxi drove along Riverside Drive, my gaze oscillated between the waterfront park on my right and rows of eclectic houses on my left, so unlike the uniform brownstones found elsewhere in the city. When finally arriving at the light stone Elizabethan Renaissance house, I craned my neck toward the rooftop garden atop the fifth story, the setting for so many family picnics and "camp outs" with my friends. Across the street, the same American elm towered above the hill that we would sled down on wintry days after school.

The low stoop entrance of my house led to a heavy wooden door framed with scroll and leaf ornamentation, all so familiar to me. However, once inside my sense of recollection dissipated. Gone were the heavily paneled walls, frieze molding, and coffered ceilings. Instead, zigzags, black lacquered surfaces, and chrome had replaced the romantic embellishments of the pre-war era. The property manager had cautioned me that, in order to generate interest among prospective tenants, the home had been modernized. Since Uncle Charles handled the financing of this remodel, I was unaware that the changes had been so extensive. My childhood home was unrecognizable. The last thread of connection to life with my parents was instantaneously severed, and I sank to my knees to weep right there in the entryway. I was advised to keep the property for financial reasons, but I now wonder if I should sell. I will make this decision on my own, for it bears emotional consequences as well as fiscal.

I return the deed to its envelope and rise from my chair to take a quick peek through the window. Mr. Snodgrass' door is closed, and only one customer remains in line. I carefully place the jewel cases and paperwork into the metal box, which I then secure in the locker with my key. Slipping on my gloves, I leave the vault and hear a sharp click, indicating that the leaden door has locked behind me.

"Hello, Ruby. I apologize for the wait earlier. Was Mr. Snodgrass able to assist you?" Howard adjusts his polka dot bow tie and greets me benevolently.

"Do you really want to get me started with that?" I joke as Howard surveys the bank lobby before releasing a titter.

"I suppose not," he whispers. Then with a raised voice he queries, "Did you find what you needed in the vault?"

"Yes, I did. Thank you for asking." I glance surreptitiously over my shoulder and lean in toward Howard. "My actual motive for visiting today, however, is to ask you some rather delicate questions about another account holder."

Howard adopts a cloak and dagger persona. "Is this for a case?" Over the years he has heard rumors about my occupation.

"Precisely that. Is the coast clear?" I do not wish to scan the room a second time.

"Clear as a whistle." He's truly enjoying this. "Give me the low down."

"Frank Graham ring a bell?" I query with nonchalance.

A coughing fit overcomes Howard who retrieves a bleached handkerchief from the inside of his coat pocket. I wait patiently. When the convulsion subsides, he bemoans, "Oh my. I had a terrible feeling about that at the time."

"So, you know then that the money belongs to Miss Graham and Miss Holmes." Placing the palm of both hands on the counter, I look directly into Howard's wide eyes. "Frank doesn't have a dime to his name."

"Yes, you are correct. All deposits have been made solely by the ladies." Howard loosens his collar while stretching his neck right and left. "I strongly advised Mr. Graham against closing the passbook account, but he insisted that it was his right as primary shareholder."

"The policy of this bank sickens me," I complain bitterly. "Or should I say, the policy of Mr. Snodgrass. What was his position with all this?"

"As soon as Mr. Graham began shouting, the boss took over the transaction." Howard casts an eye toward Mr. Snodgrass' closed door. "That aggravated Mr. Graham even further. Would you believe he dared to seize Mr. Snodgrass by the arm?" Howard continues as I shake my head with disbelief. "Was I ever thankful to be standing behind these bars. I've never seen someone so worked up."

"Did Mr. Snodgrass try to talk him out of it?" I probe, curious whether his authoritarian manner would hold up when challenged by a bellicose male.

"Not really. Mr. Snodgrass told him that the signatures of both shareholders were required to close the account. But when Mr.

Graham refused to back down, Mr. Snodgrass simply asked if Mr. Graham preferred a cashier's check or cash." Howard responds.

"He probably didn't wish to deal with him any further." Sooo, when faced with formidable provocation, Mr. Snodgrass yields his authority. I must remember that. "Please tell me that Mr. Graham accepted the check."

Howard sighs with deep regret and directs his gaze toward the counter. "That is, perhaps, the worst part. He walked out with over two thousand dollars in cash."

"And you have no idea where he went from here?"

He shakes his head, remorse written on his face. "I have not seen him since."

CHAPTER 6

A gentle steam rises from the sidewalk while the cheery afternoon sun evaporates any remaining dampness. My thoughts, on the other hand, are sober as I walk back to the car. I hadn't expected Frank to abscond with that much money in hard cash. I can understand a cashier's check or even a bankroll safely stashed in a deposit box, but simply walking outside, in this day and age, with two grand on your person is utterly irrational. Further, Howard's description of Frank's behavior confirms what Norma has already reported. For some unknown reason, Frank has gone off the deep end.

Before pulling away from the curb, I check the home address for Mr. Stan Jones, Frank's current employer, and realize that he lives two streets away from Norma and Edith. Construction, or at least contract management, must pay handsomely, for Brookdale Heights is a relatively new development and quite pricey.

My drive along Brookdale Place is pleasant as I behold an eclectic mix of architectural styles on both sides of the tidy street. I park under an acorn shaped lamp and look up toward the sharply pitched roof of a two-story Tudor style house. While exiting my automobile, a movement in the window of the house next door catches my eye. *I'm being watched.*

The neatly manicured lawn of Mr. Jones' home is elevated above the sidewalk, so I walk up a short flight of steps to the front door. After knocking several times, I conclude that no human is home, but I do hear the woebegone howl of a dog. Returning to my motorcar I nearly tumble down the steps when a wavery voice beckons, "Woooo hoooo."

At the base of the stairs a frail, kyphotic granny hovers in bright pink house slippers and a faded apron dress. She looks up at me with a chipper expression, her eyes disappearing into an abundance of wrinkles as she smiles a toothless grin. "Nobody's home except for Barclay."

"Thank you, ma'am. I discovered that." I extend my hand. "I'm Ruby Ray. Are you the Jones' neighbor?"

The fine-boned hand gives mine a weak squeeze. "That I am. My name's Luella Knox, but you can call me Lula."

"Very nice to meet you, Lula." I cannot reconcile the decidedly boxy modern house next door with this delicate octogenarian. "Have you lived here long?"

"I moved in with my grandson a few years ago." She withdraws a lacy handkerchief from a rickrack trimmed pocket and blows her nose gently. "It's a nice neighborhood. Quiet. But the folks are friendly."

"I'm pleased to hear that." Before I can ask any questions, Lula continues her commentary.

"Now Tilley and Stan Jones are very fine neighbors. Tilley's away, you may know this already, being a Gold Star Mother and all." Lula neatly folds and tucks the kerchief back into her pocket.

"Gold Star Mother?" The phrase is familiar, but I can't quite place where I've heard it.

"She's on that ship bound for Europe. They lost their only son in the war, don't you know." Her sunny demeanor briefly darkens.

"Now that you mention it, I did hear something about this on the radio last night." The news announcer reported that the US government is paying for groups of mothers to make pilgrimages to their sons' grave sites in France and Belgium. The first group sailed the other day out of New York.

"Stan's lost without Tilley here." Lula nods sympathetically. "So I've been keeping an eye on him."

"That's very kind of you." I point up at the Jones' house. "I don't suppose you know where Mr. Jones is at the moment."

"Well sure!" She beams. "He's at that new auditorium. Have you seen it?"

"I've driven past it but haven't been inside." I am about to thank Lula for her assistance when she unexpectedly changes the topic.

"Did you hear about the robberies?" Her voice quivers.

"No." I feign ignorance in the hope that she will divulge more. "Please. Do tell."

Looking right and left she lowers her voice to share the gossip. "Three months ago, the break-ins started. Here on Brookdale and over on Malvern."

"How frightening. Do you know any of the victims?" I'm certain she will tell me all that she knows.

"Yes! Stan and Tilley were robbed last month." Her rheumy eyes widen with alarm.

Now this is an interesting turn of events. "You don't say!"

Vigorously bobbing her head, she certifies. "It's true. Walked right through their front door in the middle of the night like he was an invited guest."

"Their door was unlocked?" After weeks of burgling in the area, I am astonished that anyone would fail to secure their home.

"Must have forgot." Lula shrugs. "Anyway, he was in and out lickety split. Took off with his tires screeching."

"Wait. You saw him?"

"Of course. I don't sleep well and like to look outside." She directs my attention to the wide picture window centered at the front of the cubic house where I had earlier noticed movement.

"Do the police know?" I can't imagine that she's been keeping this to herself.

"I'll tell you what I told them. He parked across the street over there where the streetlamp was out and sprinted up those steps." She glances at the flight of stairs. "Now I can't see their front door from my window, but he was out of the house and driving away before I could wake my grandson."

"What did he look like?" I inquire.

"Medium height. Slight build. It was too dark to see much else." She replies holding her hands apart to indicate a slim frame.

"Did Mr. or Mrs. Jones tell you what he stole?" I'm on pins and needles.

"Now that's the odd thing. All they found missing were Stan's pocket watch and an unopened pack of Chesterfield cigarettes," Lula declares incredulously. "Both were on the entry table by the door."

Further questions yield no additional details, so I take my leave and head toward the auditorium. I am thankful that I encountered this nosey but lonely neighbor and vow to visit her from time to time.

At a quarter to four on a Friday, the Fullerton High School campus has emptied, for the most part. A few automobiles are scattered among empty stalls in the northeast lot behind the auditorium, presumably belonging to teachers who may be completing their lesson plans for next week or catching up on grading. I meander along the red clay tiles of a covered passageway leading toward the front of the auditorium and examine the classical arches flanking the west side of the arcade. When I reach the south end of this impressive building, I head toward the curb at Chapman Avenue so that I may slowly turn around to take in the glorious front facade.

Depending on the quality of light striking the immaculate new auditorium, its surface may appear ivory at times and pale seashell pink at others. A grand porthole window with a rose motif is centered prominently above the triple archway entrance. All the more magnificent is the four-story clock tower rising above the western end of the structure. Gleaming blue and gold tiles, arranged in a Moorish design, grace the tower's octagonal domed roof and surround the open arched window above the clock face on each of its four sides. Overall, the imposing auditorium is reminiscent of the Spanish missions dotting the California landscape, although cast concrete ornamentation, such as acanthus leaves, urns, and even a cartouche, lend a classical elegance to the design.

I grip a wrought iron handrail while ascending the middle section of the stairway and enter the portico through a heavily embellished archway. Twin ticket windows greet me on my right and left, their glass papered from the inside. I tug at the central door but find it locked. Placing my ear to the door I can hear someone whistling "Sweet

Georgia Brown." So, I give the door a sharp rap and check the other two. I wait a moment before starting to descend the stairs to investigate a side entrance, when the rightmost door opens with an unnerving squeak.

"That could use oil." A barrel-chested mustachioed workman, not much taller than myself, leans against the bulk of the entryway with his stocky frame. "We're not quite ready for guests. Little things like this hinge need tending."

"Oh, I'm sorry to bother you. I can see that you're quite busy." I apologize and get straight to the point. "I'm here to see Mr. Jones, the foreman."

"Hmm...Mr. Jones." He strokes his double chin, eyes rolled with thought, then innocently meets my gaze. "Never heard of him."

"Oh...well..." I am befuddled that a worker would be unfamiliar with the construction manager. "I just thought..."

The good-natured fellow pitches forward and a releases a boisterous laugh. "Ah, I'm just messing with ya." Offering a meaty mitt he proclaims with a wink, "I'm Stan Jones. Do I owe ya money or are ya serving me a summons?"

"Neither." I return his firm handshake and smile pleasantly. "I'm Ruby Ray."

"Charles Ray's daughter?" He raises caterpillar thick eyebrows while tilting his head to the side.

"Niece," I reply. "You know my Uncle Charles?"

"Well of course!" Mr. Jones beams. "I supervised a few projects for him over the years at the oil field. Good man."

"That he is." I then redirect the conversation to the purpose of my visit. "I need to ask you about an employee. Frank Graham?"

"Frank?" Mr. Jones' buoyant affect fades as he sighs heavily. "What's he done now?"

I consider multiple cover stories but, at the moment, decide to stick with the truth, or as close to it as possible. Of course I won't mention the missing cash, but I sense that this amiable gent will be more forthcoming if he's aware of Norma's concern for her baby brother.

"His sister, Miss Graham, is a friend of mine and asked for my help with locating him."

"Frank's missing?" He starts. "Why, I just saw him the other day."

"When was that, Mr. Jones?" I inquire gently.

"Well now. Lemme see." He resumes the chin pawing and squints both eyes, no longer an act. With eyes open he conjectures, "Musta been Tuesday. He helped the painter put the finishin' touches on the beams." His face lights up with an idea, "Say, do ya wanna see 'em? Work of art I tell ya."

"Yes. I'd love that." For months I've been curious about the interior of this grand dame.

Mr. Jones hurries as we pass through the lobby, barely giving me time to notice the arched portals on both sides leading to recessed staircases. My mouth drops as we step into the ornate theater, for that is precisely what this building houses. The balcony, chandeliers, and pillared archways are adorned with sumptuous classical trimming much like a copiously iced wedding cake. Crimson swathes the floor and seats while matte gold tones overlay capitals and finials. Below each majestic balconette bounding the proscenium on both sides, a saying is prominently displayed. *Knowledge is in Every Country the Surest Basis of Public Happiness* and *This Country, With its Institutions, Belongs to the People Who Inhabit It*. Then I gasp at the magnificent stage.

Looking quite pleased, Mr. Jones remarks, "Now that's the reaction I was hopin' for."

"We could be standing in an opulent European theater." I cannot avoid dropping my jaw as I take in a myriad of stunning details. "All this on a school campus?"

"Some might say that." His head swivels as he scans the sweeping chamber. "But when I heard that Carleton Winslow was hired as the architect, I knew it'd be somethin'." He turns to catch my eye. "Have ya seen the Carthay Circle Theater in Los Angeles?"

"Why no." Of course, I've heard of the luxurious movie palace but have not yet had an opportunity to visit. "Was Mr. Winslow involved with that as well?"

"Yeah, he and Dwight Gibbs." Mr. Jones nods and motions for me to follow him. Once in front of the stage he gingerly grips my shoulders and turns me around. He points skyward toward roughhewn rafters elaborately painted in vibrant hues reminiscent of Northern European designs. "Those are the beams I was talkin' about."

I experience vertigo just thinking about the painters who work at such heights. "Did Fran…?" I begin.

"Nah, he helped mix colors on the ground. Sometimes they sent him to fetch more paint from storage." Mr. Jones saunters to the front row of seats. "I need to take a load off. Join me?"

I approach a folded seat and give him a questioning look as I notice a large clamp secured to its underside.

"For gentlemen's hats." He removes an imaginary topper from his crown. "Handy, don't ya think?"

"Very." I settle into the cozy seatback. "Are you certain that I'm not disturbing you? I appreciate your taking the time to speak with me."

"Not at all." He waves away my concern. "Not much more for me to do today. Everyone's gone home to their families. My wife's away, so I didn't hurry out with 'em. Although I should leave home to feed the hound."

"I ran into Lula when I dropped by your house earlier today. She mentioned that your wife was heading to France." I note his chuckle at the mention of his neighbor.

"That old biddy?" He laughs aloud while shaking his head. "She's a snoop, that one."

"She was quite informative, that's for certain." I join in with a smile.

"Ole Lula's a good egg. Just lonely I suspect." He softens his tone. "She mention my son?"

"Yes." I look at my hands folded in my lap. "I'm sorry for your loss."

"Thanks." Mr. Jones sniffs. "It's been rough all these years, 'specially for Tilley."

"I hope she finds solace during her journey." I offer supportively.

"Me too. That's the idea anyway." He cracks his neck on either side. "You know, Frank's brother James joined up with Junior."

"Norma mentioned that he too passed away during the war." I acknowledge. "I didn't realize he was a friend of your son's."

Mr. Jones compresses his lips as he slowly nods. "They were thick as thieves. Made sense. Ralph Graham and I were good pals so we all did a lot together."

"What was Mr. Graham like?" I'll admit, I'm curious why this wholesome family man was close friends with a drunkard.

"He was the best roofer around." He smooths his mustache with a thumb and index finger. "Now he wouldn't turn down the suds from time to time if ya catch my drift." He passes me a knowing glance. "But he never showed up blotto for work till after the boys died."

"I see." Sensing his discomfort, I gently suggest, "It must have been hard for Frank."

"Poor kid." Mr. Jones brushes at a spot of grease on the knee of his dungarees. "Broke my heart, it did."

"I understand that Frank began working shortly after Mr. Graham's death, once Norma arrived." I want to understand the course of Frank's decline.

Nodding thoughtfully, he affirms, "He was a good boy...till he started seriously hittin' the sauce himself that is."

I query, "What do you suppose changed for him?"

"That's easy. Workin' at the hotel he met all sorts, some not entirely on the up and up, if ya catch my meanin'." He lays a finger along the side of his nose. "He's not the sharpest tool in the shed. 'Impressionable' I think is the word."

"Still, you hired him for this project?" I ask with a sweep of my arm.

"I got a soft spot for him," he confesses. "Over the years, I keep tryin' to set him up with a good post, providin' he's supervised, of course."

"But he can't keep a job." I repeat Norma's words.

"Not usually. He's been showin' up for this one, though." Mr. Jones' tone betrays his surprise.

"What was he like Tuesday, in terms of his mood?" I hope to establish some sort of pattern.

"Now thatcha mention it, he was jumpy. Even a lil ornery." He states with annoyance. "Didn't seem liquored up though. Woulda sent him home if he had. Mixed paints like he was asked but kept lookin' over his shoulder. One a the painters asked him why, and he snapped at him."

This sounds consistent with his behavior Tuesday night with Norma and Wednesday at the bank. "He left home Wednesday evening after an argument with his sister. Do you have any idea where he may be staying?"

"Wish I did, but he's a quiet one. Don't give a thing away." Mr. Jones rises from his seat and pulls a key from his shirt pocket. "Better be lockin' up. Hafta return this key to the janitor."

"Don't you have one of your own?" I assume he would have an entire ring full.

"Did. Musta misplaced 'em about a month ago." He scratches the broad lobe of his right ear. "Hopin' they turn up soon. Project sup's the only other one with a key to the doors, and I don't wanna tell him mine's missing."

"Lula mentioned your home was robbed." I raise my index finger. "Do you suppose they were stolen?"

"Don't think so. Woulda noticed something wrong here by now." I find his logic a tad confusing. "Anyways, I usually keep 'em on the nightstand. Not by the front door."

I'm unconvinced but decide to let it go for now. He's far too defensive. "I thought the dedication ceremony for the auditorium was slated for next weekend."

"Was suppose to be. This wacky weather held us up. Plus, some cabinet parts for the Wurlitzer organ ain't arrived." He nods toward the stage. "Now they're talkin' beginning of June."

"Well, I for one cannot wait." I clap his shoulder as we exit down the center aisle. "You must feel so proud, Mr. Jones."

He straightens his spine and raises his chin. "That I am Miss Ray. That I am."

CHAPTER 7

Well-groomed California fan palms line the broad emerald lawn at the foreground of Fullerton High School. The expansive campus which houses both the high school and junior college sits upon twenty-two acres near the center of the city with bungalows and orange groves dotting the nearby landscape. I retrace my steps down the arcade that runs alongside the auditorium and gaze up at the pair of domed arches above the building that houses Administration, the Library, and Study Hall. These are fairly new additions to the campus and, like the auditorium, were built with a Spanish Colonial aesthetic. I cross campus to enter the passageway of a peripheral building through an arch supported by square columns. Quite familiar with the campus, I know this to be the English wing, however I am not sure where Norma's classroom is located.

"Excuse me," I catch the attention of a passing coed with sleek black hair. "Can you tell me where I might find Miss Graham's room?"

"Right behind you, ma'am." The young woman points toward a door over my shoulder.

"Thank you." I turn and knock, not wishing to interrupt Norma if she is with a student.

A moment later the door swings open, and a slim dark-haired youth with an armload of books nearly collides into me. "Oh, sorry about that." He continues down the arch-framed passageway toward Pomona Avenue.

Entering the classroom, I see Norma straightening papers and folders on her desk. She looks up, "Oh, Ruby! I apologize. I had no idea that was you knocking on the door." She walks along a row of desks to greet me.

"There's no need to apologize," I assure her. "I didn't want to disrupt your tutoring."

"Please, be seated." She motions and then perches upon a nearby wooden swivel seat with an adjoining desk. Looking at me expectantly she asks, "Is there any word of Frank?"

"I'm sorry, Norma, but I haven't found Frank yet, nor have I located the money." I feel disconcerted with my lack of progress today.

"I figured as much." Norma nods solemnly. "Otherwise, I would have already heard from you."

"I was able to speak with a few people today, however." I retrieve her list of names and addresses from my handbag. "Mr. Phillips, to start with."

"I'm curious what he had to say." A fleeting grimace crosses her face.

"Yes. Quite," I assent. It appears that Norma is also wary of "Fipps."

Refolding the paper, I look at her steadily. "He wanted me to tell you that Frank is fine."

Norma looks up hopefully.

"Nevertheless, Mr. Phillips insists that he doesn't know where Frank is at the moment."

Norma sighs and queries, "Do you believe him?"

"I can't say that I do. He seems rather..." I pause to search for a diplomatic way of phrasing my impression.

"Dangerous?" Norma offers, getting right to the crux of my misgivings.

"Decidedly so." I agree. "What do you make of Frank's friendship with him?"

"I don't really know how to answer that." Norma pauses to reflect. "He tends to show up just prior to Frank losing a job."

"Hmm…now that's interesting." I mentally file away that tidbit. "What happens when Mr. Phillips visits? What do they do exactly?"

"There's usually a great deal of hushed conversation, and then they leave in our car."

"How long is Frank typically away?" I lean forward.

"Sometimes all day, even late into the evening." A thought occurs to her. "I have noticed a distinct odor at times when he returns. Rather like rubbing alcohol."

"Was he intoxicated on these occasions?" This seems the most reasonable explanation.

"Nothing overt," she remarks.

I'm not sure what to make of this, so I continue with my report. "I also spoke with Mr. Pinney at the bank."

"He's the kind one," Norma comments.

"Yes, indeed. I've known Howard since high school, so he was quite informative." I recount his description of the transaction.

She places a hand to her heart. "Oh dear. I was afraid of that."

"I asked about Frank's affect while closing the account, and Howard reported that he was extremely agitated and hostile. Would you believe he dared to lay a hand on Mr. Snodgrass?"

Norma stifles a giggle. "Served him right."

"Precisely." I chuckle conspiratorially. "In all seriousness though, that is a great deal of cash to be carrying around."

Closing her eyes, she shakes her head. "Wherever can he be?"

"I shall press on to find both Frank and the cash," I assure her. "In the meantime, I do have news from Mr. Jones." As I disclose the behavior described by Mr. Jones, Norma's eyes begin to well.

"Ruby, I'm at a loss." She swipes away a tear. "This conduct is so unlike him. Even when he's clearly been drinking, he's usually so gentle and easy going."

I reach forward to pat her arm. "I'm very concerned about his mental state. He's been gone for nearly forty-eight hours, and Mr. Phillips is the only person who may have seen him."

"What are you suggesting?" Norma looks up with alarm.

"I would strongly urge you to report his disappearance to the police." I lock eyes with her.

She furiously shakes her head. "Oh no! We can't do that."

"But you must. Time is of the essence and," I am loath to admit, "at this point they have the resources to locate him much more quickly than I can."

"They'll lock him up as soon as they find him." She buries her face in her hands. "I just can't."

"On what charges?" I gently question. "He may have coerced the bank to bend the rules, but as it stands, he really hasn't broken any laws."

"That's true," she considers. Looking up she confesses, "I just feel as though there's much more to this and that he may have done something terribly wrong."

"Alright, but please promise that if he doesn't turn up by this time tomorrow, you will contact the authorities."

Face reddened, she nods and sniffs away her tears. "What an afternoon!"

"Is something else troubling you?" I ask with concern.

"An issue with a student." She gestures toward the door. "His college dream is within his grasp, yet now he's having reservations."

Shaking my head, I roll my eyes. "Ugh. Just like Dottie. Where was this boy accepted?"

"Northern Arizona University. Flagstaff." Norma begins to rise from the desk. "Even more impressive, Leo received an internship at Lowell Observatory out there. I helped him write his personal statement for the application."

"What is it with these kids?" Frustrated, I rake my fingers through my hair. "So many people without jobs. How can they even consider turning down such opportunities?"

"I'm as puzzled as you." She walks me to the door.

"I'd like to visit Mr. Mains, if he's still on campus." I grasp the doorknob.

"He's probably still in his classroom. Wallace tends to stick around until 5:00 or so." As we exit her room, she points southward toward the Mathematics wing. "He's in the corner room, next to the street."

"Thank you." I begin to leave, then turn abruptly. "I forgot to mention. I'll be seeing Elizabeth this evening. Hopefully she has some idea where Frank may be."

"Oh good. Please call me at any time if you learn something," she pleads.

"Of course." I give her a warm smile and wave. "Until tomorrow."

The tapping of my heels echoes sharply along the covered corridor. Students and teachers alike seem to have vacated the campus for the weekend. I walk resolutely toward Mr. Mains' door and apply three brisk knocks.

After a few seconds with no answer, I open the door a crack and call, "Hello? Mr. Mains?"

"Yes?" A tenor replies. "Who's there?"

Walking fully into the classroom, I view the bedraggled teacher, slightly older than me, holding a well-used eraser. Equations and symbols cover the surfaces of three double-hung blackboards.

"Busy day," he remarks with a guilty grin and streaks white chalk on his forehead while attempting to push back a thick blonde lock.

"Apparently so," I note with amusement.

"I'm sorry. I'd shake your hand, but…" He laughs and wiggles dust-covered digits. "Can I help you with something?"

"Mr. Mains, my name is Ruby Ray." I notice that he blinks twice in rapid succession at the mention of my surname. "I'm a friend of Norma Graham's."

"Norma?" His good humor diminishes, and he asks warily. "What's this about?"

Not wishing to lose rapport so quickly, I take three strides toward him but stumble over a book that has been left on the floor. I land with a thud on my hands and the very knee I injured yesterday. "Oof!"

Mr. Mains immediately drops the eraser and bolts toward me. Placing a hand under my elbow, he helps me to stand.

"How embarrassing!" I wave him away.

"Not at all, Miss Ray." He asks with concern, "Are you alright?"

"Physically yes," I chuckle. "But my pride is quite damaged, Mr. Mains."

"Please." He smiles reassuringly. "Call me Wallace."

"Only if you call me Ruby," I brush dust from the knee of my skirt.

"I apologize for responding so brusquely a moment ago," he offers sheepishly.

"Not to worry, Wallace. I dropped into your classroom uninvited." I tip my head apologetically. "It is I who should be asking for your forgiveness."

"Well...no...everything is fine." Embarrassed, he scoops up the book and deposits it on a nearby desk.

Glancing at the cover, I notice the title stamped in gold on blue cloth. "*The Lost Continent of Mu*?"

"Who knows." He averts his eyes as he shakes his head. "Some of my advanced pupils have eclectic interests." Walking to the front of the class, he retrieves the dropped eraser.

I follow and point to the heavily scribed boards. "Why don't your students help with that?"

"Typically they do, but the Pythagorean Club had a meeting after school today." He erases a triangle formed by ten dots next to the Greek word "Tetractys."

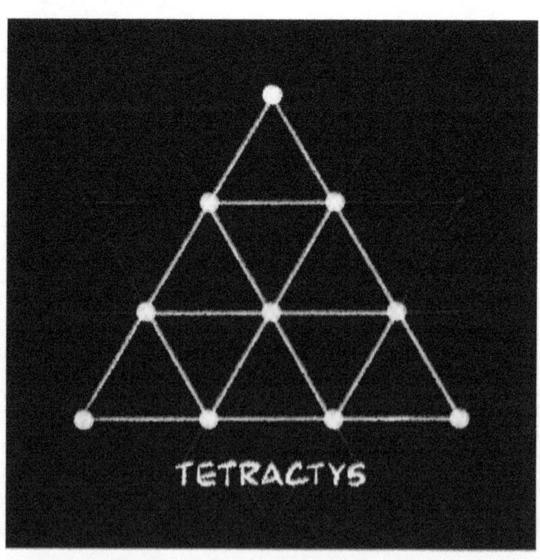

I look at him quizzically. "Pythagorean Club?"

"The elite among my mathematics students. The brightest of the bright." Wallace states proudly as he continues erasing. Once clean, he deftly pushes the chalkboard upward revealing yet another board underneath.

I peruse the room and notice a dark wooden box with numbered dials on a Bakelite control panel. "What's that?"

"Oh, nothing really." Wallace appears flustered. "Just an oscilloclast I've been tinkering with."

His reply clarifies nothing, but given his uneasiness, I don't press any further. "Can I give you a hand with the boards?" I remove my gloves and reach for an eraser lying on the desk.

"You don't need to do that."

Despite his protest, I begin gliding the felt block across integers and factorials. "It's been years since I've done this."

He confesses, "As much as I enjoy teaching, I would not miss this wearisome task were I to give up education."

"Have you been a teacher for very long?" I query.

"Off and on for a while now." Wallace exchanges the fully loaded eraser for a clean one.

"But you're new to Fullerton." With satisfaction I rub out a statement regarding cosines and tangents. "What do you think of our town?"

"It's pleasant. Very quiet, which suits my tastes." He begins to clear the final chalkboard.

"Where were you before this post?" In spite of my efforts, the board doesn't slide upward as easily as it did for Wallace.

"Here and there." He isn't particularly forthcoming.

"And now you live in the same boarding house as the Grahams."

"Yes, I moved in last fall before school started," he answers.

My attempt to segue back to the topic that riled him earlier proves successful, so I continue. "I don't wish to make you uncomfortable. But I do have a few questions regarding Norma and Frank." I return the eraser to his desk.

Wallace exhales heavily, shoulders slumped, but he doesn't turn to look at me. "Alright. Let's get to it then."

"I take it you don't care for the Grahams," I gently opine.

"Frank's usually alright." Walking to the lectern, he carefully lines the three erasers along its edge.

Taking a seat in a student's chair across from his desk, I posit, "But you're not particularly keen about Norma."

He begins sorting handwritten assignments and tests. "It's none of my business."

"She asked me to speak with you regarding Frank since he hasn't returned home in two days." I state directly. "Perhaps she's not comfortable speaking with you herself."

He looks up from his work to meet my gaze. "What's your interest in all this?" He quite fairly inquires.

I consider which approach to take and, after a brief pause, reply, "My occupation involves helping women in difficult situations. Norma and Edith came to me requesting my assistance."

"Those two." He tuts with annoyance. "You seem like a proper lady, and I don't want to offend you."

"Please," I encourage. "Go on."

He leans forward, his nose crinkled with disgust. "They're sapphists." He spits out the word as though he's uttered profanity.

Before I have a chance to reply, the door flies open on its hinges. Familiar blonde curls bounce, as Polly rushes into the room. "Mr. Mains, I forgot—" She stops abruptly when noticing my presence and turns a bonny shade of pink.

Wallace rapidly composes himself and casually strolls to the student desk. He picks up the book on which I stumbled and raises it with a shake. "This?"

Polly nods with, what? Embarrassment? Discomfort? I have difficulty reading her expression. She coughs while accepting the text. "Mmm...thank you, Mr. Mains. I have to go." Turning when she reaches the door, she murmurs. "Bye, Ruby."

When the door has closed, I look at Wallace and lift my eyebrows questioningly. "Polly is one of your advanced students?"

"You're acquainted with her?" He blinks with surprise.

"Since she was a child."

"Then I know what you're thinking." He raises both hands in protest. "But honestly, under all that frippery, she is quite possibly the most gifted mathematics student I have ever taught."

I recall my conversation with Polly last night, when she hesitatingly admitted to being "not half bad at math." Her defensiveness and compulsion to downplay her abilities saddens me, but I understand. "I was once an exceptional math student myself," I admit with regret.

"But that's marvelous!" Wallace praises. "Did you pursue mathematics in college?"

I shake my head. "Unfortunately, no. My freshman year in high school, this was in New York, I enrolled in a geometry course with older students. All male but me."

He nods, encouraging me to continue.

"The instructor was of the opinion that 'the mind of a girl is not equipped for the subtleties of mathematics beyond basic algebra.'" I have never forgotten those piercing words. "He continuously berated my attempts at the blackboard and red inked harshly worded criticism on all of my assignments. Over time, I believed him and eventually dropped the course."

Wallace sighs and examines the scuffed linoleum floor. "Unfortunately, I've encountered that attitude among quite a few of my fellow teachers."

"I'm sure." My mind returns to Polly. "You know, Wallace, my cousin is a senior here and a good friend of Polly's. Perhaps you know her. Dottie Ray?"

"That name rings a bell." He replies over his shoulder while returning to his desk. "But then there are hundreds of students on campus."

"I don't wish to keep you from your work." I comment while motioning toward the stack of papers he is sorting. "Back to the issue with Frank. Do you know where he may be?"

"I can't say that I do." With barely concealed contempt, he continues. "But I hope he's taken the money and fled far away from those two." It seems that Mr. Mains overhears quite a lot at the boarding house.

Trying not to react, I reply evenly. "Very well. Thank you so much for your time." I begin slipping on my right glove.

"I know that sounded callous." He says defensively, "I'm really not a hateful person."

"Of course not, Mr. Mains." Finished with my gloves, I grab the handle of my purse.

"So, you mentioned the Big Apple." Apparently, he doesn't wish for me to leave with a negative impression. "You must miss it. All that theater and culture. Do you ever plan to move back?"

"Not at all."

"The California weather?" he queries.

I turn with a wave to take my leave. "The avocados."

CHAPTER 8

Walking from the carport, I absentmindedly retrieve a weathered wicker basket from beneath the garden bench in order to collect avocados for Elizabeth and her family. While picking the nearly ripened fruit, I try to organize my thoughts. They've been in turmoil since leaving Wallace Mains.

First, I must alert Norma and Edna that, as careful as they have been, the nature of their relationship has been discovered. Did Wallace intentionally eavesdrop, or did he catch wind of the truth merely by chance? Second, the severity of his revulsion for the two women seems inconsistent with his otherwise affable personality. Why is that? Third, while he seems quite devoted to his students, particularly the Pythagoreans, it sounds as though he doesn't stay long at any one school. What would motivate a dedicated teacher to move so frequently? Last, despite his friendliness, Wallace holds his cards close to his vest when it comes to personal information. Does he have something to hide? Bottom line, I believe that he is unaware of Frank's current whereabouts, but I'm left with a vague uneasiness about him.

With both the basket and my handbag dangling from the crook of my arm, I reach into my coin purse for a penny. As I turn to approach the wishing well, I notice the backside of Jack, his arm fully extended into the shallow depths of the well. "Did you misplace Bob?"

Jack's shoulders jerk up toward his ears, and he freezes in place. "Naw. Ya caught me red-handed." He withdraws his arm to reveal a fistful of copper.

"You know, if you need change, all you have to do is ask." I shake my coin purse.

He drops the pennies into the pocket of his windbreaker. "Where's the fun in that?"

I laugh heartily and give his shoulder a thump. "That should be your catchphrase."

Unabashed, he shoots me a crooked grin. "Did you hear about the storm today?"

"Hear about it? I was out in it." I shiver recalling my soaked oxfords. "A lightning bolt hit the top of the Fox Theater."

"No!" Jack's eyes widen as he smiles broadly with delight. "Lightning hit a house in La Habra too. Fireball shot straight through the ceiling between a man and lady sitting in the living room."

Horror washes over me. "That's not funny Jack! Are they alright?"

"Sure!" He waves his right hand dismissively. "They're swell."

"And the house?" I picture its charred remains still smoldering in the waning light of early evening.

"A-OK!" He rounds his thumb and index finger.

I realize that the newspapers could not possibly have covered this story yet. "How on Earth did you hear about this?" I hand him the basket of avocados.

"Sal's dad." Jack accepts the basket, and we begin strolling toward the back door of the house. "He's a fireman in La Habra."

"Of course he is." That does ring a bell.

"Say Ruby," Jack lowers his voice as he holds the door for me. "Ask Nan about the hobo."

"My, this has been an eventful afternoon," I observe as Jack returns the basket to me. Something delightful is simmering on the stove, but the kitchen is empty. Depositing the avocados on the counter, I pass into the dining room, also vacant, and head upstairs.

"That you, Ruby?" Dottie's voice carries through her closed door.

Turning the knob, I see her hunched over the same volumes as yesterday. "Homework on a Friday evening? I thought you had a social life."

"Oh, just some catching up," she mutters while stacking the books face down with their spines out of view.

I notice an overnight bag on her bed alongside the beaver brown "collegiate" coat that Dottie received for Christmas. "What's with the fur? I know the weather was atrocious today, but I doubt it will snow tonight."

"We may go walking after the movie." She tosses a chemise into the open bag.

"Don't you think a sweater would suffice? It is May after all." I don't understand this "walking" past time of students her age. Basically, half of the kids promenade up and down Spadra while the rest sit in cars and watch the parade.

She shrugs. "Better safe than sorry."

Pointing toward the small suitcase I ask, "Wasn't Polly going to stay here tonight?"

Dottie sifts through the contents of a dresser drawer and extracts a pair of casual slacks and tosses them in the suitcase. "Her father won't let her." Holding up a finger she continues, "And before you ask, Dad said it's fine for me to stay with her."

"Alright," I refold the slacks and place them in the bag. "But please call us at any time if you feel uncomfortable over there."

"Of course," she replies while clicking the latches to secure the bag.

I approach the door to get ready for my dinner with Elizabeth when I remember my missing shoes. "Do you perchance have my white center-buckle heels? I'd like to wear them tonight."

She reaches under the bed and fishes out the purloined shoes.

"Please ask next time," I remind her. "Of course, I'll let you borrow them, but I'd like to know where they are when I need them."

"Sorry Ruby," she apologizes sincerely.

"Not to worry." While exiting her room I instruct, "And please set the table for three tonight. I have plans with a friend."

"Make that two," she calls back. "I'm heading out soon."

"Have fun." I turn back to give her a squeeze. "And please be safe."

"Of course, Ruby."

Back in my room, I remove my hat and gloves while kicking off my shoes. What an exhausting day filled with exhausting men! A wave of fatigue washes over me so I stretch out on the white chenille bedspread to close my eyes for a few minutes. I sigh deeply, enjoying the respite.

Drowsiness soon transitions to deep sleep, and I enter a turbulent dreamscape.

Racing down a covered corridor at the high school I desperately grasp a door handle and sprint into Mr. Mains' classroom. A handful of students are scribbling furiously with their heads bent over their work. Large block letters fill the center chalkboard, reading "FINAL EXAM."

Mr. Mains looks up from his desk and meets my desperate countenance with scorn. "You may as well leave, Miss Ray." He firmly points toward the door, and I notice a triangular ring on his index finger composed of ten garnets. "You are NOT a Pythagorean."

Looking over my shoulder at the students, I see Polly nibbling the end of a pencil as she mulls over a complex integral equation printed on her test booklet. Next to her, Dottie is scribing a letter to the University of California declining their acceptance. My pounding heart skips a beat, and I sharply whisper, "Dottie!" But she doesn't acknowledge me.

With desperation I plead, "Mr. Mains, I can explain—"

"No need, Miss Ray." He grips my upper arm. "You have been dropped from this course."

Fraught with panic, I stammer, "I-I-I forgot I had enrolled in this class." Tears begin to well in my eyes. "I need this to graduate."

"Your mind is not equipped for the subtleties of this level of mathematics," he spews with contempt.

I recoil as though I have been slapped. Looking around I realize that all eyes are now upon me. Sleek black hair is twisting around the slender finger of a young woman observing me haughtily. A thin dark-haired boy elbows the handsome fellow next to him, who snickers while twiddling a tuning fork. Polly gapes with flushed cheeks, her eyes and mouth rounded into perfect circles. But Dottie's expression breaks my heart, for she is simultaneously embarrassed and disgusted.

Mr. Mains tightens his grip and forcefully pulls me toward the door. "You have no place here." He flings open the door and thrusts me through the passage into a lightless abyss. The sound of hail roars deafeningly above me as I fall.

My eyes fly open, and my heart races. A sweeping glance at my surroundings assures me that I am awake and within the safe confines of my bedroom. I lie still for several moments taking deep calming breaths. What was that about? I haven't had the "final exam for a class I forgot" dream in quite some time. I chalk it up to visiting the campus today. Turning my head toward the bedside clock, I realize that I have about a half an hour to get ready, and I still need to touch base with Nan and Uncle Charles.

I quickly assemble my ensemble for the evening, starting with a new pair of silk stockings. Once I have changed into a floral georgette dress, I step into the white heels and select a matching beaded mesh bag. Running fingers through my soft curls I examine my reflection in the mirror on my vanity table. A touch of lipstick and pinch of my cheeks should do the trick. Using the stopper, I dab Jean Patou's new fragrance "Joy" onto my wrists and behind my ears. Feeling fully recovered from my nightmare, I place a violet beret at a jaunty angle upon my crown and fetch my coat.

Stepping into the hall I encounter Uncle Charles. "Just the person I was looking for."

"Oh?" He holds his pipe between his teeth in order to light it. "And to what do I owe this honor?" He asks around the stem.

"I stopped by Farmers and Merchants today." My tone betrays my agitation.

"This sounds like a sit-down conversation." He gestures toward the steps. "Shall we continue downstairs?"

"We can discuss this in detail later." I open my handbag to ensure I've packed everything I'll need this evening. "I'm meeting Elizabeth at six for dinner, so I'll get straight to the point."

"As you wish." He releases a cloud of sweet smoke which I find pleasant, in contrast to the repugnant odor of cigars and cigarettes.

While we stand on the landing, I state unequivocally. "I'd like to move my accounts to Fullerton Building and Loan."

"This is unexpected." Taken aback, he removes his pipe. "F&M was the first bank in Fullerton and remains its principal financial institution. I'd say it has served us quite well."

"Served." I chuckle sarcastically. "That's an interesting choice of words."

"How so?" He asks, perplexed.

After all these years listening to me grumble about Mr. Snodgrass, how can he fail to understand my perspective? "As a gentleman of means, I have no doubt that you have received exemplary service."

"I realize that Snodgrass can be intractable—" he begins.

"That doesn't even begin to describe the appalling treatment I've received because I am a woman." I inhale deeply in an effort to control my temper. "Do you realize that I am unable to remove your name from my accounts? It's 1930 yet that tyrant refuses to permit females to hold shares without a male co-owner."

Flummoxed, Uncle Charles sputters, "I had absolutely no idea." He closes his eyes and shakes his head. "No wonder you're so upset."

He nods toward the stairs, which we descend before taking a seat on the sofa. "When we opened your accounts twelve years ago, I assumed that as soon as you reached twenty-one, the shares would convert to your name alone."

"You didn't know?" All this time I assumed that he was cognizant of the intolerant policy.

"Of course not, Ruby." His face betrays a look of hurt. "I'm stunned that you would think I'd go along with this. Why didn't you say something?"

I nervously slide my fingers across the beads on my bag, feeling like the sixteen-year-old orphan who joined his household all those years ago. The residual effects of the day, not to mention the nightmare, have left me raw with emotion. "I figured that you wanted to oversee my finances...just in case."

"In case of what, exactly?" He bellows with laughter. "You are, without a doubt, one of the brightest and most trustworthy people I know, male or female."

My shoulders relax. "Thank you." I should have asked him about this a long time ago but was embarrassed to bring it up.

He pats my arm then looks directly into my eyes. "Mark my words, Monday morning we will march into that bank and close all of our accounts. I refuse to support any institution with such insufferable practices."

"What insufferable practices?" Jack saunters into the living room and plops sideways onto a cushioned chair, his knees folded over the curve of one of its arms.

"Nothing you need to worry about," my Uncle responds.

Jack rolls his eyes and shrugs.

"I cannot wait to see the look on old Snodgrass' face Monday morning." I hold a very satisfying image in my mind.

Uncle Charles reacts with a hearty laugh. "Me too, now that you mention it."

Glancing at the brass Tiffany clock atop the mantel I realize I must be leaving. "Well, I'm off to dinner. I shouldn't be too late."

"Have a nice time, Ruby," my uncle says. "If there's anything else you'd like to discuss, we can talk tomorrow."

CHAPTER 9

Dozens of early diners bustle into eateries throughout downtown Fullerton at 6:00 PM. Later, when the high school and college students descend upon the area for their Friday night escapades, parking and available tables will become scare. Mah Jong Cafe sits unobtrusively next to a cleaning business across from the brightly lit California Hotel. Despite being the sole chop suey house in our town, Mah Jong's is nearly empty when I enter the diminutive lobby.

"Miss Ray, how wonderful to see you!" Mr. Zhao greets me warmly as he walks around a strategically placed Chinese screen. "Miss Martin is already seated."

He leads me into the dining room, which is filled with black tufted-back booths and small square tables with chairs. Mr. Zhao once told us that he and his wife arrived here from Shanghai in 1924, just prior to the Immigration Act which abruptly ended the issuance of visas to people from East Asian countries. Earlier state legislation, including the Alien Acts of 1913 and 1920, had made it nearly impossible for Chinese and Japanese residents to own or rent land. Thankfully for the Zhao family, the owner of this building has been willing to extend their lease contract beyond the three-year limit. Apparently, he didn't want to travel outside Fullerton for Chinese food either. Over the years, Mr. and Mrs. Zhao and their children have become quite dear to me, and I worry about their well-being in a nativist political climate that seems to be getting worse.

Seated on a tall bench with her back to the door, Elizabeth is not immediately visible as we approach the table. Upon hearing our steps, however, she neatly slides from the booth to embrace me beneath a ceiling filled with red and gold balloon-shaped lanterns. "Ruby, I am so glad we're doing this. I have so much to tell you."

Mr. Zhao hands us both plastic covered menus and offers to bring us tea.

"Yes, Mr. Zhao, a large pot would be lovely," I reply while removing my gloves. I set my purse on the bench before settling across from Elizabeth. "I can't wait to hear your news, but first I have to ask you about that stunning frock you're wearing."

"One of the perks of managing a women's boutique." Elizabeth preens and adjusts an embroidered jabot that lies fetchingly over her slim-waisted dress. "First dibs on new merchandise."

"Well, it's absolutely lovely." I unfold and drape a red cloth napkin across my lap. "By the way, I regretted leaving this morning when that trio encircled you."

"Oh them!" She waves a hand dismissively. "Every month it's the same gripes and yammer."

"Do they buy anything?" I ask, as Mr. Zhao delivers a square jade teapot to our table.

"Ironically, they're our best customers." Elizabeth accepts a handleless cup of steaming green tea. "They each leave with at least four new ensembles."

"Figures," I giggle then peruse the familiar menu, the only change being the Chinese Zodiac. "Year of the Horse," I comment.

"Energetic and passionate," Elizabeth reads. "Hmm...I can think of a few people who fit that description."

"I'm willing to bet Hollywood is filled with them." I chuckle then close the menu as Mr. Zhao approaches.

"What will you have this evening?" He asks with a smile.

"Chicken chop suey for me," I reply with satisfaction.

"You always order that," Elizabeth teases then looks up at the kind man. "I'll take General Tso's chicken."

"How spicy would you like that?" I have never observed Mr. Zhao writing down an order. Even with large parties, his memory is impeccable.

"Medium spicy, please." She answers and hands him her menu.

"Soup for you two?" He collects my menu as well.

Simultaneously we answer, "No thank you." Mah Jong is known for its generous portion sizes, and I hate wasting food.

I wrap my hands around my warm cup and blow across the steaming surface of tea. "So, what's your big news?"

"Well," Elizabeth leans forward and places both palms on the table. "I received a call at the shop this afternoon from a talent agency."

"Really!" I take a sip and set the cup in its saucer. "Go on. I'm dying to know."

"A few months ago, a friend of mine arranged for me to meet with one of their agents." Mr. Zhao assembles an array of sauces and oils on the table before us. "I figured they weren't interested when I didn't hear back."

"What did they say?" I ask after she pauses to thank Mr. Zhao.

"They want to sign me!" She shrieks with delight. "A two-year contract. And the best part is that they represent quite a number of working actors and actresses."

"This is absolutely marvelous! It's about time." I reach across the table and squeeze her hands. "Just curious, who are these actors and actresses?"

"I'm not at liberty to say, but I can tell you that you've undoubtedly heard of them." Her smile is contagious.

"I'm so thrilled for you!" No one deserves this break more than Elizabeth. "Tell me all the specifics."

"Well, they want me to shorten my name to Liz Martin." She waves a hand nonchalantly. "All the big names are three or four syllables, and Elizabeth Martin is just too long."

I mull over the actors and actresses I can think of offhand, and she's absolutely correct. "I can see it now, 'Liz Martin' in neon lights all across the country."

She sputters the tea she's been sipping. "Easy there. I'll be happy with a speaking part."

"This is just the beginning Elizabeth, or should I say 'Liz?'" I'm filled with certainty that this moment marks her big break. "What are the terms they're offering?"

"So now you're my attorney?" She asks with a charming laugh. "The agency gets thirty-five percent."

My stomach drops. "Elizabeth, doesn't that seem high to you?"

"It is...but only for two years. Then I can try to renegotiate for half of that or sign with a different agency." She appears confident that this will work out for her. "If they can find work for me, I get exposure, and that's what I need right now more than anything."

"Will you have someone look over the contract before you sign?" I'm concerned that she's getting in over her head.

"Are you volunteering?" She jokes. "As it so happens, I know someone in the business to help me with that...which brings me to my next bit of news."

"I'm on the edge of my seat, Elizabeth. What more could have happened?"

"Well..." she replies with a blush, a finger resting on the cleft of her chin.

It dawns on me all at once. "You've MET someone!"

Nodding vigorously, she reaches inside her purse then holds out her left hand to display a square cut diamond surrounded by brightly twinkling sapphires.

"You're ENGAGED!" I grasp her hand and gape at the resplendent ring. "Oh Elizabeth!" I leap out of the booth to embrace her. "Congratulations!"

"Thank you!" Tears of joy fall down her sculpted cheeks. "I've never been so happy!"

After taking our seats, I command, "Details, please!"

"His name is Dean Larsen." She dries her eyes with her napkin. "We met at a sandwich shop in Burbank seven months ago when I was there for a casting call."

"So, he's the one who's 'in the business?'" I inquire.

"Yes, he signed with Warner Brother's a few years ago. And let me tell you, did he ever luck out." Her eyes widen. "Nabbed a small speaking part on *The Jazz Singer!*"

"No!" This first ever "talkie" ended the silent film era a few years ago.

"Yes! Zanuck was so impressed with Dean that he cast him in *Tenderloin* and *Show of Shows*." Elizabeth states proudly. "He has an amazing singing voice."

"Would I recognize him?" I think back to those three movies.

"You probably would, film buff that you are." At that moment, Mr. Zhao sets a hot plate in front of her. "Thank you! This smells simply wonderful."

"Spicy, but not too spicy for you," he responds with a grin. "And chicken chop suey for you, Miss Ray."

"Have I been missing this!" A few years ago, I learned that chop suey is not an authentic Chinese dish, but I don't really give two hoots. My mouth is salivating as I gaze at the thick brown sauce and crispy mixed vegetables.

"Please let me know if you need anything else." Mr. Zhao is satisfied with our reactions.

"Thank you." I share a warm smile with Elizabeth as he walks away. "I'm over the moon for you, my friend."

She breathes deeply and sighs contentedly. "Shall we?" Clinking our forks together, neither of us adept with chopsticks, we take a bite of our steaming entrees. "Delicious!"

After several minutes of gustatory pleasure, I revisit Elizabeth's announcements. "So how do your parents feel about your exciting news?"

I've caught her mid-bite, so she holds up a finger while swallowing. "They simply adore Dean." She washes down her food with a sip of tea. "He comes from a humble family of dairy farmers in Minnesota. Very kind and respectful. Papa's particularly taken with him."

"Have you set a date?" Elizabeth is certain to be the loveliest bride Fullerton has ever seen.

"We've decided to wait at least a year," she explains. "We're both so busy, and we want to take our time planning the wedding and finding a place to live in Los Angeles."

"Makes sense, especially with your career taking off." I nod.

After a moment she interlaces her fingers, places her hands under her chin, and queries pointedly, "What about you?"

I spear a choice morsel of chicken with my fork and ask with confusion. "What about me?"

"While I'm sure there's a long queue of gentlemen callers at your door, have you met anyone…" she examines me coyly, "special?"

I nearly choke. "Hardly a long queue," I croak. "And definitely no one special." I seize my cup and slurp several times to stifle my coughing.

"Sorry Ruby," she frowns with concern. "I didn't mean to strike a nerve."

"No, it's fine," I assure her while dabbing my face with my napkin. A few deep breaths confirm that my airway is clear. Embarrassedly I admit, "I haven't actually dated anyone in quite some time." To be honest, I don't go out all that much either, as my social circle is rather small. It's true that I find it easy to connect with people in my job. However, when it comes to my personal life, I prefer having a few close friends, like Elizabeth, rather than a large group of friends I don't know as well. And dating is the furthest thing from my mind right now.

"Why ever not?" She asks in bewilderment, her eyebrows raised. "You're hotsy-totsy and have a wonderful personality to boot."

I chuckle at her choice of slang.

"I'm serious!" She exclaims. "Men must make passes at you all the time."

How do I explain to Elizabeth that I am completely uninterested in men who make passes? Nor do I find the notion of dating strangers to be appealing. In truth, I'm not ready to open my heart to romance again.

"After Eddie…," I begin.

"Say no more, Ruby." Elizabeth shakes her fork, "He had charisma in spades, I'll give him that. But betraying you…that was unforgivable." She forcefully sinks her fork into a morsel of chicken.

We eat in silence for a few moments, both recalling the series of events that led to my heartache after Eddie abruptly ended things. It was months before I discovered that another woman was involved. I swallow a bite of vegetables and sigh, "I do miss the dancing."

Elizabeth shoots me a pointed stare. "Are you saying you haven't gone dancing in three years?"

I nod sheepishly. "I couldn't bear running into him at the dance hall…with her."

"Well for Pete's sake, Ruby. There are other places to go dancing around here."

"You're right," I nod. "But it's more than that. When you dance with a man, they're in charge. They determine everything. When you turn and how you move. Whether your steps are fast or slow. Dance was the perfect metaphor for my relationship with Eddie. He had to control everything. I just loathe the thought of another man's hand on my waist dictating my movement."

"You know, Ruby, it's not all foxtrot and waltz. As I recall, your Charleston was nothing to sneeze at."

I shrug and push my food around the plate. Given my silence, Elizabeth adds slyly, "I know just the fella for you."

My palm shoots up. "Stop right there. You sound just like Nan trying to set me up with someone."

She shrugs. "Well, it was worth a try."

"So, tell me more about your folks," I redirect the conversation. "Are they still working at the same jobs?"

"Okay, okay. It's clear you don't want to discuss your love life," Elizabeth concedes. "Yes, Papa is selling shoes at the department store, Chapman-Wickett, and Mama is still packing for Sunny Hills Fruit." She gestures south toward the tracks where most of the packing houses in Fullerton are located.

With a shake of my head, I pronounce with admiration, "I don't know how she or any of the other packers do it!"

"Or the pickers for that matter," she nods with agreement. "That's grueling work, especially in the summer heat. But there aren't many options." For most women of Mexican heritage in Orange County, employment options are limited.

"Has the strange weather affected her work recently?" I'm sure that on a day like today with lightning and hail, everything grinds to a stop.

"Not as much as you'd think." She inattentively twirls her fork with a hand resting on the table. "The foremen recognize that everyone's worried about losing their jobs so they keep upping their demands, safe or not, because they can."

"What's changed?" I can't imagine that waiting for a storm to clear would make much of a difference.

Elizabeth leans toward the table. "That appalling drought in places like Texas and Oklahoma. Those women in the shop today were saying that large caravans of families have started to arrive."

The implication of this news dawns on me at once. "And they all need work."

"Exactly." She reclines against the seat back and folds her arms.

"Just today a young man showed up on our porch seeking shelter from the storm." I retell Gabe's narrative.

"So, you see what this means for pickers and packers of Mexican descent." Elizabeth examines her dish solemnly. "Mama will be fine. She's a campiona and trains all the new packers." Years ago, Elizabeth told me that "campiona" ("champion" in English) is the prestigious title given to women who consistently pack a hundred boxes of citrus during a nine hour shift, a title which commands respect from other packers, as well as the foreman. "But the others…"

After a pause, I finish her prediction "…will be replaced."

"The Grower's Exchange must have realized this months ago when they started reducing the piece-rate pay for both packers and pickers." She shakes her head with disgust. "Mama told me that some families are barely surviving and have to dig through the garbage behind grocery stores and restaurants just to find food."

My hand slams the table with resolve. "Something must be done! For these families as well as those arriving destitute from the South and Midwest."

"I fear that this is only the beginning." She shrugs her shoulders weakly. "There's talk of repatriation. I overheard one of my customers, married to a city council member, say to her friend, 'Thomas thinks they should all go back like they did during that recession ten years ago.'"

"But many of these families have children who were born here. They're Americans!" A middle-aged couple at a table to my left glance up from their meals. I lower my voice. "As I recall, most of the immigrants that arrived after the Mexican Revolution fled violence and severe drought. California growers offered employment, housing, and education for their children. This is intolerable!"

"Yes. It is." Elizabeth nods sadly. "And there's nothing for them to go back to in Mexico. No homes. No jobs."

At that moment Mr. Zhao walks a group of diners to an adjacent booth. Sensing the intensity of our conversation, four pairs of eyes look us over with discomfort. A mask of good humor instantly replaces Elizabeth's countenance. She straightens her posture and notes, "We haven't yet discussed the purpose of your visit today."

Loathe to bring up another potentially charged topic in the rapidly filling dining room, I suggest, "Let's pay the bill and take a walk."

Elizabeth looks around. "Yes. Let's."

CHAPTER 10

Stepping outside the cafe, we secure our coats to ward off the chill of a bracing breeze. The starlit sky is mostly clear, and a waxing gibbous moon is rising in the east. Despite the abundant dinner we consumed, I find myself craving something sweet. "Say Elizabeth, how do you feel about a stroll over to Taylor's?"

She groans half-heartedly. "I really should be watching my diet, but why not?"

While walking to Taylor's Chocolate Shop we pass the former Rialto Theater, now under extensive renovation by First National Trust Bank, which will open its doors soon. The Rialto dropped its final curtain a couple of years ago when the Alician Court Theater (now the Fox Theater) became the first sound-equipped cinema in the county. The new facade of the Rialto building, all vertical lines and abstract forms, is decidedly modern in comparison to neighboring buildings.

When the Rialto was open, Taylor's was ideally located to assuage the sweet tooth of many a theater patron. Now the chocolate shop entices potential customers passing by with the rich inviting aroma of cocoa beans drifting out an open door. Once inside the chocolate shop, however, the fragrance is downright intoxicating. Elizabeth and I approach the glass front display case and visually scan the delectable options. Soon the saleswoman behind the counter finishes with her customer and proffers a sample of coconut brittle, which we accept gratefully.

"What can I help you with today?" A square of waxed paper lies on her palm.

"I'd like a half a pound of your chocolate covered dates in one of those Mother's Day boxes please." Between the candy and the corsage, I have Nan covered. Even though she never had children of her own, she is like a grandmother to me, and I like to give her a little something every Mother's Day.

"Good idea, Ruby." Elizabeth calls after the aproned woman, "I'll take the same."

While our packages are being filled and ribboned, Elizabeth turns to me, "Would you believe there's a candy shop in Los Angeles that offers delivery? Dean says that while shooting their last film, John Barrymore would call See's Candy, and a young man in a chauffeur's uniform would show up to the studio on a motorcycle with a little cab on the back filled with candy."

"I'd like to see that," I chuckle, while deciding which of the sweet offerings I will choose for myself.

Setting the boxes on the countertop, the saleswoman asks, "Would you like something for yourselves?"

"Yes, please," I reply. "I'll take a whip cream chocolate."

Elizabeth answers, "I'd love another coconut brittle, please. No need for a bag."

Once we've paid, we nibble our treats and leave the shop. "Do you want a ride home?" I ask Elizabeth.

"That would be lovely." She swallows a crunchy bite. "I rode in with Papa this morning."

We head back a few blocks toward the Mah Jong Cafe where my car is parked. While we are walking, Elizabeth broaches the subject we've been avoiding. "So, what's this business about Frank?"

"How much did Norma tell you when she called Wednesday night?" I roll the empty waxed paper into a ball and toss it into a trash bin we pass.

Elizabeth does the same then brushes crumbs from the brittle off of her gloves. "She said that he hasn't been himself lately and ran off with the money from their bank account."

"Yes, that's the long and the short of it." Stopping under a lamppost, I tuck the candy box under my arm and reapply my lipstick. "I spoke with her this afternoon, and she still hasn't heard from him. Do you have any idea where he might have gone?"

"I've been thinking about that ever since her call." She snaps a mother-of-pearl mirror closed and slips it into her handbag. "I hate to say this, but with all that dough, maybe he just left for good."

"That may be true," I admit. "But Norma insists that he's somewhere nearby. He mentioned having a plan for the two of them involving the money."

She shivers and buttons her Angora coat. "You know, he wasn't like this when we dated all those years ago."

"High school was so long ago, and we had only just become friends, so I don't remember much about your relationship with Frank." I take her cue and knot the sash of my coat. "Perhaps you can tell me what he was like before his job at the hotel."

"He was sweet...and vulnerable. A bit like a puppy who just wants to be loved." Her voice breaks. "His father was terrible to him."

This surprises me. "I hadn't heard about that."

"Frank said he'd come home from work already drunk." She sniffs. "Then he'd insist that Frank drink with him, or he'd beat him."

I'm speechless. I place a hand on her arm to continue.

"Mr. Graham died shortly before we started dating, so I never witnessed this myself." She removes a handkerchief from her coat pocket and dabs her nose. "He adored Norma when she arrived. You know, she's been his hero ever since."

"A little kindness goes a long way to someone who's been abused," I reflect.

"So true." She replaces the handkerchief. "Looking back now, I think I first fell for him because of his tragic history. I fancied myself a bit of a Florence Nightingale."

"I'm sure you weren't the only young lady to feel that way about him. As I recall he was quite handsome." Earlier today I looked up his picture in the yearbook from 1920.

"That he was! And he wanted so much to do better than his father." She smiles wistfully. "Definitely not book smart, if you know what I mean, but he was a hard worker."

"Norma mentioned that he began working while still in high school," We reach my car, and I rummage around in my handbag for the keys.

"Yes, he'd take any work he could find." She hops in the passenger seat and quickly closes the door to the evening chill. When I'm also seated, she continues. "He actually worked with my mother for a while."

"At the packing house?" I query and start the engine.

"Mm-hmm. As a hauler." She rubs her hands together as she warms up. "Mr. Baker himself hired him the summer before his senior year. He came to speak to our class about the citrus industry, and Frank approached him afterward for a job. His gumption impressed Mr. Baker."

Frank's willingness to do such back-breaking work surprises me. "How long did he work for Sunny Hills Fruit?"

"About a year. Mostly weekends and during school breaks." I begin to back out of the parking space as she reminisces. "He even picked walnuts during the fall." She chuckles.

"What's so funny?" I glance at her quickly then return my eyes to the road illuminated by my headlamps.

"Now I don't want you to get the wrong idea," she laughs. "We were very good kids, but we sometimes went to the walnut shed in the evening, if you catch my drift."

"So, was there a literal walnut shed or is that a euphemism?" I query jokingly.

"Quite literal. They'd use it to store the canvases placed under the trees, as well as the long poles used for shaking the upper branches." We stop at the railroad tracks for a moment as the sleek Red Car train passes by. "The shed was fairly good sized, and no one ever bothered to lock it because it was in the middle of nowhere."

A large vacant shed in a remote location. Now this sounds promising. "Where precisely is this shed?"

"If you head left on Bastanchury from Spadra and drive for about a quarter of a mile, you'll see a Sunny Hills Fruit Company sign on your right. There's a dirt road just past that," she gesticulates while giving directions. "If you didn't know it was there, you'd drive right past. As I recall we'd take that road for almost a mile until it ended at the shed."

"It's been nearly a decade. Do you think the shed is still there?" I ask hopefully.

"I don't see why not," she replies. "Grant you, Mama said the walnut trees were removed a couple of years ago and were replaced with persimmons, which take several years to fruit."

"So, the area is probably vacant at the moment?" I conjecture.

"There's a navel orange grove along the first part of the dirt road, but if I recall correctly, the oranges should have been harvested earlier in the spring."

"Elizabeth, I could kiss you!" I exclaim joyfully. My intuition is niggling so I think I may be on to something.

"Please tell me you're not going out there this evening," she insists with concern.

"I'll wait until the morning." I stop the car in front of her home, a small bungalow court apartment on Truslow Avenue. Reaching behind the front seat I grasp the basket of avocados and hand it to Elizabeth.

"Oh Ruby! Papa will be thrilled." She leans across the front seat to give me a warm hug.

"Elizabeth, it's been a lovely evening. Congratulations on your marvelous news!" I return her embrace.

"Thank you so much!" She swings the door open. Before exiting the car, she proclaims, "We really should do this more often."

"I agree." Once the door has closed and Elizabeth has let herself into the apartment, I put the car into first gear and begin my drive home.

A symphony of crickets serenades my brief walk from the carport to the back door. I duck upon entering the house as a formidable tan and ivory moth swoops blindly toward me. Nan must have turned the porch light on for me when she left this evening. Passing through the kitchen, I extinguish the few remaining lights while the radio in the living room booms with the syncopated rhythm of a female trio.

"Well good evening." Uncle Charles looks up as I enter and inserts a brass bookmark between the pages of a yellow novel stamped with images of pioneers and Indians.

I approach his armchair and examine the title. "*Cimarron*? Since when do you read novels?"

He removes his reading glasses and drops them into the breast pocket of his paisley smoking jacket. "Now that's not fair. I enjoy fiction from time to time."

"True, but biographies are more your cup of tea." I place my handbag, hat, and Nan's box of chocolates on the velvet cushion of the settee.

When the energetic tune comes to an end, an exaggerated bass announces, "That was the Boswell Sisters bringing you 'Heebie Jeebies.' Next up on KFWB is Paul Whiteman and his orchestra. But first, a word from our sponsor."

"Can we finish the discussion we started earlier?" I sink into the chair next to Uncle Charles.

"Absolutely." He places the novel on the end table next to him and sits up straight in his chair. "More about the bank?"

"Related to that." I stretch my head from side to side to relieve the tension in my neck and experience a click as I tilt toward the right.

"You've had quite the day today," he observes.

"And how!" After a few shoulder rolls I describe my visit to the safe deposit room at the bank and conclude with, "I think I may sell the New York house."

Uncle Charles nods slowly, deep in thought. "It's your property, Ruby. I support whatever decision you make." He extracts his pipe and tobacco from the inside pocket of his jacket.

"Thank you." I'm grateful he didn't rush in with suggestions and opinions. "I have concerns about the timing though."

"Because of the crash?" He muses while refilling his pipe.

"That and the economy as a whole." I share with him the details from a New York Times article I recently read about the conversion of houses into single room occupancy buildings and apartments. "I know there's a demand for affordable housing options right now, but I shudder at the thought of carving up that beautiful house."

He exhales three quick puffs. "I can understand your reservations. It was your childhood home."

"True. But when I visited there several years ago, so much inside had changed. The house no longer felt like my home." It helps to verbalize my reservations to another person. "What concerns me most is that the house will sit vacant when the current tenants decide to move, and then I'll be unable to sell."

"I think your apprehension is valid," he offers supportively. "Have you spoken with the property manager?"

"Not yet." I break off, lost in the thought of severing this connection with my parents.

Respecting my rumination, Uncle Charles waits patiently before suggesting, "See what he has to say. I'm sure he can recommend an agent to advise you."

"Yes, I'm sure he can." I release a deep breath, as the clock on the mantel chimes the half hour. "I'll telephone him Monday."

Jeanie Lang's childlike soprano sings a catchy tune about a "Ragamuffin Romeo" while playful horns punctuate the melody. When the descending scale of chimes marks the conclusion of the ditty, Uncle Charles asks, "Have you given any thought to what you would do with the proceeds of the sale?"

I rise and walk across the room to switch off the radio. Once I have returned to my seat, I take a deep breath and meet his questioning gaze. "I have been thinking about traveling. Of course, I'd invest a majority of the funds, but I've had my heart set on a trip abroad for some time."

With a look of mild surprise, he replies, "I had no idea. Where do you have in mind?"

"Europe." I warm to the subject. "There's a Holland America line to England, France, Holland, and Germany."

He leans forward, pipe dangling from the corner of his mouth. "My, you HAVE given this some thought."

Nodding, I continue. "After signing the paperwork for the sale in New York, I can make arrangements to leave from there."

Uncle Charles slaps both hands on his knees and proclaims, "I think this is a grand plan!"

"Oh, I'm so glad!" I beam with delight. While I certainly don't require his permission, I do value my uncle's opinion.

"If anyone deserves a tour of Europe, it is you, my dear." He approaches my chair and lends a hand to pull me up.

I gather my belongings and turn toward the stairs. "Well, I better turn in. I have an early morning visit tomorrow. Good evening."

"Sweet dreams, Ruby." He returns to the chair and opens his novel to the marked page.

As I reach the top of the stairs, I notice that Jack's door is ajar and a light is on. Unsurprisingly, he's still up. I head for my own room and plunk my load onto the bed. Once I've fished a receipt from the handbag I used earlier in the day, I stroll down the hall to chat with Jack. Before entering, I brace myself with a lungful of clean air. While I've grown accustomed to the stench of reptiles, insects, and the other fauna inhabiting this space, my heart still races when I catch a glimpse of the hairy appendages of his tarantula. The protuberant fangs don't help the matter either. Sitting on his bed, Jack's gangling form is slumped over a metal pail on the floor before him. He slowly lifts his head, a look of dejection on his typically cheerful face.

I take a seat next to him. "Is it Bob?"

He nods while blinking back tears, which reminds me of the sweet but precocious little boy I used to cuddle. "He won't eat. Just stays in his shell except when he comes up for air."

I notice the pale flesh of chicken floating like a grotesque finger just beneath the surface of the water. "What do you think is the matter?"

Jack sniffs and straightens his posture. "He's not meant to live in a bucket."

Patting his back I gently ask, "What should you do?"

He rises and shuffles to a large fishbowl teeming with California tree frog tadpoles that he caught earlier in the spring. Midway through their metamorphosis, the pollywogs' tails and legs swirl in a confused jumble. "I'm gonna let these guys go soon. I suppose I'll hafta do the same with Bob."

"I was afraid of that." I join him and place an arm around his shoulders. "But where on Earth can you safely release a crocodile turtle?"

"Alligator turtle. Good question." He continues to stare into the bowl. "I think that's why the new kid traded him." He turns and looks at me with a scowl. "Can't believe I was suckered outta my rosey boa."

"Don't beat yourself up about it." I wander over to peer into the bucket. "I'm sure it seemed like a good trade at the time."

"Yeah. It was." He approaches his desk, opens a coffee can that has been punched with small holes, and retrieves several crickets, which he quickly transfers to the cage of a blue-belly lizard. He shrugs then brightens. "At least for a while I'm the only kid in California with a pet alligator snapper."

"I like your optimism." Jack is a remarkably resilient person. When referring to him, Nan often says, "A bad mood won't stick."

I recall the reason I need to speak with him. "Jack, can you do something for me tomorrow?"

"Whadya need?" Jack queries while placing the lid back on the lizard cage.

"You know the flower shop on Spadra?"

He squints one eye while mulling over my question. "Ya mean the one by the place that sells envelopes?"

"That's the one." I hand him the receipt. "I ordered a Mother's Day corsage for Nan. Can you cycle over tomorrow and pick it up?"

"Sure!" He warms to the idea. "Maybe I'll stop by Hardy's Drugstore while I'm there."

I raise an eyebrow in question.

"Heard they got a new harmonica that's only 50 cents." The gloom has completely vanished from his countenance.

"Well with all those pennies you've pinched from the wishing well, I'd say you can afford a few harmonicas." I ruffle his hair and turn to leave. "Good night, Jack."

"Night, Ruby." He calls after me. "Don't let the bed bugs bite."

CHAPTER 11

SATURDAY, MAY 10, 1930

No sooner does my head hit the pillow than my bedside clock clangs like a toy fire alarm. Unable to fall asleep last night, I spent several hours scribing notes on the Graham case and later organizing my bookcase by hue, which I found more aesthetically pleasing than the prior arrangement by genre and author surname. The automaticity of the latter task freed my mind to mull over the limited findings thus far, as well as my growing suspicions, but fatigue rendered clarity of thought quite elusive. When I finally retired, the luminous hands of my nightstand clock suggested that I would get no more than five hours of sleep. Now those same hands, black upon a white face in the dim light of early dawn, read 5:30 AM.

A chill permeates my bedroom from the sash window left cracked overnight, and I am loath to take leave of my warm blanket cocoon. However, my determination to visit the walnut shed compels me to begin my morning ablutions. Like easing into a cold pool of water, I extricate one bare foot from the bedding at a time then methodically peel away the sheet and bedspread from my legs and torso. Once uncovered, I leap toward the foot of my bed and quickly slip my arms into my kimono.

After splashing my face with warm water and brushing my teeth in the bathroom, I return to my room and stand before the open armoire. Not sure what to expect in the citrus fields, I don a pair of navy wide-legged trousers, a cream broadcloth blouse, and a burgundy wool cardigan. Low-heeled tan and brown loafers, along with a knitted cap Nan whipped up last winter, complete my ensemble. I toss my keys, notepad, fountain pen, and wallet into a serviceable leather purse. I will forgo lipstick this morning.

While I wish to egress quickly, I cannot bear skipping a cup of coffee. I pour a mug of water into the percolator and scoop a couple of tablespoons of coffee grounds into its basket. Once the coffee is heating on the gas range, I retrieve the plate of leftovers Nan stashed in the refrigerator and nibble on a cold piece of chicken fried steak. When the glass knob on the lid indicates that the coffee has achieved the rich dark brown I prefer, I remove the percolator from the heat and pour its contents into my mug. A couple of splashes of cold cream render the coffee cool enough to consume quickly. Minutes later I am more alert and ready to follow up on the first major lead in my case.

The windshield of my car is covered with dew, necessitating a few wipes with the automatic blades. At 5:55 AM, the risen sun is hiding behind low-lying clouds which are a dull slate that many locals call "May Gray." The sun should peek through around noon, giving way to blue skies this afternoon. Unsurprisingly, the streets are empty this morning, including downtown where just a handful of cars remain parked along the curb, all evidence of Friday evening's merrymaking having dissipated after midnight.

Given the absence of traffic, I turn left onto Bastanchury Road in no time and follow the ups and downs of this hilly stretch with orchards, oil fields, and the occasional farmhouse passing by outside my windows. About an eighth of a mile ahead on my right, I spot the expansive wooden Sunny Hills Fruit Company sign supported by two sturdy posts deeply secured in the soil. Bold white letters contrast with a cerulean blue background above a display of juicy round oranges, some split in half to showcase triangular segments of fleshy pulp. As I approach the sign, a cherry red motorcycle leaves a cloud of dust while turning right from a narrow dirt road just past the sign. Unrecognizable under a leather helmet and tightly fitted goggles, the rider speeds away ahead of me. *Curious.*

I follow the dusty trail through a densely packed grove of now fruitless orange trees. Their branches shaggy with elliptic green leaves trailing down to the soil, these trees offer nary a glance of any sort of landmark beyond their border. Clearly maintained for the rugged tires of tractors, the curved road is bumpy and requires that I slow my pace dramatically. I could probably get there faster on foot. After nearly ten minutes, I spy a clearing ahead surrounded by squat-trunked annuals with wide limbs. On each tree, long tapered leaves branch outward and upward. These must be the newly planted persimmon trees.

A tall ramshackle shed nearly the size of my cottage sits on the left side of the clearing. Stacked weathered bricks form the base of the structure, while panels of corrugated tin and sun-bleached gray wood rise almost haphazardly toward a central peak. Asphalt shingles, many broken and lying on the ground, speckle the roofline. The ghostly outline of *Baker's Walnuts* is barely visible along the forward-facing side of the building, and a set of wooden doors secures the entryway. I spot no windows, per se, but a series of gaps under the eaves appear to provide some sort of ventilation.

I pull my car along the front of the shed and turn off the engine. While stepping out, I inhale deeply, and a damp earthy freshness fills my nostrils. I also detect the potent fragrance of orange blossoms nearby. Apart from an occasional bird chirrup, the crunch of my soles on gravel is the only sound disrupting the peaceful morning silence. A single line of newly made tire marks terminate in front of the shed indicating that the motorcycle has stopped here. I approach the double doors and notice a hefty padlock anchoring a length of chain between the two door handles. *Rats.*

Walking along the right side of the building toward the back, the ground is littered with cigarette butts. I search for another entrance and stumble upon a black Model T parked along its length. A preliminary glance through the windows suggests that the car is empty. I turn toward the rear of the shed, a solid wall free of doors or windows, and am stunned to discover at the far end of the structure, a pair of black loafers resting on their heels with toes angled outward. I rush forward and, rounding the corner, nearly tumble over Frank's supine form. My hand involuntarily flies to my mouth in horror as I take in his ashen face, motionless chest, and a dark wet circle on his trousers below his waist.

"No, no, no!" I can't reach him fast enough. With both hands I grasp the sides of his face and am relieved to find that his skin, while cool to the touch, is not icy cold and hard. I lay my head against his chest, my ear resting above his heart, and hear a slow thump-thump. I feel my gorge begin to rise in reaction to the pungent odor emanating from his clothing. After several unsuccessful attempts to rouse him by shaking his torso, pinching between his fingers, and squeezing his trapezius, I return to his face and manually open his eyes. His pupils do not appear to react to the light, and his eyes stare blankly. A superficial inspection of his unconscious body and the weed-covered turf around him indicate no evidence of blood or bruising.

I remove my sweater and tuck it around his arms and torso. "Frank, if you can hear me, I need to leave you in order to get help." I try to warm his scruffy cheeks with the palms of my hands. "I promise I'll be right back."

Taking one last look at his tragic figure, I race toward my car, start the engine, and drive as quickly as possible along the pitted dirt road. My thoughts are darting as quickly as my tires. *What happened to him? He doesn't appear to be injured. How long has he been lying there? I need to get to a telephone.*

Once I turn left onto Bastanchury I follow the row of tall telephone poles that runs parallel to the road until I notice a narrow line branching off toward a small clapboard farmhouse. My tires squeal as I turn sharply into the driveway and startle an incensed brood of black and white speckled hens, who cast angry glances while scrambling toward an open pen. Parking next to a green stake-body truck, I leave the car running and throw open the door. A wizened farmer in faded dungarees sloshes milk from a galvanized metal pail as he rushes from the barn.

"What in God's name?" His expression is a mix of consternation and puzzlement. "Is there a fire?"

"My apologies, sir, for disturbing you," I exclaim breathlessly. "No fire, but there is an emergency. I need to use your telephone to call an ambulance."

He motions for me to follow with a single flick of his hand and mutters, "Well I never. Not even seven o'clock. Mother won't like this 'tall." His pace slows to a shuffle, and I restrain myself from hurrying him along.

We enter through the back door into a well-worn kitchen, all gingham and scuffed hardwood floorboards that lost their luster decades ago. A snowy haired woman, adorned in a colorless but clean apron, stands at a wood-burning stove poking at sizzling sausages with a fork. She turns, utensil poised in the air, and gives her husband a hard stare.

"Where's that milk I asked for? And what's with that ruckus in the yard?" She hasn't noticed me.

"Now, Mother, settle down." His hands are raised as though this were a stick-up, and he attempts to settle his wife. Hitching his thumb over his shoulder he directs her attention toward me. "This here lady needs to use the phone. Says it's a 'mergency."

A pair of narrowed eyes, sharp with intellect, scan me from head to toe. A moment passes while she takes my measure. "Hmph," is all I hear as she turns back to roll the links in the seasoned pan.

Apparently, I have been granted permission. The farmer leads me into the adjoining living room, and my eyes require a second or so to adjust to the dimly lit space. He points toward a rectangular wooden box hanging above a small table, and I realize that I haven't seen a telephone like this in more than a decade. I gently remove the earpiece hanging on the left side of the apparatus (along with an impressive collection of wishbones). Cranking a handle protruding from the right side of the box, I wait for a response.

A scratchy nasal voice answers, "Operator. How can I complete your call?"

"This is an emergency. I need an ambulance." I feel unnerved by the open-mouthed stare of the elderly man.

"What is the nature of the emergency?" Her matter-of-fact tone suggests that the operator receives such calls regularly.

"I found a man unconscious in an orchard and was unable to rouse him." I begin to give directions regarding his location when I am interrupted.

"Do you have the man's name?"

I'm uncertain about the relevance at this time, given the urgency of the matter, but I appease the woman anyway. "His name is Frank Graham."

"Something's wrong with Frankie?" The operator's interest is suddenly piqued. "I knew him in high school."

"Yes, well so did I. Anyway, as I was saying—"

"What do ya think is the matter with him?" She asks with a gossipy tone.

"I wish I knew. That's precisely why I need—"

"Do ya think he was shot?" I suspect that she consumes a great deal of pulp fiction when the phone lines are quiet.

"No, he was not shot. Would you please—" I am exasperated by this inane exchange.

"Why's he in an orchard anyway?"

Before the conversation can be derailed any further, I insist, "Please ma'am. This is serious. I need an ambulance as soon as possible." I complete the directions and ring off, leaving the operator offended by my curt tone. Hopefully she can muster some degree of professionalism to complete her task.

I'd half-forgotten the farmer and his wife, but as I turn to leave they are standing shoulder-to-shoulder in the door frame with matching expressions of astonishment. They part to let me pass, and I thank them for their assistance. Stepping into the yard, I hear the woman remark dismissively, "Well, that's one for the books."

With as much speed as my car will safely permit, I race through the orchard, a blur of green filling the periphery of my vision. I half-expect to see the motorcycle as I pull into the clearing, the driver having also gone for help but, with the exception of my retreating tire marks in the gravelly dirt, nothing has changed. I retrieve a plaid woolen blanket from the backseat and hurry around the side of the shed. Unsurprisingly, Frank hasn't moved an inch.

"I'm back, Frank. Help is on the way." I shake the blanket to unfold its length over his still form and place my index and middle fingers along the side of his throat. A faint but steady pulse drums under their pads. *Good.*

Determined to gather as much information as I can before the ambulance arrives, I begin a search of the area surrounding Frank. Tall wild ryegrass has reclaimed this part of the clearing, creating silver blue mounds crowded tightly together. Fallen leaves from the surrounding fruit trees have become tangled at the base of these clumps, creating a haven for all manner of diminutive wildlife.

Within one such muddle, I spy the glassy surface of a mason jar. I withdraw a handkerchief from the pocket of my trousers to carefully free the vessel and hold it up to the light. I notice a few ounces of clear liquid, which may have accumulated during yesterday's storm if the jar has been here for a while and bend forward to sniff the contents. Definitely not water, the fluid smells of paint remover. I replace the jar where I found it. Surveying the remaining grassy tufts, I unearth no other clues.

I turn back toward Frank and investigate his clothing which reveals a money clip containing three dollars, a chained watch, and an empty pack of Black Jack chewing gum, all of which I return to his pockets. After a thorough search, I find no additional possessions on his person.

The ambulance could appear any minute, so I decide to quickly examine the Model T. Opening the driver's door, I am overwhelmed by the stench of stale food and unwashed body. Immediately checking the ignition, I withdraw a three-pronged key, rather like a wide trident bent at a ninety-degree angle below its prongs. Two additional keys are attached to this via a knotted loop of twine, one with a long shank terminating in a squat bit and the other a shorter key with toothlike indentations along both sides. The former is similar to my own front door key, but the latter looks promising. I pocket the set for later use and continue my search.

The front passenger floorboard is littered with discarded wrappers, cracker boxes, and emptied tins of sardines, hence the fetor. And a faded patchwork quilt, threadbare at the corners, lays crumpled in the back seat. It appears that Frank has been living rough these past few days. In the storage space under the backseat, I find a tool pouch, tire jack, and inner tube but nothing else. I slide my hand within the crevice between the front seat and its backrest and discover a large metal ring laden with about a dozen keys of various shapes, sizes, and metals, as well as a brass tag stamped with the letters "SJ".

"Oh Frank, what have you been up to?"

I place the key ring in my pocket alongside the other set, their combined weight straining the cotton. While closing the door, the loud crunch of approaching tires signals the arrival of the ambulance. The converted blue Model A pulls along the front of the shed, a red cross on a white background painted across the rear side of its extended length. As the dust cloud settles, the passenger side of the cab flies open and a sturdy young man hops out and rushes to the back of the vehicle to retrieve a cot. I can hear the tenor of the driver on a two-way radio informing dispatch of their arrival before he casually exits the cab and notices me standing nearby.

"Did you call for the ambulance?" He slowly pulls a pencil and notepad out of his back pocket and scribbles on a blank page.

"Yes, I did," I reply while trying to make eye contact.

Stubbornly fixated on his scribbling, he asks, "Your name, ma'am?"

"Ruby Ray. Listen, Frank is around the side of the—"

"There is a procedure to follow," he interrupts my response. "State the full name of the patient."

"Frank Graham. I found him unconscious—"

"Procedure, Miss Ray." He looks up with annoyance while I shoot a glance at his colleague who responds sympathetically by closing his eyes and shaking his head. "Illness or injury?"

"I-I'm not sure. If you'll let me finish, I can explain."

The driver crosses his arms and firmly plants his feet hip-width apart. A curt nod indicates that I can continue.

"I arrived about 45 minutes ago and found Frank unconscious around the side of the shed." Following my pointed finger, the young man dashes around the building.

I continue, "He doesn't appear to be injured, but I was unable to wake him. His pulse is steady but weak—"

"We'll take it from here." Snapping closed his notebook, he abruptly turns and heads toward Frank.

Bemused, I cannot decide whether to join them or head home to call Norma. I choose not to be cowed by such churlishness and join the team as they expertly lift Frank onto the cot.

The driver calls over his shoulder, "Why on God's green earth would you come all the way out here so early in the morning?"

A fair question, but I resent his tone. "It so happens that Frank has been missing, and I agreed to help his sister find him. I received a tip that he may be here."

"Hmph." He continues strapping Frank to the stretcher.

Caring little for his opinion, I kneel beside Frank and take his hand. "You're going to the hospital, Frank, where they can help you. I'll call Norma as soon as I get home to let her know."

Patting his shoulder, I stand and step out of their way so that Frank can be carried to the ambulance. The poles of the cot are slid into brackets mounted to the inside walls, and I notice seats facing backward, one on each side of the stretcher.

"Excuse me, ma'am." The friendly chap smiles at me. "Would you like to ride with him to the hospital?"

"Oh, that's very kind of you," I reply warmly. "But I think it would be best if I head home to telephone his sister. She's been distressed for days not knowing his whereabouts."

He nods his head and, with a wave, hops into the back with Frank, closing the door as he crawls onto one of the seats. The driver offers no such farewell but rather guns the engine stirring up gravel and dust as he pulls back onto the narrow track.

I bat my hand to clear the air of particles and approach the front of the shed. Grasping the lock with my left hand, I reach into my pocket to extricate Frank's keys. My fingers skip past the car and house keys, settling on the shorter key. I attempt to open the lock, to no avail. The key does not fit. A slight gap between the shed doors permits a glance inside, but the dim light reveals nothing more than nondescript forms covered with tarps. The wood on the doors appears brittle. Not much force would be required to pry off the handles. I recall the tire iron in the tool kit of Frank's car but decide to return later when I have more time to investigate. I really must be getting home to call Norma.

CHAPTER 12

A feminine voice answers the early morning call with hesitation, "Hello?"

"Edith, can you put Norma on?" I state urgently. "It's Ruby."

I overhear the somewhat muffled words, "This can't be good." Footsteps walk away from the phone.

"Norma, Ruby is on the phone," Edith calls.

Quick shuffling feet become increasingly louder. "You found him!" Not a question.

"Yes, but before I say anything else, please know that he is alive."

An extended sigh signals Norma's relief, and Edith urges her to sit down, chair legs scraping along the floor. Patiently waiting for Norma to collect herself, I can only imagine the suffering she has experienced over the past few days. The money aside, I know that she cares deeply for her brother.

"Where is he?" she finally utters.

I briefly explain his physical condition before she rings off to leave for the hospital.

Timid rapping signals someone's arrival at the back door as I hang up the phone.

"It's rather early for guests." Uncle Charles steps into the kitchen. The absence of a necktie under his V-neck sweater indicates his plans to stay home until at least mid-morning. He will no doubt don a cravat to visit one of his oil fields later on, his work ethic so much like my father's. Other than the occasional Sunday, he rarely misses a day.

"I'll see who it is." I am closer to the kitchen.

Through the door's diamond-shaped panes, I spy a grubby newsboy cap clutched to the scrawny chest of an emaciated young man. I open the door and notice a crate resting next to his feet.

"Can I help you?" I inquire, although I have an idea regarding this chap's identity.

"Um…" He colors brightly. "Yes, miss. Nan sent me over with this here box."

Everyone calls her "Nan." It wasn't until I had known her for over a year that I discovered her actual name is Henrietta Fry. Apparently, her younger brother couldn't pronounce "Henrietta" as a small child and called her "Nan," and in no time the nickname stuck.

I peek into the box. "More strawberries?"

Confused, the young man replies, "Well, I reckon they're for the pie, what with the holiday and all."

At that moment, I hear Nan's voice, "Thanks fer the ride. I'll send Gabe right back so you two can start paintin'."

I stand aside so Gabe can deposit the crate in the kitchen. That done, he gives me a bashful wave and hurries toward the car port.

"Phewie!" Nan thunks a paper bag filled with flour, sugar, and other baking necessities onto the counter. "Thought I'd get an early start on the pies." She usually doesn't arrive for another hour and a half on a Saturday. Her family is in for a lovely treat tomorrow, as Nan's strawberry pies have won awards.

"You know that you don't need to bring your own baking ingredients. You're free to use the kitchen and anything else you need from our pantry."

Holding up a finger, she retorts, "If I've told ya once, I've told ya a hundred times. I'm not gonna feed my family with yer food."

I shrug. It's a battle I gave up long ago. "I suppose then it's a moot point to mention that you're more than welcome to do your personal cooking when you're on the clock."

"My mama taught me to know my place," she sniffs.

Nan was born in Missouri (or "Missour-uh" as she calls it) during the Civil War and spent most of her life caring for others. When her father was injured fighting for the Confederacy, Nan was charged with watching her little sister and brother so that her mother could work cleaning houses. After both siblings left home to start families of their own, Nan stayed to care for her aging parents and had a side business baking for the same families who had previously employed her mother.

When both parents passed away in 1903, she rode the Santa Fe line to Orange County to lend a hand with her sister's family. She has lived here ever since.

"Have ya had breakfast?" Nan ties on her well-worn apron and grabs a skillet from below the range.

"Not so fast." I remove the pan from her grasp. "I was just about to whip up some eggs and toast. Go ahead and start your pies."

She switches on the radio, and we contentedly engage in our culinary tasks to the soothing ukulele of Cliff Edward in "Just You, Just Me."

"I claim the bathroom. Bob needs a soak," Jack informs us.

Clamping his forearm as he rises from the breakfast table, I interject, "Hold it right there. I need to freshen up before heading over to the hospital."

"Okay," he sinks back into his chair. After a moment's reflection he brightens, "Do ya think Hardy's is open right now? I don't wanna miss out on the new harmonicas." He gives me a knowing nod, acknowledging the other errand he's promised to run for me.

Uncle Charles reminds him, "Jack you need to mow the lawn before you do anything else." He opens his pocket watch. "Hmm, 9:20. I asked Dottie to be back by 9:00 so we could discuss Berkeley before I leave for work."

Rising from his chair he strides to the phone in the hallway. I hear him flip through the directory. "Number 1437, please."

His foot-tapping indicates annoyance. I am surprised that Dottie didn't return on time as she's usually compliant with her father's requests.

"Good morning, this is Charles Ray. Can you please send Dottie home?" I stand in the doorway and see him nodding his head, "She must already be on her way. Sorry to dist—." A frown flashes on his face as he listens.

"What are you saying?" A pause.

"She didn't stay over last night?" Perplexed, he asks, "Well, can I please speak with Polly?"

I shuffle toward him when I notice alarm flash on his face, "What do you mean? Alright then, please put Fred or Helen on the phone."

He glances in my direction, locking eyes with me. "Alright. Well, if any of the Bakers return home, please have them call me at once. Thank you."

"I don't know what to make of this." His hand slowly returns the receiver to the cradle. "That was their maid, and apparently neither girl slept there last night."

"This is so unlike her," I remark as we reclaim our seats at the table. "She should have called if they decided to sleep at another friend's house."

"Apparently, the Bakers both left early this morning. He had a meeting at work, and she was heading to the church." He shakes his head. "They told the maid not to worry about Polly's breakfast because she was at our house."

Uncle Charles crosses his arms in reflection. Obviously tense, he slowly releases a full breath through pursed lips. Not wishing to also become the subject of parental disapproval, Jack surreptitiously begins to retreat from the kitchen.

"Jack." Uncle Charles stops him mid-stride. "Did Dottie say anything to you about staying over at someone else's house last night?"

"No idea," Jack shrugs, but his compressed lips tell me that he knows more than he's letting on. He scurries out the back door. I'll follow up with him if she doesn't turn up before I leave.

"Uncle Charles, I can tell you are frustrated with Dottie," I acknowledge, "But I'm sure there's a very good reason for all of this."

"I suppose so." He shakes off his irritation. "More than anything I'm disappointed with her."

"That's understandable. To be honest, I feel the same."

I begin collecting the dishes, but Nan walks toward me with an outstretched hand. "Let me do the clearin' and warshin' Ruby. You best be getting upstairs 'fore Jack comes back and dirties the bathroom."

The rhythmic *ch-ch-ch* outside my open window tells me that Jack is hard at work with the back lawn. I tie the neck of the lightweight coat under the scalloped collar of my dress and study my reflection in the floor-length mirror. Not certain who I will need to speak with after visiting the hospital, I want to look presentable. A little lipstick should do the trick.

Sitting at my vanity table, I color my lips and then review the facts I uncovered during my visit to the shed this morning, starting with the motorcycle. *Who was the driver, and why didn't they return with help?* I'll ask Norma about this.

Next, I consider the mason jar. *What exactly was that liquid?* It smelled strongly of paint remover or some sort of cleaner, however I couldn't locate a lid anywhere nearby.

The most damning discovery was the large set of keys I found in Frank's car. I reach for my handbag, retrieve the hefty ring, and count thirteen keys of varied shapes and sizes, many numbered or with spots of paint coloring their surface. *Identification markings?* Laying them upon the table, I run an index finger over the recessed "SJ" on the brass tag. Mr. Jones mentioned that his keys had gone missing about a month ago. *Had Frank pocketed them while working at the auditorium? For what purpose?* Now that I think about it, I'm sure that was around the time that the Jones' house was burgled. According to Lula, the only things missing were Stan's pocket watch and cigarettes. There was no mention of the keys, yet I would think that Mr. Jones would have made the connection if they'd disappeared the night of the burglary. During our discussion yesterday he mentioned misplacing them. *Was Frank responsible for the series of thefts?*

"Don't jump to conclusions," I admonish my reflection. However, I cannot shake the unsettling feeling that I have removed evidence from a crime scene.

Extracting the twine loop of keys from my handbag, I closely examine the unidentified one. Irregular ridges and notches line each side of its squat blade, and the smooth, shiny surface of the bow suggests that it's relatively new. Both car and house keys are riddled with superficial scratches. Perhaps this mystery key is for a newly purchased lockbox. I'll ask Norma her thoughts about this as well.

Last, I consider the contents of the walnut shed. The hastily scribbled notes I made before leaving the site mention tarp-covered masses large enough to be visible in the dim light. The largest was about four feet tall and appeared to be roughly two feet wide. The shape of the object sitting to its left was cylindrical, as suggested by the convex curve of its tarp. Five remaining items, all rectangular and of a similar size, were situated to the right of the tallest mass. After visiting the hospital and finishing any additional interviews I may have later today, I plan to return to the shed and pry off the handles with a tire iron.

His bedroom door open, Uncle Charles catches a glimpse of me as he drapes a silk tie around his neck. "Any word from Dottie?"

"I was going to ask you the same question." I lean against the door frame and check the contents of my handbag to make sure I'm not forgetting anything.

He inspects his pocket watch. "10:37. I can't wait much longer for her. I'm meeting with the foreman at the southeast rig in twenty minutes or so." Returning the watch to an inside breast pocket, he runs two fingers along the side part of his hair, a familiar gesture signaling that he is ready to leave.

"And I really must see Norma at the hospital." Twisting the kiss lock on my purse, I volunteer to return home before heading back out for interviews. "I'm sure she'll be back by then."

Uncle Charles nods his head, eyes rolled. "She'd better be."

I chose to exit via the front of the house, as the clatter has migrated to the front lawn. Jack's crimson face and hurried pace indicate that he is racing through his chores, his mind (no doubt) preoccupied with the harmonica.

"Jack, why don't you take a break?" I sit on the top step of the porch and pat the space next to me.

His shoulder muscles relaxing, Jack wipes sweat from his brow with the hem of his shirt. "Not a bad idea." He flops next to me.

I survey the yard. "Your rows are very...geometric." To say that his mowing style is creative would be an understatement.

"Yeah, Dad busted my chops over the spirals last week," he proclaims somewhat proudly.

A light breeze rustles leaves on a nearby tree, and a monarch glides to one of the agapanthus blossoms at the foot of the steps.

"So, Jack, I need you to be completely honest with me about something."

He straightens his posture and leans away from me. "O-kaay."

"I know that you and Dottie tend to cover for one another, but I am concerned that she hasn't returned home yet."

"Yeah, me too," he admits.

I press on. "After the phone call, I noticed that you seemed to be holding back about Dottie's whereabouts when your father questioned you."

No response, but his posture straightens.

Trying again, "Listen, I don't want Dottie to get into trouble either, but this situation is just not like her."

His rigid form deflates. "All I know is that she and Polly had some kinda secret plans for last night."

"Did you overhear them discussing this?"

He nods.

"What exactly did you hear?" I query gently, while trying not to convey my irritation with his evasiveness.

"Well, first I want you to know that I was NOT eavesdropping." Dottie frequently complains that he is nosey.

"Fair enough." I gesture for him to continue.

"Thursday afternoon, while they were studying, I heard Polly tell Dottie, 'Earl said to bring a warm coat, but I think he's just pulling my leg.'"

There's that name again. *Earl.* Why am I not surprised that he is somehow involved?

"Go on."

"They must've noticed the step squeak cuz Dottie told her, 'Not here,' and changed the subject to their homework."

While not exactly helpful in terms of locating Dottie, at least I now know that the girls were up to something. "Did they say anything else?"

"Nah, that was it." He rises, brushing stray grass from his trousers.

"Alright, well I appreciate your honesty." I stand as well. "I have to leave for a while, but when Dottie comes home please tell her she is not to leave again until either your father or I return."

He salutes me. "Got it."

"And please don't leave either. I need you to convey the message and make sure she stays put. I don't want to bother Nan with this."

He walks back to the mower muttering, "I'm never gonna get that harmonica."

CHAPTER 13

I had intended to arrive at Fullerton General Hospital sooner, but given the unexpected disruptions this morning, my plans were derailed. Thankfully it's only a half of a mile away from our home, so I quickly cruise down Amerige and find a parking spot on the right-hand side just before the intersection with Pomona Avenue. If the otherwise congested street is any indication, the hospital is busy today.

Walking through the courtyard of the u-shaped building, I head toward the main entrance located under the pale green patina of a copper dome. Hand poised on the door handle, I pause and turn back to look at the vibrant rose garden while recalling my last visit to this facility.

About six months ago, Jack was injured while "experimenting" with his Porter Chemcraft set. Despite the messaging on the box that the product *contains no poisonous or otherwise harmful substances*, Jack managed to explode a glass tube that he was heating. Nan heard his howl from the kitchen and rushed upstairs to discover that his hands were scarlet with burns and embedded with slivers of glass. I encountered the duo as they bustled downstairs, Jack's hands encased in what looked like large wet mittens but proved to be small towels from the bathroom.

"Ruby, ya gotta take him to the hospital quick," Nan exclaimed, her eyes big as saucers. "He's hurt himself somethin' bad."

I then noticed the silent tears streaming down his pale face. Without further thought, I snatched my purse from a nearby occasional table and placed both hands on his shoulders to guide him through the front door. During the short drive I avoided looking at Jack's hands. Blood, particularly copious quantities of blood, renders me quite dizzy and, I am embarrassed to admit, I have been known to faint. However, I didn't need to look at Jack to know how he was feeling. From his silence, I knew he was in a great deal of pain. Otherwise, he would have noisily boasted about the size of the explosion.

As we entered the hospital, a white-capped woman of indeterminate years looked up from her paperwork and started to ask, "How may I hel—." But after one glance at the blood-soaked towels, she sprung up from the desk and ushered us to the emergency room where Jack was situated on a sterile gurney parked between two pale blue curtains.

I had barely settled upon a comfortless hard-backed chair when I heard a tenor voice comment, "Hey sport, looks like you've been busy this afternoon."

A lopsided grin broke Jack's otherwise somber expression as he looked up into a friendly gaze. The resident's slightly rumpled white coat and stethoscope casually draped over one shoulder indicated an easy-going confidence that immediately brought a smile to my face as well.

With good humor, he introduced himself. "I'm Dr. Armstrong, and I'll be treating you today." I imagined that he uttered those words hundreds of times each week. After thoroughly washing his hands at a nearby sink, he gently unwrapped the carmine towels and thoughtfully examined the injuries.

"These are quite impressive wounds for a young man your age. I'd ask to shake your hand, but..."

Jack chuckled and briefly described the accident with the chemistry set. Dr. Armstrong then stepped aside as an aged nurse approached bearing a metal tray laden with a kidney-shaped dish, gauze, rubbing alcohol, and an array of tweezers and forceps.

"After Nurse Furlong removes the glass, I'll return and take a closer look at those burns." Noting Jack's alarmed expression, he added reassuringly, "She's very good at this. Why just yesterday I had a wicked thorn in my finger from a rose bush outside, and she plucked it right out. I didn't feel a thing." He winked at Nurse Furlong, who colored as she began her ministrations.

I found myself admiring how the doctor's caramel blond hair fell away from his forehead in loose waves and how the cleft in his chin became more pronounced when he smiled. And before I knew it, I blurted, "I might ask you why you were picking roses instead of healing patients." *What on earth was that about?*

Eyebrows raised, he turned in my direction and, with a serious tone, asked. "Who said I was picking roses?"

Instantly appalled, I muttered, "I'm sorry…"

His face softened into a smile as he released a charming chuckle. "I'm just teasing. I'm actually a bit of an amateur horticulturist and was taking a clipping from a new floribunda for my grandma's garden. She taught me everything I know about roses."

Now at ease, I rejoined, "You'll regret telling me that. Don't get me started on my hydrangeas."

"I'm all ears." And, while a palpable energy flowed between us, we discussed the merits of ground lime until Nurse Furlong completed her work.

My thoughts return to the present moment and the task of opening the door. Norma is waiting for me and is no doubt anxious to know what I discovered at the walnut shed. I wonder if Frank is still unconscious. Hopefully the doctors have made some sort of diagnosis. Speaking of doctors, I know that residents frequently rotate through different medical settings. I wonder if Dr. Armstrong still works at this hospital.

"Enough daydreaming," I rebuke myself and, with a shrug, enter the front door.

A fresh young face resting below a peaked cap greets me and asks the name of the patient I am here to see. I notice two similarly capped young women smiling in my direction, also eager to be of assistance. I recall that Fullerton General Hospital was founded around the turn of the century to house a nursing school.

"Good morning to you as well. I'd like to visit Frank Graham please."

The greeter's fair face falls, and she steps back to allow one of her classmates access to the clipboard. Her other peer looks toward her with concern. *That's puzzling.*

"Room 133, ma'am." Leaning forward, the student points to the hallway on the right. "Walk down that corridor, and you will find the room on your left."

"Thank you so much." The young ladies, particularly the greeter, avoid my attempts to connect with their eyes as I take my leave. *What do they know?*

Concerned about Frank's welfare, I quickly traverse the passageway, taking note of the increasing numbers neatly installed to the right of each doorway. I see Edith leaning against the wall across from a closed door, head bowed and arms tightly folded. At the sound of my steps, her head snaps up, and she rushes toward me.

"Oh thank goodness, Ruby! Norma's with Frank, and we have so many questions."

I slowly open the door and see Norma slumped in a chair, one hand clasped around Frank's and the other clutching a handkerchief. His limp form alarms me until I notice that some color has returned to his pale visage. Still unconscious but better than the alternative.

Her attention roused, Norma faces the door and quickly rises when she realizes that it's me. "I am so glad to see you," she dabs her cheeks, tears still apparent at the corners of her reddened eyes.

Extending an arm around her flaccid shoulders, I lead her back to the chair and encourage her to sit. Edith stands behind her, a hand resting on Norma's upper arm, which she immediately grasps. Once I have settled opposite the two women, I begin.

"I am so sorry to have found Frank in this state." I look around the room and take in a rolling table and empty bed situated closer to the window.

"What have the doctors said?"

"Not much at this point," Edith replies. "They're waiting for the blood tests to come back."

"Has he regained consciousness at all?" I query.

Norma shakes her head and begins to cry in earnest.

Kneeling beside her, Edith wraps solid arms around Norma's trembling form and looks up at me. "Why don't you tell us what happened when you found him. Not knowing anything at all has been agonizing."

Abashed that I didn't arrive sooner, I explain in detail my visit to the walnut shed, as well as my discoveries. When I complete the narrative, the door swings open and a familiar form enters the room. His easy stride and caramel blonde waves bring a smile to my lips.

Recognition is evident by his warm grin, and Dr. Armstrong inquires, "So how's our young chemist?"

Nervous energy surges through my limbs, and I feel my cheeks flush. *What is wrong with me?* After a brief pause, I reply, "He's actually given up on the physical sciences and is now an avid zoologist."

"Sounds safer."

"You'd think so, but his latest specimen can amputate a finger."

"Ouch," he grips one hand with the other, displaying mock horror.

I apologetically glance at Norma and Edith who share a confused look, and I briefly explain our prior meeting. They nod but understandably would prefer Dr. Armstrong to focus on Frank. I don't blame them and feel chagrined.

Dr. Armstrong straightens his casual posture and assumes a professional demeanor. "Miss Graham, some of the bloodwork has come back for your brother and indicates the presence of a high level of acetaldehyde, acidemia, and probable kidney failure."

Norma whimpers, and Edith tightens her embrace.

He continues, "I wouldn't be surprised if his liver panel confirms hepatic failure as well."

I ask the obvious question. "So, what does all that mean?"

Inserting the earpieces of his stethoscope, Dr. Armstrong replies before leaning forward to place the bell on Frank's chest. "Rotgut."

"I'm sorry?" Norma responds with confusion.

"Moonshine," I clarify softly while the doctor is listening. "It would seem that Frank has been imbibing."

Norma nods with resignation. "I was afraid it may have something to do with that."

Having completed his task, Dr. Armstrong slings the scope back over his shoulder. "Not just moonshine, but poor-quality moonshine laden with methanol."

"That certainly explains the personality change," Edith concurs.

"I was going to ask about that," Dr. Armstrong interjects. "What have you noticed with regard to his behavior, mood, and so on." He lifts the clipboard suspended from the rail at the foot of the bed and takes notes while Norma describes the extreme mood changes, erratic and impulsive behavior, and paranoia.

"Definitely consistent with ingesting this type of toxic substance in large quantities or over an extended period of time." He writes a few more lines in the chart.

"I'm ordering intravenous injections of a saline solution to try and hydrate Mr. Graham." He caps the fountain pen, which he returns to his coat pocket.

Looking up at the ladies he adds, "I'll be back in a few hours with the rest of the labs. And I'll also be on hand until tomorrow morning. I'm on call tonight."

Dr. Armstrong tips his head in my direction and raises an eyebrow. "Until we meet again." Then he saunters from the sick room.

I resettle in the chair and try to curb the flustered feeling in the pit of my stomach by following up on our earlier discussion. "Now we know what was in the mason jar."

Edith admits, "I was suspecting that might be the case when you mentioned it but didn't want to say anything."

"What do you think of this?" I remove Frank's makeshift key ring from my handbag and show them the stumpy key?

Norma leans across the bed to accept the bundle. "Well, these are definitely for the Ford and the house, but I've never seen this one before."

Inspecting the key over Norma's shoulder, Edith comments, "It looks new."

"My thoughts exactly." I conjecture, "We know that Frank withdrew the money from the bank as cash so maybe he then placed the bills in a lockbox?"

"That sounds reasonable to me," Norma agrees.

"May I keep the key for now?" I extend an open palm. "I have a theory that he may have hidden the money in the walnut shed."

"Go ahead and keep the full set." Norma places them in my hand. "You may need access to the motorcar or our home."

"Thank you. I'll revisit the shed later today." I open my purse. "Now I have some difficult news to share with you." I retrieve the purloined key ring and explain that Mr. Jones thought he had misplaced them. "What would you like me to do?"

The two women gaze at one another for a moment until Edith gives an encouraging nod. Norma faces forward. "Would you take them to Mr. Jones?"

"Of course, if that's what you want."

She confirms her decision. "We'll let the chips fall where they may."

Rising to take my leave, I recall one last detail. "Do you know anyone who rides a red motorcycle?"

"Fipps," Edith immediately declares with a moue. "He always shows up at our house on that deafening contraption and then parks it on our lawn, leaving permanent marks."

"That and cigarette butts on the grass," Norma adds.

"It would appear that I need to revisit Mr. Phillips as well." I promise to return later that day once my errands are complete.

Deciding to speak with Mr. Jones before heading home, I pull up in front of the new auditorium, it's hue a dull cream in the harsh midday light. I'm certain that Dottie is home by now, and I might as well postpone my return to let her stew for a while. I glance up at the clock under the lower arch of the tower. The roman numerals read 12:15 PM, so I dash up the stairs and enter the portico. Hopefully Stan is still around. However, when I check the front entry, all three doors are locked. A trip around the glorious building reveals that the side entrances are also secure, and none of my knocks are answered. The auditorium must be empty this weekend.

I return to my car and head to the California Hotel, as it's on the way to the Jones' residence. From a distance I can tell that no spots are available on Spadra, so I head to the parking lot behind the hotel via Wilshire. A motorcycle rests in the far corner of the lot but alas, it's black, not red. I spy a service entrance at the rear, most likely opening into the hotel's kitchen given the mouth-watering aroma emanating from within. My stomach grumbles. I'll heat up last night's chicken fried steak when I return home.

Pushing open the rear door, I step into a vestibule and call, "Hello?" My eyes adjust to the dim light, and I notice the door to the kitchen, which I enter.

A red-faced woman turns away from a large commercial sink, her apron an artist's palette of viridian, sienna, and cadmium yellow. She dries her chapped hands with a dish towel and sighs, "Main entrance is around the other side, miss."

"Oh, I'm so sorry to bother you," I look around the kitchen. "I know you're very busy. But I'm here to see Floyd Phillips and thought he might be here somewhere."

"He's usually out back." She jerks her head toward the door I just passed through. "Supposed to be patrolin' but Lazy Bones is always on a smoke break."

I glance over my shoulder. "I didn't see him out there."

"Nah, it's his day off." She tucks the towel into the back of her apron. "Wouldn't be caught dead here when he doesn't hafta be."

"Do you happen to know where I might find him on a Saturday?"

"Up to know good." She cackles and then notices my serious demeanor. "Sorry. No idea." She examines my neat appearance. "You look like a proper lady. You best stay away from Fipps."

I smile politely and thank her for the suggestion. "Sorry for the interruption. Please have a nice day."

Parking under the familiar acorn-shaped streetlamp, I am pleased to see Mr. Jones is home pruning the boxy hedge between his house and that of Lula's grandson. By the time I've ascended the stairs, he's stowed the cutters atop the bush and meandered across the lawn.

"Couldn't stay away from me, could ya?" He teases while extending a hand to shake.

I chuckle good-naturedly and grip his paw. "You, Mr. Jones, are a font of useful information."

"Well, I'm glad I'm good for somethin'." He pivots toward his neighbor's house, frowns slightly and suggests, "Why don't we take this inside."

Following his gaze I observe the curtains falling into place in the downstairs window. "It would appear that your neighborhood sentry is on duty this afternoon."

He chortles. "Neighborhood sentry! Good one."

After entering the cool interior, I am immediately assaulted by a tan and white Basset Hound who audibly sniffs my shoes. "So, you're the one who was making all the fuss the last time I visited!" I lean forward to scratch between his ears.

"That's Barclay. He keeps me company while Tilley's away." Stan retrieves a knotted length of rope from a nearby chair and tosses it further into the guest parlor. Barclay abandons his inspection of my feet and trots over to the toy. He then plops his length on the floor and begins chewing one of the knots in earnest.

"That'll keep him busy for a while," Stan remarks, then pats the arm of a rose-colored chair. "Take a pew."

"Thank you." I survey the feminine salon, taking in framed samplers and a lavishly decorated upright piano, clearly one of Mrs. Jones' prize possessions. I strain to read the title of the sheet music resting on its stand. "Hearts and Flowers?"

"Our courtin' song in ninety-nine." He centers the pages. "Tilley always keeps it there." I sense that he misses her greatly.

A moment passes, and he shakes off the sentiment. "Can I get ya somethin'? I'm not too handy with a tea tray, but I can fetch a soda."

"I would love a glass of water, Mr. Jones," I admit, suddenly feeling quite parched.

"Me too now thatcha mention it."

Once hydrated, I explain the purpose of my visit. "I located Frank this morning."

Clapping his hands, Mr. Jones pronounces, "Well that's swell."

"Sort of," I caution. "He was actually unconscious when I found him and hadn't yet stirred when I left the hospital a little while ago."

His face falls. "I'm sorry to hear that."

"But that's not the reason for my call today." I place the glass atop a doily on a nearby end table. "I found something that belongs to you in Frank's automobile."

"That so?" he scratches his jaw. The weekend stubble is no doubt itchy. His eyes widen as I retrieve the keys from my handbag and pass them across to him. "Well, I'll be!"

I give him time to digest this unexpected turn of events before gently asking, "Is there any reason why Frank would have pocketed them?"

Mr. Jones holds his thumb to his lower lip and narrows his eyes pensively. "Maybe he's been sleepin' there."

"Maybe. Although the empty food containers and bedding in his car lead me to believe that he was sleeping in the backseat."

Shoulders raised with uncertainty, he responds, "I don't really know then. Nothin's been reported as stolen or damaged in the auditorium."

"Curious," I ruminate.

"Can ya tell me what's wrong with him?" he queries with paternal concern.

"It's not my story to tell." I answer gently. "I'm sure you understand, Mr. Jones. I need to respect his privacy."

"Of course, of course." His head bobs up and down. "I was just wonderin' if it had anything to do with the hootch."

"Can you please be more specific?" Yesterday he mentioned Frank "hittin' the sauce."

He leans forward conspiratorially, "Somethin' shady's goin' on behind the hotel from what I hear."

"What exactly have you heard?"

His voice lowers despite the privacy of the sitting room. "Folks don't realize we got our own pipeline of John Barleycorn passin' right through the center of town."

Startled, I exclaim, "No! I had no idea!"

"Wouldn't be the first time. Back in '24 a hotel clerk was busted fer selling whiskey. And then there were speakeasies near the hotel…."

"You don't say! I must have missed that in the news at the time."

"Yep. All the comin' and goin' at the hotel. It's the perfect set up." He taps the side of his nose. "Of course, ya didn't hear it from me. Dangerous business."

"Mums the word," I cross my heart. "So, Frank's in with the bootleggers?"

"I hope not!" He flaps in alarm. "But his boozin' seemed to start when he was workin' there. Easy access and all. Just wonderin' if that's what ails him now."

"Hmm…" I mull this over then redirect the conversation. "So what do you plan to do about the keys?"

He seems surprised. "What do ya mean?"

"Well, are you planning to report this to the police?" I add respectfully, "Of course you have every right to do so. I'm just curious what your plans are."

"Nah… I don't wanna get him in trouble with the law." He adds, "Plus, I'd have to tell my boss that the keys have been missin' for a month."

"That's very kind of you, Mr. Jones."

"Well, I'm not lettin' him off the hook," he insists. "When he's better, he has some explainin' to do. And of course, I gotta let him go. Can't employ someone I can't trust."

"Of course." I collect my handbag and rise. "I should let you get back to work. It's a beautiful day to be outside."

"Will ya let me know when he's out of the hospital?"

"I'll make sure that he gets in touch with you." I bid my farewell. "And thank you so much for your hospitality. You are most kind."

"Don't mention it," he smiles broadly. "It's nice to have a visitor now and again with Tilley away."

It's time for me to return home and have a difficult conversation with Dottie.

CHAPTER 14

Walking on the path toward our back door, I peek at my Elgin watch and note that it's now past 1:00. I feel quite peckish and opt to reheat the steak before visiting Dottie in her room. Nan is carefully placing an alluring pie on a shelf in the refrigerator.

"Would you mind handing me the leftovers you saved for me last night? I've been looking forward to them all morning." I sink onto the bench of the nook while removing my cloche and gloves.

"Let me heat that for ya," she closes the refrigerator door.

"You're an angel." I slip off my shoes and let them dangle on the end of my toes under the table.

Nan beams and sets the plate next to the range before selecting a small pan.

"When did Dottie return?" I inquire.

Nan looks at me with confusion. "She hasn't come home, far as I know."

"Where's Jack?"

"Prob'ly in his room," Nan answers as she places a pat of butter in the pan. "He's been mopin' about a harmonica."

I sigh. "It may be best if you return that to the ice box for the time being."

Disappointed, she shuts off the range and gathers up the plate.

I slip on my shoes and pluck a spherical green apple from the fruit bowl. As I enter the dining room, I nearly collide with Jack.

"Just the person I was looking for."

"What did I do now?" He whines. "Dottie's the one missing."

"Correct. And is the lawn finished?"

Jack nods. "Been finished for a long time."

I grip his shoulders and turn him to face the front door. "So, I was going to send you on your way to get that harmonica. Do you have the receipt I gave you yesterday for the you-know-what?"

Jack pats the pocket on his trousers. "Sure do." Delighted, he asks, "Really, Ruby? I can go?"

"Yes, but come home directly after your errands." I call after him, "And if you see Dottie, send her right home."

He swings the hefty door open, begins to place a foot on the porch, and then suddenly pivots. "I should warn ya, Ruby. Bob's in the tub."

"Great," I mutter sarcastically.

Peeking out the window, I watch him lift his bicycle. As per usual, it's been dumped across the porch despite repeated threats over the years that one day he will discover it missing.

Crunch. The tart apple does nothing to sate my hunger, so I place it on the telephone desk and pick up the receiver.

"How may I direct your call?" The operator's dispassionate voice is quite different from her co-worker's when I called for the ambulance. Was that only this morning? It seems like days ago.

"I need the residence of Mr. and Mrs. Frederick Baker, please."

A series of clicks are followed by the greeting, "Baker residence."

"Good afternoon. This is Ruby Ray, Dottie's cousin. I need to speak with one of the Bakers, preferably Polly."

"She's not here, miss. None of 'em are." The timid voice continues. "Would you like to leave a message?"

"I really need to speak with one of them. Where can I find Mrs. Baker?"

"She's still at the church, miss. You might telephone her there."

I open the desk drawer to extract a pencil and note paper. "Do you happen to know the number?"

"Let me check. Please wait a moment." I hear the muffled shuffling of papers. She clears her throat and returns to the call. "Here it is, miss. 9251."

"Thank you so much for your assistance. If Polly returns, would you please have her ring our house?"

"Yes, miss." A click marks the end of the call.

After swiftly lowering the cradle lever three times, I initiate my next call.

The breathy, high-pitched salutation is familiar. "Good afternoon, Fullerton Christian Church, Mrs. Frederick Baker speaking."

"Hello, Mrs. Baker. This is Ruby Ray."

"Well bless your heart, Ruby," her saccharine reply grates on my nerves. "You're lucky to catch me. I just finished the bulletins for tomorrow's special Mother's Day service," she boasts. "Sa-ay, perhaps your family would like to join us."

"We won't be available, Mrs. Baker, but thank you." There's no need to elaborate.

"Oh, that's too bad. Our service will be packed with beautiful songs and verses...and the decorations!" She exclaims with delight. "I've ordered simply stunning flowers for the narthex and podium, and after the children's choir sings 'Like as a Mother Comforteth' they'll give each mother in the sanctuary a carnation. Just darling! Not many people know that hymn, but I think it's perfect. Don't you?"

"Well—"

"Does your mother live nearby?"

"Actually, Mrs. Baker, my mother passed away some years ago." I'm certain I told her this at some point over the years, since Dottie and Polly have been friends for so long.

"Well bless your heart! I'll pray for you Ruby Ray." She then quickly returns to her preferred topic. "Anyway, Pastor Tim's sermon will no doubt inspire, but he told me it's top secret so I can't say more."

"I'm sure it will." Mrs. Baker is trying my patience. "I'd like to speak with you about Polly—"

"Well bless your heart." Never has my heart been so blessed. "Thank you so much for hosting Polly last night."

"That's actually why I am calling, Mrs. Baker."

She simpers, "Please, call me Helen. You know in all these years, you and I have never had a proper visit. We must correct that soon."

"Sure, Mrs. Baker, er Helen, that would be nice." I attempt to break the news gently, "I'm sorry to tell you this, but Polly and Dottie did not stay at our house last night, and neither girl has returned home."

Gasp. "Well where are they?" I didn't think it possible for her soprano to go any higher.

"I hoped you may have some idea about that."

"Are you saying my Polly has disappeared?" Her voice is now tinged with hysteria.

I try to reassure her. "Please don't worry, Helen. I'm sure there's a rational explanation."

Heavy footsteps sound closer and closer, as a muffled baritone declares, "Helen, I told you I need silence today so I can finish my sermon"

I hear Helen sobbing. She has put down the receiver.

"Why are you crying?" he demands as, I assume, he takes up the telephone.

"This is Pastor Tim." Perhaps the use of his first name is intended to engender trust, but he immediately rubs me the wrong way. "Helen is unavailable. How can I be of assistance?" His words convey helpfulness, but his tone implies impatience.

"Hello, Pastor Tim. I'm Ruby Ray. I didn't mean to cause such an upset but, as I was telling Helen, her daughter and my cousin have been unaccounted for since yesterday evening."

"Polly is missing? And on Mother's Day weekend!" he exclaims while Helen unleashes a fresh bout of sobs in the background.

"Well, I wouldn't go so far as to—"

"Then what's going on? Why the lamentation?" he snaps. Clearly, he's uncomfortable with Helen's agitation, and I cannot fathom the good reverend providing solace to his parishioners.

"If I could speak with Helen directly, I'm certain she and I may be able to—"

"I don't think that's a good idea," he barks.

In the background, Helen's weeping seems to abate, and I picture Pastor Tim awkwardly patting her back.

"That a girl. Now here's my handkerchief," he patronizes. "Do you feel able to speak with Miss Ray? Alright then." He sounds relieved to get back to crafting his inspiring message. Returning to the phone, he states paternalistically, "You may speak to her if there is no further upset. Can you do that?"

I almost snicker at the scolding. How does his flock put up with this sort of treatment? He's certainly not winning over any new converts today.

"Yes, sir," I reply with feigned sincerity.

"Hel-lo?" Helen's voice quivers.

"Hello, Helen. I apologize for distressing you. As I was saying, I'm sure there's a logical reason for the girls' absence."

"I pray they're alright," she laments.

"Yes, I'm sure they're fine," I remark gently. "I just want to ask you a few questions that will help us figure out where they might be. Is that alright?"

A faint, "Yes."

"Good. Now I was thinking that Dottie and Polly may have changed their plans and stayed overnight with a different friend. Do you know of any other girls in their social group? Does Polly talk about anyone?"

I asked myself this same question earlier in the day. Dottie is well-liked by her peers but, like me, has always preferred one or two close friends over a gaggle of girlfriends. In fact, I haven't heard her mention another girl's name since last fall when she and Polly fell out with their friend Ginny, who had "stolen" Polly's love interest. I learned the hard way during my own teen years that three-way friendships never work out.

"I don't think so," she replies thoughtfully. "Mr. Baker is quite strict and insists on knowing Polly's friends before permitting her to see them outside of our home."

Unsurprised, I start to ask after Polly's church friends when Helen suddenly exclaims as though she's realized something. "This has to do with that boy!"

"What boy are you referring to?"

"Leo! Leo Taliaferro." She exaggerates his last name, and I recall the conflict Dottie shared with me between Polly and her parents.

She continues, "Mr. Baker will be livid! He forbade her from seeing him anymore, but I know she's been sneaking around."

"What do you mean by 'sneaking'?"

"Well, I've caught her in a couple of lies about where she's been. Always saying she's studying with Dottie or has some math club meeting. Can you imagine that? Polly in a math club. Don't make me laugh," she declares with derision.

"Actually, Helen, she does belong to a math club called the 'Pythagoreans' or something like that. From what I understand, Polly's quite good at mathematics."

"Yes, well," she backtracks. "I suppose she's handy with the ledgers at her father's office. But that's just addition and subtraction." No wonder Polly is so insecure about her intellect.

"So, Leo..." I bring her back to the subject of our discussion. "Do you honestly think that Polly would stay out all night with a boy?" I know for certain that Dottie is too level-headed to do something like that.

"Maybe she didn't have a choice. He is Catholic after all. And Italian!"

I am dumbfounded.

"Well, you know those hot-blooded Latins. What if they've run away together?" Her anxiety is spiraling now. "What if they ELOPED?"

"Helen, that's highly unlikely," I reply calmly. "As I've already said, I'm sure there's a good explanation for this situation, and we will all share a chuckle later."

Unwilling to reign in her imagination, she disagrees, "No, I'm quite sure it's that boy."

Without a doubt, no helpful information will come of this conversation, so I make an excuse to end the call. "There's the front door now. I'm sure it must be Dottie."

"Tell her to let Polly know that I am on my way home this very moment. Just wait until I tell Mr. Baker..."

I ring off and try to roll away the tension along the sides of my neck. I'm also hungry and feel the onset of a headache. *I really must get something to eat.*

A little while later, after Nan has nourished both my body and spirit, I fill the steel watering can and retreat to the back garden to mull things over. No sooner have I stepped onto a paver stone, when a pair of ruby-throated hummingbirds nearly collide with my coiffure. Scurrying away from the chittering, I empty the can into the bowl of the birdbath that's situated next to the wooden bench. Making myself comfortable on the bench, I marvel as a mourning dove descends from the telephone wire running the length of our yard and plops into the cool water. With a series of graceful body rolls from beak to tail, the bird coos with delight.

I feel as though I have forgotten something important. I know that I should pay another visit to the walnut shed but cannot, in good conscience, leave the house until either Dottie or Uncle Charles have returned. And I don't know who else to call regarding Dottie. Feeling unsettled, I scan the yard to ensure my privacy and remove my shoes before rolling down my hosiery. Placing my t-straps and stockings on the seat of the bench, I sink my bare feet into the grass and wiggle my toes in the bending blades. With my eyes closed, I breathe deeply through my nose, expanding my abdomen to its fullest. The fresh scent of the newly cut lawn is a balm, so I hold my breath a few seconds before fully exhaling. After repeating this a few times, my shoulders and throat relax. I rest in this state of calm for a dozen or so breaths before opening my eyes. I then recall Dottie and Polly's dinner conversation about Nick Nixon. They were to meet him and his girlfriend after the movie last night. Now that I think of it, Polly mentioned Leo as well. I roll up my stockings and don my shoes. Hopefully I can get to the bottom of this by speaking with Nick or Leo. I feel energized and hopeful.

At our telephone desk, I pause before placing the receiver to my ear. It's about 3:00. Carrie should be back from her weekend volunteer work. Nick's aunt and I met when I began tutoring and, through her work with the women's auxiliary over the years, she has referred several women to me for reading lessons. When Nick's younger brother Arthur was so ill several years ago, his parents sent him with his other three brothers to stay with her. In fact, it was Carrie that broke the news of their brother's death to the children. So, it's no surprise that Nick often stays over with Carrie on the weekend, especially when he has an event at Fullerton High School. I place the call and wait for a connection.

"Good afternoon. Wildermuth residence." Her no-nonsense manner contrasts sharply with Mrs. Baker's feminine fragility.

"Carrie, hello. This is Ruby Ray."

"Well, hello Ruby. I was just heading out. Can I return your call later?"

"I'm actually ringing to speak with Nick. Is he still there? I assume he stayed over."

"Why no. He stopped by last night before his date but was planning to head home after the movie." Puzzled, she inquires, "Is everything alright?"

"As a matter of fact, Carrie, I'm trying to locate Dottie, and Nick may know her whereabouts. They had plans to meet up after the movie." I offer no additional details, as I don't want Carrie to think poorly of Dottie.

"Well, you may be able to reach him at the market." She pauses. "Here's the telephone number."

"Good afternoon. Nixon Market. Nick speaking." The connection is atrocious, even though the store is located less than ten miles away.

I press the receiver more tightly to my ear. "Hello Nick. This is Ruby Ray, Dottie's cousin. I was hoping you might help me with something."

"Well, I suppose so." He lowers his volume. "My father doesn't like for us to tie up the line."

"I completely understand. I'll try to make this quick."

"Alright…" he replies with reluctance.

I begin delicately. "There's some confusion at our house about Dottie's plans for today. Did she mention them to you last night when you saw her after the movie?"

"I didn't speak with her for very long because the show was a double feature and ran late. We only had a few minutes at the cafe. Then I had to get my date home before her curfew." His deep voice is nearly a whisper.

"I understand. What time did you leave Fullerton?"

"It had to be about 10:45."

"Do you know what Dottie was going to do after the movie?"

"I'm sorry, but I don't. The last I saw of her was when we were pulling away in my father's truck. She and a few kids left the cafe with us then headed to a parked car around the corner."

"Could you tell who she was with?"

"Well, there was Polly and Leo. I don't think I ever met the other guy." I strain to hear him.

"You know Leo Taliaferro?"

He reluctantly affirms their acquaintance. "His family lives across from my Aunt Carrie."

I sense that he dislikes Leo. Hmm…he may know more than he's letting on.

"Nick, I'm going to level with you. Dottie has still not returned home from her outing last night. I am hoping you may know something that can help me locate her."

"They didn't tell me anything," he replies uncomfortably.

"I understand. But you hesitated when you mentioned Leo's name. Anything you can tell me about him may be useful."

"To be honest, I don't think Dottie and Polly should be involved with him."

"Why is that?"

I can barely hear his response. "He's up to something," he utters suspiciously.

"Why do you think that?"

Nick sighs audibly and confesses, "Last month I was staying with Aunt Carrie for a debate at Fullerton High. That Friday night I saw Leo sneak into his house."

"What time was it?"

"It must have been 1:30." His volume increases as he defends his own purpose for staying up that late. "I was in the parlor practicing for the debate, when headlights beamed through the front window. I looked out and noticed Leo slowly opening their front door as the car drove off."

"Did you recognize the automobile?"

"Now that you mention it, the car could have been the same one they were standing around last night."

"Can you describe it for me?"

"It was a Chevrolet National...like our family car." His volume drops as he recalls that his father will be displeased.

"Thank you so much, Nick. You've been very helpful."

"I hope Dottie is alright." He always seemed to have a soft spot for her.

"Me too," I concur. "One last question. What color was the National?"

"Green." He continues with a whisper. "That's why I noticed it. Ours is black."

A gruff voice announces in the background, "There you are! You have better things to do than tie up the line all afternoon." This I hear clearly.

"I'm sorry, Ruby. I have to go."

I begin to thank him again, but the connection is abruptly severed.

CHAPTER 15

A clamorous thud on the porch startles me, and I nearly tumble from the chair in the telephone nook. Jack must be home. My mind was so preoccupied with Nick's troubling revelation about Leo that I didn't notice the squeaking of his wheels as he approached the house. I turn toward the clock on the mantle as Jack guiltily traipses through the door.

He holds up a finger, "Before you say anything, there's a good reason I'm so late."

I sigh with resignation. "I'm sure there is, Jack." Approaching his rangy form, I give him a hug.

"What's that for?" He expresses annoyance but leans into my embrace anyway.

"I'm just thankful you're home," I confess and ruffle his hair. "So, tell me why you didn't return sooner."

After handing me a small white florist box, he rummages through his pockets. "Take a look at that!" He declares enthusiastically. "I got the last one!" He then reverently opens the red and black case, *Super Chromonica* boldly printed on its side, and lifts out a modestly sized silver mouthpiece. After returning the case to his pocket, he blows a tune through the dozen or so holes. It sounds a bit like "Go Tell Aunt Rhody."

"When I got there, a guy from Hohner showed us how to play that song." With awe, he proclaims, "AND he told us they've made a SIXTEEN HOLE harmonica! I'da bought that one, but Hardy's doesn't have it yet."

I admittedly know nothing about mouth organs or any instrument for that matter. "Well, I'm glad you were able to buy one." I add, "And thank you for picking up the corsage."

"Was there ever a line at the florist!" He flings his arm dramatically. "It wrapped all the way around the side of the building."

Unsurprisingly, everyone has left their Mother's Day shopping to the last minute.

"Jack, I don't suppose you heard anything about Dottie while you were out?"

His face drains of color as he looks around. "She's not back yet?"

"Unfortunately, no." My earlier irritation with Dottie for her thoughtlessness has now become apprehension.

"Is that Dottie I hear?" Nan steps out of the kitchen into the hallway that leads to the living room.

"She's not back yet," Jack repeats.

Nan digests this information. Not wishing to upset Jack, she says, "I'm sure she'll be home any minute."

"Jack, why don't you put your parcel in the refrigerator for the time being." With Nan standing there, I am unable to be more specific and hope I don't later find the Chromonica resting amidst the eggs and butter.

When he has collected the boxes and vacated the living room, Nan grips my hand. "This ain't good, Ruby."

"I know." I sink onto the sofa. Nan joins me, patting my knee.

"I spoke with Helen Baker. She knew no more than we do."

"Can't say I'm surprised," Nan snorts.

"Nick Nixon, on the other hand, was able to shed some light on Dottie's activities last night." I retell his narrative about the late return and Dottie's group huddled around the Chevrolet.

With alarm, Nan declares, "I don't like it."

"Neither do I." Dread courses through my limbs.

"What are ya gonna do now?"

"Well, I had planned to stay here until Uncle Charles returns. But I really should pay a visit to the Taliaferros."

"Don't you worry about that." She nods and taps my arm. "I'll stay till he gets back."

"Oh Nan, I couldn't ask you to do that. You should have left hours ago. It is Saturday after all, and I know you're getting ready for—"

She holds up a hand to stop me from going further. "Now you go on. I can stay."

She wraps her arms around my shoulders, and I feel comforted by her soft, warm body.

As I pull up to the curb across from Carrie's house, I realize that I'm not exactly sure which house belongs to Leo's family. A glance at the Wildermuth's driveway tells me that Carrie hasn't returned, so I can't ask her. I examine the houses along the south side of Jacaranda Place, aptly named for the lavender canopy that lines the street each summer. Thankfully, *Taliaferro* has been stenciled in black on one of the slightly rusted mailboxes. Their walkway leads directly to a slab porch with a single steep step that I find somewhat tricky to navigate in my narrow slip. I rapidly knock four times.

Mrs. Taliaferro peeks through one of the oblong windows that frame the vertical length of the door. She opens the door, and her hopeful expression is immediately replaced with concern when she sees me. "Oh, I thought...may I help you? If you're selling something, today is not a good day."

Before she can close the door, I bravely place a hand on the casing. "Mrs. Taliaferro, I am Ruby Ray. My cousin is Dottie Ray, a friend of Leo's."

Her right hand shoots up to her heart. "Do you know where he is?"

"Leo is missing as well?" I don't like the direction this is going.

"Yes! He's been gone since yesterday afternoon. And Dottie?"

"The same. No one I've spoken with has seen her since last night." I look past her into their home.

"Oh, forgive me, Miss Ray. Do come in." She holds the door open for me to enter.

"Please, call me Ruby. And there's no need to apologize." I follow her through what appears to be an astronomy lab and enter their dining room, taking a seat at a well-used oak table.

"Ignore the scopes and charts." She waves in the direction of the adjoining room. "Leo ran out of space in his bedroom, and we told him he could use the sitting room until he leaves for college. That's what happens when you live with a genius under your roof."

Following my instinct I ask, "Is he your only child?"

"Yes." She wraps both arms around herself. "I am beside myself with worry. Leo is such a good boy. He makes us so proud."

"Did he give any indication as to his plans for last night?"

"Well, yesterday afternoon I was in the kitchen stuffing the manicotti, my husband's favorite, when Leo came in, kissed me on the cheek, and said he was heading out and would be back later."

"Did you expect him back last night? He wasn't staying over with a friend?"

"I don't think boys do that as much as girls," she dismisses the idea. "He's never had a sleepover, except for camping with his scout troop."

I try a different approach. "Does he ever stay out past his curfew?"

"He's such a good boy." She repeats. "He's never needed a curfew. As far as we know he's usually back by 11:00 at the latest."

I raise an eyebrow at the late hour.

"He's an astronomer, Ruby. He says that the constellations are clearest when most of the lights around here have been turned out."

That makes sense. I wonder if his stargazing explains the late-night return that Nick witnessed.

I query casually, "Has he ever stayed out past midnight?"

"Oh, never!" So, she has no idea of his recent late return. "Where are my manners? Can I get you some iced tea?"

"That would be lovely. Thank you."

She opens the swinging door into the kitchen, and an absolutely divine bouquet of tomatoes, garlic, and basil wafts into the dining room. I had noticed a savory fragrance when entering the house, but that was like an olfactory whisper compared to this outrageous bellow. She returns with two tall glasses. "I hope you don't mind that I sweetened the tea. Lemon?" She holds out a slice pinched between silver tongs.

"No, thank you. And sweet tea is perfect."

She returns the lemon to a brightly patterned ceramic dish. "I knew he didn't come home last night because of the bed."

"Excuse me?" I set down my glass, careful not to spill tea on the edge of a delicate lace table runner.

With a nod of admission, she confesses, "I make Leo's bed. So, when I went into his room this morning to wake him for breakfast, I knew he hadn't been home. The bed was just as I'd left it yesterday."

"You must have found that disconcerting." We didn't expect Dottie to come back last night. So, I really didn't become concerned until morning stretched into the afternoon. Mrs. Taliaferro must be in a panic at this point.

"Have you called anyone to locate him?"

"Of course. My husband visited the home of his closest friends, but no one has seen him."

"Has anyone other than myself asked after him today?" I take a sip of the sweet tea.

"It's funny you should ask that," she comments. "Mr. Mains stopped by around 1:30 asking to speak with Leo."

"Mr. Wallace Mains? The math teacher?" I don't know what to make of this. "Has he ever visited your home before?"

"No. Why would he?"

"I have no idea. Why did he want to speak with Leo on a Saturday?" I probe.

"He said something about Leo missing a club meeting today at noon."

"The Pythagorean Club?"

She nods her affirmation. "I found it strange at the time that he dropped by but didn't give it much thought since we've been so worried about Leo."

"That is odd." I will call upon Mr. Mains when I leave here.

"So how exactly does Dottie know Leo?" Mrs. Taliaferro inquires.

"Dottie's best friend is Polly," I explain.

"Polly Baker," she sighs.

"You don't like Polly?"

She hesitates. "It's actually her parents that we take issue with."

"Frederick and Helen Baker."

"The very ones." Her hands tighten around her glass.

"What sort of interactions have you had with them?" I can only imagine dealing with Mr. Baker's bluster.

"I shouldn't really say—"

I reach across the table and take her hand, which softens in mine. "I promise you. I will not repeat anything that you tell me."

She bites her lower lip. "They've been nothing but unkind to Leo, especially Mr. Baker. And then there's that other business…"

I nod for her to continue.

"A few years ago, Mattia and I were waiting to see a movie. There was a poster for a new film with Rudolf Valentino. We were talking about it when a man behind us said, 'I'm not watching anything with that Catholic dago.'"

"Let me guess. It was Fred Baker," I remark.

"Yes. Up to that moment, we knew who he was. His face is in the paper from time to time. But we'd never interacted with him before."

"Then what happened?" I can guess where this is going.

"Well, Mattia couldn't ignore such an insult. He turned around and told him to watch his mouth. That some of us are Italian."

"Oh, boy."

"Exactly," she nods. "They got into a shouting match. And before either one threw a punch, the theater manager came out and asked us to leave."

"You two and the Bakers?"

"No, just us."

I grumble in disgust.

"But before we walked away, Baker said, 'You'll be sorry, wop.' under his breath."

My hand flies to my mouth. "How horrible!"

"It gets worse. The next evening, we heard a gunshot outside our house. We know it was him."

"Was anyone hurt?"

"No. He was just trying to intimidate us."

"I have no words." As awful and bigoted as Fred Baker is, I did not expect him to be capable of this level of vicious aggression. "Thank you for sharing this with me, Mrs. Taliaferro. Did you report it to the police?"

"What could they do? We didn't actually see him. And people look up to him." She releases my hand and draws a handkerchief out of the pocket of her pinafore. "We did go to the police station this afternoon, though, about Leo."

"What did they say?"

"Kids will be kids. They didn't take it seriously."

Everything I've just heard confirms that I should visit the police as well. It's approaching 4:30 PM, and these kids have now been gone for a full day. I'll stop by after seeing Mr. Mains. Hopefully he can shed some light on this.

Before I leave, however, I have a few more questions. "You said that the Bakers have been unkind to Leo. What exactly did you mean by that?"

Shaking her head, she explains. "The one time he went to pick up Polly at her house, Mrs. Baker left him on the porch to wait. He was not welcomed inside. Then Mr. Baker came out and told him, 'You are not to pursue my daughter. Understand that? I'll not have her dating someone who is not a Christian.'"

"But your family is Catholic. Leo IS a Christian." I will never understand religious prejudice.

"That's exactly what Leo said, and then he told Mr. Baker that he had the best intentions and that his parents raised him right. But apparently this made Mr. Baker even angrier. He shook a finger at Leo and said, 'Over my dead body! You are NEVER to visit my home again, and stay away from my daughter, or else.'"

This last comment makes me wonder what lengths Frederick Baker will go to in order to control his daughter. "Does Leo know that Mr. Baker was responsible for the gunshot outside your house? I'm surprised he would want anything to do with that family."

Mrs. Taliaferro quickly replied, "Oh no! He knows nothing about that. He was shocked by Mr. Baker's words to him."

"I'm sure." I probe, "Aren't you and your husband concerned that Leo is dating Polly, given the history with her father?"

"That's a good question. He only recently opened up to us about the conversation with Mr. Baker. But you must understand, he's head over heels for her, and we don't have it in us to break them up. There's already one set of parents against them. I just told Leo to be very careful..." She trails off, lost in thought. "Do you think Mr. Baker has something to do with what's going on right now?"

"I wish I could answer that, but I'm not really sure. When I spoke with Mrs. Baker, she was undeniably shocked and distressed to learn that Polly was unaccounted for." *But what about Mr. Baker?*

"One last question for you. Other than discussing his upset over the situation with Polly's parents, have you noticed anything off or different about Leo lately?" I think about Dottie's evasiveness when the subject of Berkeley is brought up.

"It's funny you should ask. He was just accepted to Northern Arizona University. He got an internship at Lowell Observatory, that place where the young man...what was his name? Clyde something...anyway the young man recently discovered Pluto. And to think! Leo may work alongside him." Pride shines in her eyes.

"I read about that discovery." I remark. "Leo must have been thrilled about his acceptance." From my conversation with Norma, I know of his reluctance, but I want to hear what his mother has to say.

Her brow furrows. "You'd think so, but he has seemed preoccupied. And a little sad. I would have thought he'd be more excited, you know."

I do know.

"Perhaps he's upset at leaving home and being away from Polly," I comment.

"Maybe..."

"Mrs. Taliaferro, I apologize, but I must be leaving." I write our number on a page of my notepad and hand it to her. "Please call immediately if you hear anything."

She folds the paper and places it in her pocket along with her handkerchief. "Please do the same."

CHAPTER 16

The waxy petals of a magnolia drift lazily toward the ground as I view the two-story guest house from the street. I notice a curve of compressed wheat-colored grass, no doubt where Fipps routinely parks his motorcycle. A dented Studebaker roadster, rust evident just above the running boards, is parked just past my automobile. Hopefully this belongs to Wallace. I step onto the pediment and reach for the brass knocker. The door suddenly swings inward and, thrusting my palm against the doorjamb, I prevent myself from tumbling into the house.

"Oh! Ruby!" Wallace stands before me. His hair is mussed, and his tattered sweater is fastened incorrectly having skipped the second button from the top. A stack of texts balances precariously in his left arm, while an overstuffed duffel full of folders sits at his feet. His flummoxed expression suggests that he did not see me coming up the walk.

"Wallace, I apologize for startling you."

He blinks and shakes his head before regaining his composure. "No. Not at all. I'm sure the fault was mine." Bending to lift the hefty bag, he continues, "Forgive me. I'm in a bit of a rush to meet someone, but Norma and Edith are not here." His voice is tinged with scorn when he mentions their names.

"Yes, I know." I straighten my crepe coat. "They're still at the hospital with Frank."

"Frank?" His eyes widen. "Is he alright?"

"To be honest, he wasn't yet conscious when I saw him earlier." Without going into detail, I explain. "You see, I found him this morning and called for an ambulance."

"That's why the telephone was ringing so early this morning." He turns to look inside the house. "I heard Norma and Edith leave shortly after that, and they haven't been back since."

"No, I don't suppose they have."

Wallace lifts his right arm, duffel dangling under a tight grip, and examines his wristwatch. "Look, I really need to leave. Did they send you to pick something up?"

"Actually, I'm here to see you."

Wallace blinks with bewilderment. "Me? But Frank has already turned up. I don't see how I can—"

"This has to do with my cousin, Dottie," I clarify.

"Dottie?" His face pales and eyes widen further.

"Yes, they've been missing since last night after the movie."

"They?"

"Dottie, Polly, and Leo."

A gasp escapes his mouth as his eyelids quickly flutter. The bag drops to the threshold, and he flinches at the thump.

He is dumbfounded, so I continue, "I know that the kids missed their meeting with you today."

"Now how would you know about that?" Wallace's face reddens.

"Mrs. Taliaferro mentioned that you'd been to their house earlier when I stopped by to talk to Leo about Dottie's disappearance. That's how I learned that Leo hasn't returned home either."

"Look, I don't know what you want from me." He fumbles his keys while locking the door. "I need to be somewhere right now, and I can't help you." He snatches the hefty bag and strides away toward the curb.

Can't or won't. I quicken my step to follow him closely and call after him, "I'm just wondering if the kids said anything to you about their plans for last night."

He tosses the duffel and books through the open window of his car and turns toward me. "I don't know anything." His eyes tell a different story.

"Wallace...Mr. Mains. We're all quite worried. If there's anything…"

"I told you. I don't know anything!" In no time he is sitting behind the wheel and has closed the door. Despite my proximity to the car, he turns over the engine and drives away.

"Oh, I think you do," I shout as I hop in my vehicle to trail him.

He accelerates and turns right at the intersection, not even slowing to check for oncoming traffic. I manage to safely pursue him, until he bumps across the railroad tracks, at which time the wigwag starts to tilt back and forth, and a *ting-ting-ting* sounds the warning of an oncoming train. I come to an abrupt stop and pound my fists on the steering wheel. My thoughts race.

What is Wallace Mains hiding? He seems to be somehow involved with the kids' disappearance, but how? Where is he off to?

There's nothing more I can do about him at this point, so once the dozen or so Union Pacific cars have passed by and the wigwag has settled, I roll across the tracks and change course. My next stop is the Fullerton Police Station.

"As I told those Italians, kids will be kids." Police Desk Sergeant Blockhurst scowls at me, his appellation visible on the nameplate resting upon the scuffed surface of the desk. A shadow from his custodian helmet is insufficient to hide the coarse tangle of his eyebrows.

"Not these kids, Sergeant." I try a different approach. "These are honor students who have no history—"

He patronizes, "Now I'm sure they just hopped on the Red Car last night to visit that new Mexican place in Los Angeles everyone's talking about. Oliver? Aloe Vera?"

"Olvera Street? Respectfully, sir, do you honestly think they'd still be missing at," I glance at the wall clock behind him, "4:50 the next day?"

Brrring brrring

"Desk Sergeant Blockhurst." The furrow between his wiry brows deepens. "Well why didn't they report this sooner? I'm about to leave." He closes his eyes and pinches the top of his nose. "Yeah, yeah. I'll send someone over."

He drops the telephone receiver on the hook and flips open a thick cloth-bound notebook. Today's date is handwritten in script at the top of a nearly full page on which the sergeant scribbles furiously. When finished, he dots the page with a sharp tap of his pencil and notices I am still standing before him.

"Listen young lady, we're busy." His stubby, sausage-like fingers reach again for the receiver.

"But—" I am not willing to be so easily rebuffed.

"If they're not back by tomorrow morning, pay us another visit. In the meantime, don't worry yourself sick over this. Kids will be kids." He shoos me toward the door with a backhanded wave and barks into the telephone, "Tell Ike to go over to Fullerton General. It's about those robberies."

I have been dismissed.

Passing through the solid door, *POLICE DEPT* painted on its exterior surface in blocky capitals, an arm reaches forward to hold the door for me. A middle-aged man in grease-stained coveralls nods, "Ma'am."

"Thank you, sir."

As I step down from the porch, I hear the mechanic through the iron-barred windows on either side of the door. "I got a call that you found my car."

Pulling into the driveway I'm pleased to see Uncle Charles' auto, a Willys Overland Whippet. The *dinging* of its cooling engine indicates that he recently arrived home. Hopefully the same is true for Dottie.

When I enter the kitchen, Nan looks up from the task of folding her apron. She slowly shakes her head at my questioning glance.

"Any news at all?" I ask, my stomach already sinking.

"Not a peep," she replies sadly. "Your Uncle Charles just got here."

"Yes, I noticed his car. Where is he?"

Her eyes shift upward. "Upstairs."

"Thank you so much for staying here. I know you have plans with your family—"

"There's no need to thank me." Nan's hand reaches forward to give my shoulder a squeeze. "Lots of prayers for Dottie bein' sent up right now. I called and started a prayer chain just after you left."

My eyes fill with tears. Nan's use of the telephone, something she continues to view with suspicion, moves me more than anything else. At that moment, Jack flies into the kitchen, his face whitening as he notices my expression.

"Dottie…" he begins.

"Oh, Jack, it's not what you think," I pull him into a hug. "I was just thanking Nan for everything she's done for us this afternoon."

"Whew!"

His body relaxes, and I release him. "Say, Jack. Would you do me a favor?"

"Sure! Whaddya need?"

"Please go up to my bedroom and bring me the box with *Taylors* written on it. I think I left it on the chair next to the bed."

As he rushes away, I retrieve the corsage from the refrigerator and place it on the counter next to Nan's handbag. "You can't leave without this."

She reaches for the box and lifts the lid. The white carnation is surrounded by baby's breath, and the pale blue ribbon is lovely. "Oh Ruby, you didn't hafta do that. 'Specially with everything goin' on."

Leaning forward to inhale the somewhat spicy scent of the flowers, I mention, "There's one more little thing."

Jack is back lickety split with the candy, which I instruct him to give to Nan. As with the corsage box, Nan removes the lid. Her eyes light up as she exclaims, "Chocolate covered dates?!"

"You're favorite, as I recall," I comment.

"Now, Ruby you REALLY shouldn't ha—"

I hold up a hand. "As I tell you every Mother's Day, you couldn't be more of a grandmother to us if we were blood relatives."

Now her eyes have filled with tears. We embrace one another and then pull Jack in for good measure.

"What's all this?" Uncle Charles queries with alarm.

I repeat, "It's not what you think," before drawing his attention to the gifts.

"Of course," he nods thoughtfully and with some measure of relief. "Nan, Happy Mother's Day. I hope you know how much you mean to our family."

She begins sobbing in earnest, and Uncle Charles offers her his handkerchief while patting her upper back. When her tears have dried, she requests. "S'much as I dislike that phone thingamajig, please call when there's news about Dottie." She blows her nose. "Night or day."

"Of course, we'll call," I pat her on the back. "And we'll see you Monday morning, by which point Dottie will be home safe and sound."

She waves the hankie at Uncle Charles. "I'll warsh this and bring it back."

He squeezes her shoulders and smiles warmly. "You do that, Nan."

We relocate to the living room, while Jack returns upstairs to practice playing the harmonica. His approximation of "Frère Jacques" is choppy as he stops and restarts each time he misses a note.

"I'm not sure about this latest hobby of his." Uncle Charles wiggles an index finger in his ear.

"Honestly, I'll take the ruckus over Bob in the bathtub any day."

He briefly chuckles then covers his forehead and eyes with his palm. "Ruby, I just don't know what to think about Polka Dot." He looks up, "And I'm appalled that I wasn't here all day. I should have called to check in, but I was out at a derrick. And I figured she returned just after we left. You had to manage—"

"You don't need to apologize, Uncle Charles." I assure him. "I wasn't really concerned either until I learned that their friend Leo is missing too.

He rocks back in his seat. "It's not just Dottie and Polly? There's a boy involved in all this?"

I share with him the conversations I had with Mrs. Baker, Nick Nixon, and Mrs. Taliaferro.

"So, based on Nick's report, there may be a second boy involved as well," Uncle Charles surmises.

"Yes, and I think I know who that might be." I inquire, "Do you remember the young man at the diner yesterday? Thelma's nephew?"

"The one who ran in shouting about the theater sign after the lights went out?"

"The very one." I struggle to recall his full name. "Earl, something…"

"You think he's with the others?" Uncle Charles frowns, doubtlessly unsettled by the notion of his little girl socializing with a dashing older boy, and one who skips school no less.

"It's just a hunch, but his name keeps popping up. In fact, on Thursday Jack overheard Polly mention Earl to Dottie."

"Overheard?" he asks sarcastically.

"Well, so he said." I snicker. "Anyway, the conversation had to do with a warm jacket. And now that I think of it, I did notice Dottie leaving here yesterday with her fur coat. I suspect they were discussing their plans for last night."

"A reasonable assumption."

"I have more to tell you." I then proceed to recount my conversation with Wallace and the subsequent pursuit.

"You chased him WITH THE BALBOA?" I cannot tell if Uncle Charles is shocked or amused.

I downplay that last bit. "That's neither here nor there. What's important is that he knows something about all this."

"It certainly sounds that way." He silently contemplates the implications of Wallace's involvement, then states emphatically, "We need to go to the police!"

"Already been there and was told 'Kids will be kids.'"

"Did you mention this Mains fellow?"

"What would I say? 'I followed a well-respected schoolteacher with my car because I think he has something to do with my cousin's disappearance'?" I laugh bitterly. "They don't even believe there's anything amiss."

"Let me have a go." Uncle Charles marches into the hall, picks up the telephone receiver, and demands, "I need to speak with the Fullerton Police Department."

I stand next to him straining to hear the other end of the conversation. I'm genuinely curious if he will make any headway. It sounded as though Sergeant Blockhurst was leaving for the day. Perhaps Uncle Charles will speak with someone less dismissive.

"Yes, hello. This is Charles Ray, and I'm calling because my daughter has gone missing." He taps a pencil on the desk while listening. "That's correct. Her name is Dottie Ray, and she is seventeen years old. She's five foot six inches tall with a slim build. Violet eyes and dark brown chin-length hair." Another pause. "She was last seen yesterday evening outside the movie theater at about..." He turns toward me.

"10:45 PM."

He repeats the time to the officer. "No, she's never stayed out past her curfew, nor has she disappeared like this." He waits. "Yes, she was definitely with the others. Polly Baker and a boy named Leo—"

He glances my way again and asks, "Taliaferro?" I nod, and he continues, "Yes, that's correct. And there may have been another young man...Earl...but we don't know his last name."

A scowl flashes across his face. "Wait forty-eight hours? That's ridiculous. These are children!" Before slamming down the receiver, he grumbles, "Very well!"

"It was worth a try," I sigh with frustration.

"Not good enough," he glowers at the phone and then returns to his chair.

"I think I'll take a look in Dottie's room. I'm surprised I didn't think of that earlier."

"Good idea. I'll just...I don't know what I'm going to do." The look of confusion and panic on his face makes me feel sick. I have never seen my uncle like this before.

"Go check in with Jack," I suggest. "This has been hard for him as well." So, we both head up the stairs.

"Hey sport. Let's see that jaw harp," I hear him say as he enters Jack's bedroom.

I notice nothing out of the ordinary when I enter Dottie's room. Her bed is made. A few articles of clothing are on the floor, possibly rejected while she was packing yesterday afternoon. An autographed photo of Loretta Young is framed and sits upon her desk. She's been a fan of this young actress since Loretta costarred in *Laugh, Clown, Laugh*, which was quite remarkable at the time since Loretta was only fifteen, the same as Dottie. In contrast to the frivolity of the photo, several dense tomes are piled on the center of her desk, their spines facing the wall. At first, I think nothing of it, until I notice that the rest of the books are arranged neatly with their titles visible. I reorient the stack to examine the titles. A standard looking mathematics text, *Basic Harmonics*, *Quadrivium*, *The Lost Continent of Mu*, and the King James Bible.

I first open the Bible, surprised to see it among the other more academic texts. Dottie has written "*tetramorphs*" next to a passage in Ezekiel. I shrug. *The Lost Continent of Mu* seems familiar, and I recall this to be the blue book Polly retrieved from Wallace's classroom yesterday after school. From a cursory glance at the introduction, I learn that this is a narrative about a land mass in the Pacific thought to be inhabited by the Naacal, an ancient but powerful civilization. I have no idea how this pertains to mathematics, any more than the Bible. The pages of *Basic Harmonics* are covered with sin waves and other such diagrams. This makes more sense. Examining the mathematics text more closely, I see *Fullerton Junior College* stamped on the inside cover and realize that it is a college course book on calculus. Finally, a perusal of *Quadrivium* reveals the term *Pythagorean* throughout its foxed pages. I flip to the inside cover and see that a symbol has been drawn consisting of two intersecting circles with another circle embedded within the overlapping space. And a square has been sketched inside of the smaller circle, as well as a cross spanning the center of the drawing. I recognize Dottie's handwriting where *Vesica Piscis* and *Tetrad* have been scribbled above and below the figure. I have no idea what to make of this.

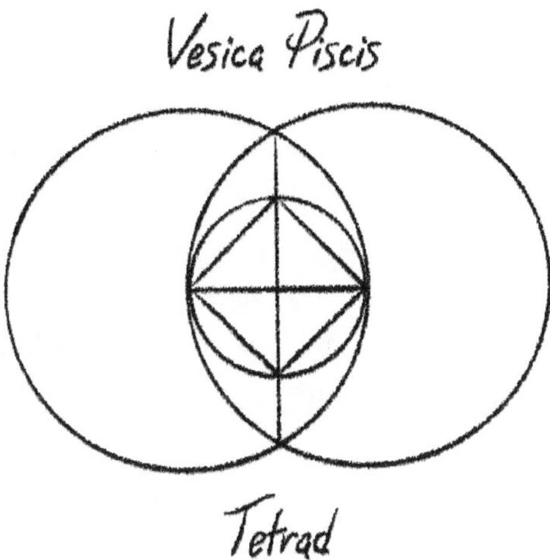

Further inspection of Dottie's room uncovers nothing else out of the ordinary, and my search for a diary or personal calendar is unsuccessful. As I close her door and enter the hall, Jack calls up to me from downstairs.

"Ruby, telephone for you."

I rush downstairs, and Jack hands me the receiver. "Hello?"

"Ruby...Frank's been arrested."

CHAPTER 17

"I got here as soon as I could," I pant, approaching the two women in the hall.

While breathless from my haste along the hospital corridors, my emotions have more of a bearing on my scattered mind than physical exertion. When I received Edith's phone call, I was loath to leave Uncle Charles and Jack at home, particularly after the puzzling clues I unearthed in Dottie's room, all of which having left me mystified and fretful. However, upon sharing the news of Frank's arrest, Uncle Charles urged me to go.

"I've got this, Ruby. Your clients need you right now."

The brief drive to Fullerton General afforded me a few moments to begin processing the observations I had made. The calculus text, book on harmonics, and *Quadrivium*, what an odd name, may have pertained to Dottie's schoolwork. I knew that she's taking advanced mathematics, however I didn't realize that included college level material. That being said, it's not surprising. She's been enrolled in an advanced chemistry course for university credit all year. I wondered if Dottie was one of Wallace's "Pythagoreans?" If so, why did he deny his acquaintance with Dottie when we first met?

The book on the lost continent may have pertained to one of Dottie's other courses, history for instance. But I was baffled by the Bible among these other books. Over the years Dottie has attended church with Polly on a few occasions, mostly holiday related, however she's never expressed an interest in religion or spirituality. In fact, based on previous conversations, I'd place her more in the camp of empiricists and would be less surprised to find the works of Locke or Hume on her desk. Which scripture had she bookmarked? Something to do with *tetramorphs*. I vowed to read those pages more fully when I return home.

I mulled over the unfamiliar terms…*Naacal, Mu, quadrivium, tetramorph, tetrad* and recalled seeing another word that began with the

Greek prefix, "tetra." Where was that? An image of Wallace erasing a chalkboard surfaced in my mind. *Tetractys.* I thought back to an English course in high school when we learned Greek and Latin roots, prefixes, and suffixes and remembered that "tetra" means "four." Actually, "quad" means "four" as well. Certain numbers are considered special or unique, such as pi, the Fibonacci sequence, and the square root of negative one. But four? With no more time to consider this puzzle, I exited my car and headed into the building.

"Yet again, I am so relieved to see you." Norma falls into my arms outside Frank's room while Edith shakes her head, eyes closed, behind her back.

Upon releasing Norma, I notice a police officer positioned to the left side of Frank's door. Under her breath, Edith suggests, "Let's take this down the hall."

"Good idea," I reply as we both slip an arm through one of Norma's.

Once situated where we can speak privately but can still view Frank's door, Norma turns toward Edith. "Why don't you explain. I'm having a hard time organizing my thoughts."

"A little over an hour ago, without warning, this officer," Edith's eyes shift toward the policeman, "Burst through the door and told us that Frank was under arrest."

"How shocking!" I exclaim. "I'm surprised that a doctor or nurse didn't accompany him."

"Dr. Armstrong was quick on his heels, but that did little to cushion the blow."

"Of course not. What reason did he give for the arrest?" I wonder if Mr. Jones decided to report the stolen keys after all.

Norma speaks up, "They say he's the neighborhood robber."

I gulp.

"Apparently the nursing student who was helping out earlier recognized the watch found in his pocket. It's her father's and was stolen during one of the break-ins a couple of months ago." Norma sniffs into her handkerchief.

"The greeter," I remark unintentionally.

"Excuse me?"

"Never mind." The awkward exchange with the nursing students this morning now makes sense. "Is Frank still unconscious?"

"Yes," Edith answers. "He hasn't awakened at all. But his pallor has improved, thanks to the saline injections, and Dr. Armstrong said the rest of the other tests confirm what he was saying about alcohol."

"I don't understand the purpose of an armed guard outside his room." I glance at the cop who is holding his baton. "Do they think he's capable of escaping in his condition?"

Edith snorts. "The officer didn't find it amusing when I made the same remark."

"I overheard him talking with his partner, and it sounded like their collective pride had been injured since they hadn't yet apprehended a suspect," Norma shared. "I think at this point, Fullerton PD is being overzealous."

"There are TWO policemen here?"

"The other one left a few minutes before you arrived."

"Are you at least allowed to see him?" I ask Norma.

"Yes, but only one of us at a time."

"And they check our purses each time we go in." Edith rolls her eyes.

I consider the charges. The robberies would certainly be deemed a felony. "Do you think Frank is guilty?"

Norma buries her face in her hands. "I just don't know, Ruby. He's been acting so strange lately."

"I don't think he's capable of pulling this off himself," Edith interjects. "Assisting, maybe, but I can't imagine him as the mastermind."

"You think he was helping someone else." This certainly sounds plausible to me, from what I've learned about Frank.

"Absolutely, if he was in fact involved at all," Edith replies.

"Of course he was involved," Norma cries, "Why else would he have that watch?"

"He picked it up at the pawn shop?" I suggest.

"That makes no sense." Norma shakes her head. "He has a perfectly good wristwatch that I gave him for his last birthday."

"We'll know more when he wakes up." I consider what other charges might follow. We know that Frank's been accessing alcohol somehow, which is illegal. Prohibition bans the sale, production, and transport of alcohol, not its consumption. Also, Frank definitely stole Mr. Jones' keys. Now I wonder if he lifted them during the robbery at the Jones' house. "Did the police say anything else when you spoke with them?"

"They were told about how he arrived here," Edith responds. "So they asked about who discovered him. We told them your name but did not offer any information about how and where you found him."

"The officer at Frank's door asked us to alert him if you arrive, as he'd like to interview you," Norma says softly. "But we didn't say anything when we saw you turn the corner."

"Thank you for that." This may buy us a bit of time. "It's critical that I check the shed for your savings. Now that the police are involved, who knows what will happen to the money."

"I was thinking the same thing," Edith concurs.

"Before I leave, though, I need you to tell you about a situation that's come up with Dottie. You may be able to answer some questions for me."

"Something's wrong with Dottie?" Norma questions with concern.

I fight back tears. "She's been missing since last night, along with Polly Baker and Leo Taliaferro. That Earl boy may be involved as well."

"Oh Ruby!" Norma takes my hands, "And here you are helping us! Please let us know what we can do."

"I'd love it if you can answer some questions for me." I retrieve my notebook from my handbag.

"Of course!"

"The first thing I need to know is Earl's last name. I'd like to see if he knows anything."

"It's Adams."

"Thank you. And I'm curious if Dottie is in Wallace Mains' Pythagorean Club."

"I wouldn't know about that." Norma responds at the same moment Edith states, "Yes, she is."

Edith explains, "I chair the faculty committee on student organizations and receive all of the participant lists."

"I'm impressed with your memory," I admit. "I'm sure you see many such rosters."

"Actually, that particular list stood out to me because it only contained four names."

"Let me guess. Earl Adams, Polly Baker, Leo Taliaferro, and Dottie Ray."

Edith taps her nose.

"I'm going to level with you both. I have some suspicions about Wallace."

"Get in line," Edith retorts sharply.

"According to Mrs. Taliaferro, Wallace stopped by their house this afternoon because Leo missed a Pythagorean meeting at noon."

"Went to their house?" Norma exclaims, "How odd!"

"Precisely. So, I visited him at your home, and he became quite evasive and agitated when I mentioned the club meeting and the kids' names."

Norma raises her shoulders. "Did he give any explanation?"

"Not at all. He quickly retreated to his Studebaker and drove away."

"Well, that was rude, although I'm not surprised," Edith remarks.

"Quite rude. I even followed him but lost him when a train passed by."

"I'm sure you put the fear of God in him when you did that," Edith snickers.

"Huntington Beach," Norma appears deep in thought.

"Excuse me?" I ask, confused.

Norma turns toward Edith, who nods, and continues, "We heard from one of our colleagues that Wallace lost his last teaching position. That was in Huntington Beach. Evidently, he was 'too familiar with the students.'"

"That may imply any number of things." My stomach turns. "Did you hear anything else?"

Both women shake their heads.

"Alright. I think it's imperative that I visit your house again and try to inspect Wallace's room."

"You'll need the key to his room," Norma declares.

"He locks his door?"

Edith smirks. "Yes, but he thinks no one knows that he keeps a spare set of keys under the pot of begonias in the backyard."

"He's notorious for locking himself out. Edith watched him fetch the keys one afternoon." Norma discloses.

I think through the logistics of my next move. "So, here's the plan. I'll head directly to the walnut shed when I leave here. Hopefully the money is there. This will also give me an opportunity to see what was covered under the tarps." I consider whether I need to return home first to change, since I plan to rip door handles off with a crowbar. However, in the interest of time, I dismiss that idea.

"But Ruby, it's getting dark outside." Norma objects.

"I agree." Edith's eyes express concern. "You have your hands full with Dottie's disappearance. One of us can visit the shed."

I remind her that their car is currently parked at the shed, so they have no way to get there. "Further, you wouldn't be able to find it in the dark. I've already been there and know where to turn."

"Then let one of us go with you." Edith suggests.

"Norma needs to stay with Frank, and she needs you here." I continue describing my plans. "After I visit the shed, I'll run by your house to check Wallace's room, provided he's still gone, then I'll come back here to let you know what I find." My thoughts are racing. and my mind is conflicted. That shed needs to be visited, ASAP, as does Wallace's room before he returns. However, I also need to call or visit

Earl Adams. Then there's Fred Baker… I have a feeling he may also be involved with the kids' disappearance. I'll ask Uncle Charles to help with that when I get home.

"Be careful," Norma pleads.

"Don't worry about me," I assure her confidently. "I'll be fine."

The rapid *thud-thud-thud* of footsteps on the marbled linoleum flooring signals that someone is approaching me from behind. I continue walking toward the front doors, pretending not to notice. The last thing I need right now is for the police to stop me for questioning. I'll talk to them tomorrow morning.

"Ruby," an urgent voice calls out.

Reflexively, I turn and see Dr. Armstrong jogging toward me, the pockets of his jacket jangling with the tools of his trade. While at any other time I would be pleased to chat with him, more pressing matters weigh heavily on my mind.

"I don't mean to be rude, but I'm off on an urgent errand." I attempt to soften my words with a smile and gesture toward the door. "Perhaps we can talk when I return in a little while?"

"Yes, of course," he nods politely. "I just wanted to fill you in on Frank's arrest. Norma gave her consent, since you're helping them with something pertaining to Frank."

"That would be great." He has my full attention. Perhaps he knows more about the police involvement, for example whether they know where Frank was found. The last person I want to run into at the walnut shed is an investigator wondering why I've traversed a dirt road in the dark.

"When Frank was transferred to the inpatient floor, Irene, one of the nursing students, was tasked with the inventory of his possessions." He digresses to clarify. "It's standard procedure. With all the comings and goings in a hospital, articles can be misplaced."

Or stolen. I've heard stories.

"Anyway, Irene recognized her father's watch immediately. It was a gift from her mother, and his initials were inscribed on the back."

"Did she let someone know?" The sight of the stolen watch must have been shocking.

"Not right away. She's quite new and probably wasn't sure what to do." Dr. Armstrong motions for us to step away from the front door as a family enters and observes us with curiosity. "The charge nurse pulled her aside after she confused the breakfast trays of several patients. I happened to be standing at the station desk and heard her confess that she had experienced something upsetting a little while earlier. I had no idea what it was about until after her father arrived."

"Did the charge nurse call the police at that point?"

"I don't think so. The hospital administrator and charge nurse discussed it out of earshot, and Irene was sent to the visitor's desk to assist a couple of her peers."

"That must have been about the time I arrived. She seemed friendly until I mentioned Frank's name."

"That makes sense."

"Did you see her father arrive? Was he outraged?" I imagine housebreaking would feel like such a violation, particularly when one's prized possessions have been stolen.

"Surprisingly, it didn't sound like it. I heard that the administrator ushered him to his office where, I imagine, they discussed how to proceed. I didn't know any of the details until the police arrived some time later."

"Not something that happens every day around here, I'd venture to say."

"You got that right." He frowns. "I would've liked to be there when the policeman broke the news to Miss Graham, but I arrived too late."

"Norma knows that."

"Between you and I, it's appalling to me that they would arrest someone in Frank's condition, not to mention place a guard outside his room. Where do they think he's going to go right now?"

"No argument here." I really need to be on my way. "Did the police have access to his patient file? More specifically, do they know where and how he was found?"

"To my knowledge, they only know that he was brought in unconscious this morning. The administrator, charge nurse, and I discussed patient confidentiality and the ethics of this situation. He instructed us to direct any inquiries to him alone. Thankfully he doesn't want to put the medical staff in a difficult situation with the police."

"That's good to hear. Did you know that the police asked to speak with me?"

"Did they?" He seems rattled. "How did they know—"

"Not to worry," I reassure him. "Norma and Edith told them."

"Whew!" He exhales sharply. "For a moment, I thought a nurse or student may have said something."

We share a smile. "I must be on my way."

"Yes. Yes. I'm sorry to keep you."

"Not at all. I appreciate that you took the time to fill me in. I plan to be back in a little while. Then you can fill me in if something else comes up."

"I promise." He lightly places his hand on his heart. "I hope, at some point, we run into each other under less onerous circumstances."

My cheeks warm, and I feel a tingle in my solar plexus. I quickly wave and head out into the twilight.

CHAPTER 18

Brilliant rose and coral clouds stretch across my windshield as I approach the walnut shed. Yet this glorious sunset does little to assuage my sinking feeling upon noticing a fresh pair of tire tracks along the right-hand side of the building.

Someone else has been here.

Before stepping out, I consider the items I will need for my task and realize that I'm without pockets. I could kick myself for not bringing a change of clothes when leaving the house earlier. Realizing that I'll have to use my handbag to carry the items I'll need, I remove most of its contents, with the exception of Frank's keys, a pen, and my notebook. Next, I reach under the driver's seat for a flashlight. *Not there.* I feel around under both seats and along the floorboards, to no avail.

"You've got to be kidding!" I growl in frustration, not knowing which of my cousins is responsible this time.

Thankfully, the twilight offers sufficient illumination for me to wander toward the back of the shed. Surely while he was living rough, Frank kept a flashlight stowed somewhere in his car. But as I turn the corner, the earth shifts beneath my feet.

The Ford is missing.

I stomp back to the Balboa, restart the engine, and maneuver my motorcar so that the headlights are shining upon the shed's weathered doors. Thereafter, I snatch a tire iron from my repair kit in the trunk and slam the lid. However, when I reach the entryway, I drop the iron bar in the dust with a clunk.

The doors are unlocked.

Once inside the structure, I nearly trip over a tarp that has been carelessly dropped. Kicking aside the filthy covering, I hear a tinny clink, and a fluted flashlight rolls into the darkness. I retrieve the torch and slide its ribbed switch forward. A strong beam of light floods the dirt floor.

"Thank goodness," I mutter and return to my car, which I move to the side of the dirt road so that way I can leave quickly if the need arises.

Back inside the shed, I slowly turn in a circle to get my bearings and immediately notice that the shrouded articles I spied earlier have largely been removed. All that remains is a coiled copper pipe and a ripped feed sack leaking golden kernels onto the dirt floor. I kneel down by the pipe and detect a sweet, yeasty odor emanating from a brownish yellow glob. A cursory pat reveals that the soil is damp to the touch. The center of the shed is completely empty, save for footprints in the dust trailing to and from the doors. Meanwhile, tangles of rods and canvases lean haphazardly against two of the shadowy corners.

The perfect place to hide a lockbox.

Peeling back one of the canvases, I am assaulted by the stench of a decomposing animal, and the messy cobwebs of black widows stick to my palm. *Ugh!* I truly loathe spiders. I make use of the copper coil to poke and pry at the poles and fabric, a time-consuming effort. The empty corners of the shed, once relieved of their contents, yield nothing further, so I begin to scour the earthen floor for any evidence of a buried object. At one point I think I hear a shuffle behind me, but when I straighten up and shine the flashlight around the interior space, nothing appears to be there. Through the open doors all I can see is the darkness of early evening. I've examined about two thirds of the floor when I notice the unmistakable smell of smoke. Pushing myself upward, I clearly perceive steps behind me.

"Who's ther—"

My arms feel bound, and something solid presses against the backs of my knees. My head throbs as my body is jostled up and down. Squinting my eyes, I see a mop of curls above me. *I'm being carried.*

"Why couldn't you just leave it alone?"

Fipps.

My attempt to scream results in a fit of coughing, as acrid particles of burning wood fill my lungs. While my mind tries to make sense of what my body is experiencing, I slip back into the dark void.

A distant glow awakens me. I'm lying upon an uneven surface, sharp objects pressing into my back and buttocks. Rolling onto my side, my palms press into the ground which is blanketed with leaves and twigs. As I rise to a seated position, excruciating pain explodes inside my cranium. The muscles in my face and neck tighten, my jaw clenches, and my eyes close tightly. When I tentatively direct a hand toward the back of my scalp, the focal point of my misery, my fingers encounter sticky, matted hair. I sniff my hand, and the uncanny tang of iron fills my nostrils. *Blood.* Gently prodding my scalp again, I sense an egg-sized lump, but the bleeding appears to have stopped.

Where am I? How long have I been out?

The scent of smoke lingers but not as strongly as before. I look behind me and glimpse a bright radiance some distance beyond the orange trees. Feeling the ground around me, I unsuccessfully search for a flashlight. Wishful thinking on my part but worth a try. Above me, a waxing gibbous moon is occasionally blurred by swirling currents of smoke. Not a full moon, but probably enough to light my way.

I need to get help.

The vivid orange hue must surely be the burning walnut shed, but it seems far-removed from my current location. Further, Fipps may still be around, and I don't wish to give him another opportunity to assault me...or worse. I decide to walk south. By keeping the moon on my left side, I should reach Bastanchury at some point regardless of how far I was carried. And the grid like pattern of the citrus trees should keep me heading in the right direction. Slowly standing, I am gripped with unbearable vertigo, my head spinning so severely that I drop to my knees. All at once my body feels unbearably hot, and my stomach revolts. My visual field begins to fill with darkness, and ambient noises around me sound as though I am underwater. Blackness returns.

I don't know how much time has passed, but my arm rests in vomit, and my body is covered in sweat. I tremble with chill. Sacrificing the little warmth that my spring coat offers, I peel my arms out of the sleeves and remove most of the sick with it. I scan the sky and notice that the moon appears higher.

I can't stay here.

With great mental and physical effort, I push myself upright and attempt to stand again. If I don't start moving now, there's no telling how long I'll stay out here. Norma and Edith are the only ones with a vague notion of my location, but they would have no reason to suspect anything is amiss for quite some time. And who knows the severity of my head wound. The next time I lose consciousness, I may not wake back up. Using a low-hanging branch for balance, I haltingly rise to my feet, stopping several times to let the dizziness pass before continuing. When I am finally vertical, I tentatively shuffle my feet forward. By keeping my head stationary, I'm able to reduce the pain and wooziness.

I trudge for what feels like more than twenty minutes but doubt that I have gone very far. Due to the bends and twists in the road, Bastanchury could be nearby or maybe a couple of miles away. I have no idea. My throat tightens, and I feel tears well up at the inside corners of my eyes. A memory surfaces, one that I had forgotten. Nonetheless, I keenly feel the emotions, as though it happened only yesterday.

Sleeping Beauty Mountain.

I am seven years old, all alone in the forest, and hopelessly lost. My parents and I had just finished lunch at Shelving Rock Falls in the Adirondacks. We were staying at the majestic Sagamore, just across Lake George from the site of our picnic, and Mama and Papa were enjoying a postprandial nap on a blanket. I was also supposed to be napping, but restlessness and curiosity got the better of me. So, I wandered off in search of the peak bearing the storybook princess' moniker. In my mind, I pictured the summit bearing a striking resemblance to a castle, all spires and turrets. I meandered about the woods, my journey dictated by the presence of flowers, for I planned to present Sleeping Beauty with an enchanting posy. However, after collecting more flowers than my petite fist could hold, I realized that I had no idea where I was. Further, my sense of time was still immature, and I didn't know how long I'd been away.

Frantic, I began running indiscriminately and stumbled upon a tree root. Landing squarely on my face, the delicate blooms I'd collected scattered around me. As I stood up, a loud rustling in a nearby clump of large bushes startled me. Whatever it was, the creature sounded gargantuan. So, of course, I concluded it must be a dragon. Screaming, I leapt to my feet and scampered in the opposite direction. When I was certain the beast had not followed me, I plopped down upon a stump and began to cry. I knew that I'd never see my parents again. I would live in the forest like Mowgli, but I doubted that the animals would help me as they did in the book Papa read to me before bedtime. No one would know what happened to me. My parents would feel so sad. They already lost my baby brother. Now they lost me too. I must have sobbed myself to sleep, for the next thing I remember was being awakened by the mad dash of a frenzied deer.

And then I heard Mama's voice.

"Ruby?"

"I'm here." I leapt to my feet and bolted toward her.

"Oh, thank goodness! She's over here, Edward!" Mama sank to her knees so that I could fall into her arms.

I recall the tears in my father's eyes, the first and only time I ever saw him cry. He too dropped to the ground and encircled us both with his strong arms. When eyes had been dried and noses blown on the seemingly endless supply of handkerchiefs from Papa's coat pocket, he looked at me sternly and scolded.

"Don't you ever wander away again. Do you hear me?"

I knew that he was afraid. Not angry. And I was overwhelmed with guilt for having worried my parents.

"I'm so sorry, Mama and Papa."

Mama pulled me into an embrace and lovingly inquired, "Why did you do it, sweetheart."

I looked into her warm gaze and answered, "To meet Sleeping Beauty."

Blotting away the tears with a scratched and bloodied hand, I am filled with disappointment and despair. What was I thinking, coming out here by myself? That's just it, though. I wasn't really thinking. Since first learning of Dottie's disappearance, I have believed that I had a plan, that every action I've undertaken was thoughtfully and carefully considered. That I was in control. But in truth, I've just been reacting. Why else would I so recklessly put myself in harm's way, not even considering that someone may return to the shed. I suspected that Fipps was connected with Frank's situation. He knew Frank was unconscious, but he just drove away to protect himself. He was undoubtedly behind the burglaries and the moonshine operation in the shed. In fact, I'm astonished that he didn't abandon me to burn, the witness to his crimes well out of the way. Speaking of burning, the smell of smoke has intensified, as has the haze. *Did the orchard catch fire as well?* Once more, with moonlight shining on my left cheek, I proceed forward, this time as quickly as I can tolerate.

A silhouette, no taller than four feet high but just as wide, materializes from behind a tree. I pause to squint at the amorphous form, but the orchard's shadows disguise its identity. It too has stopped, and I hear a humanlike gasp.

What on Earth? "Who's there?" I implore.

A startled voice squeaks, "¡Una mujer!"

As they step into the moonlight, I realize I'm looking at three small children, none older than five or six years. Given their use of Spanish, I must be near one of the villages for citrus workers, at least I hope so.

"Hola. It's ok." I hold up my hands to calm the frightened little ones. "Dónde esta?"

My Spanish is deplorable, particularly considering that I took a year in high school. In my defense, however, our teacher spent most of our class time showing photographs of his many trips to Madrid. I suppose the throbbing pain in my head isn't helping either.

I try again. "Dónde—"

"Where's what?" A little girl, her face framed by low-hanging ponytails, approaches me cautiously. The other two, a younger girl and a tiny boy, hang onto one another.

"Oh, you speak English!"

"Ye-es," she answers slowly as though I have asked a ridiculous question. "We speak English at school."

"Of course. I'm so sorry." I feel foolish. I'd heard that schools had been built on Bastanchury Ranch and Campo Pomona, the goal being to "Americanize" the children of Mexican field workers.

"Why are you here?" The other two step forward with interest as she poses this very reasonable inquiry.

"Well, that's a long story. But right now, I need help." I look around for an adult. These children surely aren't out here unsupervised with a fire burning nearby. When I turn to gaze behind me, the children collectively shriek. My hand flies up to cover the bloody mess. They've seen my injury in the moonlight and must be petrified.

"It's alright," I try to reassure them. "Well, maybe not alright, but I'll be fine."

"What happened?" the little boy asks, his mouth and eyes round with shock.

"I was injured at the walnut shed." Glancing toward the glow, I comment, "That's where the fire started."

"We know," the older girl comments. "Papi went to see."

"Why are you out here by yourselves?"

They look sheepishly at one another. The younger girl, tightly cradling a rag doll, admits, "We wanted to see."

Just then, a booming bass sounds through the trees, "¡Niños! ¿Qué estás haciendo aquí?"

The boy races toward his father. "¡Papi! ¡Ella está herida!"

At this point, a rapid exchange of reprimand and apology ensues. Meanwhile, weakness and unsteadiness overcome me, and I collapse into darkness yet again.

Someone is bathing my hands and arms with a warm cloth. I open my eyes to find a dozen or more people staring down at me, perplexed and concerned. Their faces are illuminated by a nearby fire pit. Beyond them I discern makeshift huts of corrugated iron, rusted signboards, and fence posts. A beautiful woman with full rosy lips squeezes my hand and smiles.

"Much better," she remarks. "We worry." Her accent is heavy, but I understand her perfectly.

With assistance, I sit up slowly and wait for the spinning to stop. "Where am I?"

"Tijuanita." She clarifies, "On Bastanchury Ranch."

I'm familiar with these settlements. Elizabeth once told me that Bastanchury Ranch has provided small, rent-free plots of land to Mexican families arriving, usually penniless, to find work. However, the burden of building dwellings fell to the laborers, each family constructing their home from any scraps they could find. And running water was restricted to a single water faucet for the entire village (I hate to think what the privy situation must be like). Nonetheless, I notice tiny yet tidy gardens surrounding their rudimentary shelters.

"I need a doctor." I gingerly reach toward my scalp.

"Sí." She raises an arm and points. "Mi esposo gets truck."

A few minutes later, a dust cloud arrives with the crunch of tires. *Basque Brand,* one of the labels for Bastanchury Ranch's oranges, is stenciled in navy blue across the wooden stakes of the truck's bed. A man in white collarless shirt and wide legged trousers hops out of the cab. The "papi" of the three children approaches our circle, nods when he sees me, and comments to his wife.

"Ella está despierta."

"Sí." She turns back to me and explains. "He will drive to hospital."

The trio of siblings surround their father and plead in sweet, high-pitched voices. Their mother chuckles. "They want to go."

"No!" Their father commands, but the kindness in his eyes imparts a fondness for his impetuous offspring.

He motions toward one of the other men, and they help me into the front of the borrowed vehicle. His lovely wife enters on the driver's side and scoots next to me on the bench seat.

"I go to help." She pats my leg.

In spite of the pounding in my head, I refuse to ignore social niceties, particularly with this couple who have offered me such care.

"I'd love to know your names." I place a finger upon my chest. "I'm Ruby."

"Josefina y Alejandro," she gestures toward herself and her husband.

"Muchas gracias, Josefina y Alejandro."

"De nada," Alejandro replies warmly.

"And your niños?" I ask Josefina.

"Oh," she grins with pride. "Juana...siete, Manuel...cinco, y Alejandra...cuatro."

I have expended my energy, and the bouncing of the truck aggravates my lightheadedness. So, we ride in silence for the remainder of our trip to Fullerton General, dark fields racing past our windows.

CHAPTER 19

"What in the world?" a familiar voice exclaims as I climb out of the truck. "Ruby? What happened?"

I didn't expect to see Edith in the parking lot behind Fullerton General Hospital, but I am thankful she's here. On our drive over, I considered how best to gain access to the emergency room without involving Josefina and Alejandro. Given the current climate of suspicion where immigrants are concerned, one look at a white woman in my condition in the company of two Mexican field workers, and the police would be summoned immediately. And then there's the matter of the borrowed truck…I'm not willing to take any chances with their safety.

"Edith, could you please help me into the building?"

She quickly glances at the couple standing on either side of me, and her expression signals understanding. "Of course."

"Josefina and Alejandro, this is my friend Edith."

They both nod a greeting.

"A pleasure to meet you both," Edith shakes their hands. "Thank you so much for helping Ruby."

"De nada," Alejandro replies as Josefina blushes.

"You are both angels," I reach forward and squeeze their hands. "Muchas gracias! And please thank your children for me as well."

"Si, Ruby." Josefina hugs me. "Be well."

As they return to the truck, Edith gently places her arm around my back. "We need to get you inside. Can you walk on your own?"

"I think so, but I'm feeling quite dizzy."

Just then, a woman steps toward us from a nearby automobile, her eyes round as she takes in my condition.

"Ruby, this is Ann Nordberg. She teaches chemistry at the high school," Edith introduces her friend. "Ann, Ruby Ray."

"Oh my. Dottie's cousin…" Ann stares, mouth agape, then notices my shivering in the cool night air. My jacket is still somewhere in the citrus grove. She slips her cardigan around my shoulders. "You poor thing!"

"Lean on us," Edith tells me, as Ann steps to the other side and wraps an arm around me.

My legs buckle as I shuffle forward, and they tighten their grip. We've only traversed about twenty feet when a nursing student bursts through the double doors from the emergency room with a wheeled chair.

"Oh, thank goodness!" Ann declares. "I was so worried you would fall."

Edith too looks relieved and turns toward Ann, "Why don't you go home. I'll stay with Ruby, and I'll find another way home later."

"Not a chance. I'll wait in the lobby." Ann pauses once we are inside. "But first I think I'll check on Norma."

"That would be good, Ann. Thank you." Edith follows behind me as we turn left, and Ann continues straight ahead.

After everything I've been through this evening, I'm thankful to be resting on a padded gurney rather than sitting in one of the rigid visitor's chairs. I recline on my side which alleviates the dizziness and lessens the throbbing in my head. The young nurse jots my name and vitals in a file folder and informs me that someone will be in to see me shortly.

"Ruby, you don't have to answer if you're not feeling up to it, but what in God's name happened to you tonight?" Edith hands me a glass of water.

The cool liquid is refreshing, and I realize that I'm probably dehydrated as well.

"It's a long story, but I'll give you the brief version." I fill her in regarding the shed, Fipps, my wandering, and my rescue.

"I don't know which shocks me more, the fact that Fipps attacked you or that he nearly burned down the orchard." Outrage colors her features.

"What surprises me the most is that he moved me away from the flames."

She nods in agreement and quietly reflects for a moment. "The copper coil and grain certainly indicate a still of some sort. Fipps must have set the fire to burn the evidence."

"Oh, most definitely." Recalling my search, I remark, "Based on my inspection before getting knocked out, it's unlikely there was a lockbox anywhere."

Edith winces at my reference to the assault and nods her head. "I thought as much."

Just then, a physician draws back the curtain, his badge indicating his status as a resident. *Not Dr. Armstrong.* I had briefly wondered if he'd be in the ER, but then I remembered that he's working in a different part of the hospital this evening.

"Good evening miss, I'm Dr. Collins." After I've answered a few questions about my identity, location, and the current date, he scrutinizes my wound. "It looks like you've had quite the adventure."

"You have no idea."

I startle as he places the cold bell of his stethoscope on my back to listen. "I smell smoke on you," he comments. "Can you take a deep breath for me?"

I comply without difficulty. Truthfully, I don't think I've suffered smoke inhalation. I was far enough away from the blaze and haven't coughed since I encountered the children.

"I'm going to have Minnie clean you up, and then I'll be back to examine your head more carefully." He turns back before closing the curtain. "The good news is that you won't need stitches."

Well, that's something.

While waiting for the nursing student to arrive, it occurs to me that I have no idea what time it is. I automatically reach for my Elgin but then recall leaving it in the car. My stomach sinks when I consider the state of the Balboa and my personal effects contained within, the Elgin being at the top of the list.

"Ruby, are you alright? You suddenly turned pale," Edith asks with concern.

"I'm okay. Just thinking about what I left behind at the shed." I look around the curtained area. "I don't suppose there's a clock anywhere."

Edith pushes up a sleeve and checks the time. "It's 11:23."

"Uncle Charles must be frantic!" I sit straight up and immediately regret my action. Lying back on my side, I wait for the waves of lightheadedness and nausea to fade and, after a moment, request. "Edith, can you please call him for me?"

"Oh Ruby, of course! I should have thought of that as soon as we got you settled. I'll be right back." She flies out, just as the nursing student rolls in a tray of gauze and instruments.

Tears linger at the corners of my eyes when Edith returns. I am deeply thankful that she didn't witness Minnie's thorough ministrations. The young woman will, without a doubt, score high marks on wound debridement.

"How did he take it?"

"I've never heard such despair in a man's voice before." She continues, "He said he'd be here within ten minutes."

Pangs of guilt gnaw at my conscience. With Dottie missing, I should never have taken such risks with my own safety. Poor Uncle Charles! A tear escapes and rolls slowly down my cheek. Edith offers me a paper tissue from a box on the nightstand. I have just finished blowing my nose in a decidedly unladylike manner when the curtain snaps open.

"I recall saying, 'LESS onerous circumstances.'"

"Dr. Armstrong," I quickly tuck the tissue under the sheet. "How did you know I was here?"

"That was my doing, Ruby. I hope it's alright. I ran into Dr. Armstrong after calling your uncle," Edith explains.

"No. Yes. Of course, it's fine." All at once I feel embarrassed and insecure. My cheeks are surely red.

"I shared with Dr. Armstrong the basic facts of your evening. Again, I hope that was fine." She emphasizes "basic."

"If you're going to be angry with anyone, the blame is mine." He pats Edith's back. "When I heard that you were here with head trauma, I wouldn't let her return to you until she explained what happened."

My mind is reeling, and not from the dizziness this time. He must notice my discomfort.

"I'm not going to trouble you with more questions, but at some point I would like to know the specifics. In the meantime, my buddy Dr. Collins will do an excellent job taking care of you."

"Thank you, Dr. Armstrong," I manage to say.

"Not to worry, Miss Ray." He shoots me a boyish grin. "I'll be back in a little while to check on you."

Edith refills the glass, which I gratefully accept. A little while later I hear Uncle Charles' voice. "I'm looking for my niece, Ruby Ray."

"We're in here, Mr. Ray," Edith calls out to him and settles the cup on the table for me.

The curtain is swept aside, and he rushes toward me in two long strides. "Ruby! I've been worried sick!" He gently plants a kiss on my forehead and takes my hand. When he stands back up, I notice his mussed hair and house shoes. He's a wreck.

"Uncle Charles, I am so sor—"

"Please don't apologize," he squeezes my hand. "I am just so relieved to see you in one piece. At least one of my girls is back." *So Dottie hasn't returned.*

"I figured you'd want to tell your uncle what happened, so I only mentioned that you were hit on the head and brought here." Edith rises from the chair so that Uncle Charles can sit. "I'm going to check in on Norma and will be back in a little while."

I nod to her and turn toward Uncle Charles. "I feel so foolish. I should never have ventured to the walnut shed this evening by myself."

He raises his eyebrows with alarm but refrains from interrupting my narrative. When I finish, he runs his fingers tightly through his disheveled hair and closes his eyes. After taking a couple of deep breaths, he finally opens his eyes to speak. "There are so many things I'd like to say right now, but this really isn't the time or place to discuss your choices this evening."

"I am truly sorry. You were already overwrought with Dottie, and I should never have put myself in such a dangerous situation."

"Thank you for apologizing," his voice softens, "But I'm sure you had no idea that things would work out as they did."

"I should have thought it through, but I've been heedlessly rushing from place to place, conversation to conversation, all day long." My heart sinks.

"You're anxious about Dottie, as I am." He pats my arm. "I know that you've been doing the best you can."

Relief floods my body and the muscles in my throat unclench. I've been beating myself up since I awoke at Tijuanita. Honestly, the judgment I've directed toward myself far exceeds any I'd receive from Uncle Charles.

Upon noticing my tears, Uncle Charles moves to the side of the gurney and tenderly gives me a hug. "Don't be too hard on yourself. I've been running around with my head cut off as well. Thankfully Jack was asleep when I realized you too had disappeared, so he didn't witness my frantic pacing."

"But Uncle Charles, what if he leaves the house as well?" One more thing to worry about.

"You know as well as I do, that a herd of elephants couldn't wake him. However, just in case, I left him a note instructing him to stay put." He releases me and begins to walk toward the curtains.

"Where are you going?" I'm confused.

"To call the police of course." His tone implies astonishment I even had to ask. "You were attacked this evening. They need to find this Fipps person and throw him in jail."

"Please wait." I sit up suddenly, which makes my head swim. "This situation is complicated. As the person who found Frank, the police already wanted to speak with me this evening before I ever returned to the shed." I fill him in on Frank's arrest. "My presence there as the fire broke out will, no doubt, look deeply suspicious to them."

"But you were assaulted!" Uncle Charles is incensed.

"True, and we will report that. But right now, I'm in a great deal of pain and just can't handle a police interrogation." I lie back down on my side. "Besides, Fipps is undoubtedly hiding or long gone. This can wait until tomorrow morning when I'm up to speaking with them."

"I don't like this, Ruby, but I respect your decision." He returns to his chair.

I summoned all my remaining energy during my discussion with Uncle Charles, and my body is now utterly exhausted. I close my eyes to rest and fall into a light sleep.

"Alright, Miss Ray, let's take a look at that head." Dr. Collins helps me to sit upright and releases a whistle while examining the wound. "If I didn't know better, I'd say someone took a crowbar to your head."

All at once, I picture the tire iron that I dropped outside of the shed. My body stiffens.

Dr. Collins must sense my dismay. "I'm only joking of course." He softly palpates around the swelling. "How did you get this goose egg?"

I look toward Uncle Charles who raises his eyebrows and shrugs his shoulders.

"I don't really remember," I answer somewhat truthfully while omitting the circumstances of my injury.

"That's not surprising." Dr. Collins shines a bright light in both eyes and asks me a series of questions regarding my symptoms. I choose not to mention the blackouts since the last one was quite a while ago. I really don't want to be admitted to a room.

"Squeeze my fingers as hard as you can." He extends the index and middle fingers of both his hands toward me. "Good."

"I'm going to try to bend your leg, but I want you to push back with all your might." He places his palm on the sole of my right foot. He then repeats the task on the left side.

"Let's swing your legs off the side of the bed so I can check your reflexes." Upon glimpsing the small rubber mallet, I recall a bit I once saw in a comedy where the patient kicks the physician. It's odd what the mind dredges up during moments of crisis.

When Dr. Collins seems to be satisfied with the strength and sensitivity of my limbs, he instructs me to lie back down and directs a question to Uncle Charles. "Does Miss Ray live with anyone? I'm debating whether or not to send her home with medication."

"Yes, she lives with my children and I."

Dr. Collins nods while scribbling in the chart, and I hear footsteps.

"Hello, Miss Ray. Can I poke my head in?" It's Dr. Armstrong.

I introduce him to Uncle Charles and explain the circumstances of our first meeting. "Thank you so much for taking care of Jack," my uncle shakes his hand.

"I'd say 'anytime,' but of course I don't wish to see Jack again in the ER." Dr. Armstrong motions for him to sit back down. "He's a great kid."

"I agree." Uncle Charles's smiles wearily.

On the other side of the curtain, a mature female voice directs, "Please prep bed 4. We have a volunteer firefighter coming in with burns."

Dr. Armstrong shoots me a quick glance and questions Dr. Collins, "So what's the diagnosis, doc?"

"Definitely a concussion, but I suspect it's mild. No sutures were required for that laceration."

"Glad to hear it. So, what's the plan? It sounds like you'll have your hands full in a moment."

"I was just telling Miss Ray and her uncle that I'd like to send her home, but I want to make sure that someone is on hand to monitor."

Uncle Charles stands up, "Yes, Dr. Collins, I'll get her home and sit at the foot of her bed all night."

"Excellent." Dr. Collins finishes scribing his notes and closes the file. "The nurse will explain all of the instructions and go over the medications with you."

He addresses my uncle, "If at any point the pain worsens or she starts vomiting, please bring her back immediately."

Uncle Charles nods. "Thank you, doctor."

Before taking his own leave, Dr. Armstrong leans forward and speaks quietly. "We don't usually make house calls, but if it's alright with you I'd like to stop by tomorrow morning on my way home from the hospital. Just to make sure you're doing well."

"That's so kind of you." Uncle Charles raises an eyebrow at me as he turns away from Dr. Armstrong.

Once again, I feel my cheeks flush, "Only if you have time, Dr. Armstrong. I don't want you to feel oblig—"

"It's no trouble at all, Miss Ray."

The nurse hands me a small envelope. "Take this powder every four hours for pain starting when you get home." She removes an empty cup from my other hand. "Minnie will be over soon to help you out to your automobile."

"That's not necessary." Edith arrives just as the nurse is leaving. "I'll help Mr. Ray take her out."

"Very good." She's gone before I can thank her.

"Edith, you didn't have to come back." But I'm relieved that she did, as I have a favor to ask.

"I wanted to make sure you have everything you need before Ann drives me home." She pats my knee.

Despite being strengthened by the fluids and respite, the nurse insists that I leave in a wheeled chair. I feel only slightly lightheaded when I duck into the passenger seat of Uncle Charles' car.

Edith makes sure I'm settled. "I overheard Dr. Collins telling Dr. Armstrong that he wanted to call the police. He suspects you were assaulted."

"I'm not surprised." I twist my body sideways and lean the side of my head against the seat so I can see her. "What did Dr. Armstrong say?

"He held him at bay and said that he'd persuade you to call the police tomorrow morning when he visits you at home. This seemed to appease Dr. Collins."

That's a relief. "Edith, I need you to do something for me."

"Anything, Ruby."

"If Wallace is not there, I need you to check his bedroom."

"My pleasure. I'd love to know what he's hiding in there," she states with undisguised glee. "What should I look for?"

I consider how best to advise her. "Letters for sure. Also, esoteric books that have nothing to do with mathematics. Photos, journals...whatever looks suspicious to you."

"What should I do if I find something?"

"I suppose the best thing to do is take notes. We don't want him to know that anyone's been in his room."

"I'll do just that and call you in the morning." She gives me a quick hug. "In the meantime, you should get as much rest as you can."

"That is definitely my plan."

CHAPTER 20

SUNDAY, MAY 11, 1930

Tree limbs crackle and fall around us as we frantically search for a way out. The heat is oppressive, and even though we've dropped to our knees, smoke continues to fill our lungs. No one knows we are here. I berate myself. Of course, they followed me. And now their lives are in danger as well.

"It's no use. I don't see an opening anywhere."

The little ones begin to cry and cling to one another. I look toward the sky, but the moon is well hidden behind dark gray clouds. Without warning, a thunderous hiss erupts, while gas spews in every direction. A man stomps through the steam, and my heart leaps with hope.

"Please help us!"

We scramble toward our rescuer, still tightly gripping one another's hands. But as we get closer, he pushes back a mop of curls to reveal a featureless face. It's as though his eyes, nose, and mouth have all been erased. We scream as one. I tug on Juana, Manuel, and Alejandra, but they are frozen in place. I'm only seven years old. What can I possibly do to save us? The monster lifts his right arm, and I notice the iron bar in his hand. He rushes toward us.

I sit bolt upright, but the room spins, compelling me to lie back down. Once the dizziness has passed, I reopen my eyes and register the familiar shapes of my cherry armoire and vanity table in the darkened room. The curtains are drawn, but morning light peeks in around the edges.

"Oh good! You're awake." Jack is seated on my wingback chair, his feet propped on the ottoman with an issue of *The National Geographic Magazine* resting on his knee.

"How can you even see to read?"

He retrieves a flashlight from the floor and switches it on and off. "Sorry, I forgot to tell you that I borrowed this."

Well, that's one mystery solved.

I'm still getting my bearings and recall returning home well after 1:30 AM. Uncle Charles helped me upstairs and seated me on my bed with a nightgown and damp washcloth. Somehow, I managed to change and clean myself up while he stepped out. After a few minutes, he softly knocked before opening the door, a glass of opaque fluid in his hand. I gratefully accepted the analgesic and must have fallen asleep immediately, however I remember waking up at some point in the wee hours of the morning and finding Uncle Charles seated at the foot of my bed. I readjust my head to relieve the pressure on my injury and wince. The medication must have worn off.

Jack gazes at me with alarm. "Gosh Ruby, I heard what happened. Are you ok?"

"I've felt better." To reassure him I add, "The doctor said I'll be fine."

Jack nods. "That's what Dad said."

"Where is your dad?"

"He said he had to leave for a little while." He glances at my bedside clock. "That was about a half an hour ago. But he'll be back by 9:00."

"What time is it?"

"Almost eight." He rises and picks up a small plate from the nightstand. "Mallomar?"

I can't help but smile. When Jack was little, he liked to sneak into my room early in the morning before anyone else was awake. We had an agreement that he would let me fall back asleep if I gave him a cookie and settled him in the chair with a picture book and flashlight. Years have since passed, and now he rarely wakes before ten without an alarm clock. Needless to say, my heart is warmed by his reminder of our little ritual.

"Thank you so much, Jack. That is so thoughtful of you." I accept one and take a bite, even though I'm not really hungry.

He sits next to me on the bed and, munching his own cookie, settles in for a tale. "So, is it true you were clobbered?"

"Yes, it's true, but I don't really feel up to talking about it at the moment."

Sensing his disappointment, I promise to share details of the entire saga later. Truth be told, right now I could really use a trip to the restroom and a cup of coffee. However, I'll have to wait for the latter until Uncle Charles returns. Jack is fine using the toaster, but the percolator is a different beast entirely.

"Jack, would you help me stand? I need to go across the hall."

He pops up and takes my hand. "Absolutely!"

Once I'm on my feet, I find that I'm able to move about much more easily than last night. My head no longer throbs, and the lightheadedness fades shortly after I stand. Further, a gentle inspection of my scalp suggests that the swelling has gone down. However, my quick look in the bathroom mirror becomes a double take when I catch a glimpse of puffy eyes and scratches across my right cheek. I gaze longingly at the bathtub, but now is not the time for a soak. So, I settle for carefully grooming my hair and scrubbing the remaining blood and dirt from under my fingernails. I may appear wan, but at least I'm tidy. Uncle Charles has left a glass containing the pain medication next to the sink, and I eagerly drink its bitter contents.

Crossing to my bedroom I hear Jack downstairs on the telephone. "Yes, I'll let her know. Goodbye." Rapid footsteps *clomp* up the stairs, as I tie back the curtains and lift the window sash for some fresh air. The door flies open.

"Who was that?" I return to bed.

"A teacher from the high school. She called to check on you." He examines a note he's scribed. "Miss Holmes? I told her that you just woke up."

I'm eager to hear what she found in Wallace's room, but the slip in Jack's hand appears to contain only a few words. "Did she say anything else?"

"Just that…" he peers at his hastily scrawled writing, "Mr. Mains is home. She said you'd know what that means."

"Yes, unfortunately I do." My heart sinks. Hopefully she has another opportunity later. Just then a door opens and closes.

"Dad!" Jack dashes back down the stairs, and I hear him recount the events of the morning to his father as they approach my room.

"Ruby, it's so good to see you awake." He gently kisses the top of my head. "How do you feel? You look so much better."

"Definitely better than last night. What's that?" He has placed a merchandise bag on the bed from which I extract a metal disk. "My pocket watch!"

He points toward the sack. "That's everything I found on the front seat of your car. I couldn't locate your purse anywhere, but the empty bag was in the trunk."

"The Balboa was still there? I assumed it was destroyed by the fire." My body relaxes.

"It's a shock, I know. The walnut shed was heavily damaged, but the support beams were still standing. The grove behind the shed didn't fair so well. Lucky for you, the fire moved away from your car." He tosses my keys onto the bed. "Fortunately, it suffered no more than some exterior heat and smoke damage that can be repaired. The engine was fine when I drove it home."

I am astonished by this turn of events. "But how did you know? I can't believe you went there."

"Well, that's an interesting story." He takes a seat and tugs the knee of his pants before crossing his legs. "I received an early morning phone call from Fred Baker, who was quite agitated."

Of course. The walnut shed belongs to him, after all. "What did he say?"

"I won't repeat his words verbatim," he shoots me a knowing glance, "but suffice to say he demanded to know why your auto was parked on his property at the scene of a very suspicious fire."

"Yes, I can imagine how that looked to him." He no doubt recognized my car from my chauffeuring the girls back and forth over the years.

"The police were there, as well, asking the very same question."

I nod. "What did you tell them?"

"The truth, of course." He uncrosses his legs and leans forward. "I told them you went there as a favor for a friend and were subsequently attacked by this Fipps person who then abandoned you in the burning orchard."

"Did you say anything about Frank?"

He scowls. "Ruby, for Pete's sake! You were viciously assaulted! You were left, unconscious, near a fire! You're lucky to be alive! For once you need to focus on your own well-being before the needs of others."

I flinch from his candor as much as the intensity of his exasperation. "You're absolutely right," I admit and blink back tears.

Uncle Charles moves to sit on my bed. "Please don't misunderstand. I have always been proud of your dedication to helping others. You've improved the lives of so many people."

"I just can't bear to see others suffer."

"I know that." He pats me. "And you're a doer. You've never been one to just sit on your hands and let events unfold around you. But right now, with Dottie missing..." His head drops forward, and seconds later his shoulders begin to shake. He's crying.

I swing my legs so I can join him on the side of the bed. Tears are now rolling down my cheeks, as well. I wrap my arms around him, and we sit like that for quite some time. When his sobs have subsided, I open the drawer of my nightstand and secure two clean handkerchiefs, one for each of us.

Wiping his eyes, he comments, "That was the most infuriating part of my conversation with Fred this morning."

"What do you mean?" I settle back against the pillows.

"He didn't mention Polly. Not once." His posture is rigid with indignation. "We're two fathers with missing daughters. If I knew where to look, I'd be out there in a heartbeat."

"As appalling as that is, are you really surprised? What did he say when you mentioned the girls?"

"He launched into a tirade about Polly sneaking off with 'that Italian' and told me that Dottie must be just as bad. He believes that they're hiding out somewhere until the dust settles."

"So, he didn't contact the police when he learned about her disappearance?" I ask but already know the answer to this.

"Of course not. I got the impression that he doesn't want people to know about Polly. His shed and orchard, on the other hand…"

"What did the police say about the kids when you picked up my car?" With all of the events that have unfolded over the past few days, I can't imagine that they will continue with the "kids will be kids" rhetoric.

"I get the sense that they're finally taking it seriously. The officers investigating the shed weren't really in a position to say much, but they mentioned that the sergeant now believes that it's all connected. I'm not sure what that means though."

"I'll tell you what it means. It means they'll be knocking on our door in no time." I begin to rise, but Uncle Charles encourages me to sit back down. "As far as the police are concerned, I'm the common thread between Frank's situation, the fire, and the missing kids."

"True. And hopefully they'll work with you instead of against you." He covers my legs with the sheet and blanket. "For now, though, you should rest. You're going to need it."

"I suppose so." But in truth, I cannot tolerate lying in bed while Dottie is still missing. "What do you plan to do now?"

"Me? Well, the first thing I need to do is check in with Jack to make sure he's handling everything alright." He pauses to sort his thoughts. "Then I suppose I'll start calling Polka Dot's friends. I found her address book near the telephone."

How did I overlook that? "I'll make you a deal."

"Go on," he looks at me skeptically.

"I promise to rest until Dr. Armstrong stops by. If, in his professional opinion, my wound warrants staying in bed, then I'll do so. Otherwise, I plan to get up and help you find Dottie."

"Does it even matter whether or not I agree?"

"Not really." I consider his trip to the shed, and before he reaches the door I ask, "Uncle Charles, how did you get my car home?"

"Vincent."

Our next door neighbor.

"He's an early bird and owed me a favor. Now, close your eyes and rest."

"If you say so." After the door closes and his footsteps recede, I gather a blank notebook and new pen from my desk, slide back into bed in case he returns, and begin formulating a plan to find Dottie today.

"I rushed right over when I heard!" Nan bustles into my bedroom holding a crowded breakfast tray. The pale blue ribbon of her corsage accentuates the floral hues of her best dress. She pours coffee into the porcelain cup and places the carafe on the nightstand. The plate is loaded with fried eggs over easy, soft round biscuits covered in bacon gravy, and, of course, three slices of bacon. A smaller plate contains a generous slice of strawberry pie topped with fresh whipped cream.

"Nan, you shouldn't have! It's Mother's Day for heaven's sake, as well as your day off." I slip the notebook and pen under the covers. "How did you hear about me?"

"Well, I called here this mornin' to check on Dottie, and Jack told me everything."

"But you loathe the telephone."

"Yes, well." She sniffs. "I was up all night worryin' and prayin' so when I heard about you, my nephew rushed me right over."

"But all this food?" The gravy smells divine. "Don't get me wrong, I appreciate it more than you know." I don't think I was hungry until this minute.

"I made too much for my family, you know how I do, so I brought some over to you."

"Jack's going to be jealous?" I bite into one of the bacon slices.

"Oh, don't worry about him. He and his papa are downstairs with their own plates," she proclaims proudly.

I check the time. "You better scoot or you'll be late for church."

"Are ya sure? I can stay to hel—"

"Absolutely not! You belong with your family today." I open my arms and try not to crush her corsage as she enfolds me in her warm embrace.

"You don't push yerself today," she admonishes.

"I'll try. Happy Mother's Day, Nan."

No sooner have I finished scraping the last bit of flaky pie crust from my plate than I hear a bold knock at the front door. My pocket watch, still nestled next to me on the bed, needs to be wound, so I check the bedside clock. It's 9:47.

Hopefully that's Dr. Armstrong and not the police.

I don my robe and tiptoe across the floor. While less than thrilled with the reflection I see in my dressing mirror, there's no need to primp. Under the circumstances, I'd say I look pretty good.

Uncle Charles wraps twice. "Ruby? Dr. Armstrong is here."

I situate myself against the pillows. "I'm awake. Please come in."

"Good morning, Miss Ray!" Dr. Armstrong enters with a wide smile and lovely bouquet of pale salmon and pink roses, each with at least thirty petals. I notice that Uncle Charles, taking the breakfast tray with him, has left the door open.

I raise an eyebrow while cradling the delicate blossoms in my arms. "Are flowers routinely part of your house calls?"

Merry lines crinkle at the corners of his eyes when he laughs, "This is actually my first."

"House call or flowers?" I tease, enjoying our repartee.

"House call, definitely. But I'll have you know that those are *Gruss an Aachen* blooms. A patient of mine grows them, and they are quite rare in these parts." He grins proudly, then assumes a professional air. "How is the patient fairing today?"

"Much better than last night, that's for sure."

"I'll be the judge of that. Turn your head to the left please." He gently touches the side of my head, which sends tingles along my scalp and down my spine.

Gulp. It seems wrong to have these feelings during a medical exam.

"Please sit up and lean forward." As he scrutinizes my injury, I try to answer his questions about the dizziness and pain but find myself rather breathless. "No sign of infection, and the swelling has receded."

I start to recline against the pillows. "Can I abandon my sickbed, doctor?"

"Not so fast. I need to listen to your lungs." He retrieves the stethoscope from his shoulder and bends toward me. "Who knows how much smoke you inhaled last night. Lean forward and please slip your arms out of your robe."

He rests a warm hand on my shoulder, and I shiver as he places the stethoscope's bell on my back, the fabric of my gown being quite thin.

Who am I kidding?

When he asks me to take a deep breath, all I can produce is a shallow inhalation. He removes the bell, blows on it, and taps it with a finger. "Let's try that again." He replaces it on my back, and I repeat the breath, a bit deeper this time.

Get a grip, Ruby.

After a few more attempts, he seems satisfied that everything sounds as it should. He rises and drapes the stethoscope over his shoulder, while I slip my arms into my robe. He smiles, "I have to say, I'm impressed with your recovery."

This is good news, however my stomach sinks that our moment of closeness has ended. "Can I get up and about?"

"That depends on what you mean by 'about.' As far as I can tell, you don't need to stay in bed. But you do need to take it easy and rest as soon as you feel tired."

"I'm relieved to hear that." My attention momentarily shifts to the notebook on the nightstand.

"You say all the right things, but I can see that the wheels are turning. If it's Mr. Graham—"

"Actually, it's my cousin, Dottie." I share the details of her disappearance and what we know so far.

Compassion and concern fill his eyes. "I can't imagine what this has been like for you and your family. If it were my loved one, I wouldn't rest until I found them. Howev—"

"There's always a 'however.'" I roll my eyes.

"Yes, I suppose it may seem like that," he chuckles. "HOWEVER, you cannot take care of others when you fail to take care of yourself. I've learned that lesson the hard way."

"You sound like my uncle." That's where the comparison ends.

"He's a wise man." Dr. Armstrong locks eyes with me. "Miss Ray, it's imperative that you don't overexert yourself. Head trauma is a serious business. That being said, if you feel up to making phone calls or riding in the car with your uncle, then go ahead. But if you feel pain, dizziness, or lethargy, immediately return to your bed. And absolutely no driving."

"Yes, Dr. Armstrong."

"Please call me 'Sam.'" Now he blushes.

"Only if you call me 'Ruby.'"

CHAPTER 21

A quick knock on the door startles me. "Come in."

I roll my head from side to side. My neck is stiff from falling asleep in a seated position while making notes after Sam left. *Sam.* I look down at the flowers starting to fade on my lap. *When was the last time a man brought me flowers?* This is no time for romantic daydreaming, but I find the thought of him fills me with warmth and brings a smile to my lips.

"How'd it go with Dr. Armstrong?" Uncle Charles settles himself at the end of my bed.

"Very well. He gave me the all clear to get up and about."

Uncle Charles regards me skeptically.

"Okay, he did mention a few restrictions," I confess.

"Such as?"

"I must return to bed if I feel dizzy, fatigued, or experience pain."

He raises an eyebrow. "And?" He knows me well.

"And no driving," I sigh with frustration. "Didn't Dr. Armstrong mention this to you when he left?"

"He did," Uncle Charles admits. "But I wanted to make sure you really heard his instructions."

I roll my eyes. "Yes, yes. I heard him. And I promise to follow his instructions to the letter."

"That's what I want to hear."

I reach beside me and pick up the notebook. It's time for action. "Did you make any headway with Dottie's friends?"

Given the expression on his face, I immediately know the answer. "None were home. I would imagine they're all at church. It is Mother's Day after all."

"I figured as much." I open the notebook and begin to peruse my notes from earlier. "I'd like to talk to Earl's aunt and try to reach his parents."

"I'll tell you what," Uncle Charles offers. "Why don't you get dressed, and I'll drive you wherever you think we should go. I imagine we'll fare better if we visit in person."

"Thank you. Hopefully by the time I'm ready, folks will have returned home." I really do need a bath. My earlier ablutions did little to rid myself of the smoke clinging to my body.

"Would you put these in water for me?" I pass him the bouquet.

Without saying a word, he inhales their subtle fragrance and smirks at me.

I blush, my cheeks most likely matching the hue of the blooms, and rise from my bed.

"Ruby, the police are here!" Jack charges into my room. Thankfully I am fully dressed and finishing up with my hair. I would've liked to wash away the acrid stench from my locks, but there is really no time. Instead, I settled for a spritz of *Habanita*, the fragrance supposedly used by flappers to cover the smell of cigarette smoke. Elizabeth gave it to me when she broke up with one of her exes a few years ago. Apparently, he presented a bottle to all of his girlfriends, some at the same time.

"Slow down there!" I command. "I'll join them when I'm good and ready."

Jack's eyes round with an expression of awe. "Gees Ruby! You don't seem nervous at all."

"I have no reason to feel nervous. I've done nothing wrong." I soften my tone. "Would you please ask them to give me five minutes?"

"You got it Ruby!" He bounds from the room.

I sink into my chair and prop my feet on the ottoman. Closing my eyes, I take three deep breaths, making sure that my abdomen fully expands with each inhalation. I tilt my head from side to side and roll my shoulders. Now I feel calm and ready to handle the police's interrogation, for I harbor no illusion that this will be a pleasant chat.

"…that storm the other day?" Uncle Charles has a knack for small talk, and I appreciate that he's keeping them occupied.

"We were stretched thin, that's for sure." Sergeant Blockhurst's tone is polite, nothing like the condescension I experienced yesterday afternoon. "Especially with those crates of oranges at Spadra and Wilshire. Kept us busy for quite some—" He stops abruptly and rises from the sofa when he hears me step down from the stairs.

"Please, sit back down." I motion to the sergeant, my uncle, and another officer, all of whom are now standing as I enter the living room.

Once they've settled and I've claimed a seat across from Uncle Charles' chair, he remarks, "Ruby, Sergeant Blockhurst and Officer Thompson are here to ask you some questions about last night."

"Sergeant Blockhurst. Officer Thompson." I nod to both men and recognize the younger officer as the guard outside Frank's door last night. Thankfully he's no longer cradling his baton. He must find me less of a threat than an unconscious man. "How can I help you?" I ask amiably.

The sergeant lowers his wiry brows as he scrutinizes my lack of apprehension. "Young lady, I have a lot of questions for you." He shakes a small spiral-bound notebook in my direction.

"Of course, sergeant." I smile pleasantly. I refuse to kowtow or be intimidated. "I would imagine that you do."

"Hmm. Yes. Well…" Flustered, he coughs into a stubby fist.

Uncle Charles winks at me, and I suppress a grin.

Once composed, Sergeant Blockhurst continues, "As I was saying, I have a lot of questions for you. Starting with the structure on Mr. Baker's property that burned last night."

I nod for him to continue.

"Why was your automobile," he refers to his notes, "A black Balboa, license plate number 137-524, found parked next to the structure this morning?"

"Because I drove it to the shed last night and was brought to the hospital later by some kind bystanders, thus leaving it there overnight."

"What was the purpose of your visit to the structure last night?" He scribbles while asking the follow-up question.

"I was there at the behest of a client."

His head snaps up. "Client?"

"Yes, sergeant. Somewhat like yours, my occupation involves investigations."

"What do you mean 'my occupation?'"

"Well, I'm an inquiry agent or, as some would say, a private investigator. I handle all manner of discreet inquiries for those who hire my services," I explain.

Sergeant Blockhurst's lips purse with distaste and his eyelids lower with disbelief. "Come now, young lady. You expect me to believe that people pay YOU to investigate things for them?"

Uncle Charles clears his throat. "Yes, as a matter of fact they do, and she is quite skilled at her work."

The sergeant glares in the direction of my uncle, then jots a few notes. "Fine." Once finished, he releases a deep breath and turns toward me once more. "What were you doing for your 'client' in Mr. Baker's orchard?"

"I was looking in the shed for something that had gone missing."

"And what, pray tell, were you looking for?"

"I cannot answer that," I state in a matter-of-fact manner.

He scowls, "Cannot or will not?"

"Both, I suppose," I reply candidly. "As you no doubt understand, confidentiality is a cornerstone of my relationships with my clients. They trust me with sensitive and delicate information about their personal lives. I cannot and will not disclose this information to anyone without my client's consent."

"And you, no doubt, understand that as a police officer I can demand that you answer my questions," he barks.

"Actually, Sergeant Blockhurst, without a court order you cannot command me to tell you anything about my clients," I reply calmly, while internally I am starting to seethe.

Officer Thompson emits a choking sound. So focused upon the disagreeable sergeant, I had quite forgotten that he was sitting there. Thankfully, the disruption gives me a moment to regulate my own emotions.

"Sergeant Blockhurst," I temper my tone, "I have every desire to cooperate with your investigation as much as I am able. You must understand, however, that I will not be able to answer all of your questions due to the nature of my work."

"Very well," he relents, knowing that my remark about the court order is correct. "What can you tell me about your visit to the structure last night?"

At this point, I describe what I observed during my search of the structure, while withholding details regarding the copper pipe and grain. I realize I will eventually have to mention these but do not wish to implicate Frank at this time. I continue my narrative until Officer Thompson clears his throat to interrupt.

"Ma'am, are you saying that someone set the fire and then hit you over the head?"

Sergeant Blockhurst shoots him a dirty look. He's meant to be the person asking the questions.

"Yes, officer. It is my belief that the fire was started intentionally, and that the culprit struck my head from behind." I turn so they can see swelling still evident at the site of the injury.

Officer Thompson whistles.

"That's enough, Thompson!" Sergeant Blockhurst turns toward me. "What happened after you were assaulted?"

Without disclosing the identity of Alejandro, Josefina, and their children, I vaguely describe wandering through the orchard away from the burning shed until finally being picked up and taken to the hospital by kind strangers. Given the skull trauma, the officers accept my explanation, however incomplete.

"Miss Ray," the sergeant's face softens. His opinion of me seems to have improved somewhat after my harrowing tale. "Do you know the identity of the person who struck you?"

"Yes, sergeant. Based upon his voice, as well as what I could see of him when he was carrying me away from the fire, I believe that Floyd Phillips, or 'Fipps' as he is commonly known, is the man who assaulted me."

The sergeant and officer simultaneously jump at the name, and the sergeant states, "We are familiar with Mr. Phillips. Thompson, I want you to call this in immediately and tell the station we will be a while longer." His attention returns to me. "There is more we have to discuss."

"Yes, there is, sergeant," I agree.

"Tell me about your discovery of Mr. Frank Graham."

"What would you like to know?" *Here we go again.*

"When and where exactly did you find Mr. Graham?" He flips through his notebook. "I could not locate that information in the ambulance or hospital records."

I take a deep breath. "Approximately 6:30 yesterday morning at Mr. Baker's walnut shed." They're going to figure that out at some point.

His posture rigid, the sergeant's scowl returns. "Why didn't you mention this sooner?"

I reply with a question. "Sir, have I not answered the questions you've posed?"

"You have," he concedes. "But this development changes things."

"I understand and fully intended to mention it."

Somewhat mollified, he probes, "Why on earth did you visit the shed so early yesterday?"

"A good question," I nod. "The night before, I received a tip that I might find what I was looking for at the shed. Of course, I wanted to search the premises at first light. As I wandered around the structure, I found Mr. Graham lying alongside the shed toward the back."

Sergeant Blockhurst flips through his notes. "According to the records, he was unconscious when he arrived at the hospital and, as of the last time I checked, he has not regained consciousness."

"Yes, he was unconscious when I discovered him."

"Did he come round at all when you were with him? Did he say why he was there?"

"No sir."

"He arrived at the hospital with a few items in his pockets. Were any other objects left there at the site?"

"A mason jar was lying nearby in the tall grass. Also, the Graham's automobile was parked behind the shed." If they weren't damaged in the fire, they'll no doubt find the glassware and tire marks when they return to the shed to investigate further. I don't mention the keys for the time being. After all, his question was regarding objects "left" at the shed.

Who am I kidding? It's a lie of omission.

Blockhurst vigorously dots an "i" in his notepad and looks up. "Other than your vehicle, there was no other vehicle present when we were called out to the shed this morning. What happened to the Graham's automobile?"

"When I returned to the shed yesterday evening, their car was missing."

"Do you know if Frank's relations picked it up?"

"No, they definitely did not."

His left eyebrow raises sharply. "How can you be certain?"

"I visited the hospital twice yesterday to check on Frank and spoke with both Miss Graham, his sister, and Miss Holmes, their roommate."

"Is there anything else you can tell me about your visits to the shed?"

"Actually, a few things."

He nods for me to continue.

"First, on my way to the shed yesterday morning, I saw a red motorcycle turn right onto Bastanchury from the dirt road leading to the shed."

Without looking up from his notes, the sergeant breaks from recording my testimony and rolls his hand for me to continue.

"I believe that Fipps was driving the motorcycle."

His eyes meet mine. "How do you know this? You recognized him?"

"No sir. He was wearing a helmet and goggles and was a fair distance away. However, Miss Holmes confirmed that he drives a red motorcycle, and given the circumstances, I deduced that it must have been Fipps."

"Makes sense." After a moment he catches up on his notetaking. "What else did you want to mention?"

"After the ambulance left with Frank, I looked around the grounds and peeked inside the shed through the space between the two doors. They were chained with a padlock so I couldn't go inside."

"And what did you see?"

"Well, the light was quite dim, but I was able to make out the shape of several large objects a few feet high, each covered with a tarp or sheet."

"Any idea what these objects were?"

Not ready to share my hunch about this quite yet, I fail to answer his question directly. "When I returned later, the doors were unlocked, and the objects had been cleared out."

At this point, Officer Thompson returns wearing a "what did I miss" expression. Failing to receive anything other than a curt nod from the sergeant, he returns to his seat and mumbles, "What's up with Baker's orchard anyway? First the cult thing, now this..."

With everything going on, I had forgotten about the report of Baker's employee, Bert Lemming, in the paper. I'm curious. "Officer Thompson, what exactly was found last month in the orchard?"

Pleased with my attention, the young man straightens his posture. "I was on the scene, so I saw it with my own eyes. There was a silk mat marked with weird symbols, candles—"

"Button your lip, Thompson!" Sergeant Blockhurst turns toward me. "Is there anything further you'd like to add, Miss Ray?"

Uncle Charles and I quickly look at one another before I reply, "Nothing regarding my visits to the walnut shed yesterday. However—"

As both officers begin to rise, Uncle Charles jumps in. "We need to talk about the disappearance of my daughter, Dottie."

Sergeant Blockhurst rolls his eyes and sinks back onto the sofa. "Yes, I suppose we do."

I admire my uncle's equanimity, as I know he'd like to strangle the man. "My daughter has been missing for..." He looks at his watch. "Roughly thirty-six hours."

"I understand your worry, Mr. Ray." The sergeant holds up both hands. "But until she has been unaccounted for—"

"For forty-eight hours!" Uncle Charles' patience is wearing thin. "Yes, yes, I've already been told that. But you need to realize that my daughter is a good girl. She's an honor student. She's never been into any sort of trouble. And she's always home by curfew."

"Sir, you'd be surprised how often we hear similar stories from parents at wit's end because their children have forgotten to mention they're staying over at a friend's house." Unwilling to bend but with a tone of placation, he queries, "What exactly would you have us do right now?"

"I'd like for you to look for her." Uncle Charles palms his face and leans forward. "I don't know. Start talking to her friends. Ask around..."

"Sergeant, she's not the only one missing," I interject. "At least two other students are unaccounted for, and we suspect there may be a fourth."

With a sharp flip, Blockhurst reopens his notebook. "What are the names of these kids?"

"Polly Baker, Leo Taliaferro, and Earl Adams."

"Mr. and Mrs. Taliaferro came to the station yesterday," Officer Thompson remarks.

"We haven't heard anything from the other parents." The sergeant looks piercingly from me to Uncle Charles. "Why didn't Mr. Baker mention this when I spoke with him earlier about the shed?"

"Perhaps he figures you're already working on it?" I offer unconvincingly, unwilling to mention Mr. Baker's belief that Polly ran off with Leo.

With finality, the sergeant closes the notebook and tucks it into the breast pocket of his uniform. "Look here, Mr. Ray, Miss Ray, we are stretched thin with this fire and everything you just told me about Mr. Graham. We don't have the manpower to launch an unwarranted search for kids who are, no doubt, just fine."

"Now see here—" Uncle Charles jumps to his feet.

Sergeant Blockhurst pats him on the shoulder. "I understand. I'm a father myself. And if your daughter has not returned by 10 or 11 tonight, please contact us so a formal missing person's report can be filed." He walks toward the door and turns. "But I'm sure that won't be necessary."

CHAPTER 22

"Clearly, we're on our own," I sigh dejectedly.

"Hmm, hmm," deep in thought Uncle Charles mumbles as he absentmindedly runs his fingers through his hair.

"Let's head over to the cafe to talk with Thelma. Hopefully she or Earl's parents can shed some light on where the kids may have gone." I leap to a standing position and immediately regret my rapid rise as the room begins to spin around me.

Uncle Charles notices my weaving and leans forward to steady me. "Easy there. You've got quite an egg on the back of your head."

Gingerly rubbing my scalp, I murmur, "I'm not likely to forget that anytime soon."

"Take your time gathering your things, and I'll meet you at the car."

Heading toward my bedroom I hear, "Ruby you were swell!" Legs outstretched, Jack slouches on the hall floor fiddling with his harmonica.

"Were you eavesdropping?" I quiz him playfully.

"Aw, come on Ruby! You knew I'd be listening."

I laugh, "Of course I did."

He follows as I enter my room. "You didn't let him bully you, not even for a second."

"I knew his game going into it. I've dealt with him before." I grab my notebook from the nightstand and place it into an empty handbag. Glancing around the room, I ask Jack, "Do you know where your father put the bag of my things? They were in a grocery sack."

Jack finds the bag on the floor next to the wingback chair and continues his commentary regarding my conversation with the sergeant. "What's the deal with that old shed anyway? What's it got to do with Dottie?"

"That is an excellent question." I feel as though it's all related, but I just can't fit the pieces together.

"Jack, can you get a hat box for me? The white one." I point to the top of my armoire.

"Sure thing, Ruby." He scoots the chair from my desk to the wardrobe and climbs up. He won't need the boost much longer, as he's almost taller than I am.

I mull over the stack of hats nested in the cardboard container and select the largest cloche of the bunch. Hopefully it won't put too much pressure on my wound, and it should cast a shadow over the scratches on my face, as well. After completing a mental checklist to ensure my handbag contains everything that I'll need this morning, I turn toward Jack. "Promise me that you will not leave the house until your father and I return. I know you'll be alone, but it's important that someone is here to answer the phone."

Jack salutes good-naturedly. "You got it Ruby."

When I've almost reached the door, I pivot and quickly stride back to embrace Jack, sending a silent prayer out to the universe. *Please, please keep him safe, and please bring Dottie home.*

Cruising down Spadra, I'm struck by how normal everything looks. Families pile into their motorcars after church, no doubt off to Mother's Day picnics or luncheons. Vehicles line the road signaling that the stores and restaurants are running at full capacity. I want to shout, "Stop! Don't you realize that children are missing?"

"I hope Thelma can get away for a moment to speak with us." Uncle Charles scans left and right for a parking space.

"She may be as worried as we are. I'm sure she'll be able to step away."

At that moment, a Roadster begins to back out ahead of us with two young children in the rumble seat. They wave to an elderly couple on the sidewalk. Uncle Charles brakes and extends an arm out the window to signal his turn.

"Well, fortune finally seems to be smiling upon us." He skillfully slides his car into the vacant space.

Closing my door with a solid thud, I spy a queue of hungry patrons snaking its way around the corner of McFarland's Cafe. "Looks like our luck has turned."

A portly man in a Homburg unplugs the cigar lodged in mouth and mutters, "Hey, what's the big idea?" as Uncle Charles charges past the line.

I glance back over my shoulder and mouth, "I'm sorry," while desperately trying to keep up.

Once inside, a young waitress glares at us through the thick circular lenses of her glasses. "There is a line, sir. Maybe you didn't notice."

"My apologies, miss." Uncle Charles removes his hat. "It's something of an emergency. We need to speak with Thelma."

"I got this, Lucille." Thelma tucks a pencil behind her ear and directs her attention toward us. "How can I help ya?"

I survey the congested space. "Is there a place we can talk privately? It's about your nephew."

Color drains from her flushed face. "Take a seat in the back. There's an empty table."

Cries of outrage erupt as Thelma calls to Lucille, "I'm taking a break." In answer to her coworker's confused countenance, she lowers her volume, "It's about Earl."

Lucille quickly nods and tries to appease several angry customers.

"Can I get you anything? Coffee?"

"No thank you, Thelma. Please have a seat." Uncle Charles gestures toward the chair across from him.

"Don't mind if I do," she sighs while lowering herself onto a pillow tied to the wooden seat.

"Whew! What a morning!" Thelma rolls her shoulders. "So, what's all this about Earl?"

With a look, Uncle Charles signals for me to lead the conversation.

"Thelma, we're here because we are having trouble locating my cousin Dottie."

Caution flashes in Thelma's eyes. "What's this got to do with my Earl?" she asks protectively.

"It's not what you're thinking." I raise both hands to quell her alarm. "We know that Dottie and Earl are friends, and we're hoping he can help us."

Her shoulders and expression soften. "Okay…what do you need from me?"

"Well, for starters, how can we get in touch with Earl?"

Uncle Charles interjects, "While calling Dottie's friends earlier, I asked the operator to connect me with the Adams' residence, but I reached the wrong household."

"Well, no wonder," Thelma chuckles. "Earl's stepdad is Jake Fisker. Not Adams. My sister Hattie married him when Earl was ten."

"That certainly explains my difficulty."

"Thelma, when did you last see Earl?" I inquire.

She appears to mull this over for a moment. "Hmm. Well, I guess it was Friday night. About 10:30."

"Where was this, and was he with anyone?"

"On a Friday night? Of course he was with someone," she clucks. "He was here with a few kids after the picture show. A waiter needed me to trade a shift," she explains.

"Was there a girl, slight build, about five feet six with dark hair cut to about here," he motions at his chin.

"I'm really sorry, but I couldn't say," Thelma apologizes sympathetically. "There were so many kids here that night, and they all looked the same to me."

"Of course," Uncle Charles nods.

"Thelma, have your sister or brother-in-law voiced any concerns since then over his whereabouts?" I query.

Head tilting to the side, she slowly nods, "Now that you mention it, when I stopped by their place yesterday afternoon, Jake asked me to drop him off at the police station."

Both Uncle Charles and I lean forward with interest.

Thelma explains, "I guess Earl left Jake's car over on Ellis Place Friday night, and it was towed."

"You know, I think I saw him there yesterday. Is he a mechanic?"

"Yep. He works at the Firestone station."

"Did your sister or brother-in-law say anything about Earl coming home Friday night?" I probe further.

"Nope. But then I wouldn't expect them to." She glances past us toward the other tables.

"Why is that, Thelma?"

Her eyes return to Uncle Charles and me. "You gotta understand. My sister loves Earl with all her heart, but with six little ones in the house and another on the way, she can't go worrying about Earl all the time." She sniffs, "He is an adult, after all."

I sense that there isn't much more we can learn from Thelma, so I close with the question, "Where do Jessie and Hattie live?"

She grips the pencil from behind her ear and scribbles an address on a blank sheet from her order tablet, which she quickly rips off and pushes across the table. I tuck the slip in my handbag. "I appreciate it."

My Uncle extends a hand and helps Thelma to her feet. "Thank you so much for taking the time to speak with us."

"Especially with how busy you are today." I pat her gently on the shoulder.

"Not to worry," she waves dismissively. "I hope your daughter turns up, Mr. Ray." She smiles empathetically.

"Thank you, Thelma."

She adds, "And I hope that Earl hasn't been up to mischief. He's a good boy, but you know how these kids can be."

We say our goodbyes and head directly for the door, all the while avoiding the scowls of the peeved diners.

"Remember when Orangethorpe became a city several years ago?" I remind Uncle Charles as we head over to the Fisker's house located just off of Orangethorpe Avenue.

"What a brouhaha was made about that," he chuckles.

"I was busy with my studies at the Junior College and don't remember much about it. Tell me again why they voted to incorporate?"

"Oh, there was a very good reason." Uncle Charles motions for another driver to proceed before turning right onto the relatively empty avenue. "Essentially the city of Fullerton wanted to annex land there for a sewer farm."

"Oh dear! No wonder!" I imagine the stench when the west wind kicks up.

"It was a clever move. In the end, Fullerton conceded to a sewer line directly to the ocean in '23, so Orangethorpe voted to unincorporate."

Just past Nicholas Avenue, I point to a small unpaved drive leading to a few boxy single-story dwellings. "I think we turn left here."

An array of children's playthings in varying states of decrepitude litter an unkempt yard in front of one of the homes. My uncle comments, "This must be it."

The high-pitched wail of a greatly displeased toddler carries through our open windows, as we stop on a section of broken pavement nearby.

"No car out front," I observe. "It might be best if I speak to her without you. Mrs. Fisker may be home alone with the children."

He nods in agreement. "I'll wait here."

I haven't even made it to the porch when I'm nearly toppled by two squabbling youngsters. "It's mine! Give it back!" They race through the yard.

"For Pete's sake, Michael! Bobby! You almost knocked down this nice lady!" Mrs. Fisker shifts a tearful tot across her swollen belly from one hip to the other so she can open the misaligned screen door. "Sorry about that." A blanket of exhaustion seems to envelop this woman's entire body.

"There's no need to apologize, Mrs. Fisker." I place a foot to stop the screen door, so she doesn't have to continue holding it open. "I can see that you have a lot going on so let me get straight to it."

"Some Mother's Day," she nods and snorts bitterly.

"Quite," I agree. I extend a hand but draw it back as her arms are laden with her sniffling bundle. "I'm Ruby Ray. My cousin Dottie is a friend of Earl's. That's why I'm here."

"Earl's not here, Miss Ray." Her droopy eyelids shift toward the dim interior of her home.

"I figured as much."

Bemused, Mrs. Fisker asks wearily, "What's this about? I really should be getting this one down for a nap."

At this point one of her neighbors, a scarecrow of a man dressed in a faded cardigan, wanders out his front door with a watering can and strolls to a flowering hedge that separates their properties.

"May I come in? It would be better if we discuss this indoors." This is a private matter, but I would also prefer that Mrs. Fisker is seated when I break the news that her son may be missing.

"What about that man you arrived with? Does he want to come in?" She motions toward Uncle Charles.

"He's fine waiting in the car." I give him a wave to show all is well.

I follow Mrs. Fisker into the front room and glimpse three more of her offspring, two girls who look to be about six or seven years old are reading to a smaller child who is clearly older than the toddler in Mrs. Fisker's arms, but younger than the two girls. The oldest child pauses mid-sentence as they all gape at me with curious, open faces.

"Girls, please take these two into your room and get them settled for their nap." She passes the toddler, now calm, to the older girl, and all four disappear down a hall toward the back part of the house. A door closes.

"You know, this is the first moment all day I haven't had a child attached to me." She looks down at her round midsection and chuckles, "Well except this one. He's got a couple more months to go."

"Mrs. Fisker, will your husband be back soon to help you?"

At this she belts out a laugh, "Jake? That'll be the day. He's with the guys from work, same as every Sunday afternoon."

She sinks onto the sofa and motions for me to take a seat in an armchair covered with a crocheted blanket. I settle upon the cozy chair and place my handbag beside me on the wide seat. I decide to keep my hat on. I don't want her to see my injury.

"Is there no one to help you with these little ones?" My heart goes out to her. I'm certain that if she were to lie down, she'd fall into a deep sleep within seconds.

"Earl's great with the kids, but as I said he's not here right now." She begins to rise, "Can I offer you some—"

"Oh, please don't go to any trouble." I encourage her to sit back down. "Can I get you something?"

"I could do with a glass of water…but where are my manners? You're a guest. You shouldn't be waiting on me."

"It's my pleasure, Mrs. Fisker." I am already heading to the kitchen, which I can see through a door that is ajar.

Even though the kitchen is shabby with scuff marks across the lower cabinets and a chip in the side of the sink, it is clearly well tended by Mrs. Fisker. Not a single dirty dish sits on the counter and not a crumb mars the surface of the oilcloth covering the table. I easily locate a clear glass and fill it from the tap. A window above the sink looks out onto the backyard, and the two boys are twisting among the sheets pegged to the clotheslines, both in pursuit of a calico cat. I'm tempted to say something, but I don't want Mrs. Fisker to worry about soiled linen at the moment. In fact, I'd rather not burden her with the disappearance of her son, but she needs to know.

Upon entering the front room, I notice that her eyes have closed, and she's beginning to lean to the left. Nevertheless, at the sound of my footsteps on the hardwood floor, she flinches and straightens up, eyes wide open. "Oh my. I started to doze."

Handing her the water, I reply, "I'm so sorry to wake you. It is important that I speak with you, however."

"Of course. Of course," she repeats.

"Thelma gave us your address. We stopped by the cafe to see if she knew where we might find Earl."

"My dear Thelma! She's a rock, that one. I don't know where I'd be without her," Mrs. Fisker beams.

"She spoke very warmly of you as well."

"When Earl's daddy died, she moved us into her home, small as it is. He left us broke." She sips from the glass.

"I'm so sorry for your loss," I offer. "That must have been devastating for both you and Earl."

"Thank you for that, but actually it was a blessing."

Unsure how to respond to this, I ask, "How old was Earl?"

"He was eight." She waves a hand toward me. "Please don't think I'm cold-hearted. It's just that my first husband was a cruel man."

"Ah, I see." My work experience over the years has given me great empathy for the women who suffer at the hands of those who are meant to be their protectors.

"He passed out on the train tracks, if you can believe it. Didn't hear the train." She takes another sip. "I married Jake two years later. He may not be great with the kids, but he loves me and would never lay a finger on me or our children."

"I understand." Looking at the pendulum clock on the wall, I realize that it's nearly 1:45. This day is slipping away from us, and we still have no leads. I'm determined that not another night will pass without Dottie safely home. "Mrs. Fisker, when did you last see Earl?"

"Please call me Hattie." She appears to give my question some thought. "I guess it must have been Friday evening. He asked Jake if he could borrow the car. That's a whole other story, that car..."

"And please call me Ruby," I return before continuing. "Thelma told us that your husband had to pick it up at the police station. In fact I think I may have run into him there yesterday when he entered the station."

"It was odd that Earl didn't return it. He's usually very good about that and had to know how angry Jake would be if he didn't bring it home Friday night."

"Any idea why he hasn't been home since then?" I inquire gently.

"He must have stayed over with friends. I'm sure he told me his plans, but in all the chaos around here it slipped my mind. To be honest, my brain goes all fuzzy when I'm pregnant." She yawns. "I thought he'd be back this morning, maybe watch the kids so I can rest today, it being Mother's Day and all."

I wish I didn't have to break the news to this exhausted woman, but the situation calls for it. "Hattie, I'm so sorry to tell you this, but my cousin Dottie has been missing since Friday night, and we have reason to believe she was with Earl the last time she was seen."

Panic flashes across her face. "Do you think something has happened to them?"

"Unfortunately, I do, Hattie. Two other students are missing as well."

Her eyes fill with tears. "Oh, Ruby! This is terrible!" She draws deep breaths and shakes her head as though trying to clear her mind. Reaching into a pocket of her threadbare pinafore, she withdraws a bleached white handkerchief and dabs her eyes.

I lean forward and pat her knee. "Hattie, I'm distraught about this as well, but I'm hoping that between the two of us we can figure out someone who may know their whereabouts."

She nods, "Yes. Me too."

Thinking back to the hailstorm on Friday, I recall a detail I'd forgotten. "Doesn't Earl tune pianos for people?"

"That's right. He's a genius with anything musical. Can pick up an instrument for the first time and play it with ease within minutes."

"Interesting." *This fits, but how?*

"Thelma has a piano, and when we moved in, Earl couldn't stay away from it. He was playing chords with both hands within a week all on his own."

"Is that so?" The connection is hovering in the periphery of my mind but darts away just as I zero in on it.

Maternal pride compels her to continue. "Yep. He started playing by ear, but Thelma taught him what she'd learned from the lessons when we were kids. Then when he entered school, one of the teachers noticed his talent and worked with him after school for years. He learned to play horns, stringed instruments, drums, just about everything. But the guitar is his passion."

I let go of my distraction and focus more fully on what she is saying. "Does he perform locally?"

Sharing Earl's gift has energized Hattie, and she scarcely resembles the drained woman I met on the porch. "Yes! There's a little band he put together, and he sometimes plays the organ or piano for churches."

"Now that's something! Did he have anything scheduled this morning for any of the Mother's Day services?"

"Maybe. I know that he worked on the piano at the Methodist Church Friday just before that downpour. I guess their piano just hasn't been the same since it was moved to their new building last year"

I retrieve my notebook and jot a note to visit the church next. "Can you tell me the names of any of his band members?"

"I'm afraid not. They never come over here, as you can imagine." She looks toward the window and shakes her head. The boys are at it again.

"How about teachers? Is there anyone at the high school that has encouraged Earl with his music?"

"Yes, the music teacher has been wonderful to Earl. He dropped out of high school for a while because he wanted to help out around here as much as he could. But Mrs. Hopper encouraged him to graduate so he could study music composition in college."

"Composition?"

"He writes songs all the time. She said he has a real talent for it." She mulls something over for a moment. "There's also Mr. Mains."

I nearly topple out of my chair. "Mr. Wallace Mains?"

"I think that's his first name. Anyway, Earl's always been pretty good at math, and Mr. Mains told him to join the Pythagorean Club. Now that I'm telling you this, I remember him mentioning a meeting yesterday afternoon. You should talk to Mr. Mains. Maybe he knows something."

"Mr. Mains is definitely on my list," I mutter.

"Maybe Earl's with one of the kids from the club," she suggests.

"Oh, I definitely think he's with other Pythagoreans. All four students who are missing belong to that club."

Hattie tears up at the word *missing*. "Ruby, please find my Earl. He's my sunshine. I don't know what I'd do without him," she sobs.

I stand and walk to sit beside her. With a hand on her shoulder, I try to offer what reassurance I can. "I promise I am doing everything I can to bring those kids home. In the meantime, I encourage you to contact the police about Earl's disappearance."

She blows her nose into the handkerchief while nodding. "I'll go next door and use the neighbor's phone as soon as you leave."

"Please call me if he returns home or if you hear anything." I give her one of my business cards and bid her farewell.

Walking to the car, I hear her call out the back door, "Michael! Bobby! Get away from those sheets and come in at once! I need to go next door to make a phone call, and I don't need any more grief from you today."

CHAPTER 23

Wave upon wave of fear, hope, and disappointment send our minds tumbling to and fro during our drive home. At the corner of Pomona and Commonwealth, I interrupt the oppressive silence before Uncle Charles drives past the newly constructed Methodist Church, a Spanish Colonial style building that sits on the corner. "I should run inside to see if, by some longshot, Earl played during today's Mother's Day service."

Uncle Charles turns right and glides to a stop across the street. He removes his handkerchief and quickly dabs the corners of his eyes. "I'll wait here."

My heart sinks further as I look both ways before crossing. As much as my stomach twists with anxiety, I cannot begin to understand the terror my uncle must be feeling. I pass under a lovely rosette of oblong hearts and enter the portico of the church through the central arch. I pull the handle of each door. *Locked.*

"I'll have a go at the back door," I bellow across the street to Uncle Charles, who waves me on through the open window.

While walking up Pomona, I spy the crenelated red brick of the lovely gothic sanctuary across the street that housed this faith community until very recently. Despite being built a mere twenty years earlier, the original chapel feels hundreds of years old. It's a pity that the congregation outgrew the space. I've long felt that its flying buttresses and stained glass make it seem somehow "holy."

Turning into a gravel strewn parking area behind the new cathedral, I realize that there's no need to continue knocking on doors. The lot is empty, so I retrace my steps to the car.

"Well, it was worth a try," Uncle Charles remarks.

My head pounds as I nod, "Let's just go home. Hopefully someone has called." I could use another dose of headache powder right about now.

"Dottie?" The front door flies open, and Jack sprints toward the carport as we exit the vehicle.

Uncle Charles catches him mid-stride and pulls him into a hug. "Fraid not, sport."

"But you're back so soon." He looks at his wristwatch. "It's only 2:00. I didn't think you'd be back till you found her."

I pat his back. "I'm disappointed too, Jack. There's nowhere else for us to go at the moment, so we came home to make some phone calls."

"Speaking of calls, are there any messages?" Uncle Charles asks.

My cousin kicks the turf and shakes his bowed head. "Not a peep."

I wrap an arm around his shoulders. "It must have been hard waiting here all by yourself."

"Yeah," he mutters slowly.

"Tell you what." Uncle Charles ruffles Jack's hair. "The next time we head out, you can ride along."

Jack's face lights up, "Really?"

"On one condition."

"Anything," he exclaims enthusiastically.

"If we need to go speak with someone, you must stay in the car and wait." Uncle Charles instructs.

Jack's face falls slightly, but he rallies nonetheless. "It beats sitting around here doing nothing."

"Uncle Charles, I'd much rather have Jack with us, but who will answer the phone if someone calls?" I query.

He considers this then declares, "We can ask the operator to forward the calls to Vincent next door. He won't mind."

"Great idea!" Once inside I drop my handbag on a side table and retrieve my notebook. "Speaking of calls, I should try to reach Mrs. Hopper. She's the music teacher that's close with Earl. I also need to touch base with the Taliaferros."

"Sounds good. I'll head over to see Vincent about the phone." Uncle Charles turns toward Jack, "And I think it's time we put your talents to good use. How'd you like to help me look through Dottie's room for clues?"

"Are you sure, Uncle Charles? What about her privacy?" I question.

"Needs must. We'll apologize to her once she's safely home." He calls toward Jack, who is already thumping up the stairs, "Not a toe in Dottie's room until I return. Understand?"

Jack salutes but continues his march. "Got it."

"Good afternoon operator. Please connect me with the Hopper residence."

A disembodied voice informs me, "There are three Hopper residences nearby. Do you have a full name?"

"Oh dear! I hadn't thought of that." I think through my options. "Well, the Mrs. Hopper I want to speak with is a teacher at the high school if that helps."

"Listen, ma'am, I'm new to the area. Unless I have a full name, all I can do is give you the numbers, and you can connect to each one, if you'd like."

I mull this over and decide not to interrupt Mother's Day for these families with so little to go on. "I'll call back if I get more information."

"It's up to you, ma'am," she says dryly. "Anything else?"

"Yes, actually. Can you connect me with the Taliaferros? Let me find their information." I flip through my notes.

"No need. There's only one of them in Fullerton." After a pause she utters, "Have a nice day."

The operator's matter-of-fact tone is replaced by a frenzied, "Hello? Leo?"

"Mrs. Taliaferro, it's Ruby Ray. I'm so sorry you thought that this was Leo calling."

"Oh, Miss Ray. Please tell me you've found them," she pleads.

"I wish I could, Mrs. Taliaferro. I was calling to see if you've heard anything from Leo's friends."

"Nothing," she replies dejectedly. "No one's seen him since Friday night. And I tried the police again first thing this morning, but they put me off. Something about a fire in the orchard."

"Yes, that's a whole other story unrelated to our missing kids," I inform her.

"Have you gotten anywhere? You must have spoken with someone..."

"I'm afraid not. But I have discovered that the tally of missing students is now up to four."

"Four?! Leo, Polly, your cousin Dottie, and who else?" she inquires.

"Earl Adams. Have you heard of him?"

"Earl Adams," she repeats slowly and considers the name for a moment. "Can you hold for a moment?"

Her voice is muffled as I hear her shout, "Mattia, have you ever heard Leo mention an Earl Adams?"

She returns to our call. "I'm afraid neither my husband nor I have heard of him."

"I spoke with his mother a little while ago. Here's the thing," I lean forward as though she's sitting across from me. "All four kids are members of Wallace Mains' Pythagorean Club."

"So basically, they're all smart kids," she deduces.

"Exactly!" I slap a hand on the desk. "Which I find very troubling. If even one tended to get into trouble, I might believe that the others could somehow be persuaded to follow along."

"But..." she encourages me to continue.

"But I've been told by both you and Mrs. Fisker, Earl's mother, that the boys are good kids. And I know that Dottie and Polly are, as well."

"This is so out of character for them," she concurs.

"Which is precisely what we tried to tell the police."

"And look where that got us," she remarks.

"Incidentally, they were over at my house this morning about another matter, and Sergeant Blockhurst absolutely refused to look into this until they've been missing for 48 hours."

"It makes me want to curse."

"Indeed."

After a pause, she utters, "I wonder if the Bakers have gotten anywhere."

"Hmm," I grunt. "My Uncle spoke with Mr. Baker this morning. The loathsome man made it very clear that, in his opinion, the kids have run off and are hiding out."

"And Mrs. Baker? She must be frantic, even if her husband isn't concerned."

"Dottie and Polly have been friends since grammar school, and I've observed that Mrs. Baker holds Mr. Baker on a pedestal and believes whatever he tells her." Not to mention she's most likely been preoccupied with her cherished Mother's Day service.

"So what next?" She voices my thoughts.

I shake my head, even though she cannot see me. "I'm at a loss for the moment."

"So are we." Sagely, she advises, "We should keep the lines clear. Please call if you hear anything."

"Same here. Thank you, Mrs. Taliaferro."

"I've looked everywhere, Ruby, and can't find her diary anywhere!" Jack proclaims as I peek into Dottie's room.

Uncle Charles is sitting on her bed with a drawer that has been removed from her desk. He looks up, "Nothing."

"Jack, she may not even keep a diary." I advise, "Instead of focusing on a specific item, cast a wider net to see if anything jumps out at you as unusual or if the names 'Earl' or 'Leo' are written anywhere."

"But she DOES have a diary!" Jack insists.

"You seem quite certain. Why is that?" Uncle Charles gives me a meaningful look.

"Well…umm…" Jack mumbles. If he found it at some point, I'm sure Dottie's hidden it well since then.

I tap my lower lip while giving the room a visual sweep. "Watch out for 'Pythagorean Club' and 'Mains,' as well, while you're searching."

"Anything from the phone calls?" Uncle Charles asks.

"I couldn't reach Mrs. Hopper, but then I doubt she would know anything. And the Taliaferros have hit a wall with their contacts."

Meandering over to Dottie's desk, I pick up a children's book from the hanging shelf. *Anne of Green Gables* was also my favorite as a child, and I recall reading it with Dottie when she was small. I think that as a child without a mother, Dottie identified with Anne. I replace the book and find the current issues of *Scientific American* and *Popular Science* tucked next to *Stars of the Photoplay*. I chuckle at the juxtaposition.

"What's this?" Jack holds up a golden object he's found on Dottie's dresser.

Uncle Charles glances up from where he's seated. "That's Polka Dot's National Honor Society pin. It's important to her, so be careful with it."

Jack gently places it back on the dresser.

I refocus my attention to the desk's surface and reach for the stack of books I saw yesterday, starting with the Bible. Flipping to the page she has marked in Ezekiel, I read the passage adjacent to where she's written *tetramorph*. The prophet describes a vision of four creatures with four faces and four wings. I set aside the scripture and open *Quadrivium* to the inside cover where Dottie has written *vesica piscis* and *tetrad* around the drawing of a geometric form. This is all so confusing.

Once again, my head begins to throb, and my eyes glisten with tears. I sink onto the desk chair. "Uncle Charles, how long did the nurse say to wait between doses of the headache medication?"

He looks up with concern, "Four hours. Are you okay?"

I rub my forehead. "That explains it."

"Shall I mix you a powder?" He offers kindly.

I rise and head toward the door. "No need. I got it."

"You should lie down after you take the medicine," Uncle Charles suggests.

"That's not a bad idea," I concede. "That'll give me an opportunity to mull things over."

"OR you could rest," he states as though this should be obvious.

"That too," I reply to pacify him, however rest is the last thing I want to do.

My bed feels far more comfortable than it ought to, and I fear I may easily slip into slumber. I rest on my side to avoid pressure on my wound, as well as to write while reclining in bed. Closing my eyes, I take a few deep belly breaths, careful to blow them out slowly through my mouth. Once my heart has slowed and the muscles around my skull have softened, I gradually relax the rest of my body from neck to toes. I sigh and listen to a mockingbird run through its litany of calls outside. Through the shared wall between my room and Dottie's, I perceive Jack and Uncle Charles moving about. They seem to have things in hand, although I doubt they'll find anything. I was fairly thorough yesterday.

After a moment or two, I redirect my attention to my thoughts and allow them to percolate without trying to consciously reason or analyze. Words begin floating into my awareness, some of which I perceive as written in block text. *Quad, tetra, Pythagorean*, all mathematical terminology. I record these in my notebook. It can't be a coincidence that various forms of the word "four" keep surfacing, particularly since we now know that four kids are missing. As I recall, Pythagoras was the Greek mathematician who discovered the well-known eponymous formula for the hypotenuse of a right triangle. *Wasn't he also a philosopher?* I make a note to look into this and feel abashed that I don't know more. Ancient Greece was, admittedly, never a subject that held my interest during my school days. The Bible passage now fits with its reference to "four." However, the book about the lost civilization is confusing. What was it? *Mu?* A Greek letter. Perhaps that has something to do with Pythagoras. I jot these observations, as well, in the notebook.

Closing my eyes, another word surfaces. *Genius*. Mrs. Taliaferro described Leo as a "genius," as did Mrs. Fisker today when speaking about Earl. I know that many proud parents may boast about their children's talents, but I don't often hear them throw around the term "genius." Is Dottie a genius? She's highly intelligent, that's for certain, and she always gets top marks when it comes to the physical sciences, but I can't imagine Uncle Charles telling people that she's a genius. Still… And then there's Polly. Mrs. Baker was quite dismissive about Polly's mathematical prowess. However, Wallace Mains called her "gifted." And what did he say about the Pythagorean Club? "The elite among my students?" "The brightest of the bright?" All of this seems to come back to Wallace. He knows something, that's for certain. And after his cagey behavior yesterday afternoon at their house, I am deeply suspicious that he's involved with their disappearance. But if he knows where they are, why visit the Taliaferros when Leo didn't show up for the club meeting yesterday?

I complete my notes and close my eyes to rest, hoping the pounding in my head will dissipate. The next thing I know, a tap at the door awakens me.

"Come in," I swing my legs off the bed and carefully rise to a seated position. "I can't believe I dozed off! There's no time for that!"

"Don't be so hard on yourself," Uncle Charles gently admonishes. "I'm amazed you've been up and about all day with that head injury."

"What time is it?" I look at my bedside clock and, with horror, exclaim, "3:15!"

My uncle extends a hand that prevents me from jumping to my feet. "Easy there."

"But we must head over to Norma and Edith's boarding house right this minute! I have to check Wallace's room! Maybe he's even there!"

Just then, Jack bolts into the room and breathlessly announces, "Ruby, it's for you."

"I didn't even hear the phone ring," Uncle Charles remarks.

"Neither did I." Slowly standing, I grasp my notebook and follow Jack down the stairs. "Any idea who it is?"

"Some girl who knows Dottie."

For the first time in hours, hope settles upon me like a warm blanket.

"Hello, this is Ruby Ray."

"Hi, I'm Elsie Pivens. I sure hope it's okay to give you a jingle on Mother's Day. Mrs. Fisker told me to call you," a melodious contralto replies apprehensively.

"Oh, it's no trouble at all. Is this about Earl?"

"Yes, he's my boyfriend, and I've been worried sick," she declares.

So, Dottie isn't dating him.

The girl continues, "He was supposed to watch my solo at church this morning but never showed up. So, after leaving my grandma's, I asked Dad to drive me over to Earl's place to make sure he wasn't sick or something. His mom just told me no one's seen him since Friday night."

"That's right. He's gone missing along with a few other students, including my cousin Dottie." I had hoped she might be able to add something to what we already know. "When did you last see Earl?"

"Friday night at the cafe," she answers quickly.

"What time was that?" I wonder if she saw Earl before or after Nick spotted the kids by the car.

"Around 10:45?" She guesses. "We were with our band sharing fries, when Mains' Brains got up from a table and left. Earl made some pathetic excuse and followed 'em."

"Mains' Brains?" I have an idea what that might mean.

"Yeah, those smart kids in the math club. I don't know why Earl bothers with them," she huffs with irritation then suddenly changes her tone. "Oh sorry! I guess Dottie's one of 'em."

"That's alright. You must have been quite frustrated."

"And how! I couldn't believe he'd ditch us like that. And with our gig coming up…the band I mean."

"A gig?" I'm unfamiliar with the slang term.

"Yeah, we're playing at a school dance. Mrs. Hopper fixed it up."

"Who was with you? From the band?" I begin jotting notes.

"Well, there was Louie, our drummer, Rex…he plays trumpet…and Georgie who plays bass."

"Are you the singer?" She certainly has the voice for it.

"Yeah, and Earl plays just about everything else."

"So, what exactly did Earl say when he left?" I sense both Uncle Charles and Jack standing behind me, but when I look over my shoulder, they each take a step back. I don't blame them for listening.

"He said, 'Forgot I got something with these guys. See ya tomorrow.'" She releases a *tsch* sound testily. "And that was it. Haven't seen or heard from him since."

"Were you worried at all? Before speaking with Mrs. Fisker?"

"Nah, I figured he was letting me blow off some steam. Didn't want me to let him have it for being such a heel."

"That's understandable."

"But now I'm frantic. And you said other kids are missing too?" Her pitch rises.

"Yes, Dottie, Polly, and Leo. They were last seen outside Earl's car just after you saw them leave the cafe."

"Oh, that musta been before we walked to Louie and Rex's place. They've got an apartment there on Ellis. We saw Mr. Fisker's green Chevy in front of the complex, but no one else was there."

I'm familiar with the courtyard of charming bungalows built several years ago, as I had a friend who lived there. I think it's called "Rose Court."

"What time was that?" I ask.

"About 11:30. Some other kids stopped by the cafe, so we stayed for a while. Then Rex offered to drive me home. Boy, were my folks sore. I was supposed to be home by 11:00," she confesses.

So, sometime between 10:45 and 11:30 the kids disappeared. *Why didn't they take the car? Did someone pick them up on Ellis? Where could they possibly be?*

"Elsie, can you do me a favor? Would you please call the others from your band and ask if Earl's been in contact with any of them?"

"No problem, Miss Ray!" Then with a soft, girlish voice she murmurs, "Please find him."

And the call is disconnected.

CHAPTER 24

Brrring brrring

No sooner have I summarized what little I could glean from Elsie's recount to Uncle Charles and Jack, when the telephone rings urgently.

"Ray residence. This is Ruby." The receiver is still warm from my previous conversation.

"Ruby, it's Edith! Am I glad I reached you! I've been trying to call for several minutes." She is uncharacteristically agitated.

"I'm sorry, Edith. I was speaking with Elsie Pivens, Earl's girlfriend," I apologize.

"So Earl IS involved, and they're still missing?"

"Yes," I sigh despondently.

"I'm so sorry!" After a silent pause she exclaims remorsefully, "Oh Ruby! I didn't even ask how you're feeling."

"Not to worry, Edith. I'm feeling much better than last night, that's for sure, but I seem to have hit a wall with finding the kids."

"That's exactly why I'm calling!"

"What's happened?" I sit up straight in the chair at the telephone desk, while Uncle Charles and Jack move closer behind me.

"Wallace has moved out of the house!" Edith declares.

"Moved?! Did he leave anything behind? What happened?" I am stunned.

"Well, about a half an hour ago, Ann drove me home to pick up some things for Norma." She adds as an aside, "No change with Frank, unfortunately."

"I was about to ask you that." My heart sinks further.

She continues, "As we pulled up, we noticed that Wallace's car was gone, so I decided to sneak into his room to take a peek."

"The key from the begonia pot?"

"The very one. In his haste he must have forgotten about it. Anyway, when I entered the room, the drawers of the dresser and desk were all open and empty. And the closet was filled with empty hangers."

"Did he leave anything behind?" I recall the books and folders he tossed into his car window yesterday afternoon before peeling off. He must have been in the process of vacating the house even then.

"Not that I could tell, but I didn't look for very long. I tried to call you immediately. I figured you'd want to take a closer look." I hear her speak with someone else, "You don't need to stay Ann. I'll find a ride back. Thanks so much."

Meanwhile Jack takes advantage of the pause and demands, "What happened? Who left?"

Uncle Charles shushes him. "She'll tell us everything when she hangs up."

I nod toward them with my palm raised, then ask, "When do you think he left?" From her message this morning it sounded like Wallace was still home.

"I really don't know. Ann picked me up at about ten this morning, and he was still there. I heard him moving around in his room. I haven't been home since."

It's now half past three. That gave him plenty of time to clear out. "We'll be right over."

Edith is racing down the steps from the broad porch as we stop in front of the house. "I looked around a bit after we rang off and found something very strange."

I instruct my uncle and cousin, "You two wait here and keep an eye out in case Wallace returns while we examine his room."

"Righty-o, Ruby!" Jack responds enthusiastically. "Dad, I shoulda brought my binoculars," I hear him say as I follow Edith into the house.

She leads me through a proper Victorian parlor past a well-tended potted fern and an antimassacared armchair with claw-and-ball feet. Looking around, it's evident that the landlord has maintained the gentility of times gone by. We exit the parlor and venture to the end of a narrow hall where a small semi-circular table holds a double-handled, porcelain urn. Two closed doors face one another on either side of the table.

Edith grips the knob of the right-hand door and says, "Wallace's room."

I'm on tenterhooks about her discovery but first take a quick look around. The room has clearly been abandoned, and the curtains have been drawn. I open them to bring more light into the dim space and observe that the sheets have been bundled and placed at the foot of the bed alongside a folded blanket and a down pillow. The tops of both the bedside table and writing desk are empty save an ivory doily and floral blotter, respectively. The floor is lacking any sort of detritus that I can detect, and all four drawers of a chest have been closed. I hear a squeak and turn. Edith is opening the mirrored doors of the armoire.

"I don't know what to make of this," Edith remarks and points to the floor of the closet where two rectangular boxes are resting, each with multiple dials.

"I recognize this." I pick up one of the devices and set it on the wooden desk chair nearby. "Wallace had one in his classroom when I visited the other day."

"What are they?" Edith reaches in to retrieve the other black, metallic box. This one has three wires dangling from the side which are connected to hollow tubes with fluted ends.

"I don't remember what he called it, but he said it was something he'd been tinkering with."

"These look a bit like a telephone receiver," Edith holds up one of the tubes.

I nod and look past her into the armoire. "Is there anything else? It's odd that he would leave these behind. I'm sure they cost a pretty penny."

"They were under a few decorative pillows. I didn't see them at first." She reaches on the other side of the bed and stacks three, good-sized ruffled pillows on top of the matching folded blanket. "Perhaps he didn't notice that he forgot them."

I examine the bed and flip up the skirt, which also matches the pillows. The landlord has left no decorative detail overlooked. I spy a piece of paper under the head of the bed against the wall. While straining to reach the stray page with my right arm, I bump my head against the railing of the bed, my cloche offering little protection. "Oof!" I cry out.

"Oh Ruby, you should let me do that," Edith declares and kneels down next to me. "Besides, my arms are longer." She swiftly retrieves the sheet and places it on the surface of the desk blotter.

My eyes sweep over the page. "The number four again," I mutter to myself.

"Oh bother! Just something for one of his classes," Edith steps back and crosses her arms.

"Actually, this may be something of interest." I take a closer look.

The page contains a diagram of the triangle made of ten dots that I saw on Wallace's chalkboard along with *Tectractys* and T_4 written above it. Around and below the object are scribbled notes: *Pythagorean symbol of the cosmos, represents the four dimensions of space: point, line, plane, tetrahedron. 10 points reflect order in its highest form. Tetragrammaton, God's spoken name. Kabbalah.*

"I found the number four and prefix *tetra* written in some of Dottie's books. *Pythagorean* was repeated as well," I comment.

"So, this is related to that club?" Edith posits.

"I believe so." I flip the page but find nothing further. "I think it's no coincidence that the Pythagorean Club consists of only four students, all of which are missing."

"Ruby, this is troubling, deeply troubling,"

"I agree." Lifting the bed skirt again, I carefully look underneath, determined not to hit my head again. "There's nothing else down here."

"You know, despite their heavy handedness with Frank at the hospital, we really should call the police." Edith begins to walk toward the door.

"Just a moment," I stop her. "We should take a closer look at the chest of drawers and the desk."

"The drawers were all pulled open when I entered earlier, but maybe I missed something," she agrees and turns toward the chest.

"This will be our only chance to investigate here. Once the police take over, this whole room will be cordoned off."

"Oh, I hadn't thought of that," she pauses to mull this over.

"Tell you what." I suggest, "Why don't you throw a few things together for Norma before the police descend en masse. You mentioned that she asked you to pack a case for her at the hospital. I'll finish up here."

"Good idea." Edith says worriedly, "Suppose Norma and I can't get back into the house for a few days."

"Hopefully that won't be the case, but maybe you should throw some things in a bag for yourself as well," I try to assure her. "Would you have a place to stay?"

She thoughtfully considers my question. "I hate to impose on Ann any further. She's been such a help. There are a couple of other teachers with whom we have good relations."

"I'm sure, under the circumstances, they would oblige, but if you do find yourselves without a place to lay your head, you are always welcome at our house," I offer.

"I wouldn't hear of it!" She declines. "You and your family have enough to deal with at the moment. On top of that, I wouldn't dream of asking you for anything else. You've been such a help to us."

"Edith, given what's happened over the past couple of days, I would hardly say, 'It's been my pleasure,' but I'm glad to assist Norma and you." I gently palpate the back of my skull, "However, next time I'd make sure to have backup."

"I'll say!" She crosses the hall to her own bedroom, and I hear her rustling about.

I systematically pull out each drawer in the chest all the way out and tip them over, examining their underside for anything that might be secured with tape. Except for a lavender sachet, no doubt the landlord's special touch, the drawers and inside of the chest are clean. I turn toward the desk and repeat the process with the drawers running down both sides. *Nothing.* I then notice that the desk has a shallow central drawer and give it a tug. Something crackles so I attempt to withdraw the drawer completely, but it appears to be jammed. Then I realize that there's a catch that must be depressed. Pushing down on the metal tab, I slide the drawer all the way out.

"Hmm," It too is empty. But I distinctly heard crinkling of some sort. I reach a hand into the restricted space, and my fingers bump against paper. Unfortunately, the crumpled page is tightly jammed in the back corner. I need something to wrench it out, so I cross the hall.

"Edith, can you get me a shallow wooden spoon? I'm trying to extract something that's lodged inside the desk."

She looks up from her traveling case with interest, "I'll be right back."

Quickly returning with the requested cooking utensil, she kneels before the desk. "Let me have a go." After a couple of attempts, she hands me a wadded ball of stationery.

I smooth out two pages of a letter dated March 2nd of this year and read aloud both sides of the first page,

"Dear Josiah, I have the greatest possible news to share! I've found them! I've found the Four that the Tetramorphs described to the Prophet, 'There exist four children whose births narrowly preceded the last great plague. Born in the new land on the coast of the great sea whose waters contain Mu, their life force pulsates at a frequency higher than all other humans born to date. As an ideal vessel for one of the Tetramorphs, each of the Four will achieve super consciousness and thus be capable of communication without words, the mental control of matter, and interaction with higher dimensional realms. The land on which the children reside demonstrates geothermal and electromagnetic forces strong enough to withstand their combined super consciousness.'"

"Oh my God!" Edith's hand flies to her mouth.

I choke back a sob and attempt to continue reading, but I cannot speak as a wave of nausea overtakes me.

"Let me," Edith holds the second page and reads aloud,

"There are two boys and two girls, all of whom are brilliant. The girls excel at arithmetic and geometry, and the boys are prodigies in music and astronomy. The quadrivium, as predicted. Unsurprisingly, they were skeptical at first but eventually embraced their lives' purpose, to bring forth the permanent physical presence of the Divine Quaternity."

She abruptly stops reading, "Oh Ruby, this is terrible!"

"Please continue," I urge her, even though I cannot bear to hear more.

"Alright, if you're sure." Edith resumes,

"The radionic device detected high levels of subtle energy in each one. I nearly wept with joy when completing the final test. Since then, I've been working with them after school and on weekends to prepare them. It is my hope that they are ready for the Channeling Ceremony in the next month. There's so little time before the window closes. Thankfully, they have found a location that suits, one in which they are close to the earth."

"The orchard. That was in April," I whisper.

Edith glances up at me with confusion.

"One of Baker's employees encountered a group of, what he called, Satan worshipers in the orange grove late one night in April and scared them off by shooting blanks into the air," I explain.

"That's right! Norma and I read about it in the *Fullerton Daily*. Didn't the police find ceremonial objects and things?"

"Yes, and something was marked with obscure symbols." I think about the drawings, Wallace's *tetractys* and Dottie's *tetrad*. Nausea rises again, but I encourage Edith to finish the letter.

"There's not much more." She completes her reading,

"'This cannot fail. With the Prophet's detention—' It just ends there." Edith ponders this. "Perhaps he started the letter, had to stop writing for some reason, and couldn't find it later because it was wedged in the back of the drawer."

"A cult! Dottie joined a cult!" I'm stupefied. Then I recall the *New York Times'* article and shudder. The details of sacrifice, both human and animal, were gruesome. My throat closes and tears run down my cheeks, dropping onto my tensely clenched hands. A growl starts low in my throat and is released as a bellow of outrage, "That monster!"

"I'm calling the police this very moment!" Edith storms to the parlor.

I want to scream. I want to hit something. I want to rip his head off. But I settle for pounding the mattress until I collapse in a heap on the floor. "What have you done with them?" I murmur with exhaustion.

A few minutes pass, and Edith returns, "They'll be over in the next half an hour."

"I must tell Uncle Charles and Jack," I rise to my feet.

Edith wraps an arm around my shoulders, leading me into the parlor. "I'll tell you what. You sit here, and I'll bring them in. If you'd like, I can tell them what we found."

"Thank you, Edith," I squeeze her hand. "I'm not sure how much Jack should know so I should probably be the one to break the news."

"What did you find?!" Jack bounds into the room while Uncle Charles follows, slowly shaking his head, eyes rolled.

"Please have a seat," Edith gestures toward two armchairs.

Jack lowers himself carefully onto the pristine ivory damask and appears uncertain about where to put his hands. He settles for his lap. Uncle Charles locks eyes with me. His expression conveys that he understands something must be amiss.

I inhale deeply, making sure that my abdomen expands fully, and release the breath slowly while speaking. "I have some news that is going to be difficult to hear."

My cousin, who has been bouncing to test the spring of the seat's cushion, instantly halts. His face whitens as he gulps audibly.

"Perhaps you and I should speak in the other room," Uncle Charles shifts his gaze toward Jack and back toward me.

Edith quickly suggests, "Jack, why don't you help me put together a tray of refreshments."

"But—," Jack begins to protest, but after a look from his father, he reluctantly trails Edith out of the parlor.

Uncle Charles bends forward, elbows on his knees and hands on his temple. "For days I've been yearning for some crumb of information that can lead me to my daughter. But now I find myself reluctant to hear what you have to say."

"I understand completely."

He lowers his hands and looks up, tears in his eyes. "Is it…?"

"No, Uncle Charles! It's not that!" *At least I hope not.* Hot tears well in my eyes, and I feel my neck muscles tighten around my throat. But I cannot drag this out any further for either of us, so I get right to the point. "A letter in Wallace's room indicates that Dottie is involved in some sort of cult."

"WHAT?!" Uncle Charles bolts upright, shock registering on his countenance. "That's the last thing I expected to hear!"

"That's exactly how I felt!" I unfold the papers on my lap and hand him the letter. "You should read this yourself."

He snatches the letter and begins reading while pacing about the room. I sense when he reaches the part about the ceremony. He pivots toward me and, through clenched teeth, declares, "I will murder him!"

Never in my life have I seen my affable uncle so enraged. But I completely sympathize, having felt his fury myself just moments ago. I rise and lay a consoling hand on his arm. "There's not much more, and I think I may be able to shed a bit of light on this."

He quickly releases his breath with a mighty *whoosh* and sits back in his chair. When he finishes the letter, his tongue stumbles over his myriad questions. "W-w-why? H-how could—"

"How could an intelligent, well-adjusted young woman fall for this gibberish?" I complete his question.

"Yes! Exactly!" He deposits the pages on the end table beside him as though they are hot to the touch.

"We won't know the answer to that until we get her home, but let me fill you in on what I've found so far…"

"What did I miss?" Jack sets a plate of shortbread cookies on the dark walnut table beside the letter.

Edith hands each of us a glass of lemonade from a round serving tray then arranges several lace doilies on the table's waxed surface. She retires to a corner of the room, not wishing to intrude upon this private family discussion.

I'm curious how my Uncle Charles will respond. Jack is, after all, still a child, and the way this is handled could have a bearing on his emotions and mental state for years to come.

My Uncle places the cool crystal glass he is holding on one of the doilies then shifts in his chair, so he is facing Jack. "We don't know where Dottie is at the moment, but we have an idea about what she may be doing."

Registering his father's solemnity, Jack nods for him to continue.

"We believe that Dottie has joined a…well a club of sorts."

"A club? So, what's the big deal?" Jack huffs.

"Well, it seems that she may have gone to some kind of ceremony." Uncle Charles pauses to think carefully about how to proceed. "It's likely that she was detained because of the activities that were part of this ceremony."

"What activities?" Jack queries, confused by the cryptic nature of his father's explanation.

"We don't know exactly," Uncle Charles admits. "But—"

"Well, is she okay?"

I empathize with his fear and frustration and wish we could reassure him with certainty. "We are extremely hopeful that she is fine."

"Then why hasn't she called to let us know where she is?"

"If we had the answer to that question, we could figure this whole thing out," Uncle Charles rubs his forehead.

"We do know that her math teacher recruited her and her friends to join this club and most likely knows their location," I explain. "Unfortunately, he has moved out of his room here at the house, and we don't know where he's gone, as of yet."

At that moment, a brisk knock at the door signals that the police have arrived.

"Uncle Charles, I think it would be best if you and Jack wait in the car while I speak with the officers," I suggest.

Edith quickly rises from her seat in the corner and gathers the cookie plate and napkins. "Take your drinks and cookies with you." She hands the plate of shortbread to Uncle Charles.

CHAPTER 25

"This had better be good," Sergeant Blockhurst charges through the door. "The Mother's Day flowers I bought for the little lady are wilting." He glances outside toward a black and white Model T with *POLICE* and 5 centered in blocky letters on the passenger door. The windows have been left open.

Edith and Ruby step aside for the sergeant and Officer Thompson to enter. It's almost 5:00 PM, and both men appear fatigued and ready to call it a day. Edith gestures for them to take a seat in the parlor. I imagine this formal sitting room is getting far more activity today than it has in quite some time. Once they are situated next to one another on the sofa and have placed their custodian helmets on their laps, Thompson leans toward the sergeant and mutters something under his breath. Blockhurst sits up and, with a grin, declares, "Officer Thompson tells me you are friends with the Grahams." He is looking directly at Edith.

"Yes, that's true but—"

"Great!" he claps his hands. "Does this mean you've uncovered something about the fire at the shed?" He directs his query to me.

"Sergeant this is not about Frank Graham nor the fire in Baker's orchard." I raise my hands to calm him as his face reddens. "This pertains to—"

"Don't tell me this is about those blasted kids!" he bellows.

Officer Thompson's eyes widen at his supervisor's outburst, and Edith exclaims, "Well, I never!"

Once again, I attempt to appease the sergeant. "Sir, we would not have called you if it weren't important. We have evidence to show that—"

"Why on earth would you call us out to the Graham's residence…this is the Graham's residence, is it not?" Puzzled, he glances at Edith.

"That's correct," Edith affirms. "But I live here as well."

"As I was saying, why would you call us to the Graham's residence if this has to do with those delinquent teenagers?" He is utterly stupefied.

"If you'll just let me explain, I can answer all of your questions." Despite trying to remain calm, my tone expresses my own exasperation.

He folds his arms and leans against the antimacassar draped on the back of the sofa. "Be my guest," his raised eyebrows and narrowed eyes mirror his unctuous tone.

"Very well." I breathe deeply and try to organize my thoughts, hoping to provide a clear-cut explanation, while avoiding another explosion. "Edith, Miss Holmes," I nod toward her, "and the Grahams have another roommate. Another high school teacher named Wallace Mains."

The sergeant's flat expression conveys apathy, but Officer Thompson motions for me to continue.

"Mr. Mains abruptly moved out sometime this morning and left evidence that suggests that he recruited Dottie, Polly, Leo, and Earl into a cult. Further, we believe that their participation has put them in danger." I hold my breath, anticipating the sergeant's indignation, but a moment of absolute silence passes.

Officer Thompson shifts his gaze from me to his commander and back again, while Edith shrugs her shoulders. Suddenly, Blockhurst's body rocks forward as he releases a booming guffaw. His arms tighten around his paunch, and tears stream down his face. His helmet rolls across the throw rug to the edge of the hardwood floor. Unsure how to react to this display of hysterics, Thompson snickers halfheartedly. A minute or more passes before the sergeant regains control of himself. Wiping his eyes with stubby fingers, he settles down and shoots me a patronizing glance. "My dear, that head injury of yours has clearly rattled your brain."

"Now see here, sergeant!" Edith objects. "She's telling the truth. Here, you read the letter we found." She retrieves the papers from the end table and hands them over.

Blockhurst's eyes quickly shift from line to line. At one point he chuckles, "Higher dimensional realms." I fear he is on the verge of another fit. When he finishes reading, he passes the letter to Thompson and, with a condescending tone, pronounces. "This is obviously a work of fiction. A…a play or short story or something. You said this Mr. Mains is a teacher."

"A math teacher," I clarify.

He dismisses this. "Yes, yes. Anyway, why in the world would either of you ladies assume this is true. And why would you think it has to do with your cousin and her friends? He mentions no names."

"There's more to it than just this letter." I describe the books and notes I found in Dottie's room, along with Mrs. Taliaferro's concerns regarding Leo's recent behavior and Wallace's visit to their home Saturday. I describe the Pythagorean Club, and my interactions with Wallace.

"Well, there you have it!" he declares. "Obviously they're going to put on a play about math or something." He stands and scoops his helmet from the floor, depositing it on his head and looks down at me, still seated. "Miss Ray, you need to stop this obsession. I'm sure the kids are fine. Now, I should be scolding you for distracting Officer Thompson and I from other REAL investigations, but that hee-haw you gave me just about made my day." He wipes at a corner of his eye. "I really needed that." Turning to the young officer he commands, "Let's go, Thompson."

"Wait sir," he rises, pointing a finger at a line in the letter. "*Music and astronomy*. We found a tuning fork and a star chart in Baker's field last month."

"The ceremony that Bert Lemming reported?" I ask eagerly.

"Now just a minute!" Blockhurst interrupts. "I know what you're thinking."

"It all fits, sergeant," I plead. "The letter, the evidence in the orchard. This can't be a coincidence."

"Look," the sergeant softens his tone. "I know you'd like to believe that, but the evidence, if you can even call it that, is skimpy. If your cousin has not returned by tomorrow morning, then please give us a call. In the meantime, I must get home to my wife and kids. It is Mother's Day, after all."

Edith and I walk dejectedly outside with the officers. Noticing my expression, Uncle Charles exits the car and approaches. "Well, sergeant, what do you plan to do about my daughter and her friends?"

Blockhurst gazes at him with a modicum of paternal comradery. "Mr. Ray, I'm sure if I were in your shoes, I'd be pulling out my hair as well. But there's nothing to go on. As I told your niece, please call us tomorrow morning if your daughter has not returned, but I'm sure that won't be necessary." He looks at his wristwatch, "It's dinnertime on a Sunday. She's probably home waiting on all of you."

My heart aches at the hopelessness on Uncle Charles' face, but he perseveres. "Perhaps if we call the Chief?"

Shaking his head, the sergeant advises, "Not going to happen. He's away on a long weekend with his family. I suggest you take this little lady home and encourage her to get some rest. That head wound has muddled her thinking, and I'm afraid she's gotten you and Miss Holmes here wrapped up in her crazy notions as well."

At that, both officers get in their vehicle, but not before Officer Thompson turns toward me with a compassionate nod.

"Looks like we're still on our own," I moan to Uncle Charles as I step toward his car. Edith returns to the house to finish her packing, although there probably isn't any point to it. It's not like Wallace's room or the house will be cordoned off for evidence any time soon.

"So, they're still not gonna help?" Jack's expression is as cross as his arms. "I feel like they're the bad guys here."

"I understand that you're frustrated and disappointed," I sympathize. "Your father and I feel the same way."

"They're supposed to be the heroes. This kid in my class is always bragging about how great his dad is cause he's a policeman," he grumbles and hugs his knees to his chest.

Uncle Charles ruffles his son's hair. "I get it, sport. I'm ready to strangle Sergeant Blockhurst, but that would complicate matters…"

After a chuckle, Jack mumbles, "I just don't understand. They're meant to help people."

I bend forward into the car so I'm level with Jack. "I happen to know that most of the officers in our city are good men. But Sergeant Blockhurst has his own unique way of looking at things. I do believe he's trying to do the right thing."

"As exasperated as I am, I can see where Blockhurst is coming from on this," Uncle Charles sighs thoughtfully, stroking his chin.

"I suppose," I admit. "So far, the evidence is scant. Without personally knowing Dottie and the circumstances that have led up to our finding the letter, it looks as though a bunch of inconsiderate kids ran off to have a high time and are now reluctant to return home and face the music."

"So, what next?" My uncle weakly shrugs his shoulders. "Do we call the other parents?"

"Not quite yet." *I have a plan.* "I need to check on something with Edith, and then I'll let you know where we'll go next."

I tap lightly on Norma's partially open bedroom door, and Edith answers, "Come in." She turns toward me, a folded sweater in her hand. "I called our landlord, but they've not heard a thing from Wallace."

"Just as I suspected." I mull this over. "He must have given references with his application to rent the room."

"I doubt it. When Norma heard that a new mathematics teacher was moving to the area, she sought out his contact information and wrote to him about renting the room. It had been sitting vacant for quite some time, and the landlord was beginning to grumble about selling the place."

"Let me guess. The landlord was so thrilled to find a tenant, no background information was requested."

"That's my understanding." She opens a drawer and selects a couple of handkerchiefs.

Giving her a moment to finish packing, I survey my surroundings and note that the landlord's fondness for floral frills and flounces extends into this space as well. That being said, Norma has personalized her room with modern paintings, including a dappled expressionist landscape and an oil painting where boldly colored geometric shapes allude to bodies in motion. "These are stunning." I squint at the illegible signature in the bottom right corner of one of the paintings and ask Edith, "Your work?"

"Alas no," she sighs and looks around. "With the exception of this."

I examine the delicate watercolor that depicts a woman gazing out a window at a lady and gentleman walking past arm-in-arm, waving to other similar couples passing by. The subject's face is shadowed by her hat, but her posture is wistful. Furthermore, her arm hangs limply at her side, a letter enfolded in her grasp. Next to the window, a framed photograph rests on a table, depicting two young women in high-collared frocks, their arms linked together. "It's lovely," I comment softly. "And quite moving."

She nods with sad eyes, the corners of her mouth curving into a regretful smile. "And autobiographical."

"You have a gift, Edith." I look around the room, "Are the rest of your paintings in your room?"

"A collector in Boston offered me fifty dollars for all of my work before we left for California. I wasn't sure how I'd transport the paintings, and we really needed the money at the time."

"He noticed your talent," I remark. "But I'm sure you'd rather have at least some still in your possession."

"She," Edith emphasizes the pronoun, "was kind, and the theme of my work appealed to her."

"Well, I'm sure that Laguna Beach will bring you opportunities to continue your art," I encourage brightly, thinking about the artists' colony.

"If we can move there," she says doubtfully.

"Oh, Edith, please don't lose hope." I take her hand and give it a squeeze. "I'm confident that once Frank wakes up, he'll tell you both where the money is."

She shrugs. "Not much we can do as far as that goes but wait."

I know the feeling. "Have you decided to take much with you?" She has closed the small case. "I don't think you'll have a problem returning home tonight."

"I just threw a few things in there for Norma." She lifts the case and motions for me to leave the room before her.

"I do have a question for you, Edith." We pause in the hall.

"Of course. Anything I can do to help," she smiles sincerely.

"I'd like to take a look at Wallace's classroom. Maybe there's some sort of clue there about where the kids have gone, if they were indeed performing this ceremony he referred to."

"That's a good idea. What do you need me to do?"

"Would you happen to have a key?" I cross my fingers hopefully.

"You're in luck," she brightens. "Ordinarily, teachers only have a key for their own classroom, but my department had a campus-wide event a few weeks ago, and I borrowed a master key." I follow her into her room where she opens a drawer in her desk. "Lucky for you, I forgot to return it."

"Oh, that's terrific!" On our way through the living room, I retrieve Wallace's letter and the page with the tetractys diagram.

When we reach the car, Uncle Charles places the case in the trunk and asks, "Where to now?"

"The high school, please. Park on Pomona. It'll be closer to the mathematics wing." I lean my head against the cool glass of the window and watch the long shadows of trees and buildings pass by on the pavement. The sun will be setting soon.

Cabinet doors are open, while students' tests and assignments are haphazardly piled on Wallace's desk and on a few student desks nearby. *He wasn't here for very long.* I turn my gaze toward the table positioned under a window near the desk. The oscilloclast, I now remember its name, is missing but has left a dustless mark on the table's surface.

"He didn't waste any time," Edith observes. "He was so meticulous at the house."

"He probably stopped by after leaving there." I remove the lid from a box under the table. More exams. "Hopefully he left us a clue in his rush."

Most of the student's papers are covered with numbers and symbols, but a stack (neatly arranged on a small two-drawer file cabinet in the corner) appears to contain written reports. I flip through the first dozen and stop when I see Dottie's name typed in the upper right-hand corner next to an $A+$ marked in red pencil. The title reads *Music of the Spheres* and begins with a quote by Pythagoras. *There is geometry in the humming of the strings. There is music in the spacing of the spheres.* Double-spaced typed print covers five pages. I skim through the text. Most of it has to do with mathematical theory and harmonics. I turn over the last page and see a note in red. *A brilliant exposition, Dottie. You have eloquently explained the subtleties of the hierarchical dimensions, specifically arithmetic, geometry, astronomy, and music. The success of your upcoming endeavor is certain.* I flip back to the cover page. The date reads *April 7, 1930*, just a few days before the ceremony in the orchard.

"Edith, can you help me with something?" I hand her half of the assignments.

"Of course. What am I looking for?"

"Papers written by our four students." I carefully remove each report from the stack and create another pile. I don't want to accidentally skip over anything. Unsurprisingly, Dottie's work is far more advanced than her peers, judging from the titles and content on the first pages I peruse.

"Aha!" Edith passes me a hand-written paper titled *Number in Time*. "The subject is harmonics. A+."

"This is Earl's." I examine the back. "More glowing praise." The red-penciled feedback ends with *You will no doubt lead the others to triumph.*

"Edith, we should carefully scan all the reports for anything that stands out. Perhaps more students are involved than we thought."

After about fifteen minutes have passed, we both reach the final paper in our respective piles. Edith found both Leo and Polly's papers in her stack. Leo, of course, reported on the mathematical aspects of astronomy, while Polly's addressed geometry and the three linear dimensions. Both contain feedback from Wallace alluding to success and an impending event.

"The subjects and level of the other reports are what I would expect from high school students," Edith declares. "It doesn't look as though any others are involved with the Pythagorean Club."

"I agree," I show her a paper marked *D-*. "None of the assignments received a grade higher than a B. And the feedback on many seems overly harsh."

"Listen to this." She reads, "*Next time, actually study your textbook. Your lack of understanding is appalling.*"

"What's appalling is his treatment of his students, both those he praises and those he condemns."

Edith points to a quotation by Pythagoras written on the leftmost corner of a row of blackboards. *A man is never as big as when he is on his knees to help a child- Pythagoras.* "His hypocrisy astounds me."

"He is deeply disturbed, that's for sure." *And that's what worries me the most*, I think to myself. I wander over to his desk and begin upending drawers, most of which have been emptied. Unfortunately, no stray notes or papers are jammed inside. "Nothing here."

Edith discovers a sport coat in the space behind a tall file cabinet that has been positioned at an angle in another corner of the room. She digs in the pockets and withdraws a business card.

I look over her shoulder and exclaim, "Bingo!" The manila card displays the contact information for one Josiah Colby, whose electrical repair shop is in Seal Beach. The city's name triggers a memory. "The article in the *New York Times* a few days ago about cults in Southern California mentioned a self-proclaimed prophet who was arrested in Seal Beach."

"That fits with Wallace's letter to Josiah," Edith remarks. "He mentioned a prophet."

"That's right! Perhaps that's where Wallace was headed." I'm not sure what to do with this information, as of yet. I put the card in my handbag and remove my notebook to list our findings from the classroom. Thumbing through the previous pages, I spot Mrs. Taliaferro's report regarding Wallace's visit to their house yesterday. "If Wallace knows where the students are, why would he go to Leo's house yesterday after he missed a club meeting?"

"I've been thinking about that as well." She looks puzzled. "Maybe he was trying to appear innocent, in case everything backfired."

"Maybe." I consider the most obvious explanation. "Or maybe he, in fact, doesn't know where the kids are."

"I'm not sure if that's a good thing or not," Edith replies uncertainly.

"I don't think there's anything more to be found here." I look around and then gather the reports Dottie and her friends wrote. We exit the classroom to join Uncle Charles and Jack, who we left waiting in the car.

CHAPTER 26

"Finally!" Jack races down the hallway toward me. "I wanted to come find you, but Dad said I shouldn't interrupt your search." He frowns at his father.

"Jack, it hasn't been that long," Uncle Charles rolls his eyes.

"What's this all about?" I hand Edith the reports. "I thought you were waiting in the car."

"We were, but someone got bored and wanted to look around," my uncle answers good-naturedly.

Jack extends a fist, his fingers curled around some sort of round object. "Look what I found!"

I accept the metallic disc and realize that it's a woman's compact case. Turning it over, I note the filigree flowers and vines engraved on both sides, along with a set of initials. The interlocking letters are elaborate whorls, and I find it hard to identify the letters in the dimming light of sunset.

"It's Polly's!" Jack proclaims. "I found a clue!"

"Polly's?" I squint to get a closer look. "I'm sure there are many girls whose name starts with P."

"Polly Baker! See that's a B." Jack points to the symbol in the middle. "I don't know what the O is for."

Now that Jack has drawn my attention to it, I'm surprised I couldn't discern the *P*, *B*, and *O* to begin with. "Jack, this could still belong to someone else. Maybe there's a girl named Pansy Ophelia Brown."

Jack chokes out a laugh. "I hope not! Can you imagine being saddled with that?"

"Ruby's right, Jack," Uncle Charles remarks. "It could belong to someone else. Why are you so certain."

At that, Jack's cheeks flush. "I'm just sure."

Knowing full well that there's more to the story, I probe, "Jack we need more information if we're to make any use of this clue. How do you know it belongs to Polly?"

"Okay, okay." Jack draws in a breath. He clearly has something to confess. "Polly lost it at our house a few weeks ago, and I…well…"

"Go on," Uncle Charles prompts.

"Well…I sorta…Okay I found it and kept it for a few days," Jack's entire face is furiously red, and he avoids eye contact with all of us.

"Oh Jack," I sigh and share a sympathetic smile with Uncle Charles. "I understand. I know you're quite fond of Polly." I examine the outside of the case more critically. "It's definitely silver. Most likely a special gift from her parents. I'm surprised she didn't realize it was missing immediately."

"She and Dottie were rushing out the door when she dropped it, and then she didn't come back over for a few days." He admits, "Then I kinda put it in her bag when she wasn't looking."

"Oh, there's a picture." When I open the case, a small photograph of a dark-haired youth slips out and floats to the ground.

Jack retrieves it and hands it back to me. "Yeah, I think it's that Leo guy she always talks about." He says the name scornfully.

"Where on earth did you find this," I look around the hallway.

"Over there by the other building." We follow Jack through the covered, arch-lined hallways to a two-story building in the middle of the campus. A cupola sits atop each of the front corners of the structure. "I was looking at the dates on these plaques here when I saw it on the sidewalk." A series of years mark the walkways along campus, beginning with 1896, the first year that the high school had a graduating class. "Dottie told me that there's a time capsule under each one and that her class is planning something swell. But she wouldn't tell me what it is," he explains with some disappointment.

"That's right!" I point toward another walkway a bit further north. "Mine is over there. 1920."

"What's under yours, Ruby?" Jack questions enthusiastically.

"I have no idea," I laugh. "All I know is that I didn't put anything in there." I scan the sidewalk around us. "Where exactly did you find this?"

Jack takes a few steps and points. "Right there where the sidewalk hits the wall of the arch."

I realize that Jack is proud of his discovery, but I have to ask, "Why do you think this is a clue, Jack? She may have dropped it on Friday between classes."

"That's precisely what I told him," Uncle Charles comments.

"Actually, Jack may be correct," Edith interjects, to Jack's delight, and we all turn toward her. "Since this building is Study Hall, the corridor gets a great deal of traffic throughout the day. I'd be very surprised that a case this nice (and this expensive) would be left here. Someone would certainly have picked it up. To turn it in, if they're honest, or keep if they're not. Either way, valuables have a way of disappearing with roughly 1,500 students roaming around campus."

"If that's true, then she must have dropped it after everyone left campus. Edith, when does that usually happen?" I query.

"On a Friday? Unless there's a game or some other special activity, the place clears out by 4:00 at the latest, including the staff."

"Was there anything going on Friday afternoon or evening?" Uncle Charles asks.

"Not that I know of," Edith replies.

"That means Polly was here after 5:00!" Jack insists. "That's when Dottie was picked up."

"Did Polly and her mother pick her up?" It's still unclear how things unfolded between the time she left our house and when she was seen downtown.

"No, it was a green Chevrolet. Polly was already in the car because I saw her get out to help Dottie with her things," Jack explains.

"Polly could have dropped this case after school before picking up Dottie with their friends. I saw her in Mr. Mains' class after 4:00 that day. She had come back to pick up a book." I report.

"I doubt she would have walked by this area if she was returning to campus after school. Most likely, she was dropped off on Pomona," Edith suggests.

"I suppose so. But we can't rule that out," I agree. "There's always the chance that all of the kids came back here after leaving our house."

"Everything would have been locked up by then," Edith informs us.

I have a hunch that Jack is correct. "Alright, you've persuaded me. Jack, I have to thank you for finding this clue."

He beams proudly and salutes, "You got it, cousin!"

But what does the clue mean?

Bells chime from the tower of a nearby church, and Edith looks at her wristwatch. "It's seven," she announces. "Mr. Ray, would you mind dropping me off at the hospital? Norma's probably wondering where I am by now."

"Of course, Miss Holmes."

"I only told him what was absolutely necessary," I inform Edith. During our quick drive to the hospital, I've been giving her a brief recap about my conversation with Sergeant Blockhurst this morning. "I didn't mention the missing money, nor keys I found."

"Did you tell him that Fipps attacked you and set the fire?" Edith inquires.

"Oh, most definitely! Hopefully he's locked up by now at the police station." A thought occurs to me. "I'm surprised you didn't say anything to the sergeant about your missing Ford. Surely, it's turned up by now if it's been abandoned somewhere."

"To be honest, Ruby, I didn't want to draw any additional attention to myself personally. I considered asking when the officers were at the house, but Sergeant Blockhurst kept giving me suspicious glances after he discovered that I share a house with Norma and Frank." She picks at a loose thread on her cotton gloves. "I'd prefer that he not think of me any further."

"Makes sense." If the sergeant took it into his head to dig around into Norma and Edith's relationship, the results could be catastrophic for them.

"Bottom line, the car is the furthest thing from my mind at the moment," Edith confesses.

We arrive at the front of the hospital just as the streetlamps flicker on. "I'll help you with your bags."

"I got it, Ruby, but thank you." We both slide out of the back seat and wait for Uncle Charles to open the trunk. "What will you do next about Dottie and her friends?"

The question weighs heavily upon me, and I can tell that Uncle Charles is wondering the same thing. "I feel like the clues are all pointing to something, but I just can't put my finger on it. I suppose we'll try to reach Dottie's friends again. Hopefully they're back from their Mother's Day activities."

Edith pulls me into a warm embrace. "Well, you know where to find Norma and me if you need anything. She'll no doubt stay the night here tonight, and I'll most likely hunker down on an uncomfortable chair in the lobby in case she needs me."

"Please call me if Frank's condition changes. Hopefully he'll wake up soon."

"I'll do that," she promises and releases me with a compassionate smile. "But please don't give us another thought. You have more important things to concern yourself with, not to mention healing from your injury."

Now that she's brought it up, I notice a dull throbbing in my head that I'd been too preoccupied to notice. I'm probably due for another dose of medication soon. "Thank you, Edith, for all your help today. We couldn't have done it without you."

"The same goes for you, dear Ruby." She turns and passes between the rose bushes to enter the building.

"Where do we go now?" Jack asks eagerly.

"Home for the moment," Uncle Charles answers. "I for one could do with a bite to eat, even though my stomach is tied up in knots."

"Eating's always fine by me," he chirps and fiddles with Polly's compact. I told him he could carry it home for me but that it would stay in my room for the time being.

As we approach our house, lights are visible through the living room windows. "I'm quite sure the lamps were off when we left this afternoon," I remark.

"Dottie's home!" Jack doesn't even wait for his father to stop the car, nor does he close the door before sprinting up the steps to the front door. I hear him shouting, "Dot-tie…"

Uncle Charles and I, also heartened, rush to exit the car, just not as speedily as Jack. However, our hope is dashed as Nan steps onto the porch and shakes her head. I slip an arm through his, and we slow our pace. "How are you holding up?" I question softly.

"Honestly, I'm trying to focus on what's immediately in front of me. If I allow my mind to stray…"

"Same," I squeeze his forearm and change the subject. "I'm surprised Nan is here."

"Are you really?" He raises an eyebrow.

"No, not really," I admit.

When we reach her, Nan pulls us both into a tight hug. "I've been prayin' for ya all day!"

Her love for our family moves me, and I brush away a tear. "It's your day off, Nan. You should be with your family."

"Already been there," she waves away my comment. "Better I'm on pins and needles with you all than on pins and needles away from here."

A savory aroma fills my nostrils the instant I enter the house. "What have you been up to, Nan?"

"You shouldn't have, but I'm glad you did," Uncle Charles pats his stomach.

"Well, what else am I gonna do with myself?" Nan pronounces as though nothing could be more obvious. "Already set the table, so have a seat. I'll bring in the food."

Jack is already situated at the dining room table with a buttered roll in one hand, and a glass of lemonade in the other. "Sorry," he apologizes through a mouthful of biscuit. "I'm starving!"

"You had a plateful of cookies at Edith's house!" I remind him and ease Nan's burden by taking a bowl of green beans from one of her hands so that she can place a chicken pot pie on a trivet with the other. A hole in the center of the flakey golden crust reveals a bubbling creamy sauce. A wave of hunger so keen I feel momentarily lightheaded passes over me. The last thing I ate was the hearty breakfast Nan prepared this morning.

"This looks and smells wonderful, Nan. Thank you!" Uncle Charles begins spooning mashed potatoes onto his plate.

"Kept it warm in the oven till ya got home," Nan cuts the steaming pie with a triangular server and scoops a generous portion onto each of our plates.

"For land's sake!" Our silent feasting is interrupted by Nan scurrying from the kitchen. "Can't believe I forgot!" She smacks her forehead. "Ruby, you had a telephone call." She says *telephone* with disdain.

My fork drops on my plate with a loud *ping*. "Who was it?" I am already rising from my chair.

"A boy from the school," she directs me across the hallway to the phone nook and hands me a scrap of paper with the name *Gordon* scrawled at the top followed by a number.

"I assume this is about Dottie and the others," I accept the slip from her age spotted hands.

"Didn't say. But said it's important and ta call him back right away." She begins twisting at her apron. "I'm so sorry, Ruby! If my head weren't screwed on…"

"Not to worry." I reassure her and walk to the phone nook to place the call. Meanwhile, Nan wanders back to the dining room to, no doubt, refill empty plates and glasses.

"Stewart residence," a hypo-nasal baritone answers.

"Yes, may I please speak with Gordon? This is Ruby Ray." I had only begun to sate my hunger, but my appetite has disappeared to be replaced by an uncomfortable tightness in my abdomen.

"Oh, hey Miss Ray!" he replies casually. "Glad ya called back. Leo's mom told me to call ya. She rang my house a while ago."

"Leo? Do you happen to know where he is?" My spine tingles and a lightness radiates upward from my neck. Over the years I've learned to recognize this unique feeling, as it often heralds a discovery from which all the pieces of the puzzle start to fall together.

"Nah, I haven't seen him since Friday night," he says casually.

That's okay. There may still be something here. "What time did you see Leo?" I search through the telephone desk for more paper.

"Huh, lemme think." A pause. "Guess it was around midnight. I know that cuz I thought it was weird seeing him so late. He's not one to get into trouble, if ya know what I mean."

So, Gordon's the last one to see them. "Where did you see him, and was he with anyone?"

"Yeah, a couple of lookers and some other guy. Saw 'em at the school."

One of those "lookers" happens to be my cousin. My feathers are ruffled. "Why were you at the high school so late?"

"Uh…" he mutters sheepishly. "Cuttin' through there to get home." *Yeah, right. Boozing is probably more like it.* I recall avoiding cigarette butts and broken glass from empty bottles while arriving at school early on Monday mornings for 6:00 AM classes during my first semester at the Junior College. Not to mention other unsavory objects lying about. "Where exactly on campus did you see the kids?"

"On the quad by Study Hall. Standin' around one of those concrete benches."

I picture the treeless seating area and remember nearly burning the backs of my legs on a hot June day. "What were they doing?"

"It was pretty dark, so I couldn't really tell." *Couldn't tell or don't want to tell?*

"Did you talk to them?"

"Nah, we decided to scram. One of my pals didn't wanna be seen." The pal was probably "blotto" as we used to say.

"If it was so dark, how did you know it was Leo?" *And how could you tell the girls were "lookers?"*

"Well, I guess I could see their faces ok. Could barely tell what they had with 'em, though," he backpedals.

"How much did they have with them? What size were the objects?" I probe.

"Look, I dunno. Maybe a few bags? I didn't stick around long enough to get a good look." He's beginning to sound irritated.

"Could you hear what they were saying?" I'm determined to get as much information as possible before he disconnects.

"Leo asked if it was time. Or maybe he asked for the time." He hesitates. "Now that I think about it, he musta asked IF it was time cuz that church clock just chimed midnight."

I quickly list the details in pencil while mentally processing their implications. So, the kids were on campus at midnight, at the quad, near the location where Jack found Polly's compact case. And it sounds as though they had bags of some sort with them. "Is there anything else you can tell me? Any other detail, even if it doesn't seem important."

"Fraid not," he answers quickly, eager to end our conversation.

"Alright, thank you so much, Gordon, for getting in touch with me. You've been very helpful."

A sharp *brrring* erupts from the telephone the instant I replace the receiver. "This is Ruby," I answer eagerly, unwilling to waste time with a formal greeting.

"Ruby, it's Edith. Frank's waking up and muttering the word 'kids.' You need to get over here. Pronto."

CHAPTER 27

"I could wait in the car, but I absolutely must go in with you," Uncle Charles insists as he backs out of the driveway and immediately turns onto Amerige.

"Of course you will! I hadn't thought otherwise." I gaze out the window. The moon is slightly fuller than last night in the orchard and definitely more visible since the air is free of smoke.

"I'm glad Nan stayed with Jack. I don't think he should be with us when…if…" He breaks down into silent tears. He's at the end of his rope, and frankly so am I.

"There is no IF. We will find Dottie, and she's going to be fine!" I summon hopefulness for us both. The acorn-shaped streetlamps highlight an open space at the curb just before Fullerton General. "Over there," I direct Uncle Charles.

He throws open the driver's door before I even have a chance to reach for my handbag. "All set?" he asks impatiently.

"This way." I lead him through the lobby and down the right-most corridor. Edith is pacing to and fro, glaring at two young policemen guarding the door each time she passes. I don't recognize either officer, but they're all business and one has even rested a hand near his gun holster. "Officers," I nod politely and approach Edith, who grips my arm and pulls me a few doors down.

"What's going on?" Uncle Charles joins us and nods toward the young men. "Will they let us in?"

"Now that Frank's beginning to regain consciousness, they've amped up the police presence hoping to get a testimony. There's even one in Frank's room," she explains.

"Do I need to request entry?" I assume they are still limiting Frank's visitors to one at a time.

"Yes, but before you go in, I have something to tell you." Edith leans in and lowers her volume. "They think his vision has been impaired, and he's quite incoherent."

"As I recall, rotgut will do that to you. Has he said anything more about 'kids?'"

"I can't say for certain. Norma hasn't been back out since I returned from my phone call with you."

"Alright, I'm going in. Uncle Charles, wait here with Edith and Norma when she comes out. I'm going to try to question Frank." This will be tricky with a policeman in the room. I want to safeguard Frank's rights, but I need to ascertain whether he knows something about Dottie and her friends. I can't begin to imagine how he's involved with them. Surely, he's not joined the cult as well. I decide to approach the officer who is not toying with his weapon. "I'd like to see Mr. Graham, please."

"Who are you?" he snaps while looking me over.

"I'm a friend." Best to keep it brief.

"Just a minute," he huffs and opens the door to speak with the guard inside. After a somewhat involved conversation during which both repeatedly shoot glances in my direction, the door closes and I hear, "Visitor for Mr. Graham. You'll need to step outside."

"Oh, Ruby!" The door swings open, and Norma rushes toward me, tugging me into a hug. "You've been through hell over the past 24 hours!" She holds me at arm's length and critically examines my face and head. "Are you okay?"

My hand instinctively touches the back of my cloche. "Physically I'm much better, but we're in agony not knowing where Dottie is. And you? How are you holding up? What's the latest with Frank?"

She passes me a serious look and jerks her head toward Edith and Uncle Charles a few doors down. "Let's speak over there."

Uncle Charles nods a solemn greeting to Norma as we approach, and Edith places a comforting hand on her shoulder. "What's the latest?" Edith inquires. "I've already filled them in on the police and Frank's vision."

"Well, when the doctor arrived, just after you left to call Ruby, Frank stirred and repeated the words 'tunnel' and 'dark' a few times." Norma shrugs her shoulders. "The doctor said Frank probably has something called 'tunnel vision' where he can't see what's on the periphery."

"Ruby thinks it's the moonshine," Edith says under her breath.

Norma nods, "That's what the doctor said as well."

"Has Frank said anything about 'kids' again?" Uncle Charles asks anxiously. He is gripping his hat with such ferocity that the brim will never be the same again.

"I'm afraid not," Norma answers regretfully. "Edith had snuck into the room and was telling me about Wallace in front of Frank. We thought he was unconscious when he suddenly mumbled, 'Kids,' then passed out again." She peeks at the officers. "Unfortunately, that's exactly when the one with the gun opened the door and realized that Frank was waking up."

"He called for reinforcements immediately," Edith adds.

"Has he said anything else?"

"Not a peep," Norma sighs.

I don't know how I'm going to get anywhere with him. Then an idea occurs to me. "If it's alright with you, Norma, I'd like to see if I can get him to answer some yes/no questions nonverbally."

"Yes, please. Give it a try." She walks me to the door and knocks. When the officer answers, she informs him I'm going in.

Frank's color has markedly improved, as has his breathing. I sink into the chair next to his bed and grip his hand. "Hi Frank, this is Ruby Ray. I don't know if you remember me, but I found you at the shed yesterday morning."

His body stiffens, and he turns his head toward me, squinting his eyes.

"Dark," he grunts.

"I understand that you're having trouble seeing."

My comment seems to agitate him for he thrashes his head side to side and repeats, "Dark." Then he bellows, "Tunnel."

"I know you're having trouble seeing, but I need to ask you—" He abruptly closes his eyes and drifts off.

I tap his forearm to wake him. "Frank, you mentioned kids earlier. Squeeze my hand if you were trying to say something about kids."

His hand lies limply in mine.

"Were you trying to say something about Wallace?"

Nothing.

I give his shoulders a shake, and his eyes fly open. His head swivels, searching for something.

Let's try this again.

"Frank, squeeze my hand if you know something about kids. Maybe they're in danger?"

His hand tightens around mine, and he exclaims, "Kids!"

The guard looks over with interest. "What's going on here?"

"Officer, my cousin and her friends have been missing for days. I believe that Frank may be trying to tell us something about them. If you could let me continue…"

"Go on," he responds slowly, his expression suspicious.

"Frank, are kids in danger? Four teenagers?"

He turns toward my face, his eyes wide, and implores. "Tunnel! Dark tunnel!"

With that, all the pieces of the puzzle click into place. I rush out of the room and grab Uncle Charles' arm, dragging him toward the exit. "We need to go see Stan Jones immediately!"

"Ruby, what's happening?" Norma calls after us.

"I think I know where they are!"

Despite the urgency of the moment, I notice that the streetlight is still out across from the Jones' residence, just as Lula described. A fierce hypervigilance has overtaken me, and my senses are acute, perceiving every sight, sound, and smell around me. I burst out of the vehicle and experienced a wave of dizziness, having forgotten that I am still concussed. Shaking it off, I take the steps up to Stan's house two at a time. Uncle Charles is right on my heels. Dispensing with social niceties, I pound on the door, and Barclay begins to bay.

"What in the world?!" A lock clicks open on the door. Stan isn't taking any chances after the break-in. "Charles! Ruby!"

"Stan, I'm so sorry to bother you on a Sunday evening, but this is an emergency!" I'm winded and rest my hand on Uncle Charles' arm to keep my balance.

His eyes round with alarm, "What happened?"

"I have to ask you…is there a tunnel under the new auditorium?"

He stares back dumbfounded, hesitating for a moment, then chuckles, "Is that all? Ya shoulda called me instead of comin' all the way over." His shoulders relax. "It's no secret. Just not many people know about 'em."

"Them?" Uncle Charles and I ask at the same time.

"Sure!" Stan waves a hand dismissively. "It's like a rabbit's warren down there. Must be miles of tunnels. Say, what's this all about?"

"Stan, my daughter and her friends may be trapped down there. They've been missing since Friday night!" Uncle Charles' voice breaks with emotion.

"My God!" The color drains from Stan's face. "Come right in while I get my keys and some flashlights. It must pitch black down there. Electrical switches are in the buildings, not inside the tunnels," he calls over his shoulder as we follow him in.

"May I use your phone?" I plead.

"Of course! It's over there." He points to a table near the piano.

"Operator, please connect me with the Taliaferro residence." A moment later, "Mrs. Taliaferro, this is Ruby Ray."

"Ruby! Tell me you've heard something!" I can hear her muffle the phone and speak to her husband, "It's about Leo!"

"Yes, I think I know where they are, but it's not definite," I caution her. "Can you and your husband meet me in front of the new high school auditorium immediately?"

"The auditorium?" She's perplexed. "Of course."

"Bring flashlights or lanterns, as many as you have," I insist. "I need to ring off to place another call."

"Yes. Yes, of course."

"I'll see you soon." The line goes dead, and I click the receiver three times. "Police Department, please. It's urgent."

"Fullerton Police," a lethargic man yawns into the phone.

"Yes, this is Ruby Ray. I believe that a group of students are currently trapped in the tunnels underneath the high school."

"Now hold on there," he barks. "What makes you think so?"

"Sir, I was at the hospital just now with some of your fellow officers. I have reason to believe—"

"Look, Miss Ray. Sergeant Blockhurst warned me about you. He said to tell you that unless you know something for certain, you have to wait until tomorrow morning to file a missing person's report. Then we'll start looking," he tries to pacify me.

"You're not letting me finish. I was told—"

"Good night, Miss Ray." *Click*

"OHHHH!" I scream with frustration.

Uncle Charles shakes his head. "Did you expect a different outcome?"

I inhale deeply and blow out my ire. "I guess not."

"Look, we can do this without them." He gently nudges me aside. "Now I really should call the house before we head over. There's no telling how long we may be, and I want to make sure Nan can stay."

"For the life of me I can't figure out how they'd get into the auditorium, much less know about the access door to the tunnels. It's pretty plain but is handy for us. Storage for the theater was created down there and we've been usin' it for supplies." Stan, who is seated next to Uncle Charles in the front seat, turns around to speak with me. "I made sure all the doors of the building were locked Friday before I returned the key to the janitor."

"Who else would have keys to the auditorium?" Uncle Charles asks.

Stan pulls at his chin. "Just the project supervisor."

"You mentioned there's more than one tunnel. Are there other entrances?" I visualize a labyrinth running under the campus. They could be anywhere down there.

"Yes…but I was told they'd all been locked up with chains." He runs a hand over his mustache. "Don't know much more about 'em than that."

I exhale audibly and wonder if Wallace somehow secured a key. But if he knew they were going down there, why bother visiting the Taliaferros Saturday afternoon? An alibi, as Edith suggested? I suppose it's unimportant now. We just need to find the kids. I'm sure they'll fill us in later…provided they are able.

"Who'd you say is with your daughter, Charles?"

"Polly Baker—"

Stan whistles. "I'll bet Baker's hoppin' mad. He's hired me over the years for some projects, and you do not want to mess with him."

Uncle Charles clears his throat. "So…um…Polly, Leo Taliaferro, and Earl Adams."

"Earl Adams!" Stan slaps his head. "How'd I forget?!"

I perk up. "You know Earl?"

"Yeah, I'll say. Been tunin' Tilley's piano for years. In fact, she told me to ask him to give the Wurlitzer a whirl." Stan notices Uncle Charles solemnity and apologizes, "Sorry about that. It usually gets a chuckle. Anyways, I couldn't stand the thought of it sittin' there not being played while we're waiting for replacements for those damaged cabinet parts. And I knew Earl sometimes fills in for church organists around town."

"So, Earl's been visiting the auditorium?" I probe.

"A few times. And it's been beautiful! Music fillin' the eaves."

"When did he last visit?"

"That's the thing. He was there Friday afternoon. Arrived just after you left, Ruby. I wanted to lock up early but didn't have the heart to ask him to stop. So, I told him to use the side door backstage when he was done. Asked him to turn the lock on the door handle and just close the door behind him. Can't believe I forgot about that." Stan looks at both Uncle Charles and me remorsefully. "He's done it before, and he's always been a good kid. At least Tilley and I thought so. I didn't think twice about leaving him alone there."

"Well, that explains it." I mull this over.

Uncle Charles parks on Harvard, the street that runs along the east side of campus. Under the streetlights I can see that the Taliaferros have arrived before us. I shiver while exiting the car and wish that I'd worn a warmer coat than the lightweight sweater I grabbed on our way out. After all, it's been unseasonably cool this past week, as evidenced by the hailstorm Friday afternoon. I tug my cloche sharply for warmth and wince, having momentarily forgotten my wound.

As soon as we approach them, Mrs. Taliaferro throws her arms around me. Her body quivers, and she begs, "Please let them be here. And please please let them be alright."

I can't tell if she is addressing me or sending up a prayer. Perhaps both. I comfort her, "My instinct tells me that they are in the tunnels somewhere. And my instincts are rarely wrong." I don't add that my instincts have been silent when it comes to the kids' well-being.

She nods and wipes her eyes with her gloved hands. Mr. Taliaferro, a tall slim man with a thick head of wavy dark hair, drapes a protective arm around her shoulders. He offers his other hand to shake and introduces himself, "I'm Mattia Taliaferro. Thank you so much for everything you've been doing to find our Leo." He chokes up.

"Of course," I grip his hand. "I'm Ruby Ray, and this is my uncle, Charles Ray. His daughter Dottie has also been missing."

The two men exchange handshakes and politely murmur their regards.

I accept a flashlight from Stan and introduce him as well. "This is Stan Jones, the foreman for this building project. He can get us inside and lead us into the tunnels. Apparently, there are quite a few below."

Mr. Taliaferro holds up two lanterns. "We also have an extra lantern for whoever needs one." Uncle Charles accepts it from him.

Mrs. Taliaferro has a third lantern sitting at her feet. She opens the knapsack she's been holding and reveals two Thermos flasks. "We brought water too. Who knows when they last ate or drank."

"Good thinkin'" Stan replies

"Before we go down, Mr. and Mrs. Taliaferro, there is something I need to tell you." I have no idea what the conditions will be and don't want them to be blindsided. "This afternoon we visited the home and classroom of Mr. Wallace Mains."

"The math teacher who stopped by our house?" Mr. Taliaferro is taken aback. "What's he got to do with this?"

I pause to consider my words. "Many of the clues we uncovered have led me to conclude that Mr. Mains knows something about the kids' disappearance."

"What did you find?" Mrs. Taliaferro is eager for answers.

"Several things. But the most compelling was a letter that Mr. Mains drafted to a friend. The long and the short of it is that he successfully recruited the kids into a cult."

"God help us!" "Mary, Mother of God!" The Taliaferros exclaim at the same time, both as horrified as I felt earlier today.

"My Uncle Charles and I are as shocked as you." I glance in his direction. He has raised a hand to cover his closed eyes.

"What does this mean?" Mrs. Taliaferro demands.

"Well, they had planned to participate in a ceremony to summon or channel some sort of mystical force." I cringe at the way that sounds.

"Blasphemy!" Mr. Taliaferro cries. "How could my son do such a thing?"

"No doubt about it! Polly Baker's behind this," Mrs. Taliaferro pats his arm, her face livid.

"Speaking of the Bakers, shouldn't they be here too?" Stan suggests and receives scornful glares from Leo's parents. He holds up his hands and shrugs. "Their daughter is down there too."

"For that matter, Earl's mother and stepfather should be here as well," Uncle Charles adds.

I close my eyes and breathe deeply to settle my frustration. Every part of me is itching to race down into the tunnels. But Stan and Uncle Charles have a point. "I guess we can wait for them to arrive..."

My uncle groans.

"And that may take a while since Earl's family doesn't have a phone," I continue. "Or we could go down immediately and contact them once we've found the kids."

"Well, I for one am not waiting another minute. Mr. Jones, please unlock the door and show us the way." Mr. Taliaferro marches up the steps.

Stan's eyes meet mine and, with another shrug, he ascends the steps toward the portico, his keys in one hand and a flashlight in the other.

CHAPTER 28

Claustrophobia aside, it's the ominous silence that unsettles me most from the moment we step through the doorway into the dark cramped tunnel. Ordinarily I relish moments of silence as a balm for my nerves when I'm feeling unraveled. But now, the stillness pricks and scrapes, exposing my every dread and terror. I suppose I had expected to hear shouts for help or some sort of commotion.

"Leo!" Mr. Taliaferro bellows. His call, both a command and a plea, carries along the concrete tunnel until it hits some barrier and echoes back.

Everyone else joins in shouting names, but the cacophony of voices booms and reverberates unpleasantly.

"Stop!" Uncle Charles beckons. "If we continue like this, we'll never hear them answer."

"He's right," Stan affirms.

I sweep the space around us with the beam of my flashlight. It looks as though shallow alcoves line the right side of this main tunnel. The closest alcove is chockablock with makeshift shelving laden with paint cans, roller brushes, and trays. I stroll a bit further and spy ladders of various sizes, sawhorses stacked in threes, and a table with wheels. Odd bits of furniture and neatly arranged crates fill the remaining alcoves as far as I can see. There's no evidence of the kids anywhere nearby. I flash my beam down the passageway and notice another tunnel on the left.

"A fork?" Uncle Charles inquires.

"Yeah, not sure where either tunnel goes from there," Stan replies.

"You've never been any further?" Mrs. Taliaferro asks with alarm.

"Sorry, ma'am. I've never had any cause to wander down here," Stan sniffs. "I'm sure some of my men have snooped around. But I've got plenty a other things to keep me busy."

"Of course you do, Stan," Uncle Charles assures him. "I wonder though…there must be some sort of diagram for this space."

"Oh, I'm sure there is. The architect no doubt has one. But my job is finishing the auditorium. We only use this space for storage. I've only been down here a couple other times. To be honest it gives me the willies," Stan confesses.

"Great!" Mr. Taliaferro remarks sarcastically. "What do we do now? Wander aimlessly until we stumble upon them?"

I empathize with his mounting panic, but reacting to our fears will get us nowhere. "We need a plan. If the kids can hear our calls and can answer, they would have done so. Which means they're further along the tunnels." I pause, refusing to consider the chilling alternative. "Anyway, we have two options. One is to go back and try to get a hold of someone who knows the layout down here. The other is to continue the search on our own but in a systematic way."

"Agreed." Mr. Taliaferro suggests, "My wife and I can take the tunnel on the left, you three keep going on this one."

"Oh, just a minute." Stan shuffles away from them into one of the alcoves, rustles through one of the crates, and then rushes back a moment later. "Here." He hands something to Mrs. Taliaferro. "It's chalk for marking the walls."

"Good idea," Mr. Taliaferro replies. "If we—when we find them…"

"One person can stay with the kids if necessary and the other can follow the chalk markings to locate the other team," Uncle Charles recommends. "I mean, how far can these tunnels go? I doubt they extend past the school."

"Unless they branch further into town," Stan broods.

"Is that true?" Mrs. Taliaferro snaps.

"Well, somma the guys were talkin' one day about all the construction nearby—" Stan begins.

"Let's keep our heads," I interject and reach into my handbag for my watch. Shining a beam onto its surface, I note the time. "It's 8:50. I propose that in 30 minutes we turn around and head back here. If one group finds the kids before that, then send one person back to retrace the steps of the other team to let them know."

"That's a good idea, Ruby." Uncle Charles adds, "Limit our calls to every few minutes. That way we can better hear their reply."

"You should take water." Mrs. Taliaferro reaches into her knapsack and retrieves one of the flasks. "At least whoever reaches them first can give them something to drink while waiting for help."

"Good thinking," Stan accepts the container with his free hand, and we part ways.

"Oh!" I jump. "You didn't have to do that!" Uncle Charles has draped his coat around my shoulders.

"I can hear you shivering. Who'd have thought it would be so chilly down here."

"Well, thank you." I slip my arms through the sleeves and roll the hems to free my hands. The temperature is in the 50s, if that. My lightweight spring sweater isn't cutting it. I mark the wall with chalk, and we continue our steady progress, stopping to call out the kids' names each time we hear the Taliaferros do the same. After a little while, I realize that the Taliaferros' calls are no longer audible. Judging from the distance we've already covered, I'd say we are under the football stadium. The passageway has been a straight course since the earlier split. Alcoves continue on either side, although they are becoming less frequent. And the network of pipes and ducts along the ceiling has thinned to a single tube. While exploring one alcove, I hear the scuff of a shoe.

"Oops!" Stan warns, "Watch out. There's some loose dirt on the path."

The crunch of granules underfoot marks the transition from the paved floor to packed dirt. A larger alcove opens on the right. Footsteps indicate that this space has been in use, perhaps recently. I examine them closely. "There are at least three different sets of prints here." I shine my flashlight on an area where a larger print is situated next to a smaller one. A male and female. Both with wide heels, like a loafer or oxford. Another set clearly belongs to a female wearing shoes with a pointed toe and dime-sized heel. There's a fourth set of prints, also large, but they aren't as clear as the others and may be from the same shoes as those I already noticed. Geometric shaped depressions in the earth mark the center of the alcove. Nothing more can be gleaned from this space, but it appears that the kids may have been here.

As we venture further down the passage, the quality of the sound changes. Our footsteps are muted to dull thumps, and the air smells musty. I mark the wall with chalk.

"Dottie! Polly!" Uncle Charles beckons.

"Leo! Earl!" I join in.

Silence.

"Feels like we're well past the campus boundary," Stan remarks quietly.

"I thought so too," I agree. The passage abruptly turns left. A little ways further, we are unexpectedly assailed by a strong antiseptic odor. I swing my flashlight left and right, stopping when the beam lands upon a heap of toppled crates strewn throughout a recess. "Careful here. There's broken glass."

Both Uncle Charles and Stan sweep their lights around the niche. Stan whistles. "John Barleycorn," he murmurs while lifting a mason jar.

"Not only that," Uncle Charles points toward a bulging duffle in a corner. When he opens it, silver and crystal twinkle brightly under the gleam of our flashlights.

I reach forward with my free hand and snatch the handle of an ornate urn, under which I spy a lengthy strand of pearls and a small gold ormolu clock.

Oh, Frank.

I understand now. This must be where he stashed the loot from the neighborhood thefts, as well as the moonshine they produced. Clever really. No one would find this space. It's well past the alcoves in use beneath the auditorium. He had the keys and could let himself, and Fipps for that matter, inside late at night. I wouldn't be surprised to find a hand truck around here somewhere to move these heavy boxes.

I shift my beam to the other corner of the recess where shards of broken glass sparkle back.

"Hold on." I take a couple of cautious steps toward the jagged fragments and bend down to get a closer look. "There's blood here. Quite a lot, in fact." While retracing my steps around the minefield of sharp-edged pieces, I lose my balance and begin to tumble forward. My hands are splayed, ready to stabilize my fall, as the cloche drops off my head onto the sticky mess. Thankfully, a pair of hands grip me around the waist and spare me from an injurious landing.

"Easy there," Uncle Charles holds me upright until he's certain I've got my sea legs. "Are you alright?"

"Just a bit lightheaded," I confess.

"You've been going nonstop all day. I keep forgetting that you should be recuperating from your injury." He peers around to the back of my head.

Stan joins us and, to my astonishment (and irritation), shines his light directly into my face. "You're injured?" With everything going on so far, he must not have noticed the scratches on my face.

"Look, there's no time for that now," I brush aside their concern and quickly bend down to retrieve my hat so we can continue our search. But in my haste, everything around me starts spinning, nausea wells up in my throat, and darkness rapidly fills my visual field despite Stan's beam shining directly upon me.

"Uggh!" I open my eyes and try to sit up. Uncle Charles releases me once he's sure I won't topple over again. Energy surges into my limbs as panic surfaces to my conscious awareness.

We don't have time for this!

"We need to get going!"

"Not until I'm sure you've recovered." Though he's in shadow, I sense he's watching my every move.

Why this? Why now? I berate myself. Of all the times to faint. I reach toward my head.

"Your hat's a lost cause," Uncle Charles focuses the lantern upon my cloche, which has rolled back into the mess.

"Probably for the best," I mutter. I don't think I could have worn it a moment longer. Having forgotten to take another headache powder when we returned home, the pressure of the hat on my wound was becoming unbearable. It's remarkable how adaptable we can be to chronic pain when we are preoccupied with more compelling concerns. We don't notice the severity of our pain until it's gone.

"There's a trail of drops across the floor here leading into the passage." Stan's beam redirects our attention toward a line of regularly spaced dark spots. "Ruby, are you alright?"

"You go, Stan. Ruby and I will follow in a moment," Uncle Charles urges him onward.

In no time my unsteadiness dissipates completely. I call out to Stan, "I'm fine. We're right behind you."

"Are you sure?" Uncle Charles' tone conveys doubt, but he accepts my determined canter forward, sticking close to my side just in case.

The tunnel bends to the right, then after about two hundred feet the trail suddenly hits a dead end. "That's odd. It's as though—"

"Drat!" Uncle Charles curses. Now only two sources of light are visible. Mine and Stan's.

"What happened?" I shine my light upon him and see that he's jiggling the lantern.

"Out of kerosene," he sighs with frustration.

"Probably wasn't full to begin with," Stan remarks.

"That's ok, Uncle Charles." I loop my arm through his. "We'll share mine. We need to keep moving." I scan the unusual contours and shiny specks of minerals on the wall before us. "That's odd. It's as though there's a natural cavern down here."

"Maybe there is," Stan points out. "We're probably near that big hill northa campus. Hillcrest Park. Wouldn't be surprised if there are caves inside."

My beam chases the wall's length to the left, and another tunnel is discernible. I mark the wall with chalk, and we enter the mouth of a narrow passageway, its ceiling barely six feet high. Uncle Charles has to bend his head slightly. The air is tinged with a metallic, earthy scent, and the opening seems to be constricting. My claustrophobia kicks in with a vengeance, but I breathe through it. "I wonder why the trail of blood stopped there?"

"I sure hope this tunnel's been reinforced," Stan remarks.

"Should we turn around?" Uncle Charles raises his wrist into the beam of light. "It's been thirty minutes."

"I suppose so," I concur. Hopefully the Taliaferros have had better luck at their end.

"Shh," Stan quiets us, and I detect a voice further along the tunnel. "Keep going," he whispers.

The passage twists and turns, narrows and broadens, slowing our pace here and there. I begin to doubt the direction of the call when we hear it again, thankfully closer.

"Here! They're here!" Mrs. Taliaferro's howl is perceptible.

We race along the tunnel until we encounter a fork in the passage. "No!" I fume, exasperated by this hindrance. "Which way now?"

"They're here!" Mrs. Taliaferro shouts again.

"This way!" Uncle Charles swings our flashlight to the left and we continue our sprint.

A glow begins to brighten in the distance, about fifty yards away. As we approach, we see a large cave lit by both lanterns the Taliaferros were carrying. Mrs. Taliaferro is on the ground, her arms tightly gripped around her son who looks up weakly while drinking from her flask. Mr. Taliaferro is holding Leo's right hand while wiping tears from his own eyes.

"Polka Dot!" Uncle Charles leaps forward and scoops up his daughter as though she were still a child of six. They cling to one another, shaking with sobs.

She's not dead. She's not dead.

This fear has been propelling me forward, driving my every action since I first realized the implications of Wallace's letter. I rush over and wrap my arms around them both, basking in relief, that giddy warmth that floods your body with a happiness you can only experience on the heels of great anguish. But the moment passes more quickly than I'd like.

"We need help," Stan redirects our attention to Polly, whose pale form is arranged on the floor beneath a pile of fur.

Earl sits near Polly, his back against the wall and his knees bent. He looks stunned, his face a mix of shock and confusion. "How? Who?"

"Earl, I'm Ruby. Dottie's cousin. Are you alright?"

He nods at me, confused.

I kneel beside Polly and retrieve her limp hand from beneath the coverings. She's breathing but doesn't react at all when I squeeze her arm. "What's happened to Polly?"

"She…I mean…her ankle," I hear Earl mumble.

Pushing aside the fur, which is stiff in spots and sticky in others, I realize that the lantern light is insufficient to closely examine Polly's injury. So, I direct my flashlight toward her feet and see that blood has pooled on the ground beneath. *Gulp*. A large, deep gash slashes across the inside of Polly's left ankle from front to back. Her delicate shoe has been removed and lies on its side next to her foot, its silver marred by crimson stains. The wound appears to have stopped bleeding, but her foot is an unnatural pale gray, nothing like her usual lovely porcelain complexion. Brushing modesty aside given the circumstances, I lift her skirt and feel that a belt has been tightened around her thigh as a tourniquet. Unsurprisingly, one of these kids knows a thing or two about first aid. My mind flashes to the jagged shards of glass, and I wonder how on earth she managed to make it through the passage all the way to this cave. I'm sure the story will unfold in due course.

"Oh, Ruby," Dottie squeezes me from behind. I drop my flashlight and turn to hold her quivering figure. "I thought she was going to die."

"I'll go back and call for an ambulance," Stan turns toward the tunnel but is momentarily stopped.

"Wait…water…please," Earl gasps.

Uncle Charles retrieves the flask Stan dropped by the entryway on his way in and helps Earl take a sip. "Not too much at once or it won't stay down."

Stan pats Earl's shoulder. "I'll bring more for all four of you. There's a phone in the auditorium, so I won't have to dilly dally."

"I'll go with you," Mr. Taliaferro steps away from his little family. "You may need a hand."

Stan nods and both men charge away, sharing Stan's flashlight between them as Mr. Taliaferro has left his lantern to help illuminate the cave.

"Earl hasn't had a thing to drink since Friday night," Dottie releases her embrace and sits next to Earl against the wall. "We had a flask of water, but Earl wouldn't take a drop. Insisted that we drink it instead."

Uncle Charles reaches down and squeezes Earl's hand. "That was a valiant thing to do, young man. We owe you a debt of gratitude."

Earl smiles frailly. "Don't worry about me. Polly's the one who needs your help."

"What happened to her," Mrs. Taliaferro asks from across the room, determined not to release her firm grasp on her son.

"Did she cut her foot on broken glass in the alcove with the crates?" I turn toward Dottie for affirmation.

She averts her glance and looks at her hands. "Please don't think poorly of her."

"Polka Dot…" Uncle Charles rises and places a reassuring arm around her. "We're not going to judge Polly or any of you. We just need to know exactly what happened so we can help her."

"She drank from one of those jars, sir," Earl replies.

Uncle Charles sighs. "I think I get the picture."

"We were so thirsty, Dad. And Polly…you know how she is…she must have been desperate because while we were sleeping, she took one of the flashlights and snuck back there."

"She must have been gone for a couple of hours," Leo looks guiltily toward Polly. "I shoulda noticed. I coulda stopped her. But I was asleep. I'm so tired." He waves away the flask his mother is pressing upon him, preferring to recline against her.

"You're all dehydrated, and I doubt you've had any food either," I look at Dottie who is drinking from the flask Uncle Charles has placed in her hands. "This isn't your fault. NONE of this is your fault."

I lock eyes with Earl and Leo as well. "And as for Polly, well we all know that once Polly sets her mind on something…"

"Listen to her, Leonardo," his mother advises him. "You're not to blame for any of this."

"Dad, I…" Dottie begins.

"No need to explain anything right now, Polka Dot," Uncle Charles counsels. "There will be plenty of time for that later. What can we do to make you comfortable right now?" He tightens his hold on his daughter and encourages her to sit back down, "You're shaking. It was thoughtful of you to warm Polly with your coat, but you must be chilled through."

"Here, Dottie." I remove my arms from Uncle Charles' coat and hand it to her. "You need this far more than I do."

She accepts the coat with a grateful smile and drapes it across the front of her body, bending her knees so they too are covered. I turn toward Polly, and Dottie gasps. "Ruby! Your head!"

Mrs. Taliaferro winces. "What happened to you?!"

My hand instinctively flies up to my scalp. "I'm fine. That's a story for another time." I redirect the question, "Has Polly woken up since you found her?"

Dottie doesn't look convinced by my response, but she lets it go for now in the interest of her friend. "She'd start to rouse from time to time, but she hasn't really said anything."

"She vomited a few times when we found her," Leo adds. "And she was crying when we carried her back."

"We had to make the belt pretty tight to stop the bleeding," Earl explains.

"Ahh…that explains the trail stopping in the passageway." The kids look at me questioningly, so I clarify. "That's how we found you. We followed a trail of blood drops from the alcove with the alcohol." I turn toward Leo and his mother. "How did you find them?"

"We actually just stumbled upon them," Mrs. Taliaferro explains. "The main tunnel ended and there was, what looked like, a natural opening in the rock. We still had a couple of minutes before we needed to turn back so we decided to take a look. We'd only walked about fifty feet in the small tunnel when I heard Leo call, 'Mom.'" She looks lovingly at her son.

"I couldn't believe my eyes! I thought I was hallucinating or something," Leo smiles back at his mother, wiping a tear from his eye. "I don't know how long we've been down here. All our watches stopped because we forgot to wind them. We didn't know how long we'd have to wait before someone answered that door."

Puzzled, I look at Dottie questioningly. She clarifies, "Every so often a couple of us would go back to the door leading into the auditorium. That man locked it when he left Friday night."

"That man?" Uncle Charles asks, although I know exactly who Dottie is referring to.

"We were in another part of the main tunnel, closer to the door, when we heard a loud crash." Dottie explains.

"We turned off our lights right away." Earl confesses, "We didn't want to get caught again." Both Dottie and Leo shake their heads at him, eyes wide.

"It's okay, kids," Uncle Charles assures them. "We have a fairly good idea what you were doing down here."

Earl continues, "A few minutes after the crash, the man was heading back down the tunnel and found us with his flashlight."

"We were so scared," Leo admits. "His eyes looked crazy, and he started yelling, 'You shouldn't be here,' along with some other words I won't repeat." He glances apologetically at his mother,

Dottie picks up the thread of the story. "We held onto each other while he ran off toward the door."

Her father gives her a squeeze. "How terrifying for you."

"Looking back, I'm sure the four of us could have taken him down," Earl comments. "But we didn't know if he had a gun or anything. His clothes and hair were messy, and he looked like a madman."

"We waited until we were sure he'd left, but when we tried the door to the auditorium, it was locked," Leo explains. "We weren't sure if or when he might return, so we decided to find a place to hide."

"It took us a while, wandering all over these tunnels, but eventually we found this pla—" The sound of vomiting interrupts Dottie.

"Oh Polly." I rush toward her as Mrs. Taliaferro hands me a handkerchief from her bag.

"So-o-o co-o-ld." I lean close to hear her voice as I wipe her face.

"Give her some water," Uncle Charles hands me the Thermos.

"I don't know if that's a good idea quite yet." I tuck the coats more firmly around her. "I doubt she can keep it down."

"She's unconscious again anyway," Dottie strokes Polly's hair.

Placing two fingers on her cool neck, I realize that her heart is racing. Her shallow breaths have become more rapid as well. "She's in shock."

Uncle Charles looks at his watch, "They've been gone for about 20 minutes. It may be a while longer until the paramedics can reach us."

"We may not have that long," I reply urgently. Polly is now shaking violently. "Uncle Charles, can you carry her out? I hate to move her, but under the circumstances...."

He immediately scoops her petite, frail form into his arms. "Put your flashlight in my hand."

I comply but begin to question whether he can manage her on his own with the convulsions. "I'm not sure tha—"

But he's out of the cave before I can finish.

CHAPTER 29

MONDAY, MAY 12, 1930, EARLY MORNING

The clamor of voices and clanging equipment in the emergency room contrasts sharply with the tomb-like silence of the tunnels. I attempt to loosen the tightness in my body by tilting my neck side to side and rolling my shoulders. There hasn't been a moment to reflect since finding the kids, and my nerves feel raw. Uncle Charles is propped on the edge of Dottie's gurney, encouraging her to sip water every couple of minutes.

He notices my stretching and asks, "How are you feeling Ruby? You were in this same bed not twenty-four hours ago."

"It feels like weeks," I confess. "I'm beat, as I'm sure you both are too."

"How's your head?" Dottie hands the cup back to her father. I had given her a synopsis of my own misadventure during our ride over to the hospital.

"To be honest, I could do with another headache powder."

"I'll go get a nurse." Uncle Charles begins to rise, but I hold up a hand to stop him.

"They're swamped right now. I'm sure someone will be in to see Dottie when they have a spare moment." He looks at me with uncertainty, so I add, "I can wait. Really."

Appeased, Uncle Charles nods and redirects his attention to Dottie.

I settle back into the stiff chair as best I can and mull over everything that transpired this evening. After Uncle Charles left with Polly, all conversation in the cave came to an abrupt halt. The kids were exhausted, and we were all preoccupied with concern for Polly. Uncle Charles later told me that he had just made it into the auditorium with the fragile girl when Stan intercepted him and reported that the ambulance was on its way. Stan and Mr. Taliaferro then reentered the tunnels to bring more water for the remaining children. Not long after that, the emergency crew arrived, including paramedics, a fire truck, and two police cars. Polly was immediately loaded into the ambulance and taken to the hospital, while Uncle Charles helped the others carry additional stretchers and first aid equipment through the tunnels. Earl's dehydration and physical weakness required that he was transported via ambulance, as well. However, the paramedics agreed that Dottie and Leo could ride to the hospital in their parents' cars. Around midnight we arrived at the emergency room. I was impressed by the well-orchestrated actions of the hospital staff. All three remaining students were immediately situated into partitioned rooms next to one another, and either a physician or nurse began their initial work up with each patient within minutes. That was over two hours ago, however.

A commotion just outside the filmy privacy curtain snaps my attention back to the present moment. Metallic clatter and pings suggest that someone has dropped an equipment tray. "Get that cleaned up immediately!" The head nurse chastises.

"I think we're going to be here a while longer," Uncle Charles sighs.

Dottie groans, "I'm starved!"

"I'm sure you are, Dottie." Now that her body has received some hydration, the audible rumbles in her stomach signal the awakening of a fierce appetite. I attempt to distract her. "I'd like to hear more about your experiences after finding the cave. You mentioned searching the tunnels once you realized you were locked in."

She nods. "Yeah, at first, we tried to find a good hiding place. We were worried he'd come back right away with a weapon or something. But after a few hours, we started searching for other exits."

"There must be several," Uncle Charles suggests. "Those tunnels have been there for quite some time."

"There were a couple. But they were locked from the outside. Earl tried to kick through one since it opened outward, but that was a bust."

Uncle Charles raises his eyebrows, "I'm sure those doors are reinforced with steel. He's lucky he didn't injure himself."

"That explains why they couldn't break down the door with all that equipment stored near the exit," I declare.

"Exactly! After a few hours, we started taking turns to check the auditorium exit. See if by some chance it had been unlocked." Dottie looks at her hands folded in her lap, no longer pale from the cold. "By Saturday afternoon or so, we realized we were in it for the long haul. We'd hoped workers might be in on Saturday, but there's no way they'd go to work on Mother's Day."

"How in the world did you find out about the tunnels in the first place?" her father asks. "I honestly had no idea about them, and I've lived here for nearly twenty years."

Dottie appears reluctant to answer, so I encourage her. "Dottie, we know about Mr. Mains and suspect what he might have asked you to do."

Her head snaps up, eyes wide with shock. "How did you—"

Uncle Charles clears his throat. "We don't need to get into all that right now." I suspect he is as reluctant as Dottie to discuss Wallace Mains and the Pythagorean Club at this moment.

"Your father's right," I reassure her. "There's plenty of time to talk about that later."

Dottie's body relaxes, and Uncle Charles passes her the cup of water, lovingly patting her shoulder. She dutifully sips instead of gulping down the remains of the cup, as I'm certain she'd prefer to do. Once she's settled back onto the gurney, she answers her father's question. "Earl's been practicing lately on the fancy organ in the auditorium. One day he noticed that the door to the tunnels was ajar, so he took a peek. Later he explored them after everyone had left for the day. Mr. Jones let him stay and practice, as long as he locked up each time."

"Don't they lock the door to the tunnels each night?" I query.

"No, Earl said it was always left unlocked." Dottie explains.

"Maybe a key was required to secure the lock," I suggest.

A key on Stan's keyring?

Dottie continues her story. "Friday afternoon after everyone had left for the day, Mr. Jones told Earl he could stay and practice but asked him to turn the lock on the handle of the side door when he left."

"But he didn't do that," Uncle Charles adds.

Guilt flashes across Dottie's face.

"We already deduced that, Dottie," I pat her hand.

"Back so soon?" Dr. Collins parts the curtain and notices me immediately. "I'm glad to see you're upright this time." He then turns his attention to Dottie and runs through the usual diagnostic drill. *Pulse. Stethoscope. Pupils.* "How are you feeling, young lady?"

"Better now. I'd love to eat something though," she confesses. "And sleep in my own bed," she mumbles under her breath.

Dr. Collins chuckles. "I see no reason to keep you here. Compared with a couple of your pals, you're in pretty good shape."

Relieved, Uncle Charles asks, "So, can I take her home?"

"In a bit. The nurse will need to come in with instructions." Dr. Collins then turns toward me. "You, on the other hand, promised me you'd take it easy this weekend."

"There were more pressing matters…" I begin to rise from my chair.

"A head injury like yours is not something that can be ignored. I'd like you to stay until I have a moment to give you a more thorough examination." He motions for me to sit back down. "Unfortunately, that may be a while given my patient load this evening." He turns to Uncle Charles, "Feel free to take your daughter home once the nurse has finished up."

"Thank you doctor."

"And you, young lady, go easy on the food at first." He winks, "I'm sure you'd like to keep it down."

Dottie chuckles, "Yes, doctor."

"Miss Ray, you'll be taking your cousin's place. I'll be back as soon as I can." With that, Dr. Collins pulls aside the curtain and leaves.

About fifteen minutes later, a harried nurse arrives and rapidly instructs Dottie and her father about resuming food and liquid intake, as well as signs to watch out for in case of complications. As she's about to leave, Dottie inquires, "How are my friends?"

The nurse's stern countenance softens. "As good as can be expected, given what they've been through." She approaches the bed, bending close to Dottie. "I shouldn't really be telling you this, but your friend Leonardo will be going home like you in a little while. However, the other two…let's just say they'll be here for a while longer."

I help Dottie into the wheelchair the nurse has left.

"I don't need that," Dottie grumbles.

"Hospital policy." I make a face and whisper, "They made me ride in one last night."

She giggles.

"I'll get Dottie settled at home and come back as soon as I can," Uncle Charles leans in for a hug. "I'm sure Jack and Nan will fuss over Dottie the moment they hear us pull into the driveway."

"Don't worry about me," I assure him. "I'm fine and will have them call you when I'm ready to go home."

"You're sure?" he asks uncertainly.

"Positive. Now off you go. This brave young woman is in dire need of comfortable pajamas and her cozy bed." I give Dottie a warm squeeze. "I'll see you soon."

"Alrighty then. Let's go, Polka Dot." Uncle Charles wheels her out of the room.

I glance at the wall clock. It's just after 3:00 AM on Monday. A nursing student hustles in to change the bedding on the gurney and clear the items from the bedside table. She returns with fresh linen, a sterile glass, and a pitcher full of water. Once the gurney has been made, neat hospital folds at the corners, she finally speaks to me. "You're supposed to lie down, ma'am." I catch her staring at my head wound and the abrasions on my face as she assists me into the bed.

"Thank you, Olive." I read the badge on her uniform. "You've been most helpful."

She smiles bashfully. "The doctor will be in soon." She looks out the door. "Hopefully. Is there anything else I can get you in the meantime?"

"Actually, there is." And I request the headache powder I've been longing for since we arrived.

"She's right in there, ma'am." I hear Olive's voice outside the partition.

I stretch my arms as Norma enters. I must have fallen asleep. A glance at the clock tells me it's now 3:41 AM. Norma approaches the bed and squeezes my outstretched hand. "Oh Ruby! Are you okay?"

"It would appear that the good doctor is not convinced I followed his orders yesterday to rest."

"I should say you didn't," Norma admonishes. "Ruby, what were you thinking? After you left last night, Edith filled me in on everything that happened yesterday at Wallace's house and in his classroom. But you should have let others manage things."

"Story of my life," I confess. "What was I to do Norma? I couldn't lay in bed all day while Dottie's life was on the line?"

She nods with sympathy. "I know. I was sick with worry when Frank was missing."

"How did you know I was here?" I query.

"While returning from the restroom, I overheard two nursing students discussing Dottie and her friends. I thought I'd come by to see how they are. I wasn't expecting to find you in bed though."

"This hospital's been a hive of activity this weekend," I comment as she takes a seat by the bed. "How is Frank doing?" My stomach turns as I recall what the kids said about him, and a fury begins to bubble within me. Nevertheless, I understand that Frank was unstable and under the influence of the toxins he'd ingested. My heart aches for Norma and can only imagine what she's going through. I'm sure she's conflicted. She adores her students, the very ones her own brother locked away.

"He's under arrest for child endangerment," she looks down at her hands. "The sergeant mentioned that he may be charged with bootlegging as well."

"Blockhurst?"

"That's the one." Norma's shoulders slump forward. "He's banned all visitors from the room, including me."

I nod with empathy but understand that decision. It sounds as though the sergeant is finally doing his job. "Norma, I need to tell you that while I've been able to insist upon client confidentiality up to now, given the investigations that will ensue, I'll need to tell him about finding Stan Jones' keys in Frank's car."

She bobs her head. "I figured as much. I'm just a wreck about what Frank did to those kids. I'm so sorry." A large tear rolls down her cheek. "That was so unlike him. He's truly not a bad person."

"I know that," I reply gently. "But he is responsible for his choices and must be held accountable."

"Of course." Her response is barely audible. We sit in silence for a few minutes when she asks apprehensively. "What do you think will happen to him?"

I carefully consider how to respond. "That will depend on many factors. I cannot say with any certainty what's in store for him. While it's easier said than done, try to take things one step at a time. Focusing on what might happen in the future will only bring you grief."

"You're right, of course." Some of the tension leaves her shoulders.

"Nan often says, 'Worryin' is practicin' pain.'"

"Wise words," Norma smiles.

Then we both nearly jump from our seats as a booming baritone in the hallway roars, "Get out of my way, wop!"

"How dare you!" I recognize Mr. Taliaferro's voice.

"It's because of your brat that my daughter is on her deathbed!" Baker continues.

"Uh oh," I murmur to Norma. "It sounds like the Bakers have arrived."

"Our son?!" Mrs. Taliaferro joins in. "He wouldn't be lying in that bed if it weren't for your spoiled daughter!"

An ear-piercing wail announces Helen Baker's entrance into the melee. "Fre-ed! Don't let them say such things about our Polly!"

"It's the truth!" Mr. Taliaferro interjects. "You're horrible people and even worse parents! She's been here for hours and NOW you choose to turn up?!"

"We didn't hear the pho—" Helen whines.

"That's it!" Mr. Baker bellows as the screech of shoes scuffling on the flooring echoes along the corridor. Grunts and thuds suggest that the altercation has become physical.

"Stop!" Multiple female voices thunder at the same time.

"What's going on here?" A third woman, most likely the charge nurse, intercedes. "This is a hospital, for Pete's sake. You and you." I assume she's pointing toward the men. "If you cannot control yourselves, you will be escorted out of the hospital and banned from returning as a visitor."

"But our baby girl—" Mrs. Baker begins.

"—will not enjoy the company of her parents if your husband cannot manage his anger," the nurse completes Mrs. Baker's objection. "And the same goes for you, Mr. Taliaferro."

"Yes, ma'am," he answers, chastened.

"I'll have you know—" Mr. Baker is unable to complete his declaration as a male voice down the hall shouts, "We need a blood donor. Stat." Footsteps pound past my doorway.

"Clear the hallway! Mr. and Mrs. Taliaferro, your son has been released. Please return to his room until the wheelchair has arrived to transport him to your vehicle," the charge nurse commands. "And you two! We need one of you to donate blood for your daughter."

"My baby!" Mrs. Baker sobs.

"Not to worry, Helen. I'll save her." Mr. Baker proclaims then shouts down the hall, "I'll donate my blood."

"Very good." The nurse's no-nonsense voice restores order. "Olive, will you please escort Mrs. Baker to the waiting room and sit with her?"

"Of course, ma'am,"

I hear Mrs. Baker's voice trail away, "We need to call Pastor Tim. He should be…"

"NOW they're worried about their 'baby,'" I exclaim with irritation. "Had the Bakers taken their daughter's disappearance seriously, we may have convinced the police to respond sooner, and her life wouldn't be in danger."

Norma tsks, "That man is frightening."

"And I'm sure he'll never stop crowing about 'saving' his daughter." I shake my head.

Norma nods in agreement. "That poor girl. I always say, 'I love my students. It's some of the parents I could do without.'"

"Her wound looked very deep. There's no telling how much blood she lost, and she's so petite as is. I'm deeply troubled for her."

"Have she and Dottie been friends for very long?"

"They have. I've always had a soft spot for Polly. Partly because of her home life, but also because she lacks confidence. She's an intelligent young lady who has no idea of her worth. It's always been about her beauty, not her brains."

There's not much more to say, so we wait in silence for the doctor to examine me. I don't expect that to happen anytime soon, and after a while, my eyes begin to droop as fatigue overcomes me.

I have no idea how long I've been asleep when Norma shakes me gently. "I'm going to leave and let you rest."

"Thank you so much for stopping by. I'll check in with you and Edith when I'm able."

"Don't you worry about us," she reassures. "There's nothing further you can do for us or for Frank, and your family needs you now. Again, I'm just so sorry that Frank caused you all so much grief."

I stretch out an arm and grasp her hand. "No need for you to apologize. This was not your doing." I squeeze and release her hand. "Take care of yourself, Norma. I'll be in touch."

With that, Norma waves and leaves through the curtains just as Dr. Collins steps aside to let her pass.

"Is Polly alright?" I immediately inquire.

Dr. Collins sighs and nods thoughtfully. "Thankfully yes. For the moment. I cannot say much more than that."

I nod my understanding. "I really don't need to be here, Doctor. Especially with everything going on this evening." I look at the clock. 4:10AM. "We'll, morning."

"You're not getting away that easily," he smirks. "How are YOU feeling?"

"Much better than yesterday, that's for sure. My head was aching, but not terribly so. I took a powder an hour or so ago, which helped."

"Dizziness? Lightheadedness? Weakness?" He asks while shining a light into each of my eyes.

"No weakness. And no dizziness since last night when we were in the tunnels."

He gently probes my skull and asks me to carefully sit up. "How's that? Dizzy?"

"Not as long as I take it slowly."

He nods, "You'll no doubt experience orthostatic dizziness off and on for a little while. Take it slow when rising up. And continue with the headache medication, as needed. We discussed what to watch out for when you were here yesterday. If you notice any of the red flags, come back here immediately."

"Does that mean I can leave?"

"I see no reason to keep you any further." He jots a note in a bedside file. "I'll send in a student to help you arrange for a ride home."

Uncle Charles arrives within minutes of being called. I'm sure he didn't get any rest since returning home. It's raining as he wheels me out through the parking lot, and I fumble with an umbrella, trying to cover us both. We don't notice Sergeant Blockhurst until he's nearly upon us.

"Mr. Ray. Miss Ray?" He raises an eyebrow, undeniably perplexed by my presence in a wheeled chair.

"The good doctor insisted I stay for an exam given my injuries over the weekend." I shouldn't have to explain, but I want to remind him what I've been through in case he chooses this moment to bombard me with questions.

Instead, he addresses my uncle, "How is your daughter, sir?"

"As well as can be expected, Sergeant. Had we found Dottie and her friends sooner—"

Blockhurst raises his palm. "I know what you're going to say, and before you go any further, I want you to know that I am truly…that is to say…I could have…."

Uncle Charles and I offer no assistance as he struggles to apologize.

"I'm sorry," he mumbles words that have probably not crossed his lips in years. "I should have listened to you and the boy's parents."

We both nod our agreement and wait for him to continue.

"I'll have some questions for you, Miss Ray, given Mr. Graham' involvement in the case and your investigation on his behalf."

"Yes sergeant, I understand and intend to assist you with your own investigation. However, under the circumstances, I'd really like to go home."

"Of course. Of course," he mutters. "I'll stop by your house sometime today."

"We'd prefer that you wait until the late afternoon or early evening. It's been a long night, and none of us have gotten any rest," Uncle Charles insists.

"Yes. Well. That'll be fine." At that he proceeds toward the hospital entrance, and Uncle Charles navigates the wheelchair around the newly formed puddles.

CHAPTER 30

The honking of a car horn on the street outside my window stirs me from a deep, well-deserved sleep. According to my bedside clock, it's almost noon.

Sigh.

I'd hoped for a bit more rest. When we returned home in the wee hours, the sun was due to begin rising soon. Dottie was sound asleep in her room, but Jack and Nan met us at the door.

"Why aren't you in bed?" Uncle Charles asked Jack.

Running a hand through his tousled locks, my cousin drawled, "Gees, Dad. How's a fellow supposed to sleep when his cousin's on her deathbed."

I titter. "Deathbed? I'm sure your father explained that the doctor just wanted to give me a once over before sending me home. Hardly a life-or-death scenario."

"It didn't feel right, you bein' gone," Nan interjected. "There's no way I could catch any winks til yer all safe and sound at home."

Safe and sound.

The realization struck as I leaned in to be enveloped by her warm embrace and was all at once overwhelmed by relief and comfort. My body softened as a small sniffle escaped from me. Nan tightened her cuddle. After a moment of relishing this sense of security, I mumbled into the cushion of her shoulder, "It's all fine now, Nan. Dottie's fine. I'm fine. It's over."

She gave me one final squeeze, then held me at arms-length. "You must be tuckered out. I laid out yer gown and turned down yer bed. Do you wanna nibble before headin' up?"

"Honestly, I may just fall into bed as is." Fatigue gripped me and even the task of walking up the stairs seemed beyond me. "Thanks so much, Nan."

She pecked me on the cheek, and Uncle Charles patted my back, as I slowly ambled upstairs.

Now I ponder rising from my cozy haven to check on Dottie. Should I try to slip back into a restorative slumber? I sink back into my pillows, but a dull throbbing in my skull prevents any further rest. So, I carefully rise to a seated position and swing my legs around the side of the bed. No dizziness or lightheadedness. That's progress. I glance at my bedside table and notice a box of headache powder, a glass of water, and a spoon.

Again, what would we do without Nan?

I rise to drop the powder into the glass and stir. I've never grown accustomed to the bitter taste, so I quickly drain the glass without pause. Now that I'm sitting up, a ravenous hunger overwhelms me.

When was the last time I ate?

I may have managed a bite or two last night for dinner before dashing off to the hospital when Frank awakened. Hopefully Jack hasn't devoured all the leftover chicken pot pie.

I carefully stand then tighten my kimono around me. The house is quiet outside my room, and when I near the bottom of the stairs I realize that Uncle Charles is sleeping in his favorite chair, his feet propped on the ottoman. He's still dressed in the same clothes he donned yesterday morning, and a dark stubble shades his jaw. In all these years, I have never seen him so disheveled, a testament to his weariness after days of dread and strain. I forget to tread on the right side of the bottom step and a pitchy squeak disrupts the silence. His eyes fly open, and Uncle Charles looks around, dazed, as he tries to orient himself. At the same moment, I hear the metallic scraping of a utensil across a plate in the kitchen.

Someone else is up.

Uncle Charles checks his pocket watch. "Ruby, why aren't you in bed?"

"I could ask you the same question." I hand him his handkerchief which has fallen onto the floor next to his chair.

"Nan didn't want to leave, and I insisted that she rest upstairs in my room." He folds the handkerchief, which he tidily stashes in his pocket.

"Of course, you did," I reply.

At that moment, Jack thumps downstairs, for once more presentable than both Uncle Charles and I. He has smartened his hair, and his clothes are wrinkle-free. As soon as he notices we are both awake, he cheerfully pronounces, "This has to be the best day ever!"

"Come again?" His father remarks.

"Dottie and Ruby are both home," he answers as though it's obvious, and I realize the full impact that the past few days must have had on him. Most of the time, he was left at home while Uncle Charles and I were off searching for Dottie. Which is remarkable since Jack's not one to wait idly under the best of circumstances.

"I have to commend you, Jack, for your maturity and cooperation while your dad and I were away," I compliment. "It couldn't have been easy for you. In fact, I would not have been surprised if you'd snuck out to look for Dottie yourself."

He grins sheepishly. "Well, the thought did cross my mind."

Uncle Charles snorts.

"I'm sure it did, Jack. What made you stay back?" I ask.

"Well, it's like this," he gives his father a look so full of love, I feel my eyes begin to well. "If something happened to me too. It'd just about kill Dad."

Uncle Charles pulls his son into a tight hug, which Jack gratefully accepts, clutching his father in return. "You're right Jack. This is the best day ever," my uncle murmurs while kissing him atop his head.

"What's all this?" Dottie races over to encircle her brother and father. I can't resist, so I join the familial embrace. At the center of the enfoldment, Jack releases a strangled plea, "Can a guy get some air?"

Laughing, we release one another and head into the kitchen. "I don't know about all of you, but I could eat a horse," Jack exclaims.

"You have no idea," I groan. "And there better be some pot pie left."

"Too late," Dottie chirps brightly.

"So much for the toast and broth the doctor prescribed," I remark.

"Oh, I had those too," she grins.

How I have missed that smile!

"Youth!" Uncle Charles musses Dottie's hair and opens the refrigerator. "Let's see what's left."

"This is Charles Ray," my uncle speaks into the telephone. "Oh, my goodness! Please accept my apologies. No, Jack will not be at school today." He pauses to listen then replies, "There's been a family emergency. He will definitely be back tomorrow. Thank you. Goodbye."

Dottie slides over to let her father return to his place at the breakfast nook after sneaking a strip of bacon from his plate. "I saw that, Polka Dot," Uncle Charles playfully admonishes. "You might consider taking it easy with the food for a while. I'd hate for everything to come back up."

"Eww! That's revolting, Dad," she scrunches her nose with disgust but sits back smirking. Perhaps she'll take his advice. It's comforting to see the spirited and lighthearted side of Dottie again. For months, she's seemed so preoccupied and serious. Now we know why.

"I forgot today is Monday," I comment.

"To be honest, so did I. But then I was in no condition to wake up and call in the absences," he admits.

"Would you like for me to call the high school?" I offer, finishing my last bite of eggs.

"Would you? I dare not leave my plate again," he winks at his daughter.

I sit down at the hallway desk and dial the operator. "Fullerton High School, please."

After a moment the school secretary answers, "Good morning, Fullerton High School. Mrs. Fields speaking."

"Oh, hello, Mrs. Fields. This is Ruby Ray. I'd like to report an absence." Mrs. Fields has been the office gatekeeper for over 20 years. While loathed by many students because she doesn't miss a thing, I've always been fond of her.

"How is Dottie?" She immediately inquires. "We've all been so worried about her and the others."

"She's much better this morning, thank you. Leo was released from the hospital with Dottie last night. The others didn't fare quite as well, particularly Polly." I dare not elaborate, knowing that anything I say will quickly spread among both faculty and students. Mrs. Fields is also a notorious gossip.

She tuts, "What in heaven's name were they doing down there? I had no idea there were even tunnels under our school. And I've been here for 24 years." The fact that she was unaware of the subterranean labyrinth doesn't surprise me. Had she known, then surely we all would have heard of them by now.

I ignore her question. "Obviously Dottie won't be in today or the rest of the week for that matter."

"That's understandable," she remarks. The clack-clack of her typewriter implies that she's already completing an absence form. "I'll let her teachers know, as well as Principal Mason."

"She'll no doubt wish to stay on top of her studies, as best she can. Would you please ask her teachers to assemble a home study packet? I can pick it up tomorrow morning."

"That's a Pleiad for you!" Mrs. Fields proclaims approvingly. "That won't be a problem at all." The Pleiad Society is part of the National Honor Society, for which Dottie's been a member since her first quarter of high school.

"Thank you so much for your help." A sudden thought occurs to me before I hang up. "Mrs. Fields, how did you hear about what happened to Dottie and her friends?"

"Well," she lowers her voice conspiratorially. "The police were here first thing this morning. When they left, Principal Mason told me everything."

"Oh?" I wonder what exactly "everything" entails.

"Yes! They explained how the students snuck down there and were trapped by a madman. But we still have no idea how they got into the tunnels, much less found out about them in the first place."

I breathe a sigh of relief that the full details aren't yet coursing through the school's rumor pipeline. "Yes, well, I'm sure we'll know more when the kids are well enough to talk about it."

"Of course," she utters sweetly. "Please tell our dear Dottie that everyone at school is pulling for her and her friends."

"Thank you so much, Mrs. Fields. Goodbye."

"Bye, now."

So, it would seem that Frank's identity as the "madman," as well as Wallace Mains' involvement, have not yet come to light. Nor has Polly's condition been made public. That will no doubt change, however, as the day progresses, I'm certain. And when the press finds out about this…

I return to the kitchen in time to hear Nan bemoan, "Why didn't someone wake me up? Ya didn't need to get yer own meal! That's why I'm here."

"Your here, Nan, because we love you, and you're a member of this family." Uncle Charles drapes an arm around her shoulders and maneuvers her to the breakfast nook. "Now sit down so I can get YOU some lunch." As she's about to protest, he adds, "You haven't eaten a thing since last night. I don't want to hear another peep about it."

She presses her lips firmly and sits rigidly next to Jack, who grins with amusement at the entire exchange. He loses his composure entirely when his father begins to tie a bright yellow gingham apron around his waist. At that, his father tosses a second apron towards him (this one with crochet trimming around a floral tea towel) and orders, "You help."

I head upstairs for a soak in the tub just as Dottie emerges from the bathroom. "It's all yours."

"Thanks, Dottie," I check the tub to make sure it's reptile-free and turn both faucets. "I'll be quick. I'm sure you'd like a bath as well."

"Oh, don't worry about that. Nan had one ready for me as soon as I got home last night," she strolls down the hall to her room. "Have a nice dip."

After a lengthy and delectable soak, I slip my arms into a lightweight cardigan then secure a belt around my trousers. The rain from earlier this morning appears to have dissipated, but the air is still a bit chilly for a May day. Thankfully my back and limbs feel much looser, the bath salts having done their job. Out in the hallway, I knock on Dottie's door.

"Come on in," she beckons lazily. I find her sprawled on her belly across her bed, a copy of *Screen Play* magazine open to a full-page advertisement with *We are looking for Miss Columbia* printed boldly across the top third.

"What's all this?" I examine the ad over her shoulder.

"Creepy. That's what it is." She pushes herself up and sits with her legs crossed, handing me the magazine. "See for yourself."

As I read the ad more thoroughly, I'm appalled that Columbia Pictures is soliciting "girls" to send in a photograph, along with personal information such as their measurements (including thigh and bust) for the chance to win a $250 film contract and become the new face of their studio. I can only imagine the lecherous men reviewing their applications then summoning unsuspecting young women for an "interview." Elizabeth has filled me in on the harassment and even assault that takes place in the moviemaking industry, all without consequence.

"Appalling, but I've seen this sort of thing before. They prey on young women hoping for their big break," I reflect.

"But who'd ever fall for that?" Dottie shakes her head with disgust.

I consider how best to respond, as this may segue into a discussion about the Pythagoreans. "We all have weaknesses that could potentially be used by other people. For the young ladies responding to an ad like this, it might be insecurity or an obsession with fame. It may even be a need to escape from their life circumstances. The point is, our weaknesses can be exploited by those with ulterior motives."

"I guess so," she shrugs, but curiosity plays across her face.

She seems open, so I decide to dive right in. "It's not so different from how cults recruit members. Cults fill a need for people, a need tied to their weaknesses."

"Oka-ay," Dottie says, puzzled by the topic change.

"I imagine cults offer answers, a sense of purpose, or maybe the feeling of being part of something much bigger, all of which provide a balm for souls that have suffered."

She impatiently turns to face me, "I don't know where you're going with this, Ruby. It seems like you're talking about something else."

What's that old saying? *A fish can't see water unless it jumps out of its bowl?*

I gently take her hands between mine and softly gaze into her eyes, for I know this will come as a shock to her. "Dottie, I know about the Pythagorean Club, and I have to say that it has all the qualities of a cult."

"How can you say that?! What do you know about it anyway?" She crosses her arms and rolls her eyes.

The fact that she didn't laugh off my suggestion implies that, at some level, she knows what I'm saying is true. I understand her defensiveness, her need to shield her friends, her actions, and especially Wallace Mains. But the first step forward begins with recognizing the cult for what it is. "Dottie, I've been to Mr. Mains' house and his classroom. I've read his letters. Seen the machines and notes."

"Then I'm sure he explained it all to you," she settles a bit and waves her hand. "I get why you didn't understand the math, Ruby, but he must have told you what it was all for."

"Dottie, he lied about you and your friends when we were looking for you. In fact, when I first met him for the first time last Friday, he claimed he didn't even know you. Then when I started asking questions Saturday about your disappearance, he took off in his car." I sigh.

"That doesn't make any sense!" she declares with confusion.

"And yesterday, Miss Holmes discovered that he moved out of their house. After that, we knew he had something to do with the four of you, so we searched his rooms."

"He just…left?" Stunned and hurt, she draws her knees up to her chin.

"Yes, he seems to be involved with a cult led by a self-proclaimed prophet in Seal Beach. I just read about this group the other day in the paper. The prophet was arrested," I explain. "Once Mr. Mains realized I was close to figuring all this out, he packed up his things and left town."

"I don't understand. Mr. Mains never mentioned anything about that or about a prophet. We were studying advanced mathematics." She gestures toward the tower of books on her desk. "He showed us how our universe isn't limited to the four dimensions we know. How we can connect with these other planes of existence." She shakes her head with her eyes closed. "I'm not explaining it well. I know it sounds like baloney, but it all made sense. I studied the proofs and equations."

"I'm convinced of that, but there's more to it." I rise and head toward the door. "Wait here a moment. I need to show you something, but it's in my room."

When I return, I hand her the letter Wallace wrote to his comrade Josiah. She reluctantly accepts the missive and slowly begins to read. Her eyes convey rapidly shifting emotions. *Bewilderment. Alarm. Betrayal. Revulsion.* She rereads the letter twice and looks up at me, tears glistening. "This is just…" She looks down, one hand gripping her head. "We didn't know…"

"Take your time. This is shocking news," I pat her back and wait for her to continue.

"How could we, I, be so stupid?" Dottie implores with disgust.

"You weren't stupid at all. In fact, it's precisely your intelligence that he took advantage of."

"Ruby, we didn't mean any harm. Truth is, we were trying to do something good. Something that would fix everything."

"I know you did," I tuck a stray lock of hair behind her ear. "He probably thought he was doing good as well. His letter implies that he believed in this nonsense. However, he manipulated all of you by appealing to your academic strengths and curiosity."

"But he mentioned none of this malarky," she blurts angrily. "He used us!"

"Yes, he did," I agree bitterly. "Wallace Mains is a persuasive person who wields flattery and an odd charm to get what he wants." I recall my first meeting with him. "Until he has no use for someone, that is. Then his cold and abrasive personality surfaces."

She bobs her head. "I think I know what you mean. Lots of kids hated him. But most of the time with us, the Pythagoreans, he was so encouraging. He seemed genuinely thrilled when we understood a difficult concept or solved a complicated math problem. But every now and then he would snap with a harsh comment. And we never knew when it was coming. It kept us on our toes."

I recall studying Thorndike's Law of Effect in my psychology class at the Junior College. "It sounds like Mr. Mains used his praise and criticism to control you." I gesture toward Dottie's desk. "While I now understand the hefty tomes you and Polly have been pouring over, I'm curious about some of them."

She glances at the books and cringes before responding. "*Quadrivium* explained the grouping of four academic studies: arithmetic, geometry, astronomy, and music. Plato wrote about these. So did the original Pythagoreans. And *Basic Harmonics* is really all about mathematics. The proportions among intervals in music."

"That makes sense I suppose, but they seem more appropriate for a university course. What about the others though? The Bible? And what is this about Mu?"

"That's where things seemed a little strange. Mr. Mains said that some of the authors of Hebrew scriptures were brilliant mathematicians and disguised their work in religious texts. During his captivity in Babylon, where math was pretty advanced, Ezekiel wrote about four creatures with four faces and four wings. They've been called tetramorphs since then, but Mr. Mains explained that they were referring to the quadrivium Plato later wrote about. He wanted us to study the text to find a hidden equation. Honestly, I thought it was a waste of time, but Polly was obsessed."

"I can understand why," I comment. "And Mu?"

Dottie snorts dismissively. "*The Lost Continent of Mu* was about an ancient and powerful civilization thought to suddenly vanish. Mr. Mains was convinced that they had discovered the other planes I mentioned and thought the book might give us some clues. I never believed that, but he really did."

"Clues about what? I now understand the references to 'quad' and 'tetra' among your notes and his. They all have to do with the number four. But what exactly did Mr. Mains want you to do?"

Dottie draws in a full breath and releases it slowly. "I think this is where things went haywire."

I nod for her to continue.

"Mr. Mains told us the other planes were sources of unlimited energy that could be tapped if we discovered the algorithm. We spent countless hours working out equations and studying theorems he'd found by decoding ancient texts. We thought we finally found the answer," she blushes.

"If this were true, what on Earth did he expect four high school students to do about it? I'm confused."

"I thought the same thing until he tested us."

The image of the radionic device flashes in my mind. "The oscilloclast."

"How did you know about that?" Her eyes are round with astonishment.

"I saw it in his classroom the day I met him and asked what it was. His response was vague. How did it work?

"Well, a couple of months ago during lunch, he invited a bunch of students from all his classes to his room. One by one he hooked us up to this machine. Apparently, he'd modified it so it now gave readings of a specific type of energy linked to the other planes. He said that all four of us in the club had readings that were massive. It was so believable. We all saw the flashing lights and could read the measurements."

"But what were these readings supposed to mean?"

"I'm embarrassed to answer that," she confesses.

I squeeze her upper arm reassuringly. "Dottie, I'm not going to judge you."

She averts her gaze and starts to pick at a hangnail. She only does this when she's distressed. "You have to understand. By the time he used the device on us, we'd spent hours and hours studying, solving nearly unsolvable problems, and staying up late to get our other schoolwork done. We were exhausted but also committed to seeing this through. We trusted Mr. Mains."

I gently separate her hands before she pulls the hangnail so far that it starts to bleed. "Please continue."

"Okay." She pauses and gulps some air. "He told us that we were the perfect people to make the connection to the other planes because of the readings on the device, but also our interests and intelligence. He told us that, in a few short months, we'd accomplished what others hadn't been able to do for thousands of years." Her eyes are now full of tears as she looks directly at me. "Then he told us what we needed to do."

I lean forward apprehensively when a shave-and-a-haircut knock suddenly startles us both.

CHAPTER 31

"Dad, you must think I'm a complete idiot!" Dottie buries her head upon her bent knees, her body contracting further into a ball.

Stunned, Uncle Charles takes a moment before responding and eventually places a hand on her curved back. "Polka Dot, the last thing in the world you are is an idiot."

When he entered the room a little while ago, I persuaded Dottie to share what she'd already told me about the Pythagoreans and their activities. Her reticence required coaxing and reassurance on her father's part. She cares deeply about his opinion of her. But once she began describing the actual ceremony, words gushed unimpeded from her mouth. The confession provided a cathartic release of the strain she has been shouldering. In a nutshell, she and her friends were convinced that the future of the world and all its inhabitants depended on them. She described how they had planned to mark symbols and formulas on a large square of silk and arrange objects and books pertaining to the four disciplines of the quadrivium. Specific harmonics were to be played, and they were meant to recite a Greek chant, which Dottie admitted seemed to have nothing to do with mathematics.

"You are most definitely NOT an idiot, Dottie," I concur. "All of this was taught to you in a very gradual way, and you dedicated so much time and energy to the process. So, by the time Mr. Mains instructed you to do this ceremony, I'm sure it didn't seem nearly as bizarre as it would have at the beginning of your work with him."

"You trusted him," her father adds.

"I did." Dottie looks up and wipes the tears from her cheeks. "He told us there would be endless energy for everything we need. No one would starve anymore. The four of us would know everything there is to know." She pauses then murmurs softly, "And no one would ever have to get sick and die."

"Oh Dottie." Both Uncle Charles and I wrap our arms around her, for we know she's referring to her mother.

The weakness that Wallace Mains exploited.

"That's a monumental responsibility to shoulder. For anyone, much less a student," her father remarks.

"It really was," she straightens up and scoots back. "A part of me was so relieved when we didn't go through with it. Both times."

"The orchard?" I question.

"Yeah, how'd you know about that?"

"I first read about it in the paper. Then I realized you kids were involved when I spoke with one of the police officers," I explain and tell her what Officer Thompson had to say.

"We didn't even begin the ceremony this last time. We heard the crash before we had a chance to start."

"Did Mr. Mains know where you were going Friday night?" I think about his visit to the Taliaferros.

"No, Earl suggested that we keep it hush hush. He thought that maybe Mr. Mains wouldn't approve, since it was technically breaking and entering."

I consider her answer. So, they were willing to defy Wallace when necessary.

Would they have, ultimately, chosen not to go through with the ceremony if they hadn't been interrupted? And what would they have done when it failed?

After quietly listening to our conversation, Uncle Charles states, "So, all this is why you were reluctant about attending Berkeley."

"Well, yes," Dottie answers. "I mean, if the ceremony had gone like Mr. Mains said it would, we'd be all-knowing. I realize now how ridiculous that sounds, but at the time I figured there wouldn't be any point in going to college?"

"They better find that monster! He manipulated and controlled you for his own sick reasons," Uncle Charles declares.

The evidence I found strongly suggests that he believed this nonsense too. Yet for a seemingly intelligent and reasonable person to buy into all this, he himself must have been manipulated and controlled by the prophet. That being said, it is downright vile that he would risk children's lives in his quest to connect with something so powerful and potentially dangerous. "Thankfully the prophet who started all of this is behind bars. But Wallace is 100% responsible for his own actions and belongs in jail, as well, to protect other young people he may try to trick in the future, if nothing else."

"Do you think they'll find him?" Dottie asks.

"I sure hope so. One thing for certain, it'll be hard for him to find a teaching job again, even if he changes his name." I think about his photo in the articles that will ensue once this story breaks in the press. It's precisely the sort of turmoil newspapers love to print.

"Dad! Ruby! The cops are here," Jack bellows as he watches the headlights dim on the Model T in front of our house. Uncle Charles and I join him at the window in the living room and, even in the darkness of evening, we can make out two forms approaching.

"I guess we should get this over with," I sigh.

Sergeant Blockhurst is much friendlier this evening and speaks to me with, dare I say, a cautious respect. Once he and Officer Thompson are settled on the sofa, iced tea in their hands, the sergeant apologizes for intruding. "It's been a rough weekend for you all, and I know you're still recovering, Miss Ray."

"Thank you, sergeant. I suppose you need me to divulge details pertaining to my case with Mr. Graham."

"I hope you don't expect my daughter to speak with you this evening," Uncle Charles interjects defensively. "She's been through enough."

Thankfully, Dottie is upstairs in her room. She was exhausted after her confession.

"No, no," he raises his hands in appeasement. "Actually, I'm here with news for you."

Taken aback, I remark, "Do tell."

"Well, Mr. Graham woke up fully a couple of hours ago. He can't see all that well, but he was fully conscious and has confessed to everything. The neighborhood thefts, bootlegging, stealing Stan Jones' keys, locking the kids in the tunnel."

"I'm glad to hear he's recovering, despite all this," I admit. "Did he mention why he locked them down there?" I have my suspicions but want to hear what he has to say.

"Apparently, he'd been drinking the hootch he and Fipps have been making. Taking nips of the first drops of each batch to test it. The fool poisoned himself."

"We suspected that was the case, sergeant."

"Yes, well, he claims he went into the tunnels to drop off more jars, but he heard music."

"Dottie said Earl was playing his guitar before they got trapped," Jack informs the officers.

"Is that so?" Sergeant Blockhurst turns and glances suspiciously at Jack, who's been sitting quietly on the stairs. "This isn't really the place for—"

"Jack, go up to your room," Uncle Charles commands. "And stay there until the officers have left."

"Yes sir," he trudges up the stairs with disappointment.

"As you were saying, sergeant," my uncle urges.

"Anyway, Graham says he got spooked when he realized someone else was in the tunnels and decided to lock the door to give himself time to find Fipps and figure out what to do with their stash."

"Hmm…" I murmur.

"I know, it doesn't make much sense, but he claims he was confused and that everything was a blur for him."

"Given the state he was in when I found him a few hours later, I'm not surprised. In fact, I'm shocked he remembered anything at all from that night. What else did he say?"

"Only that he went to the shed after leaving the tunnels to wait for Fipps, but he blacked out. Between you and me, I think he started drinking again as soon as he reached their distillery. He doesn't remember anything after that."

I mull this over. I'd hate to see Frank held solely responsible for the break-ins and bootlegging. "You know Fipps is the ringleader in all this, right?"

The sergeant barks a laugh. "That goes without saying. Don't know how bright Graham was before all this, but there's no way he could have done it alone. He's not the mastermind type."

"I assume Fipps hasn't turned up yet." I gently rub the back of my head.

Officer Thompson, who's been silent until now, chimes in. "His bike was found outside a diner in Anaheim. No one there remembers seeing him, so we have no idea where he went."

"How about the Graham's car? He had that at some point Saturday afternoon or evening."

"Still missing," the officer replies. "Most likely stripped for parts and dumped somewhere. We do know that Fipps used it to empty out the warehouse prior to the fire."

I direct my next question to the sergeant, "Does Miss Graham know about all this? You weren't permitting any visitors."

He nods. "We allowed her to sit with him when it was clear he wanted to confess."

"What do you think will happen to Frank?"

"He could be charged with kidnapping or entrapment, not to mention the robberies and manufacturing, transporting, and selling alcohol. He'll surely be in jail for a long time. However…"

"However?"

"Now, I'm just speculating here, but so far, he's been cooperative with the police. The district attorney's office would really like to reel in Fipps and his cronies. If Graham helps with that, he may get a reduced sentence."

"I'm conflicted about this, of course," Uncle Charles joins the conversation. "My daughter could have been seriously injured or worse because of what he did. But I also understand he wasn't in his right mind."

"I have to say, Mr. Ray, as a father I'd feel the same way. Mr. Baker on the other hand…"

"He's already been in to see you?" I query. "If only he'd been as concerned when he learned his daughter was missing."

"I was waiting outside Mr. Graham's room when he came looking for an officer," Thompson explains. "He demanded that Graham be charged with attempted murder."

"Why am I not surprised?" I roll my eyes.

"Not only that," he continues, "He insisted that both Leo Taliaferro and Earl Adams be arrested for kidnapping the girls."

"That's a lie!" Dottie exclaims.

All heads swivel toward the stairs, where both Dottie and Jack have apparently been eavesdropping.

"So glad to know that my children do as they're told," their father mumbles under his breath.

The sergeant reassures her, "Not to worry young lady. No charges will be filed against the boys nor you girls for that matter."

Dottie quickly descends the stairs and sits on the arm of her father's chair, gripping his hand. "Charges?" she asks nervously.

"Did you think you could go galivanting down there without permission?" The sergeant informs her sternly.

She visibly gulps and her eyes begin to tear.

The sergeant must have daughters, for he softens his tone. "There, there. It's all fine. Nobody's pressing charges."

"And what about Wallace Mains?" I'm surprised that the sergeant hasn't asked about him.

"We've contacted all the other stations in the area informing them that he's wanted for questioning."

"If anyone is responsible for our being in the tunnels, it's him," Dottie exclaims vehemently. "He tricked us!"

The sergeant examines her with interest. "Is that so? Are you prepared to answer some questions, young lady?"

"Absolutely!"

WEDNESDAY, MAY 14, 1930

"Why do YOU need to go?" Dottie moans as Jack piles into the backseat of my Balboa.

"I got something to give her," he replies innocently. He asked me earlier if he could go with us to visit Polly under the pretense of giving her the compact he found on campus. I don't think Dottie has yet realized that her baby brother is quite smitten with her best friend.

"He's fine, Dottie," I wink at Jack through the rearview mirror.

Polly called Dottie Wednesday afternoon to inform her that she'd been discharged from the hospital. Given the seriousness of her condition Monday morning, I was quite astonished that she was ready to go home. Polly insisted that she needed to see Dottie immediately. For the time being, Uncle Charles has forbidden Dottie from going to the Baker's residence unattended. I agree wholeheartedly.

"Why do you think she wants to see you? Was she upset?" Jack is concerned.

"None of your business," she responds acidly.

Sigh.

The sibling truce following Dottie's return seems to have dissipated. "Dottie, please don't talk to your brother that way. You went through hell this weekend, but so did he."

"Yeah! Do you know how worried I was?" Jack exclaims.

"I guess," she reluctantly replies, but I notice that she has tempered her tone.

A few minutes later, Jack sticks his head out of the window as we pass a glorious two-story Mediterranean-style mansion surrounded by lush green grass and palm trees.

"Admiring the Muckenthaler's place?" I query.

"Yeah! It'd be swell to live there," he declares dreamily. He would be in heaven running amok on the nine-acre grounds that surround the hilltop home. "Dottie, you're so lucky you get to go there so much."

"You're right about that," she declares. Dottie frequently babysits their young son when Walter and Adella attend galas and other community soirees.

We turn right on the street just past the Muckenthaler mansion and ascend a steep road up the hill. At the top, we pull in front of a monumental house with an elaborate balustrade around the second story porch. An ornamental cornice crowns the roof line and proclaims that someone of great wealth and power resides here. We walk up marble steps and pass through imposing columns before arriving at the carved mahogany door. Dottie lifts and raps the polished brass knocker.

"Oh, Dottie. Please come in," a wispy young woman in a dove gray service uniform ushers us into the entrance hall. "I'll tell Mrs. Baker that you're here."

Jack whistles. "Take a look at this!" His eyes follow two symmetrical staircases that curve upward and join at a landing on the second floor.

"Have you never been here?" I'm surprised.

"Nope. Dottie never let me," he shoots her a quick look of annoyance. "Just the outside."

"Well, now that you're here, behave yourself," she commands.

I hear Helen Baker's high-pitched whine in the next room. "Well, why did you let them in? Polly's in no condition to receive guests." Whispering is not her strong suit. A moment later she waltzes into the entryway with a forced smile. "Hello, Dottie. Ruby…young man?"

"We're sorry to bother you, Mrs. Baker. But Polly called and asked me to come over," Dottie explains.

In response to Helen's confused gaze toward Jack and myself, I clarify, "I wasn't comfortable with dropping Dottie off, as she's still recovering from the ordeal."

She relaxes slightly and nods in sympathy. "Of course."

Oblivious to Mrs. Baker's discomfort, Jack announces enthusiastically, "I'm Jack. Dottie's brother. I have something to give Polly."

Helen sighs and surrenders. "Well, I suppose if Polly called you. But please don't stay for very long. She's still weak, and the doctor ordered bed rest."

"We won't be long," I assure her and follow the pair up the stairs.

Polly's petite form resembles a doll surrounded by fluffy down pillows and blankets in a massive canopy bed. Every shade of pink has been included somewhere in the room, from the rose tasseled lampshades to the cerise velvet chaise at the end of her bed. It's been years since I've visited this room and have forgotten how exceedingly feminine it is. An engraved sterling silver tray rests on the mattress beside Polly and contains a crystal carafe of water and delicate drinking goblet in blush pink.

"Dottie! Am I glad to see you!" she exclaims weakly while extending a hand to her best friend. "Ruby and Jack. I wasn't expecting you."

"We're so sorry to intrude, Polly. You must be exhausted, and we won't stay long. Jack has something for you."

He bashfully approaches the bed and reaches into the pocket of his trousers. As soon as he raises the delicate case, Polly's eyes widen. "My compact! Wherever did you find it?"

Jack's cheeks redden, and he hands her the filigreed case without making eye contact. "By the Study Hall building Sunday evening. Next to those dates on the sidewalk."

"I thought it was gone forever!" she exclaims. "And I'd only just found it after losing it a few weeks ago."

Jack winces and looks my way.

That'll be our secret.

"Polly, this clue was what led us to finding all of you," I inform her.

"Oh Jack!" She beams. "You're a hero! Tell me exactly how it happened."

He squares his shoulder proudly and dares to look at Polly directly while recounting his discovery. He embellishes a detail or two, but I don't say a thing.

Once his tale has been told, Dottie reminds us all of the purpose for her visit. "Polly, you said on the phone that you had something you could only tell me in person."

I notice Polly's bedside phone. That would come in handy at our house. It's time to give the girls some privacy so I excuse Jack and myself. "Jack, let's wait downstairs while Dottie visits with Polly." He hesitates but concedes when he notices my raised eyebrow.

When we reach the front hall, the maid informs us that her employer is waiting for us in the living room, a formal space I remember from prior visits. As we enter, Helen rises and invites us to join her for refreshments. She doesn't have to ask twice before Jack accepts a plate of cookies and a glass of milk. I accept a cup of tea and wave away the sweets. We take a seat on what has to be a Biederman sofa. I hope Jack can keep cookie crumbs off the ivory upholstery.

"How are you holding up, Helen?"

She exhales wearily. "It has been quite a tribulation."

"I can only imagine," I empathize, all the while internally chastising her for not taking the situation seriously when I first told her. "What did the doctor have to say?"

"She suffered an arterial laceration to her ankle."

"That explains the blood loss," I comment.

"Speaking of blood, my husband saved her life, you know."

"I did hear that he was transfused." I'm sure everyone in the hospital heard him at the time.

"Yes! If it hadn't been for him and Pastor Tim's prayers, my baby would have died."

I know this experience has been traumatic, but I find it hard to muster compassion for her, given the way she's overlooked her husband's reprehensible words and actions. So, I offer the most honest words I can articulate. "I am so thankful that Polly is going to be alright. I was terrified for her when we found the kids in the tunnels."

"You were there?" She startles. I'm surprised she didn't know this already.

"Yes, my Uncle Charles, Stan Jones, the Taliaferros, and I went looking for them late Sunday night."

"The Taliaferros!" She blurts hatefully. "Their Leo is the reason I almost lost my baby."

"I know that's what you believe, but the truth is—"

"I can't discuss this," she sniffs as though she will begin to weep at any moment.

"Alright, but you should know that—"

"My Bible study group is organizing a fundraiser for the poor in our community. Would you be interested in helping us ladies?"

The abrupt topic change leaves me reeling for a moment. "What? Oh…well…what?"

"We need people to sell tickets to our luncheon."

"Mrs. Baker, I'm not really sure I'm the right person," I try to discourage her.

"Why of course you are, let me tell you more about it." She spends a solid ten minutes detailing where they will buy the miniature cakes and finger sandwiches for the luncheon and who will be arranging the flowers. It occurs to me that she hasn't mentioned the people who will benefit from this fundraiser even once.

"Where will the money you raise go, exactly? You mentioned the poor, but how do you identify people who need help?"

She opens her mouth, stunned. I can tell she has absolutely no idea who they'll be helping. Then I have an idea. "Helen, I know of a small community of families in desperate need of basic necessities. They need clothes, nonperishable food, blankets, and so on. Is there any way you and your friends can help?"

I've put her on the spot, for no upstanding Christian woman could possibly refuse such a request. So, after a pause to regain her composure she replies, "Of course we can." She then raises her head and straightens her spine, settling into the idea of helping these families. "And, how do you know them?"

A question that I, for one, can actually answer. "They're migrant farm workers on Bastanchury Ranch. I met them the other night when I was assaulted at your husband's walnut shed while looking for a client."

Her mouth hangs open. It's the first time I've ever seen her completely speechless. You'd think that I told her they were from the moon.

"So that's a 'yes?'" I confirm brightly.

As soon as we get settled in the car, Dottie launches into a tirade against Polly's parents. "He threatened to shoot him! Shoot him if he dares step foot on their property! Can you believe that?"

"I assume we're talking about Leo," I shake my head with disgust.

"Yes! Polly's so afraid he'll come over, and her dad will actually shoot him…gosh it's just so shocking to say that. She needed to tell me in person to warn him. She doesn't trust her mother not to eavesdrop on her phone conversations if she tries to call him."

"I can believe that. How did she plan to explain your visit though? I mean, she just got home from the hospital."

"She's going to tell her parents that she was just so excited they'd agreed to let her attend Fullerton College, that she had to tell me in person."

"She talked them into it?" I'm surprised her father would change his mind.

"When she first woke up, they were making all sorts of promises," Dottie explained.

"Figures." I turn right on Spadra. "What do you think will happen with her and Leo? Will they sneak around?"

Dottie exhales slowly. "I don't know. Leo went through all of this because of her. He never would have joined the club if she hadn't begged him."

"I assumed that was the case. What about Earl? Why was he involved? He seems more serious about music than mathematics."

Dottie chuckles, "You know Dad thinks he's my boyfriend."

"I did too until Elsie called me," I confess.

"She did? When?" Dottie is openly curious.

I chronicle my conversations with Elsie, Earl's mother, and his aunt.

"That makes sense." She pauses to reflect. "To answer your question, I don't exactly know why Earl joined the Pythagoreans. But my guess is that he liked the attention he got from Mr. Mains. Just like the rest of us. Earl's a smart guy, he just doesn't usually apply himself at school. But Mr. Mains made us all feel like geniuses."

I consider what his mother, Hattie, told me about his childhood. His father, a cruel man, died when he was young. And his stepfather is absent, even when he's home. Earl hasn't had a strong male role model in his life. I can understand how he could be taken in by Wallace's encouragement and charm. I wonder if he knows yet about Wallace and the cult, so I ask Dottie.

"I talked to Leo yesterday. Mr. and Mrs. Taliaferro told him when they got home Monday. I guess Leo went to the hospital later that day to check on Polly, but Mr. Baker was in the hall. So, he ducked into Earl's room and visited with him instead," she explains.

I assume Earl's home now. His condition wasn't nearly as serious as Polly's. "What did the boys make of it?"

"Leo said he wasn't too surprised and thought the dimensional energy stuff was probably phooey. But he was willing to give it a shot, just in case." She shrugs. "Sounds like Earl was as shocked as me, though. And Polly flipped."

"You told her?" I look away from the road to quickly glance at her.

"Of course! She needs to know!"

"Given her condition, I thought you might wait a bit."

"She's bound to hear about it, and I'd rather it be from me." She sighs, "I expected her to become hysterical. She really liked Mr. Mains and was fully committed to this thing. But her biggest concern was what her parents would think of her."

"Yes, I can see why. I tried to broach the subject with Mrs. Baker, but she refused to discuss it." More like she refused to admit that Leo was innocent.

"Polly's worried her mom will think she's possessed or something."

"Yes, well…." I can only imagine what Pastor Tim will have to say about all this.

We ride in silence for a bit, when Dottie suddenly announces, "I'm going to call Dad when we get back to make sure he sent the telegram to Berkeley's admission department today."

"I'm sure he did. The deadline to accept is tomorrow, after all," I reassure her. "But if it would make you feel better, then give him a call."

We pull into our driveway, and Jack bolts from the car as soon as we are parked. "Gotta feed Bob."

CHAPTER 32

SATURDAY, MAY 17, 1930

"I think Bob's gonna die," Jack mutters quietly from the seat next to mine. He's been atypically silent since we began our drive.

"Why's that?" To be honest, I'm surprised the turtle has lasted this long living in a bucket.

"He's not moving much, and he won't eat anything at all now." He sniffles, "I just don't know where to take him."

"I think I may have an idea about that."

Yesterday, just two days after being asked, Helen Baker stopped by our house with an impressive collection of donations for the residents at Tijuanita. I suppose she just wanted to be done with it. However, I was overjoyed yesterday afternoon to take the food, clothing, bedding, and even books printed in Spanish to Josefina and Alejandro's family, as well as the other residents of the settlement. While I was chatting with the children, they mentioned a small lake near their ranch school. Apparently, the ranchers use it to water their horses, but the kids like to swim there after school and sometimes catch frogs. Alejandro said that someone dumped a bunch of catfish in the lake a while back, which have adapted well to its murky waters. I suggest the lake to Jack.

"That sounds perfect! And I can visit him sometimes," he proclaims happily. "When can we take him there?"

"Oh, I'm sure your father would want to take you. That way you can say goodbye together. Why don't you ask him later?" There's no way I'll allow that rock monster in my car, even if he's riding in a bucket.

"We can go on our way to the airshow next weekend!" Jack's enthusiasm is palpable. His father promised to take him to the Fullerton Municipal Airport for a biplane exhibition. That'll soften the blow of releasing Bob into the "wild."

When we arrive at Farmers and Merchants, the rest of our family is already waiting outside the bank. After his morning at the oil field, Uncle Charles collected Dottie from Leo's house, while I picked up Jack from his friend's home. When the kids heard what Uncle Charles and I were going to do, they insisted on joining us and participating.

"Ready for this?" Uncle Charles asks me with a wink.

"More than you'll ever know," I declare with delight.

We barely enter the bank when Mr. Snodgrass sprints across the lobby toward us. "Good afternoon, Mr. Ray," he simpers and extends his hand.

Uncle Charles returns his shake. "Mr. Snodgrass."

"And young Ruby," he smiles falsely.

"Clifford," I riposte and take pleasure that his cheeks have reddened.

He collects himself by coughing into a handkerchief. "Yes…well…how may I help all of you today." His eyes sweep to Jack and Dottie then return to Uncle Charles.

"I'll let Ruby begin," Uncle Charles gestures toward me.

"Is there someplace private where we can all sit to discuss this?" I ask. The lobby is quite full for a Saturday afternoon, and while embarrassing Snodgrass would please me to no end, I have nothing against F&M as an institution and don't want to make a scene.

"Of course. Of course." He leads us past the teller window to an office in the back corner of the first floor.

Four chairs face an imposing desk of highly glossed dark wood. We each take a seat as Mr. Snodgrass installs himself in a high back rolling chair. He places his folded hands on the surface of the desk and attempts a smile that does not reach his piggy eyes. "Please tell me how I may be of assistance today."

"I'd like to close my accounts and collect my possessions from my safety deposit box. I'll take the balance of my accounts in the form of a cashier's check." I push my bank book across the desk. "And yes, I know I need my uncle's signature to do so."

Mr. Snodgrass' head snaps toward Uncle Charles. "Surely, you can talk some sense into her. Farmers and Merchants is a solid financial institution. Why Mr. Chapman himself—"

"Yes, Mr. Snodgrass, I am aware of the history of this bank. However, until recently I was quite unaware of the policies you enforce for women," Uncle Charles calmly replies.

"Now see here, not all women. But you have to admit, young things like your niece need supervision. If not, there's no telling what they'll do," Snodgrass wags a finger in my direction.

"While I agree that young people of BOTH genders who have not reached the age of majority should be guided by a parent when making important financial decisions, my niece is a mature woman and has been capable of managing her finances for many years."

"Thank you, Uncle Charles," I beam toward him.

"Furthermore, I will not have my children saving their money at a bank whose manager holds such condescending views toward women." Uncle Charles is on a roll. "Nor will I continue to entrust my own funds to you. That includes both my personal and business accounts."

The weight of my Uncle's proclamation settles visibly upon Mr. Snodgrass, and he sinks back into his chair. My Uncle's wealth is quite respectable, and I'm certain the bank has benefited greatly from his investments over the years. "But Mr. Chapman—"

"I have nothing against Mr. Chapman, nor F&M. But YOU, Mr. Snodgrass, are the sole reason my family will be changing banks." Uncle Charles rises from his chair. "Please wire the funds to Fullerton Building and Loan. And I'd be more than happy to explain my decision to Mr. Chapman or anyone else from the board of directors."

Throughout the exchange, Dottie and Jack swivel their heads back and forth, totally engrossed. When their father finishes his tirade, Jack stands next to him, proclaiming, "And the same goes for me!" before dropping his savings book on the desk and following his father out the door.

"I'll be just a moment," I shout after my uncle. I am not yet willing to let this go without one final retort. "Mr. Snodgrass, this was all so avoidable. If only you had followed the actual policies and procedures laid out by your employer. You could have avoided alienating one of the most prominent oil men in the county. Perhaps you need someone to guide your decision-making in the future. I suggest that you seek counsel from your wife. Good day."

With that, Dottie and I link arms and march toward the vault housing the safety deposit boxes, which Howard Pinney has already opened. He whispers, a huge grin shedding years from his countenance, "That was the bee's knees!"

"I'll see you in a bit. I have something I must take care of first," I tell my family outside of the bank.

"Take your time, Ruby," Uncle Charles assures me. "Jack tells me there's already a new harmonica display at Hardy's."

"Do I have to go too?" Dottie's groan trails as they walk away along the busy street.

I don't want to waste a moment before opening an account *by myself,* so I quickly walk down Amerige to approach the newer, yet less impressive, Fullerton Building & Loan office. Its long rectangular structure resembles a train car more than a financial institution.

"Norma! Edith! Fancy meeting you here," I proclaim while entering the building.

"Ruby! We were just talking about you," Norma smiles as she finishes tucking something into her purse.

I tilt my head toward a private corner then ask, "How's Frank?" once we've moved away from the line.

"He's feeling better and will be released on Monday," she pauses. "But they'll be taking him directly to jail."

I picture the small concrete cube with rocks piled outside. I've heard that drunks are often given a small sledgehammer and instructed to smash the rocks into tiny pebbles. A tedious but back-breaking chore that, hopefully, Frank avoids given his physical condition. "The charges?"

"Bootlegging, larceny, and child endangerment," Edith replies. "The charges could have been a lot worse, but he's cooperating with the police and district attorney's office as they pursue Fipps."

Just as Blockhurst predicted. "Any sign of him?"

Both women shake their heads. Then Norma gazes at me earnestly, "I am so very sorry about what happened to the kids. I know Frank wasn't in his right mind, but I am wracked with grief about what they had to go through…what all of you went through."

"Me too," I nod. "I suppose, in a way, his actions brought to light Wallace Mains insane plan for the Pythagoreans."

"That's quite a silver lining for a very dark cloud," Edith observes.

"Did Frank give any explanation for the thefts and alcohol?"

Norma leans toward me and further lowers her voice, "He did. Apparently, he planned to buy a house for the two of us. Make a fresh start somewhere…"

"Somewhere far away from me," Edith adds, her arms crossed. "He's been jealous of my closeness with Norma since the very beginning, despite my best efforts to win him over."

Norma explains, "Apparently Wallace recently told him about the nature of our relationship. I think that, coupled with overhearing our plans to move to Laguna Beach, compelled him to take the money."

"He was trying to 'save' you from me," Edith interjects.

Norma turns toward me but averts her gaze. "I didn't mention his dislike of Edith to you, Ruby, when we first met because I didn't think it was relevant at the time. I now see it was the cause of all of this."

I nod toward Edith, who has placed a hand on Norma's shoulder, and reach forward to squeeze Norma's hand. "It wouldn't have changed the investigation, nor would it have prevented Frank from doing what he did. You have done your very best to care for your brother over the years under very challenging circumstances. It's time to live your life the way YOU want."

"Thank you for saying that," she looks up.

"Tell her our good news," Edith encourages her.

She brightens, "Well, Frank told us he put the money in a safety deposit box at this bank."

"The third key," I realize.

"Yes, exactly. Since Frank can't come in person to open the box, the bank was kind enough to send a notary public to the hospital this morning. He signed a form giving me access."

"You'll be able to buy the house in Laguna Beach!" I clap my hands with joy.

"Yes! We've been in touch with an agent," Edith smiles broadly. "And one of the artists from the colony is going to help us get jobs with the local grammar school since there's no high school in Laguna."

"The older students attend Tustin High," Norma clarifies.

"And you get to paint, Edith!" I declare.

"That's the idea," Edith replies somewhat bashfully, but I can tell she's thrilled by the prospect.

"This all sounds marvelous! But I confess, I'm somewhat envious. It would be lovely to live at the beach."

"Oh, you must come and visit. You could stay for a weekend," Edith enthuses.

"And meet the kitten we plan to get," Norma giggles like a schoolgirl. "I've always longed for one but could never have one. No pets at the boarding house."

Edith turns to look at the line. "We should let you go before it gets any more crowded."

I hug them both and promise to stop by before they relocate. I then join the back of the queue.

Hopefully this won't take too long.

"Sorry I'm late," I hurry inside the police station, having walked over directly from the bank. The Taliaferros, Earl, and Hattie have already arrived and are visiting with Uncle Charles, Dottie, and Jack. "That took longer than I expected."

"It's no problem, Ruby," Mrs. Taliaferro takes my arm. "The sergeant has asked us all to wait until he finishes with another interview."

At that moment we hear an angry voice bellow, "And you see that he's caught and thrown behind bars or so help me—"

"Mr. Baker, you have my word that we have every man available looking for him," Sergeant Blockhurst tries to appease Polly's father, and I am taken aback by his obsequious tone.

"It's okay, Leo," Mr. Taliaferro placates his son who has started to bolt from the building. "You've done nothing wrong and have nothing to fear from that man."

Leo nods unconvincingly and stands behind his father just in case.

Fred Baker storms into the lobby and notices all of us, his face darkening further. Without a word he shoves a hat upon his head, tightens his coat and pushes through our assemblage. The door slams and rattles the barred windows as he exits. Sergeant Blockhurst sits at his desk, wiping his brow with a damp handkerchief before directing his attention to our group. Officer Thompson has followed him and, after a glance in our direction, whispers something into his ear. "Yes, yes that's fine," the sergeant replies while shooing him off with a flick of his hand.

"Alrighty then," Blockhurst says curtly, attempting to regain his composure and authority. "Who's next?"

"If it's alright with you," Hattie looks timidly at the rest of us, "Perhaps, Earl and I can go next. My sister is watching the kids and needs to get to work soon."

"Of course, Mrs. Fisker," Uncle Charles gestures for her to join Sergeant Blockhurst. The Taliaferros both nod reassuringly.

"Makes no difference to me," the sergeant mutters as he leads the pair through the door.

Moments later, Officer Thompson arrives carrying a tray filled with mugs of coffee and a few bottles of soda pop. "We don't usually do this, but you've all been so great about coming in at such short notice…and on a Saturday."

Jack gladly swipes a glass bottle of Coca-Cola and pops the top with a key from his pocket. "Ya want one, Dottie?" He reaches for another.

"No thanks," she replies nervously and leans her head on her father's shoulder.

"I'll take one Jack," Leo accepts the bottle and retrieves an opener from the tray. Jack rolls his eyes as he turns away, no doubt irritated by the boy he views as his rival for Polly's affection.

"Thank you, Officer Thompson," I accept the coffee, as do the other adults. "That was very thoughtful of you."

His cheeks blush and he quickly occupies himself by setting the third bottle on the small table beside Dottie before exiting the lobby to join the sergeant.

"I'm relieved that they're finally taking this business with Mains seriously," Mr. Taliaferro remarks.

Uncle Charles agrees, "It's about time. However, I'm not surprised that it took threats from Baker to make it happen."

When we received a call from Sergeant Blockhurst last night, it became evident that Polly had finally told her parents about Wallace Mains, at which point Mr. Baker called the police station to demand justice. The sergeant asked Uncle Charles to escort Dottie, since she's a minor, to the station at 3:00 sharp this afternoon to make an official statement. I'm certain the sergeant has more questions for her than the cursory interview he conducted Monday evening. I was asked to give a statement as well and bring the documents and evidence I collected from Wallace's classroom and bedroom.

Uncle Charles continues, "Unfortunately, Baker will still try to find a way to blame your son." He smiles apologetically at Leo. "But I for one will do what I can to organize…how best to put this…pressure among his colleagues in the local business community so that he'll back off and leave you all alone."

"We appreciate that, Mr. Ray." Mrs. Taliaferro gives her son an encouraging smile.

"Please, after all we've been through, call me Charles."

"Thank you, Charles," Mr. Taliaferro firmly shakes his hands. "And please call us Mattia and Sofia. That goes for you as well, Miss Ray." He directs his last comment to me

"Ruby, please," I reply. "Thank you, Mattia." Now that we're finished with pleasantries, I ask Leo, "How are you feeling with all this?"

He releases a long breath. "Gees, I'm still trying to wrap my head around all of it."

Dottie agrees, "It's a lot to digest. For now, I'm just trying to focus on finishing our classes with straight A's, so I have a shot at valedictorian. And then there's Berkeley."

"Are you planning to attend Northern Arizona University this fall, Leo?" I inquire. "Your mother mentioned your acceptance to me."

"There was never any doubt about that," Mattia answers for him, but Leo looks at me and nods.

After a while, Earl and his mother return to the lobby while the Taliaferros take their turn. Uncle Charles stands to give Earl a seat next to Dottie on the bench. Earl collapses and admits, "That was rough."

"What did he ask you?" Dottie's eyes widen with alarm.

"I had to pretty much tell him everything." He glances nervously at the rest of us. "Even the bit about the orchard."

"We already knew about that, Earl," I reassure him. "You must be exhausted." I turn toward his mother. "Hattie, I don't know how much Earl has told you about their time in the tunnels, but your son is a hero."

She leans forward and gives his arm a squeeze. "I always knew that."

"It's true, Mrs. Fisker. Earl refused to eat or drink anything and insisted the rest of us take his portion," Dottie shoots him a look of admiration.

"I'm just relieved the sergeant didn't charge me with something," Earl confesses.

"What on Earth would he charge you with?" Uncle Charles asks with surprise.

"Well, I'm a couple of years older than the others. I'm the one who suggested the tunnels in the first place and let us in without permission."

"First, you are under 21 so you are still a minor. Secondly, the choices all of you made were due to the manipulation and machinations of Wallace Mains," I insist. "The way I see it, none of you are guilty of anything more than trying to save the world."

"Well, when you put it like that..." The worry lines vanish from Earl's face.

"Hey, ya wanna see my new harmonica?" Jack doesn't give Earl an opportunity to respond before handing over his new prized possession.

While the guys are discussing chromatic notes, I pull Hattie aside. "How are you holding up?" I think about her recent turmoil on top of her ongoing fatigue, unhelpful spouse, and houseful of children.

"Right as rain now that Earl's home. And he's going to take some composition courses at the Junior College in the fall." She attempts a cheery facade but it's clear that nothing has changed with her circumstances at home.

"Hattie, I wanted to let you know that several women I tutor have started a babysitting collective. They take turns watching each other's kids so they can have a bit of time to themselves to rest, if nothing else." She seems interested so I continue, "If you'd like, I can put you in touch with one of them."

She blinks sharply at my unexpected offer. "Why...that would be wonderful. Thank you so much, Ruby."

"Any time, Hattie."

Not too long after Earl and his mother leave, the Taliaferros rejoin us in the lobby. They briefly describe their interview, then they too depart for home. Officer Thompson enters the lobby with an empty tray and, before beginning to collect the cups and bottles, informs us, "The sergeant will see you now. Just head through that door and turn right at the first hallway. You can't miss it."

"I'll stay with Jack while you take Dottie in for her interview," I suggest. "Then you can drive both kids home while I chat with the good sergeant."

Uncle Charles agrees while I settle next to Jack on a second bench. I smooth a stray lock of hair at his crown, and he immediately pulls away. "Hey, watch it," he complains playfully.

"So, what's this about a new harmonica? Don't tell me you have another one."

"Sure do." He retrieves it from his coat pocket and passes it over to me. "That Hohner guy didn't mention that the sixteen-holer was coming out THIS weekend. Ain't she a beaut?"

I turn the silver mouthpiece over in my hands and cannot see how it differs from the one he bought last week. But I'm pleased that he's so content. I dare not bring up the topic we discussed earlier, but he mentions it himself.

"Dad said he'll take Bob and me next weekend to that lake you mentioned before the airshow." He blows a few notes through the harmonica.

I immediately shush him. Blockhurst was not in the best of spirits, even for him, and I don't want to irritate him further before I've had my interview. "I'm glad you're ready to release Bob. He'll be much happier."

As the last interviewee, I expect that what little patience Blockhurst possesses has been depleted by now. So I am surprised when he pulls out my chair and offers me a glass of water from the pitcher on the table. "I know you've been waiting a while. Can I get you anything else to make you more comfortable?" He inquires genuinely.

"No, the water is fine. Thank you."

I'd really like to wrap this up as soon as possible.

Office Thompson enters the room and deposits a stack of file folders and two boxes marked *Evidence* on the table. "Do we need anything else, Sergeant?"

"No, that'll be all for now."

Officer Thompson takes a seat across the table from me, while the sergeant sits at the head.

I glance at the files and boxes. "Looks like you've been busy."

"Oh, this isn't all for the Wallace Mains case," Blockhurst waves his hand dismissively. "Some of this pertains to Frank Graham. As you well know, the two are connected, and you, Miss Ray, hold the evidence we need to unravel this mess."

I place my hand upon my chest in mock astonishment. "Are you, sergeant, asking for my professional assistance with these cases?"

He shakes his head, "Now let's not get carried away. While I have to admit, you're a pretty good investigator, the discussion we are about to have in no way indicates that the Fullerton Police Department is formally engaging your services."

"God forbid!" I declare sarcastically.

He clears his throat uncomfortably. "Yes…well…"

"So, who shall we start with? Frank, Fipps, or Wallace?" I reach into the case I brought to retrieve my own notes and folders.

Officer Thompson clears his throat. "Sir…Miss Ray…I took the liberty of taking notes during each of our meetings over the past week," he informs us.

"And?" Blockhurst urges him to continue.

"Well, I…" The young man is flustered and reaches into a coat pocket. "I was thinking that Miss Ray could look them over, as they pertain to Mr. Graham and Mr. Phillips. If everything's there, it could save us some time."

"Excellent point, officer," I praise and accept the hand scribbled notes. After thoroughly examining them, I add a few minor details in the margin with a pencil and pass them back to the officer. "I think that does it as far as the bootlegging, my attack, and the robberies are concerned. You must be relieved that the burglaries have finally ended."

"You have no idea," the sergeant nods to Officer Thompson who has handed him the notes. "The residents' panic reminds me of the chloroform burglars during the summer of '27."

"I remember that well." A group of robbers pumped chloroform under doors and through open windows into their victims' houses to knock them out. One famous victim was none other than Ralph Ince, an actor and director, who was asleep in his room at the California Hotel when he was robbed. Other hotel guests, as well as the residents of nearby homes, were also targets in these bizarre crimes that went unsolved for weeks. A headline in the *Los Angeles Daily News* on the Fourth of July that year broadcast "New Terror Reign Arrest in Fullerton" when the final culprit was captured.

"I wouldn't be surprised if this situation with Mains gets the same sort of press," the sergeant speculates.

I present the sergeant with a copy of my own notes, the papers we found under Wallace's bed, the students' graded reports, the letter I retrieved from the back of his desk drawer, and Josiah's business card. "The only evidence I didn't collect were the two devices that Miss Holmes found in his bedroom."

"We've already cordoned off the house and his classroom. I'm sure our officers have retrieved the devices." The sergeant flips through the documents I provided. "I don't get all this *quad* and *tetra* nonsense."

I try to give him a layperson's summary of Wallace's crazy ideas, but he just shakes his head and drops the notes on the stack before drawing the business card into his hand. "Thompson, did we get anything on this Josiah Colby guy?"

"I'll check," the officer swiftly vacates the room.

"One of our investigators found a similar card in Mains' classroom, so we contacted the Seal Beach PD to pay a little visit to his electrical shop. Haven't heard anything back yet." Blockhurst explains.

Officer Thompson rushes in breathlessly. "He's cleared out too."

"Damn!" The sergeant barks before remembering my presence. "Oh…sorry, Miss Ray."

"No offense taken, sergeant. I happen to share your sentiment."

"Sir, with everything going on today, I forgot to tell you that I spoke with a Seal Beach officer who worked on the 'prophet cult' investigation a little while ago and confirmed that the names of both

Mains and Colby were found among some of the evidence retrieved," Thompson reports.

The sergeant looks at me sheepishly. "You already knew this, didn't you?"

"I strongly suspected this, but you wouldn't listen to me last Sunday at the Graham residence."

The sergeant ignores my pointed remark. "So, it sounds like Mains knew what the kids were doing Friday night."

"Absolutely. Although, according to Dottie, he didn't know where they'd be. And when they didn't show up at their prearranged meeting Saturday at noon…"

"He panicked and did a runner."

"Yes, especially after speaking with both Mrs. Taliaferro and me Saturday afternoon."

The sergeant nods thoughtfully and appears to be lost in thought. After a moment, he declares, "Well, why not?" and hands me an envelope.

"Just came in this morning," Thompson informs me.

Before I have an opportunity to open it, Blockhurst looks at me sternly and says, "Not a word of this to anyone. Got it?"

I nod and gaze at the front of the envelope. *The Prophet, care of Orange County Penitentiary.* The return address states *Wallace Mains*, along with his Fullerton address.

"Look at the postmark," Officer Thompson advises.

"Saturday, May 10th."

Sergeant Blockhurst replies, "Exactly. It was posted the evening after the kids disappeared."

"But how—" I begin to ask.

"Apparently when Mains split, he informed the post office to hold his mail until a forwarding address could be provided. Since that envelope was addressed to The Prophet instead of Daniel Hightower, the guy's actual name, it was returned to the Fullerton post office," Blockhurst explains.

"But how did you get a hold of it?" I ask.

"When Mains became a person of interest, we asked the Fullerton postmaster to let us know if he received any mail from Josiah Colby or the county jail. He called us immediately when the returned envelope arrived."

"Can I read it?"

The sergeant nods. "That's why I gave it to you. Maybe you'll see something there that suggests his whereabouts. We're stumped."

"I'll try," I pledge hesitantly and begin to read.

Most Reverend Prophet, I had hoped to never write this letter. If the Channeling Ceremony was successful, you would have been released from your unjust bondage, and all of us would be communing with the Four, the students now vessels for the Tetramorphs. The Divine Quaternity would be among us.

But I've spoken with all seven of the others in our group, and none of us have sensed a thing. What's worse is that the students have not contacted me either. Nor have any returned to their homes. Their families are beginning to ask questions, and I don't know what to do.

Through the years, you have been my teacher and friend. Had we not met when I returned from the war, I surely would be dead by now. I could not have lived with the guilt and pain. As you know, my family cut off all ties with me after my little brother was killed. I was there, in the bunker next to him, and still could not save him. I never told you this, but I encouraged him to lie about his age and enlist with me. Two brothers saving the world. My parents never forgave me. I don't blame them.

But you led me to see the truth, the greater reality. You showed me my divine purpose and persuaded me to teach so that I could find the Four. That's why I was born at this time and place. That's why my brother lost his life in that bunker. So that, in my grief, I would find you.

We were supposed to change the future of humanity. There would be no more sin, no more suffering, no more war... We could have actually saved the world. But the window has now closed. I have to assume that we failed.

I am leaving Fullerton to gather with the other seven and await your advice. We'll be at the temple. The police never found it when they arrested you.

Yours in Truth,

Wallace

I take a moment to reflect on what I've read. "This certainly answers many questions I had about Wallace, but unfortunately, I have no idea where this 'temple' could be located."

"Well, it was worth a shot," Blockhurst sighs regretfully.

When we've completed my interview, he grips my hand in a firm shake. "I have to admit. You have talent, Miss Ray."

"Thank you, sergeant." I take some pleasure in his discomfort paying me a compliment.

His face then transforms into his typical gruff demeanor. "That said, I hope we never have the opportunity to work together again. Good afternoon, Miss Ray." And with that he leaves.

CHAPTER 33

MONDAY, MAY 19, 1930

"Our brother got Gabe a job!" May gushes as she plunks a bucket of cleaning rags on the floor.

Her unexpected announcement throws me for a moment until I remember the "hobo" who took shelter on our porch. It's hard to believe that it's only been 10 days since that fateful Friday. "Is that so?"

"Yep! He's gonna help at Coleman Machine Shop. The owner lost his prentice—"

"Apprentice," Addie corrects her.

"As I was saying," May snaps with irritation, "And he's giving him room and board."

"Well, I'm glad to hear the poor boy is finally settled." In the last week I've heard of two other cases like his where families from the Great Plains have sent their children to California. According to the papers, farmers are being hit with extremely dry weather and are losing crops. Hopefully this is just temporary.

"You girls best be gettin' to work," Nan commands gently then sets down a basket on the counter. May and Addie scurry into the dining room to begin sweeping and dusting.

I rise from the breakfast table to refill my coffee. I got up early to look over some brochures and books I picked up from a travel agency in town a few days ago. I notice Nan struggling with her apron, so I offer, "Let me help you with that." Her knuckles appear swollen, and I fear her arthritis is acting up.

She waves me away. "The day I can't tie my own apron is the day I hang it up fer good."

"Well let me help you with breakfast," I insist and remove a bowl of eggs, butter, and sausage links from the refrigerator.

"I reckon ya can," she gives in easily, so I know her hands are hurting this morning. She removes the tea towel covering a basket and sets out a pie and a lovely loaf of squaw bread. "This'll do fer toast I suppose."

"It'll be perfect, Nan." And we set to work preparing the meal.

Jack has already finished his breakfast and fled from the kitchen to head for school, lunchpail and books in hand. He usually requires at least three forceful nudges to leave his bed on a school day, but not this morning. I imagine he plans to show off his new harmonica to his pals. Uncle Charles strolls into the kitchen and, seeing me alone at the breakfast nook, raises his eyebrows.

"Jack's already left, and Dottie has yet to make an appearance," I inform him.

"Well, she better come down soon." He pours coffee into a mug. "I promised her a ride to school, but I need to head out in the next few minutes."

"Sit down there and eat sum'n before ya leave," Nan orders him.

He pushes aside my stack of brochures and books to clear a spot for his plate but pauses when he spies a *Baedeker's Guide to Great Britain*. "I take it you're moving ahead with selling the New York property."

I nod affirmatively, "That's the plan. Later today I'll phone the property manager and instruct him to arrange the sale. Based on my initial communication with him late last week, the whole process should happen fairly quickly. But in the meantime, I'll move forward with reservations for the cruise."

"Ruby, I'm so glad you're doing this. You deserve a vacation more than anyone else I know," he says warmly.

"Ain't that the truth?!" Nan interjects from across the room.

"There's a Holland America cruise that sets sail from New York on June 9th. Hopefully I can sign all the papers to finalize the sale the day before I board."

"The timing's going to be tight, though. It's already mid-May, and Dottie's graduation is June 6th." Concern furrows my uncle's brows.

"It will. But if for some reason the sale falls through, I have plenty of money to cover the trip and can finalize things when I return."

"When will that be?" Uncle Charles spreads boysenberry jam on his toast.

I hesitate. My absence will impact quite a few people, especially my family. "August 10th."

Startled, his head jerks up mid-bite. When he has swallowed, he asks, "Two months? That's quite a cruise."

"I know I'll be leaving you in the lurch with the kids—"

"That's not it at all, Ruby. I'm thrilled that you have the opportunity and means to travel. I just need to reconcile your plans with a trip I'd hoped we could all take as a family before Dottie heads off to Berkeley at the beginning of September."

"Did I hear something about a trip?" Dottie waltzes in, a black tie dangling around the neck of her white sailor-neck blouse, indicating her membership in the California Scholarship Federation. Given the school uniform policy for girls, her shiny new patent leather heels and expertly coiffed bob are the only elements of individuality in her ensemble.

"Dottie, you don't have much time to grab a bite," her father advises.

I fill her in on our discussion while she wraps a sausage link inside a slice of buttered bread and begins munching while still standing.

Nan tuts her disapproval. "Guess I'll put the rest a these eggs in the frigerator."

"But I thought I heard Dad say something about a family trip," Dottie pops the last bite into her mouth. She already knows about my cruise and is helping me assemble a list of things to see at each port.

"Well, I was thinking it would be nice if we could all fly somewhere for a week or so this summer." Uncle Charles thinks aloud, "You, Jack, and I could go someplace, of course, but it won't be the same without Ruby. Of course, I already invited Nan to join us…"

"I ain't flyin'," Nan insists. "But thanks for includin' me."

"I have an idea!" I exclaim and propose that they meet me in New York City when I disembark in August. "Then we can tour Manhattan.

I've always wanted to take Dottie to a Broadway show and visit a Yankee game with you and Jack. They've had quite a season so far."

"Oh, can we, Dad?" Dottie pleads.

Uncle Charles' face lights up, "That sounds like a grand plan! We'll talk more over dinner this evening." He drops his fedora on his head as he rises from the table and retrieves his keys from his pocket.

"Jack will be over the moon!" Dottie comments enthusiastically before picking up her handbag and books to follow him out the back door. "See you, Ruby. Bye Nan."

Brrring brrring

I've no sooner deposited my travel materials on the desk in my room when the phone rings downstairs. I hear Addie answer, "Ray residence, Addie speaking." A moment later she calls upstairs, "Ruby, it's for you."

I quickly retrace my steps downstairs and speak into the headset, "This is Ruby."

"Ruby, you'll never guess!" Elizabeth's ebullience is contagious.

"You got a part!" I shout.

"Yes! And I get to sing a solo during one of the ensembles. I even have a speaking bit."

"Oh Elizabeth, or should I say 'Liz,' I'm so thrilled for you!" I enthuse. She's worked so hard for this over the years. "That new agent of yours really means business."

"And how!"

"So, when does it start?"

"I just got the call, and would you believe I have to be in L.A. tomorrow morning? I'm going to be so busy I just had to call you before I start packing."

"Packing? Are you moving?"

"Yes, the film's going to shoot at the Warner Brothers Studio almost daily for the next two months, so I'm moving in with a couple of other girls who already have a place near Hollywood."

"Well, I'm sure Dean will be happy to have you so close," I point out.

She laughs, "Yes that'll definitely be a perk. He'll be filming two lots over, so hopefully we can sneak visits."

"I take it I won't be seeing you for dinner Wednesday evening," I joke. We had made plans to return to Mah Jong's.

"I know, Ruby. I'm so sorry about that! It's why I called immediately," she laments.

"I'm just teasing you. Honestly, Elizabeth, I am so proud of you and have a good feeling about this. It'll launch you to stardom, I just know it."

"Before we hang up, I have to know how you're doing," she asks with concern.

"The head injury is improving. No more dizziness or lightheadedness, and the pain is bearable, so I no longer need medication."

"That's so good to hear," she sounds relieved.

"In fact, I'm feeling so good, I've decided to reopen my reading parlor later this week." I put my tutoring on pause when I took on the Graham case, and I have no idea where we left off, so I need time to prepare.

"Oh, that's swell, Ruby." She pauses. "There's something else I wanted to mention."

My stomach sinks as I sense her discomfort. "Is everything alright with your parents and brother?"

"Oh, my yes. It's nothing like that. I only hesitate because when I've tried to bring it up before…"

Then it sinks in. She wants to set me up with someone. "Let me stop you right there. I am not nor will I ever be interested in a blind date."

"Ru-by! But he's so sweet. I know you'd think the world of him. Unless…have you met someone?" When I don't respond, she exclaims, "You have! Ruby Ray, you've been holding out on me."

I laugh, "It's nothing like that. More like the potential for something."

"Well, who is this potential man? I need details."

"His name is Sam Armstrong. He's a doctor—"

"A doctor! Ruby! How clever you are!"

"Let me rephrase. He's a resident currently on rotation at Fullerton General. We've met a few times, and he brought over a bouquet last Sunday when I was home from the hospital." I try to make light of the gesture, but my heart still skips a beat when I think about it.

"Have you been out with him?" She inquires.

"Not yet," my tone sinks. "To be honest, I haven't heard a peep from him since he stopped by. I don't know what to make of that." Thankfully, I've been so preoccupied with everything else, I haven't given it much thought.

"Hmm, that's frustrating." She has an idea. "Can you think of a reason to stop by the hospital and 'bump' into him?"

With a chuckle, I brush off her suggestion. "I'm going to wait and see how this plays out. As it is, I'll be away for two months this summer anyway. Probably not the best time to start a new relationship."

"Away? Where on Earth are you going?"

"Well, let me see…England, France, Holland, Germany…and I'll spend some time in Manhattan before and after the cruise." Just talking about my trip fills me with a delightful anticipation.

"Wow! Well, you've earned it, pal, that's all I have to say."

I notice two heads peeking around the corner. When Addie and May realize I've spotted them, they pop back into the kitchen. Then I hear Nan scold, "Girls, give Ruby some privacy. Were ya born in a barn?"

"I'm sure you need to get started on your packing, Elizabeth. I should hang up," I suggest.

"I guess you're right," Elizabeth sighs. "Well, it sure was great chatting with you. I'll call you when I know my phone number. And don't be a stranger," she begs.

"Never. And I'll send you a postcard from each country I visit," I promise.

"That would be swell! Bye." And she disconnects.

On my way to the backyard, I pass through the kitchen. "May. Addie." I nod at the twins. Their cheeks color as they return my greeting before promptly refocusing on their cleaning and scrubbing.

Once in the backyard, I stroll to the avocado tree to collect a few alligator pears for a face mask. This immediately makes me think of Bob. Only a few days left, and I'll no longer have to worry about sinking into the tub with him. Birdsong in the trees relaxes my body and mind. Out of the corner of my eye, I spot the cobalt blue of a scrub jay. We don't see them very often, but I know Jack has been leaving peanuts outside in hopes that they'll pay a visit. In general, the weather has warmed since the hailstorm a week and a half ago, but this morning the sky remains "May Gray."

I shiver and head back inside only to hear Addie saying, "Just a moment please. I'll go get her." Seeing me pass into the kitchen, she says, "The phone is for you, Ruby. Sergeant Block-something."

I leave the avocados on the counter and step into the hall to retrieve the receiver. "This is Ruby."

"Miss Ray. Sergeant Blockhurst here. Do you have a minute?" His tone sounds urgent.

"Yes, sergeant. What can I do for you?" I sit down and search for a pencil and tablet in the desk drawer.

"I have news I thought you'd want to hear."

"Of course. What's happened?" I sincerely hope he's about to tell me they located Wallace.

"We got Phillips last night," he proclaims.

"That's fantastic!" I'm relieved to hear that Fipps is finally behind bars. While not particularly worried about my own safety, I've definitely been uncomfortable knowing he was still on the loose. "How'd you catch him?"

"Bert Lemming tipped us off. He's the night watchman working for Baker at Sunny Hills Fruit Company."

"Yes, I recall his name," I reply. "What has he got to do with Fipps?"

"Well, we found out that he knew about the bootlegging operation at the walnut shed but had turned a blind eye…provided they give him a flask or two every so often. Lemming was scared stiff when we brought him in and confessed everything, including Phillips' whereabouts."

"Where was Fipps picked up?"

"A speakeasy in Santa Ana, if you can believe it. He was trying to fence some of the equipment from the still they had in that shed." He laughs darkly. "One more count against him."

"I hope he's in jail for a long time." I tick through the multiple felony charges I know they'll throw at him…*bootlegging, larceny, aggravated assault, arson, burglary.* I'm sure there are others. Who knows what else he's been up to.

"San Quentin for sure," Blockhurst replies. "The district attorney will be in touch with you in the next few days to discuss Phillip's attack. But it sounds like he's pushing for an arraignment by the end of the week. He's already pled guilty to some of the charges, including his assault on you. So, I doubt you'll have to appear in court."

That's a relief.

"What about Wallace Mains?" Although I'm thrilled that Fipps is behind bars, I cannot feel any closure on the suffering we've endured until he's locked up as well.

The sergeant clears his throat. "That's the other thing." He wavers before continuing. "There's been a…development this morning."

"Go on," I urge, apprehension washing over me.

"This is pretty grisly," he warns me.

My mind considers myriad possible scenarios, so I press him to continue. "Please, I want to know what's happened."

"Well, here's the thing. Early this morning in Sunset Beach…you know the place?"

"Yes," I reply impatiently. The small community sits between Seal Beach and Huntington Beach.

"Well, a group of eight people, including Wallace Mains and Josiah Colby, climbed up the eighty-seven-foot water tower and…"

"And?" I demand.

"And…jumped."

I gasp even though I've already guessed what he was going to say. Blood seems to flood out of my head and torso and rushes into my limbs. I grip the desk and close my eyes as the room begins to spin.

"Miss Ray, are you alright?"

After a moment I reply, "Yes, I…this is shocking news."

"It is. I'm sorry to tell you over the phone. I should have come by," he apologizes.

"No, you have a great deal to do today. What about Daniel Hightower, the 'prophet.' Is he still behind bars?"

"He's dead too. They'll have to do an autopsy, but the coroner thinks he ingested some sort of poison. Probably cyanide. No idea how he got his hands on it, though."

"This is all so tragic." I feel a lump form in my throat. "I appreciate that you called me."

"I'll let you go then." His voice starts to trail.

Before he has a chance to hang up, I ask, "Will you be contacting the other families?"

"Yes, I'll do that next. Goodbye, Miss Ray."

Still reeling, I mumble a hasty goodbye. I close my eyes and sit for quite some time at the desk, considering the ramifications of the group's actions.

How far would Wallace have taken things with the kids? Would he have tried to persuade them to jump as well?

I wrap my arms around my chest as my body begins to shake.

"You look like you need a good soak in the tub," Nan stands next to me, wringing a dish towel between her hands.

"Thank you, Nan," I mutter weakly. "But I need to call Uncle Charles." I'm sure he'll want to pull Dottie from school so she can hear the news directly from him.

"Number 723, please," I tell the operator and wait for the line to be connected. "Uncle Charles..." I then break down and sob.

FRIDAY, MAY 23, 1930

A familiar jingle gives me pause.

Sigh.

I return the box of Mallomars to a bin in the cabinet and turn off the stove. The coffee has not yet percolated, but I don't want it to burn if I step away for very long. I wonder who's at the cottage gate. I've already met with the district attorney about Fipps, and the press stopped noseying around yesterday morning. Apparently, the grand jury indictment of Benjamin Tatem, a Hollywood financier, for stealing a quarter of a million dollars has upstaged the "Cult Mass Suicide in Sunny Sunset Beach" headlines that have dominated the press throughout the week.

Dottie and her friends seemed to take the news remarkably well, but I worry about the long-term ramifications of all this. However, in true adolescent fashion, the other Fullerton High School students found the story titillating at best. Mr. Mains was not well-liked, and many claimed they always thought there was something "fishy about that guy." While deeply saddened for the cult members and their loved ones left behind, I feel equally guilty for the relief I experienced once the news sunk in and I realized that Wallace was no longer a threat. It's taken me all week to get back into my usual routine, but the prospect of finally resuming my tutoring this evening has given me the lift I need. Not to mention the plans for my upcoming travels.

I turn down the radio on my way to the Dutch door, its top half already open, and encounter a rosebush, of all things. Most of the flowers are tight buds, but a couple have begun to open into gorgeous champagne blooms. A familiar tenor behind the foliage laughs, "I may need a hand with this."

My heart skips a beat. I haven't had much time this week to think about Sam and wonder why I haven't heard from him. That being said, I have felt somewhat bruised.

"Floribunda I presume." I hope my reply sounds lighthearted.

"You are correct." Sam steps back so I can open the bottom half of the door. After entering the cottage, he places the ceramic pot on the floor, then leans out the door to brush terra cotta dust from his hands.

"These are lovely," I bend to smell one of the open blossoms. "To what do I owe the honor?"

He ducks his head in mock shame and gazes up at me beseechingly, "An apology."

"Apology?" I blink sharply.

Sam straightens and leans against the entryway wall. "Apology for my radio silence this past couple of weeks."

"I did wonder about that," I confess. "Please come in and take a seat." I head toward my kitchen nook. "Do you want a cup of coffee? I was just about to brew some."

"That'd be great." He unbuttons his cardigan and sinks into the rattan chair. "I noticed an empty spot next to those hydrangeas as I walked up," he comments. "The light would be perfect there for the roses."

"Good idea. I just removed an overzealous rosemary bush there a few days ago." The water in the percolator was already hot and takes no time to brew the coffee. "Do you like Mallomars?" I query.

"As a matter of fact, I do." He begins to rise, "Can I help?"

"No, no. Sit back down," I motion to him. "I'll just be a moment. Cream or sugar?"

"One spoon of sugar, please. Thanks." He sits back in the chair. I can feel his eyes watching me as I finish in the kitchen. A warm tingling blossoms in my face and chest.

Once I've placed the tray on the coffee table, we both grab a cookie from the platter. Sam holds his up in a formal pose. "A toast?"

I imitate his gesture. "What are we toasting?"

"Hmm…" He strokes his jaw then has an idea. "To less onerous circumstances." He leans forward to tap his cookie against mine.

"Hear, hear!"

After a brief silence while we consume our treats and take a few sips of coffee, Sam looks at me earnestly. "I really do want to apologize. I was planning on seeing you sooner, but I was called away by a family emergency."

I set down my mug and lean forward. "Oh dear. I'm so sorry to hear that. I hope everything's alright now."

"It will be. Thank you. My grandfather—"

"Please don't feel like you have to explain. I understand. Believe me." I smile reassuringly. "Clearly, I know all about family emergencies."

"I'd like to explain. My grandfather fell from a ladder just after I came to see you. I'm all they have. He and my grandmother are the ones who raised me, and my grandmother was just beside herself." He runs a hand through his caramel waves. "He was pretty banged up but, thankfully, didn't break anything. However, persuading him that he needs to let other people help with clearing pine needles from the rain gutters…well, let's just say that conversation needed to be in person."

I think about how stubborn Nan can be when we try to help. "Giving up pieces of one's independence must be brutal."

He exhales and glances at me with appreciation. "You understand then."

"Of course, I do. So where do they live?" I figure he's from someplace nearby.

"In the Sierras," he sips his coffee. "A long drive."

"I'll say!" That explains the extended absence.

"I was just finishing a rotation and was able to push out the next one a couple of weeks."

"Oh? What will you be doing next?" I hope he'll be staying in Fullerton.

He replies reluctantly, "Arizona. Rural medicine. There's an Indian reservation that needs help."

It hadn't occurred to me that he may not be staying in Southern California for the remainder of his training. Disappointed, I ask "For how long?"

"I leave tomorrow and won't be back until early August," he says forlornly. "I applied for it a year ago. I never expected…"

"I never expected either," I echo.

"It's rotten timing," he laments.

"Well, I'm going to be away as well, if it makes you feel any better," I offer.

"Really…" He asks playfully, "Are you jetting off to some far-flung locale?"

"Sailing off is more like it," I laugh.

"Sailing off? Well, that's much more romantic. Should I be worried?" He asks jokingly, but I sense that, at some level, he means it.

"Not at all." I then describe my plans and itinerary.

"That'll make it difficult to write. You on a ship, cruising around Europe, and me at a reservation whose mail service I'm still unsure of."

"You can send letters to the house here," I suggest. "Once you get settled in Arizona, write to me with a return address."

"Good idea."

"Then I'll have a lovely collection of notes to read when I return. Meanwhile, I'll send you postcards from afar."

"I'll hold you to it," he wags a finger.

I chuckle. "Will you be coming back to the area once you're through there?" I ask hopefully.

"That's my plan," he confides. "But I won't know until the tail end of the rural medicine rotation. The good news is that I only applied for placements in Orange County."

I breathe a sigh of relief. "I'm glad to hear that."

The radio begins to play "I'm In the Market for You." Sam rises and extends a hand, one eyebrow raised. "Do you foxtrot?"

"May-be," I reply coyly and take his hand. Electricity courses up my arm as soon as our fingers connect. He places a hand on my lower back, and I feel as though I could melt.

There's not much space in the room for dancing, but as he steps back, I follow him with my right foot. We bounce about to the lively tune, as Fred MacMurray croons about a couple who've just met and are attracted to one another.

"How about a spin?" Sam suggests, his warm breath blowing across my ear.

Speechless, I just nod.

The truth is, no one's ever asked me my opinion while dancing before. They usually twirl me two and fro, oblivious to the fact that I'm getting dizzy. Sam raises our hands above my head and applies slight pressure to my lower back, signaling a right-hand turn. I glide easily in a circle and comfortably return to arms. We attempt a promenade and bump into a chair.

"Oops," I giggle.

"Not much room here," he laughs.

"I don't suppose you know how to Balboa?" I learned this dance a few years ago in Newport Beach where the dance originated as a solution to tightly packed dance halls.

"As a matter of fact, I do." He leads me back into the closed position, and we finish the rest of the song with quick steps and kicks, both laughing merrily at our exuberant attempts.

"Whew!" I wipe my forehead with the back of my hand. "It's been a while, and I forgot how energetic that one is."

"And how!" Sam pretends to pant. We share a smile of delight, but after a moment his grin starts to slip. He releases one of my hands and guides me to the door. "Unfortunately, I need to be off. I only meant to stop by for a few minutes, and I have a lot to do before I leave tomorrow…" he trails off.

"Of course," I agree, even though I'd love for this moment to go on a while longer.

When we reach the door, he turns to stand directly in front of me. It's plain to see that he's also disappointed, but a different emotion shines in his eyes too…hope. "I know that right now is not a good time to be starting something new, but perhaps when we both return in August…"

I squeeze his hand. "I'd love that, Sam."

He brings my hand to his lips and gently kisses the flat expanse below my knuckles. His eyes remain locked upon mine. "I'll miss you, Ruby," he whispers, then releases my hand. But as he walks down the path, I notice a bounce in his step.

My heart expands. "I'll miss you too."

AUTHOR'S NOTE

On the first day of my junior year at Fullerton Union High School, I walked into chemistry class and was delighted to discover that the kind-hearted, well-dressed boy I'd been crushing on for more than a year was also in the class…and sitting alone. I mustered my courage and casually asked him to be my lab partner. We were married five years later. This is one of many reasons why Fullerton holds a special place in my heart.

Growing up in this "historic" town (well, historic by California standards), I felt transported to another time, especially around old homes and buildings. My imagination would take flight with stories about life during bygone eras. So, when this same imagination introduced me to Ruby a few years ago, it made perfect sense that she was from Fullerton. I decided that the date should be at the cusp of the Great Depression and, through my research, learned that the high school auditorium (a structure that has captivated me since childhood) finished construction in 1930. Perfect.

While I strove for historical accuracy when describing places, events, and objects, it was necessary at times to take liberties in the interest of the story. Similarly, the campus buildings on the cover illustration and the maps within the book have been modified to fit the narrative. That said, references to state and national events, newspaper articles, fashions, entertainment, even automobiles, are largely based on true events reported in digital archives and books. The information that follows is included for folks from Fullerton and those with curious minds like mine.

Which locations in Fullerton actually existed in 1930?

Most buildings and businesses mentioned in the book did exist in 1930. While researching information for the story's settings, I greatly depended on several sources. The book *Fullerton: A Pictorial History* by Bob Ziebell, as well as digital articles from *The Fullerton Observer*,

Fullerton News Tribune, and historic ads in the *La Habra Star*. In addition, the websites for Fullerton Heritage and Fullerton History.com (see QR code at the end for links to these sites). And last but not least, the Local History Room at the Fullerton Public Library was a treasure trove of print and digitized copies of old articles and records, including city directories.

Downtown Fullerton

I should first point out that some of the names of major streets in Fullerton have changed since 1930, particularly Spadra Road, which later became Harbor Boulevard, and Harvard Avenue which became Lemon Street. According to digital copies of newspapers and phone books from that time, all the buildings, shops, banks, restaurants, the Fox Theater, Stedman Clock, the California Hotel, and Fullerton General Hospital existed in downtown Fullerton in 1930. Exceptions include the florist, the stationary store, and the church that the Bakers attended.

Early in its history, Fullerton became a hub for railway lines. The Atchison, Topeka, and the Santa Fe Railroad (yes, just like the song) opened a station in the late 1800s which was later replaced with the Santa Fe Depot, (a Spanish Colonial Revival structure built in 1930) and remains Fullerton's main train station. Pacific Electric, known for its Red Cars, built a depot in 1917 to connect Fullerton with nearby cities, including San Bernardino and Los Angeles. This station closed its doors to passengers in 1938 but now houses the charming Hopscotch Tavern. The third railroad to construct a station in Fullerton was the Union Pacific in 1923. This mission-styled building was physically moved in 1980 and ultimately became the Old Spaghetti Factory.

Beyond Downtown

Outside of the downtown area, several locations mentioned in the book are factually based, including the community of Orangethorpe and the Muckenthaler Mansion (which now serves as a local cultural center). The residences of the remaining characters are fictitious but were inspired by actual homes in the area.

Bastanchury Ranch did exist and was established by Fullerton's founding father Domingo Bastanchury, an immigrant from the Basque region of France who began his career as a sheep herder. Over time he amassed between 8,000 to 10,000 acres in Fullerton and nearby La Habra, which supported sheep and cow herds, as well as crops (chiefly oranges, lemons, and tomatoes). But in 1931, not long after *Felony in Fullerton* takes place, the Bastanchurys announced they were two million dollars in debt, and the ranch was placed into a receivership. It should be noted that Baker's orchard, which bumps up against Bastanchury Ranch, is entirely fictitious, as are the boundary lines for Bastanchury Ranch depicted on the map at the beginning of the book.

Which historic events actually happened in Fullerton?

While most of the happenings in this novel are entirely the invention of my overactive imagination, some were, in fact, true, and a few were downright strange.

Richard Nixon

Notable in the annals of Fullerton's history is former President Richard Nixon's attendance at Fullerton High School during the late 1920s. His family home, now the location of the Richard Nixon Presidential Library and Museum, was in nearby Yorba Linda. Given Richard Nixon's notoriety, it would have been easy to portray him through a nefarious lens. However, after reading about his early history in *Nixon: A Life* by Jonathan Aitken, I felt only sadness and compassion for the child and adolescent "Nick" and, consequently, chose to portray him accordingly.

Labor for the Citrus Industry

Oranges were big business for Fullerton in the early days. In fact, Orange County was a major supplier of citrus throughout the United States and worldwide until after World War II. The book *Labor and*

Community: Mexican Citrus Worker Villages in a Southern California County, 1900-1950 by Gilbert Gonzales was key in my efforts to paint a picture of Ruby's rescuers and the labor community where they lived.

Early on, Chinese immigrants provided labor for the citrus industry in Fullerton until the Chinese Exclusion Act of 1882 prohibited Chinese labor in the USA. Over the next two decades, orchard owners hired Japanese laborers until they too were excluded by the California Alien Land Law of 1913, which impacted all immigrants of Asian descent. At that time, the Mexican Revolution was in full-swing and many Mexican citizens immigrated to the USA, particularly border states like California.

Since oranges and lemons require hand-harvesting, the Mexican immigrants were welcomed by crop growers, including owners of large orchards like the Bastanchurys. The wages were low compared to other jobs in the area, and the work was physically brutal at times, resulting in injuries and physical ailments. Labor was quite organized in terms of pickers, packers, and haulers, as well as those who tended the trees and packing houses. Some growers constructed houses for the field laborers since many were married with children. While Bastanchury Ranch provided plots of land for settlements, including "Tijuanita," laborers were left to construct homes on their own out of any materials they could find. Each settlement typically had access to just one water faucet and the latrines were makeshift. Disease ran rampant through the labor camps, and infant mortality rates were much higher than those outside of the camps. Segregated schools were built near some of the camps for the purpose of "Americanizing" the children of the laborers. However, despite (or perhaps because of) the hardships, strong communities developed within the villages.

Bootlegging in Fullerton

Fullerton was a "dry" town even before prohibition began but, unsurprisingly, that didn't prevent the sale and consumption of alcohol within city limits. And like elsewhere in the United States, speakeasies existed, including a pool hall (now known as the Continental Room), which is considered to be the oldest bar in Fullerton. Speakeasies weren't the only source for those who wished to imbibe. According to a recent article by Debora Richey, librarian emeritus at CSUF (see Fullerton Heritage Newsletter dated February 2023), a clerk at the California Hotel was arrested in 1924 for selling alcohol to hotel guests. So, it was no stretch of the imagination to write about the "pipeline of John Barleycorn passin' right through the center of town" (as Stan Jones describes in the novel).

The Chloroform Burglars

And speaking of the California Hotel, Ms. Richey's article also described the series of burglaries that took place over a weeklong period in the summer of 1927, including an attack on actor and movie director Ralph Ince (brother to the famous producer mentioned in Chapter 3) in his hotel room. Two men used chloroform to render their victims unconscious in order to rob them. A headline in the *Los Angeles Daily News* on the 4th of July read "New Terror Reign: Arrest in Fullerton" and detailed how the two men were finally nabbed.

Lightning and Hail

The unseasonal storm described in the book on Friday, May 9th did in fact occur, but it happened one day earlier. An article in the *La Habra Star* on May 8th, 1930, entitled "Lightning Strikes La Habra Heights Residence: Freak Storm" described a "ball of fire" that descended from the ceiling of a couple's home and landed between them as they sat in their living room. I cannot fathom how no damage was done to the house, but according to the article both the couple and their residence were safe and sound.

Balboa Motor Corporation

Growing up in Fullerton, I never heard about the Balboa Motor Corporation. According to Ziebell's *Fullerton: A Pictorial History*, the company exhibited prototypes of their touring car and sports brougham at the California Hotel in early 1924 and promised to build a thousand cars over the next year at the plant it had just built in Fullerton. The five-seater touring car was priced at $2,900, a luxury car at the time. And an ad for the brougham boasted 100 horsepower and eight cylinders, as well as the ability to get 25 miles to the gallon of gas. This "supercharged engine," however, wasn't ready in time for the Orange County Auto Show, and engines from a Continental were substituted, prompting critics to suggest investor fraud. Other than the two prototypes, no Balboa automobile was ever produced.

"Bob"

Perhaps the strangest fact (and definitely the most fun to write about) was "Bob" the alligator snapping turtle. For decades, Fullerton residents reported sightings of a prehistoric-looking monster who lived in the murky depths of Laguna Lake. From time to time, he was observed stealing fish from people's fishing lines and latching onto ducks then pulling them down to his aquatic lair. In the novel, Laguna Lake is no more than a pond near the village school on Bastanchury Ranch where the kids like to cool off and catch frogs. In truth, it began as a watering hole for horses, but over time the lake was expanded for recreational use. "Old Bob," the name given to him by locals, was captured in 2004 when the lake was drained as part of a restoration project. He was measured to be four feet in length and weighed 100 pounds. Experts estimated that he was 50 years old at the time of his capture, but alligator snapping turtles can live to be 120 years or more in the wild. They are not native in California, living mainly in the southeastern United States, including western Tennessee where the Bob in our story hails from. "Old Bob" was thought to be abandoned in Laguna Lake in his youth, so it made sense for Jack to release his Bob at the small lake on Bastanchury Ranch. Sadly, "Old Bob" was relocated after his discovery and died a few years later.

What about the high school?

Several people and sources allowed me to be as historically accurate as possible when writing about the high school. Cheri Pape, the local history archivist at Fullerton Public Library, was immensely helpful. She has digitized a vast array of records for the city of Fullerton, including FHS yearbooks that date back to 1909. Similarly, Fullerton College (formerly known as Fullerton Junior College) was located on the same campus as the high school until 1936. Their library has created digital records of the college newspaper dating back to 1923, which are all available on their library's online archive. Last, Diane Oestreich's book *The History of Fullerton Union High School 1893-2011* offered key information which helped me create an authentic version of the high school in 1930. References to clubs, the dress code for female students, time capsules, and descriptions of classrooms are factual and based on photos and text from these sources. A few additional features of the high school warrant further explanation.

Auditorium & Clock Tower

The auditorium and clock tower were, in fact, built in 1930, and the auditorium was opened to the public on June 1st of that year during a dedication ceremony. Musical selections by Haydn, Bach, and Mendelssohn were played on the Wurlitzer organ, which was comprised of 3000 pipes and was considered at the time to be one of the largest pipe organs in the western United States. Ruby's description of the auditorium's interior is accurate, including the Spanish-style paintings on the beams, which remain to this day. It should be noted that the clock faces on the tower, as described in the novel, did not exist in 1930 but were donated by the graduating class of 1932.

Tunnels

The existence of tunnels running under Fullerton High School was the stuff of legends when I was a student there. Several of my classmates claimed to have located an access point and made a few trips down. As I recall, someone brought back a package or two of old rations. And some students and residents thought the tunnels were haunted. According to archival information, the tunnels were installed in 1922 and housed pipes connected to a boiler room, as well as conduits for wiring. The novel describes the tunnels as "pitch black," however electrical switches would have existed to control lights along their length. Further, I found no evidence to suggest that an entrance existed within the auditorium itself. An article in the Junior College's newspaper in 1926 reported that the tunnels ran in a two-mile circle under the campus, so they were nowhere near as extensive as described in the story, nor did the tunnels extend past the campus perimeter at that time. The tunnels were extended under Harvard Avenue (now Lemon Street) in 1935 to connect with utility tunnels under the new site for the Junior College. In fact, for several years after the new campus was built, Junior College students would traverse through the tunnels to the high school campus on rainy days, since that was the only place they could purchase lunch. Apparently, students also utilized the tunnels for extracurricular events like haunted houses at Halloween. It is unclear today if any tunnels remain under the high school campus due to modernization projects that began in 2002 and included filling in sections of the tunnel system because of safety concerns.

Readers from Fullerton may have guessed sooner than others that Dottie and her friends were trapped in the tunnels. While conducting research for the story, I did not encounter any information that students had ever been trapped in the subterranean passages. In fact, information about the tunnels was scarce. However, after I finished the first complete draft, Jesse LaTour published a post on Fullerton History.com that referenced an article from 1926 in the Junior College's newspaper. The article entitled "Betty Miller Is Tunnel Heroine" described how, one evening, a school employee working in the engine room heard screaming coming from a nearby tunnel entrance. A search party found a group of twelve students who had been trapped. One young man had attempted to dig his way out with a comb, of all things, and the aforementioned Betty Miller screamed at the top of her lungs continuously. The others were apparently incoherent when they were rescued. The article was laden with hyperbole, so I'm uncertain how serious the situation actually was, but

I felt compelled to share this story as an amusing counterpoint to the grave situation in the novel.

What about the cult?

The cult idea came to me early in the book's development. I ran across an article from March 1930 in *Time Magazine* about cults that had popped up suddenly in Southern California, including the Blackburn Cult mentioned in the novel. I'd already decided that the story would involve a group of honor students trapped in the tunnels, and I needed to come up with a reason for them to enter the underground space. A cult ceremony seemed to be a promising and interesting notion, but how could a group of intelligent students be recruited into a cult in the first place? The idea for a pseudo-spiritual ideology grounded in mathematics came to me while reading about Pythagoras and ancient Babylonian mathematicians. I then recalled a passage in the Bible about Ezekial's vision while he was exiled in Babylon. This suggested a way to inject spirituality into the otherwise mathematically grounded ideology of the cult. I also remembered a few books I read in the 1990s about a purported ancient civilization (similar to Atlantis) called Lemuria, or Mu, which suddenly vanished during pre-history. The book *The Lost Continent of Mu,* quite popular in its time, was first published in 1926, which fit with the timeframe for my story. While the cult material was very numinous and ridiculous, I have to say, it was quite fun to write.

Still curious?

Links to additional information and other sources related to the book can be found online by clicking the following code.

Coral Cloche Press

sites.google.com

ACKNOWLEDGEMENTS

This section was challenging to compose only because there were so many people I wanted to thank. My heart is full of gratitude, and I could fill an entire book with special messages for those who have touched my life. However, I decided to limit my acknowledgements to those who have directly assisted me with this novel. For friends and family not specifically mentioned, please know that I am profoundly grateful for your ongoing encouragement, companionship, and love.

First, I'd like to thank the librarians and historians whose help was critical throughout the development of my story. Local historian Jesse LaTour's websites about Fullerton's history saved me hundreds of hours digging through archives. Further, my discussions with him helped shape key aspects of the narrative. Debora Richey, librarian emeritus at CSU Fullerton and board member of Fullerton Heritage, went to great lengths to track down information for me. In addition, her writings for Fullerton Heritage, as well as her interviews in the *Fullerton Observer*, were instrumental in making the story as historically accurate as possible. Similarly, I'd like to thank all of those at Fullerton Heritage whose efforts have resulted in the vast collection of information available online, as well as during walking tours. Finally, Cheri Pape, archivist at Fullerton Public Library's Local History Room, has digitized an impressive array of documents, which saved me from making multiple trips to the archives when I was physically unable to leave my home due to illness. Additionally, she quickly responded to all my requests for information and was willing to go the extra mile to track down obscure bits of information.

A huge thank you to my early readers, Lesley, Amanda, Christine, Jennifer, Julie, Janis, Monika, and Katie Ann. Your thoughtful feedback and marvelous suggestions were crucial as I polished the narrative. I am also thankful to Ana for helping ensure the accuracy of the Spanish dialog in the book. Special thanks to Kim for her words of wisdom and support throughout the entire writing process. And profuse thanks to authors and dear friends Katherine Morse and David Drake for their support and expert advice.

To my son, Charles, thank you for the love and encouragement you've given me throughout this writing journey. Your creativity and dedication to your art continue to inspire me. I enjoyed bouncing ideas off that imaginative brain of yours and appreciate the assistance and advice you gave me while I developed the illustrations for the novel. Most of all, I want you to know how proud I am to be your mom.

My dearest Lance, where do I even begin? You've been my rock for nearly forty years and literally saved my life. I adore our life together and am endlessly grateful for you. Thank you for lending an ear when I needed to talk through elements of the story that were giving me trouble. Thanks too for reading an entire draft of the manuscript while we were vacationing in Maui (that did not go unnoticed). As I tell you all the time, I don't just love you. I cherish you.

ABOUT THE AUTHOR

Photo by Katie Ann O'Keefe

Southern California native Debra Brunner writes historical mysteries and has contributed to academic publications and websites as a speech-language pathologist. She received an M.A. from UC Irvine, where she worked as a statistician for several years before realizing her calling to help children with communication disorders. She subsequently received an M.A. from CSU Fullerton, where she later taught undergraduate and graduate courses.

A self-described bibliophile since childhood, Debra adores feeling immersed in the worlds created by the minds of authors. She strives to give her readers the same experience while aiming for historical accuracy as much as possible. Having grown up in Fullerton, Debra's research for *Felony in Fullerton* took her down many enjoyable rabbit holes (such as perusing the Fullerton High School yearbook from 1930) thus enabling her to infuse true places and events into her story.

A few years ago, following a brush with death mid-way through her breast cancer treatment, Debra vowed to embrace joy whenever possible. To that end, when not writing novels or working with children, Debra enjoys sartorial adventures with her husband, some involving swing dancing at local Art Deco venues.